TAP IN

by Tom Berliner

Dedication and Thanks

First and foremost, I give thanks to my Lord, Jesus Christ. He patiently waited for me to awaken, to accept His invitation and to put my troubles at His feet. I could accomplish nothing without Him.

This book is my most favorite of the several that I have written. You know why? Because I didn't write it...sort of. When I sat down to write a novel, I didn't have any idea as to what it would be about, much less where the storyline would head. I simply sat down at my computer and started to write. But, instead of conjuring up ideas and laboriously converting them to text, it absolutely (and I mean absolutely) felt as though I was reading instead of writing. It was the most amazing thing. I felt more like a scribe than an author.

No, I'm not suggesting that I was a scribe like someone who contributed to the writing of the Bible. No, indeed. But I did feel that I could thoroughly enjoy the way the book was unveiling and that I didn't have to 'worry' about its destination.

I'm guessing that you, too, have had similar experiences (not necessarily with writing something) where you felt peacefully directed and that all you had to do was follow the path. If such is the case, then you know what I mean.

I want to thank my family – wife Carlene and kids Julie, Jason and Bina. I am especially appreciative of Carlene. I couldn't find the time, the privacy or the inspiration without her. None of the books that I have authored could have been written without her support and love. Thank you, Honey.

I also owe a ton of gratitude to informal editors Rand York, Dave Bledsoe, Ron Gajewski, Susie Gans and Gerry Mravik. Thanks, too, to Bill Coons of CustomerExploders who helped guide me through the publication process.

Maya Angelou produced a great quote: "There is no greater agony than bearing an untold story inside you." It would have been agony had I not listened to a higher power when it came to writing *Tap In*.

Other Books by Tom Berliner

Arnell

Beedra

Carson

Choices

Debatable Death

Easy-Peasy (with Ron Gajewski)

Exilon

Faithful Connections (with Ron Gajewski)

Forensic Detectives

I Say Forever

Needing a Planet

Novak (with Ron Gajewski)

Posse

Somewhere (with Ron Gajewski)

Tap In II

Tap In III

Tat (with Rand York)

Tidi's Dream (with Dave Bledsoe)

Unexpected Return (with Ron Gajewski)

Wolf

For additional information and titles, please visit

https://tomberliner.com

Cast of Key Characters

Main Individuals

- Conner Ramsey – Central character
- Esther Conrad – Conner's girlfriend
- Shedrick Harris – Conner's roommate and teammate

Brantley University Basketball

- Jason Wright – Coach
- John Deerman, Athletic Director
- Gary Dixon
- Clyde Forrester
- Wes Harmon
- Kenny Kline
- Injujai Obumje
- Levon Walker

Brantley University Faculty

- Evan Calhoun, President
- Reginald Cook, Professor
- Bartholomew Andrew Greene, Professor
- David Ving, Professor

Brantley University Boosters

- Chet and Liz Applegate
- Justin Goudas
- Gordon and Doris McKenzie

Others

- Pete Carlyle – Conner's childhood friend
- Richard Means, *Sentinel News* reporter

- Tony Weston, *Chicago Tribune* reporter

Chapter 1

Conner struggled to complete his final set of bench presses. He sat up, took a deep breath, retrieved his clipboard and marked off this last exercise. It was Saturday evening, going on 8:00 P.M. The last person in the weight room had left over an hour ago. A bold sign on the upper part of the wall of mirrors warned: 'When using free weights, have a spotter.' Conner ignored the advice.

He took his towel and walked into the gym. It was empty but the lights were on. He took a basketball from the rack on the floor and looked up. Even though he was a shade taller than six feet, the basket always looked miles away.

He dribbled the ball to the foul line. Five shots, he told himself. He bounced the ball three times and focused on the basket. His first shot didn't reach the rim, bouncing harmlessly under the basket. "Nice shot," he said out loud.

He got the ball and returned to the foul line. His next shot barely touched the rim. His third shot went well off to the left.

"Annoying," he called out to no one.

His fourth shot was relatively straight but hit the front of the rim and bounced straight back to him. He caught it and semi-slammed the ball down, catching it on the way back up. His fifth shot hit the right side of the rim and caromed off in that direction. Retrieving it, he pretended to be guarded by an All-American defender. His first dribble hit his foot and rolled to the other bleachers.

He rolled his eyes and smiled sarcastically, reclaiming the ball and dribbling toward the basket. His attempted layup wedged itself between the basket and the backboard. Conner stared at it angrily.

"Pathetic," he said.

He went back to the ball rack, got another ball and walked to the basket. On his third attempt, the wedged ball came free, the two balls going in opposite directions. Conner recovered one and put it in the rack. He did the same with the other.

"Basketball is a spectator sport," he said sarcastically.

With one last look over his shoulder, he went into the locker room.

----- ----- -----

The next day held promise for Conner. He counted on a particular contract coming through. Excitedly, he called to schedule time to get the very last t's crossed and i's dotted. That was when he heard the dreaded "We've had a change in direction. I'm sorry to tell you that we won't be initiating that project we discussed…now or in the foreseeable future." Feeble protests fell on deaf ears. The contract was gone. Adios. Auf wiedersehen. No matter what the language, it was time to move along.

Making his way to his car after work, he looked up to see that someone had sideswiped the driver's side. A horrendous gash decorated the car from the front left bumper all the way to the rear left taillight. Putting icing on the cake, he was unable to open the driver-side door.

"That's just super!" he said, wanting to scream but containing himself. Instead, he spun around on one foot as though centrifugal force would send his frustrations into outer space. It took him a couple of minutes to maneuver himself into the passenger seat, over the gear shift and then into the driver's seat. When he was settled in, he slapped the steering wheel and then gently put his head against it.

Arriving home, he banged the front door open with such force that a treasured antique plate that had been hanging on the living room wall vibrated itself loose and broke into a million pieces, scattering every which way. He spent the next hour trying unsuccessfully to retrieve all the shards.

This hadn't just been a terrible day. The entire week had been terrible. Heck, as he really thought about it, this month had totally stunk. It seemed like one thing after another had schemed to torment him. And succeeded.

Conner ended the day with "Lord, give me a break. Please turn on the 'abundance' tap. I'm ready to drink from *that* faucet!" It was a selfish prayer but he excused himself from any feelings of guilt and went to sleep.

Chapter 2

Conner awoke the next morning at 4:30. He arose with a curious feeling running through his head. For a while, he couldn't put his finger on it. Then, just when he had begun to dismiss it, he recalled his previous evening's bedtime prayer. "Lord, give me a break. Please. It's time to turn on the 'abundance' tap. I'm ready to drink from *that* faucet!"

The wording played in his head like a melody one can't shake. It was like *Jingle Bells*. When one sings it a few times, it seems impossible to forget. Same thing for the Mickey Mouse theme song ("M---i---c---k---e---y, M-o-u-s-e") or *Take Me Out to the Ballgame* (the one sung in the bottom of the seventh inning). They rattle around one's brain vacuum like a coin in a tumbling jar.

Arriving at work through the revolving door, Conner passed a bizarre-looking chap. He wore a deerstalker cap, like the kind Sherlock Holmes was known to wear. He also wore a black leather jacket, orange high-top sneakers, tan shorts and a shirt that had a distinctive western flair to it. He accented all that with a bright blue bowtie.

The man never looked away from Conner, not from the moment that the two met eyes, which was almost immediately upon Conner entering the building. The man didn't seem to be looking at Conner in an accusatory manner, only looking at him very intently.

As Conner passed him, the man said, "The tap is always on."

Conner stopped and turned to him. "Were you speaking to me?" Considering that the two of them were separated by at least fifty feet from the nearest person and the man had spoken softly, it was a rather rhetorical question. Nevertheless, Conner felt compelled to inquire.

The man smiled. "Of course," he said with a warm smile. No antagonistic inflection, no body challenge, nothing other than a welcoming look.

"What do you mean?" Conner asked.

Again, the man smiled. "We can talk. Anytime you wish."

Conner stared at him. Here was this odd person speaking to him as though it was the continuation of a conversation they had started at another time. Yet he made no sense.

"I'll even participate in a 'person' sort of way."

"What?" Conner challenged. "What the heck are you talking about?"

"Whenever you wish," the man added. Then he gently turned and walked away.

Conner stared at his back. There was something both eerie and pleasing in that brief exchange. He stood there for a few moments after the man left the building and thought about it.

How had he known about "the tap," the one to which Conner had referred in his prayer? Conner figuratively shook his head free of insane thoughts and proceeded to his office.

He couldn't quite leave the oddity of the whole thing behind.

Chapter 3

Friday passed uneventfully. A few times throughout, though, Conner came back to his conversation with that eccentric man in the lobby. It even crossed his mind that he had been speaking with an angel. Then he laughed it into dismissal and moved on.

After work, Conner met a friend at the gym, had a strong workout, grabbed a salad at a favorite café near his apartment and opened his front door with what felt was his last bit of energy. This would be a "me" weekend, he thought. No nuthin' except me, myself, and I.

Preparations for bed were minimal. Once under the covers, he read a few more chapters of his favorite C. S. Lewis book, *Mere Christianity*. He could read and reread that thing and still not fully understand it. Yet he always benefitted from reading it. Each time, much like the Bible, he took different things from the reading. He often said that, if he were to be stranded on an island with only two books, they would be the Bible and this Lewis book.

As he marked his stopping point and put the book aside, he turned to prayer. "Lord," he said, "thank you for the many blessings you provide." He named off some that came to mind. "Thank you, as always, for your mercy and grace." For Conner, mercy was the underserved forgiveness of sins and grace was undeserved gifts. He briefly reflected on them. "Thank you, too, for the unbelievable gift of salvation. Just knowing that a wonderful eternity lies before us is incredible peace of mind."

He thanked God for other things. He asked for blessings over friends, family and others fighting physical, emotional and spiritual issues. He also thanked God for the interesting day he had experienced. He thought again about that strange man and their very brief exchange. He ended with "Please show me how to access this tap. I am definitely ready to fill my cup from it."

----- ----- -----

When he awoke the next morning, Conner was surprised to see that it was almost 7:00 AM. He was even more surprised to realize that he hadn't gotten up once during the night. He confirmed that by having to race to the bathroom. "Whew" was about all he could offer when the floodgates closed.

Before he had much more time to think about it, he heard noises in the kitchen. Considering that he was the only one home, this was not a good thing. He ran through his checklist of reasons for any noises: Open window – All closed. Pet – Had none. Left TV on – Didn't. Girlfriend – I would have remembered. Family member – No access keys. Burglar – Likely.

He looked around and grabbed the first thing that came into view. It was a broom. Now Bruce Lee, Jean-Claude Van Damme or Samson might be able to whip entire armies with a broom but Conner had no idea how to use it as a weapon, except against spiders. He set it aside and looked for something else.

Aha, he thought, there is a Louisville Slugger in the closet. If I'm really quiet, I can get it and thus be armed. Conner tiptoed silently to the closet. He carefully took the door handle and began to open it. Almost expectedly, it squeaked like an alarm.

That won't do, he thought, and quickly pulled the door open to lessen the length of time that the squeak was in play. He listened carefully to see if he had alerted the trespasser to his action. Nothing. Apparently, the invader hadn't been tipped off. Without moving his feet any further, Conner leaned into the closet, knowing exactly where the baseball bat stood, even though he hadn't swung it for a good nine or twelve months. There it was! He took hold of it and gently pulled it out of the closet and into both hands. Someone doesn't want to be on the bad-boy end of this thing, he thought.

Then, again, he considered that maybe the burglar had a pistol, a rifle, a shotgun or maybe even a bazooka. Oh, gosh. If this invader had a broom, I'd be okay, Conner thought, but not a real firearm. He stood there considering his options, one of which was not to move and hope that the person would simply exit. He adopted this strategy only because he couldn't think of what else to do. When in doubt, play ostrich.

Unfortunately, all his stealth went for naught. He heard the clearly audible instructions: "Come in here." It carried no malice, no anger and no urgency. It was simply a directive.

Had he not already gone to the bathroom, that three-word command would have been the moment he would have emptied his bladder. Instead, he tried to decide what to do with the bat. If I set it down, I will be completely defenseless, he thought. If I bring it with me, it might raise the level of conflict, probably to my own detriment. He started to put it on the bed, then stopped, then started again, then stopped. Finally, he set it on the bed and stepped around the corner into the living room. From there, it was but one more room into the kitchen. He was frightened but also drawn by the calm command he had been given.

As he stepped into the kitchen, not knowing if it was going to be his last step forever, he saw a man sitting on a stool at the wooden island in the middle of the kitchen. On the island were odds and ends — magazines, sections of the newspaper, some mail, HP Sauce Conner had forgotten to put away a couple of days ago and a screwdriver (for whatever reason). In spite of the circumstances, he felt a little embarrassed about the mess and would clean it up right after the man left.

If he left.

And if Conner was still alive.

On the other hand, Conner noticed a few things about this home invader. For one thing, the man was sitting rather casually at the island. His right elbow was on the wooden surface with his chin sitting comfortably on the outside of his right hand, sort of a variation of Rodin's sculpture. His left arm was simply resting on the island. Conner didn't see any weapons.

Then Conner looked up at the man's face. He was stunned. It was the same coconut who had approached him at work. This time, though, the man's attire was considerably more casual, almost as though he had taken a break from tennis to come over.

Conner was speechless. He felt relieved, although still concerned, violated and, eventually, angry.

"What the heck are you doing here?"

"Omnipresent," the man responded.

"What?" Conner yelled. "You've broken into my home and now you're, you're…"

"…having a conversation with you. Only if you wish to, of course," the man added.

The man suggested that Conner sit down on the only other stool available. It was on the other side of the island. Although not exactly knowing why, Conner did as he was told.

"Can I get you some juice or something?" came the man's inquiry.

Listen to that! The man breaks into my house and offers me my own food. Confusion would not even begin to describe Conner's current condition.

"No thank you," Conner responded, not knowing why he was being polite.

The man remained silent while Conner gathered his thoughts. No longer frightened, simply bewildered, Conner blurted out "Why are you here? How did you get in?"

"I had a sense that you wanted to chat."

"About what?" Conner asked, not yet seeing any logic to the conversation.

"The tap, of course," he said, as matter of factly as though they had just been talking about it ten seconds ago.

"The tap," Conner echoed.

Then, suddenly putting some pieces together and with the immediacy of a firecracker, Conner exploded "The tap! The tap?" He stood up. "Why on earth would you break into my house to *chat* about the tap?"

"You were the one who brought it up," the man replied, as easily as if he had just been asked for the sum of two plus two.

Conner was quiet. There was something surreal taking place, perhaps even supernatural.

"Okay, really, who are you?" Conner asked.

"God," the man answered.

Conner sat there and stared, dumbfounded.

The man looked back and smiled. It had just been one word: "God."

"God with a capital G?" Conner asked.

"There is only one," he answered.

"And why are you talking to me?"

"Actually, I have a wheel at home that has every living person's name on it. I spun it and your name came up."

Conner started to roll his eyes and then stopped.

The man laughed. It wasn't a Santa Claus ho-ho-ho laugh but it was inviting. Conner couldn't help but smile, too.

"You have this thing with your eyes. Do you always do that?"

Conner could have played dumb but, really, what was the use? If he was God (with a capital G), then he already knew whether the truth was being told. And, if he wasn't, then the truth probably didn't make a difference.

"Yes," Conner answered. "It's a bad habit. I even do it when I'm by myself."

"Interesting. You know that I was just kidding about the wheel, don't you?"

Conner ignored the question. "Why are you talking to me?"

"You know, that's an interesting question. In a manner of speaking, I talk with everyone who wants a meaningful relationship with me. In most instances, it's what I call Guiding Dialogue. I hate to tell people to *do* things." He emphasized the word 'do' in a way that conveyed his dislike for giving orders.

"Sometimes, though, I have to give very explicit instructions. But those few instances have been the result of unique circumstances. Most times, I let individuals hear the conversation very much through reflection. Not being told something in black and white still leaves them with choices."

"Free will," Conner chimed in.

"Something like that."

"Well, what's unique about these circumstances?"

"I'm afraid *that* information is only available on a need-to-know basis and…"

"…I don't need to know."

"Bingo."

The man - God - had hardly moved at all. Conner suddenly had the urge to be a good host. "Can I get you something?"

The man tilted his head and looked at Conner.

Both of them smiled. "Okay," Conner conceded.

"But, really, God, if you are God, why are you here?" Conner suddenly realized that he was now talking to this man, this apparition, this spirit as though he was actually the Big G. Other than mysteriously showing up in his kitchen and knowing that something had been said about a tap (maybe a coincidence), there was no proof that he was even an angel, much less God. He might even be the Devil.

"You prayed about abundance and I thought it best to help you explore what that means."

Oh, man, he's the real deal. I mean he's really the real deal, Conner thought.

"Out of millions and millions of people, you just happened to…what? Like my prayer?"

"Something like that. Actually, it's a bit more complicated but understanding the engine isn't essential to being able to drive the car, if you know what I mean."

Conner was about to ask him how they were going to go about exploring abundance when the man said "I'll bet that you're wondering how we are going to explore abundance."

Now it was Conner's turn to tilt his head.

Again, both smiled. "Okay," he conceded, "no more of that."

"So, what now?"

"We take a break. I'll be back."

And, with that, he was gone.

"Wow," Conner said aloud.

Chapter 4

Conner spent much of the day trying to decide if he should tell anyone about this experience. He finally decided against sharing it. Among other things, nobody would believe him. But, above all ed to undertake this experience himself.

.t all certain why he had been chosen but,

.ad wanted others involved, he would have

.ed them.

Conner was preoccupied throughout the day. Even during his run, his involvement with this puzzle caused him to run his twelve-mile route instead of the one covering seven miles, never once thinking about the distance at all. He was fixated on the word "abundance" to such a degree that it almost became a mantra.

When he returned home, he checked his watch and was stunned to learn that he had covered this route in a full five minutes less than he had ever run it.

"Weird," he said out loud.

That's the way it was for the whole day. Whatever he did, he seemed to be on autopilot.

He went to bed that night with a very light heart. He didn't sense stress about anything – money, work, health, relationships, nothing. It was incredible.

"Thank you, Lord." He paused. "To be continued," he added. "Amen," he concluded. And then he smiled, knowing that God was probably smiling, too.

Conner awoke on Sunday with a good feeling, partially expecting, definitely hoping, that his visitor would be in the kitchen again. No such luck. He tried to act casually as he walked around the house but, alas, God was nowhere to be found.

Bummer. Conner was ready and rarin' to renew their conversation. This time he would ask God some of the questions about things that he really wanted to know. Like…Are there other worlds like ours? How much do dogs think? Do we go straight to heaven or do we have to wait until Judgment Day? Aside from Jesus, who is the greatest person who ever lived? Do we really use only a small percentage of our brains? Will animals join us in heaven? Can you give me an easier explanation of the Trinity than the one about a pretzel? And, of course, the quintessential one…Why does our pee smell funny after we eat asparagus?

He could probably come up with a few others, too, but that was a really good start.

Realizing that God was going to show up when he was good and ready, Conner tried to make the most of the day. Although he didn't intend to go to church, he reconsidered and went, figuring that God might be insulted if he stayed home and played solitaire on the computer. He also put a few extra bucks in the collection basket, just in case.

When Conner got home, he created a computer file to organize his thinking.

1. *God didn't mean for us to have abundance in all facets of our lives. Different people receive abundance in different aspects of their lives. For example, one person might receive loads of money while another might be given surprising health recovery after being diagnosed with something quite severe.*

2. *We can't choose which area will be impacted. Perhaps we can influence it with prayer, but we can't say, for example, "I'll take my abundance in money."*
3. *We don't get to choose when, where or how we take delivery of this abundance, if we even get it.*
4. *Not everyone is gifted with abundance, at least not in the way mortals typically judge it. I am hard pressed to view someone with birth abnormalities or someone truly homeless as having abundance.*
5. *Abundance means different things to different people. A lot of money to me is likely to be different from what that same amount means to someone else. For some, abundance may have no meaning at all. Someone wishing to be childless would not consider it wonderfully abundant to be told she was going to have twins.*

Following that, Conner stayed busy by working out, watching the tail end of a track meet on ESPN, doing some laundry and continuing to read a novel that he was having a tough time getting into. He finished the day with a light dinner, and then went to bed.

Once again, he thanked God for this incredible time of his life and easily drifted off to sleep.

Monday morning Conner jumped out of bed and checked the kitchen. No visitors. He did his get-ready chores around the house, then left even earlier than usual. He was in a particularly chipper mood. Maybe God will return today and we can continue our dialogue. Conner felt much more knowledgeable now than earlier when his mysterious guest had visited.

This morning, Conner looked at people differently. He began to wonder if any of them was *The Man* in disguise. From time to time he had prayed to see Jesus in more people but it was more prayer than practice. Although he intended to do it, he would forget almost immediately. This morning he was more attentive to it.

As hard as he looked, he didn't see God anywhere.

Conner determined to stop daydreaming. When God was ready, Conner would be ready. Conner needed to focus on those things that were within his world, to concentrate on that which he could impact. The rest, as they say, is simply noise.

He did that and had a very productive day.

And that's the way it was throughout the week.

When Conner left his office building, he merged into a sea of humanity, each person on his or her way somewhere with the utmost urgency in mind. He wasn't half a block into his walk when he heard his name called. "Conner!" He turned around only to be looking into a collage of unfamiliar faces. It seemed as though everyone who lived or worked in the city was now either coming or going on that very block, all at the same time. It was much like trying to find Waldo in the popular book series or newspaper entries.

"Conner. Over here."

He continued to look and saw a hand waving above the heads of the masses. He began to make his way in that direction, not understanding how that man could see him but that he could not do the same. Conner still didn't recognize anyone. Then there was a tug on his sleeve and he turned to face someone he was sure that he had never seen before.

"Conner Ramsey, old buddy. Long time no see." The man's face lit up and Conner didn't really know what to do. Pretend to remember him? Pretend to almost remember him? Act as if he didn't remember him? Walk away? Conner finally selected the 'almost there' approach.

"Ohhh, no. You don't remember me, do you?" the stranger said.

"I'm almost there," Conner lied, pleased that this approach had worked. He added the exaggerated body contortions that one manifests in such situations. "It must have been quite a while," he added.

"It's me."

Great. Thanks for the help.

"God," he added.

"What?" Conner exploded. He stepped back and looked at him. This certainly wasn't the nut case from the office building or the person who had been in his kitchen. This was a dapperly-dressed man in his early thirties. He had a full head of dark hair, very fashionable glasses, was clearly in good physical shape and, judging from his attire, was successful at whatever he did.

"What's this? Your Body-of-the-Day outfit?"

The man laughed. For a split second, Conner wondered if this was God or maybe someone who really did know him from way back when and had, coincidentally, called himself the Divine One. He decided to check.

"Last time we were together, what was our primary topic of conversation?"

As soon as the man tilted his head, Conner confirmed his identity.

"Okay, never mind. I just wanted to be sure."

God smiled.

"What are you doing here? I thought that we were going to meet in my kitchen."

"Well, you know we can meet anywhere. I thought that we shouldn't get too rooted into a single spot."

Makes sense to me, Conner decided.

"But I don't have my list."

"What list?"

"I spent time considering the word *abundance* and came up with a list that helps me explain my thoughts on the subject."

"Conner, this isn't a test."

Just then a fire engine, sirens blaring, drove by. Both of them looked at it.

"Why don't you do something about that?" Conner asked.

"Because those aren't the rules," he said calmly.

"Since you're the one making the rules, why don't you change them?"

God took Conner by the elbow, like a grown child takes his elderly parent, and guided him away from the stream of humanity all around them. Up to that point in time, they had been like large rocks in a rushing river. Everyone was forced to make his or her way around them while they stood immovable. Now they were out of the way. Just before starting to answer his question, God noted that a table was being vacated in an outdoor café. He took Conner's elbow again and directed them to it. They sat down.

Quirky fellow that he was, even if he looked like Sean Connery as James Bond, God cleared the table and then sat back down. Conner was relatively dumbfounded by all this.

"Now," he said. "You want to know why I don't...I think you called it 'change the rules' around here, right?"

Suddenly aware of the enormity of what was taking place, Conner could only nod his head.

"Sorry. That's classified. If I told you, I'd have to kill you." God looked at his table companion very seriously. This exchange could be part of a spy script in a movie. The tension was palpable.

Conner looked back at God. He didn't know whether or not to be terrified.

"Just kidding," God added lightly. "You wouldn't understand."

Conner's shoulders slumped. Here he was on the verge of being given the answer to one of the most intriguing questions in the universe and God had been teasing.

"Try me," Conner boldly asked.

"Can't," he tersely replied. "Not now, anyhow."

"Meaning?"

"Not while you're mortal."

So, he wasn't kidding when he said that Conner would have to be dead to know.

"Besides, let's stick with one topic at a time. I think that 'abundance' is sufficient for the moment, don't you?"

Conner nodded obediently.

"So, from the best of your abilities, try to recall the list you created about abundance. That will be a good place to begin."

"I'll do my best."

"That's a good soul," he said.

"One, abundance isn't all inclusive. Two, we don't choose the area. Three, we don't choose when or where it happens. Four, not everyone receives abundance. And, five, abundance means different things to different people."

"That's good. Very good."

"Thanks."

God didn't say anything further. He just looked at his tablemate. It was a look filled with warmth, like a father reflecting on the joy of his newborn son.

"What?" Conner asked, breaking the silence.

"That's a mighty good list. Now, having thought about this subject a bit more, do you want to amend your prayer?"

Conner flashed back to the request he had made that had seemingly kicked this whole thing off: "It's time to turn on the 'abundance' tap."

Conner believed that he now was beginning to understand the lesson. "Yes," he responded.

With that, once again, God was gone. Nobody at the café seemed to notice.

Conner made his way home, alternating between elation and frustration, but much more to the former.

Chapter 5

Conner thought more about his 'chats' with God. "You may be an undigested bit of beef, a blot of mustard, a crumb of cheese, a fragment of an underdone potato," as Charles Dickens' Ebenezer Scrooge had put it in *The Christmas Carol.*

Deep inside, though, Conner knew that it was God.

He wondered what to do now and determined to pray more specifically, starting with what was meant by abundance. He resolved to ask for one thing. His major problem was deciding upon that thing.

Conner sat down at his computer and, as he had done with his assumptions about abundance, listed areas that he should consider. In effect, it was a nomination slate. Once listed, he put them into alphabetical order. His logic was to review each and not be clouded by some sort of subconscious preference. As much as possible, he wanted to be objective. He came up with ten entries: faith, fame, fun, good will, health, long life, love, money, peace and wisdom.

Now came the matter of culling the list...all the way down to one entry. After much soul-searching and inner turmoil, he boiled it down to two entries: Faith and love. The first sounded a whole lot like a winner. The second, although less spiritual, seemed to have hold of Conner, as well. He knew that he had to ponder this further and took yet another break.

Surprisingly, he remembered a passage from Mark. He grabbed his Bible and thumbed through it, in due course coming to rest at Mark 12:28.

> One of the teachers of the law came and heard them debating. Noticing that Jesus had given them a good answer, he asked him, "Of all the commandments, which is the most important?" "The most important one" answered Jesus, "is this: 'Hear, O Israel, the Lord our God, the Lord is one. Love the Lord your God with all your heart and with all your soul and with all your mind and with all your strength.' The second is this: 'Love your neighbor as yourself.' There is no commandment greater than these."

Great, he thought. Faith is one and love is two.

He went to bed determined to ask for abundance of faith. He wanted to have the kind of faith that allowed him to walk on water and sustain it, something Peter was not quite able to do. That was the essential message in his prayers that evening. He slipped off into a peaceful sleep.

He awoke the next morning, once again fully refreshed. He did not expect God to be in the kitchen. Or anywhere else in the house for that matter. Thus, Conner was totally taken back when his visitor was at the kitchen island once again, this time adding half and half to his coffee.

"I usually put in too much," God commented, substituting that for a good morning salutation.

"Too much what?" Conner asked.

"Too much cream," he answered. "Not good for you."

"The cream?"

"Too much of anything," he answered.

Conner thought about that, intuitively not agreeing. He even shook his head.

"Name something," God challenged.

"Wealth."

"Do you know what happens to virtually everyone with money to burn?"

"Lots of things. All good," Conner responded, trying to be funny.

"Not really," God said.

"Okay," Conner acknowledged. "Health," his replacement for wealth.

"Think about it," God invited.

Confused, Conner asked "About what?"

"How would you answer *too much health* in a way that I addressed *too much wealth*?" He emphasized the word 'too.'

Deciding not to banter with him, Conner put serious thought into this. Obviously, God wanted Conner to discover something. By then, Conner had also sat down at the kitchen island. He closed his eyes and let his chin fall onto his chest. Sometimes, Conner found this to be a good posture for prayer or reflection.

"Well," he began, somewhat uncertainly, "perhaps too much health will result in someone becoming fearful of losing what he or she has and obsessing about it, to the exclusion of other things."

"Bingo," God said.

"Point taken," Conner acknowledged.

"You're still not convinced, are you?" God asked.

"I'm not quite there yet."

"Okay," God began.

Before he could get into that sentence, Conner blurted out "Faith!"

"Too much faith?" God paused. "Good one. Good one, indeed," he added. "Well, there ya have me," God said. "I don't think that there is such a thing as too much faith...in me, that is."

"I thought that you're omniscient," Conner commented, more interested in learning than in being right or clever.

"Your point?" God asked.

"Well, if you are all knowing..."

"I *am* all knowing," God corrected. Conner chose not to argue.

Conner thought for a second, then restarted his thinking. "As an all-knowing being, why did you enter into a conversation without thinking that I might identify faith as an element to prove my point?"

God smiled. It was the smile of a proud father.

"Excellent question," he said.

The two briefly held their eyes in a sort of visual embrace. It was every bit as good as if they had physically hugged one another.

God continued. "Do people learn more from being told something or from discovering it for themselves?"

"Bingo," Conner said, adopting God's expression. Both smiled. "I get it," he said with no sense of victory. "Man, do you have patience," Conner commented.

"I've got all the time in the world. And beyond. All the time," he added just for good measure.

"True. Me, too," Conner said, somewhat showing off.

"Yes, you do, my son."

Wow. My son. Double wow…with whipped cream and a cherry on top. Unbelievable.

Conner's head began to spin. "I must confess that I've lost track of where we are and what needs to be done."

"You were seeking to identify what you wanted to get in abundance."

"Oh, yeah. I got it down to two things, faith and love, just like Jesus declared."

God smiled. He smiled often. That was nice. When Conner had been growing up, many religious illustrations portrayed the people in them as serious, even sour. They appeared to be judgmental rather than encouraging. Although Conner hadn't been inundated with paintings of Jesus, the ones that he had viewed portrayed him as either condemnatory or vulnerable. God seemed much more cheerful than that, almost to the point of being, at times, mischievous.

"I'll go with faith," Conner concluded.

"You got it," God said, much like the genie who granted a wish to the finder of the lamp.

"Now what?" Conner asked, hoping not to be done.

"Now go convince others."

Conner was too dumbstruck to speak.

And then God was gone.

Chapter 6

Two mornings later, God was back at the kitchen island.

"The last time we were together…"

"We're always together," God corrected.

"You know what I mean."

"Go on."

"The last time we were together, you instructed me to influence others."

"Actually, I said convince others."

"How many others?"

"How many people are on earth?"

"What?"

"Mark 1:17."

"Which is?" Conner asked.

"*Come, follow me*, Jesus said, *and I will make you fishers of men*."

Conner nodded and smiled, remembering the verse.

"So you're good with this?" God asked.

"Are you really asking? I mean asking *asking*?"

"Son, it's entirely up to you whether or not you come forward on this."

Conner thought for a few moments. "You didn't really mean everyone, did you?"

"I did."

"Oh, come on," Conner whined.

"Ever hear of the story of David and Goliath?"

"But Goliath was just one man."

"How about my prophets?"

God was obviously ready to provide many more examples. Conner's silence conceded the point.

"How can I reach everyone?"

"Three ways. One is through disciples. My Son did so."

Conner nodded in agreement.

"There are other ways."

"Like what?"

"Like the use of electronic media. Today's message sharing has quite a bit more potential than what Jesus had at his human disposal."

"You want me to be your publicist?"

"No."

"Am I supposed to be today's Moses?"

"Oh, no. That would never do. Mo wouldn't appreciate something like that."

"Mo?"

"In heaven, everyone is on a first-name basis."

He seemed to become lost in thought, then snapped back.

"Nobody is too important. Everyone is equal. For example, nobody is called saint, pope, rabbi, doctor, professor or anything like that. Everyone has punched the same ticket, in a manner of speaking."

"Have you always spoken like that?"

"Spoken like what?"

"With phrases like 'punched the same ticket' for example."

"Oh, that." He stopped and chuckled. "I speak in the language most familiar to the person with whom I am speaking."

"You can speak all the languages of the world, now and through all time?"

"Of course. Who do you think handled the Tower of Babel?"

"Then speak with me in a remote language of the Australian bush."

God smiled. "Is this a test?"

A sudden flash of fear raced through Conner. Who was he to test God? The last question had come from God. Protocol dictated that Conner be the next one to speak.

"No," he lied.

God looked at Conner with a do-you-want-to-reconsider-that-response gaze.

"Okay, yes."

"I don't do tests," God said with a smile.

"I figured as much. You said that there were three ways," Conner prompted.

"So I did," God said, pleased that Conner had paid attention.

"And it is…?"

"Become bigger than life."

"Bigger than life? What does that mean?"

"Become a celebrity, one that many will want to emulate."

"Right. I can see it now. Conner Ramsey, the man who can recite the Bible forwards and backwards in seventeen languages." Conner smiled, pleased with himself. When he looked at his guest, he didn't see any smile. Oh, oh, he thought.

After fidgeting a bit, he asked "I still don't know what you want me to do with this information. It's not every day that someone speaks with God."

"Actually, that's not quite right. Do you know what omnipresent means?"

"Of course."

"I know that you know," he said, without a hint of frustration. "I'm just allowing you occasion to reflect on what it means."

"It means that you are everywhere."

"And do you know that I offer everyone both my attention and love?"

Conner was silent.

"You're skeptical." God looked at Conner without expression.

For the most part, Conner disliked it when his thoughts showed through. Here they seemed totally transparent.

"Well, truth be told..."

God interrupted. "Don't you normally tell the truth?"

Conner listened to the replay of that phrase. It really sounded foolish.

"Okay, let me begin again," Conner said. "It strikes me that you have been inattentive and not loving in the past." Then he quickly added "...sometimes."

Conner could have been looking at the Mona Lisa because all he saw was a beautiful but impassive face. God didn't try to defend himself. He simply nodded.

"I see. And from where, may I ask, are you drawing this observation?"

"Huh?" came the ineloquent reply.

"Is this your reading, your being influenced by others or your own thinking?"

Conner's initial reaction had been to blurt out "The Bible!" Upon further consideration, though, he realized that all three had contributed to his thinking. "All three. My reading, being influenced by others and my own thinking."

"Good," God observed.

"Good? Why good?"

"Had it only drawn from what you have read or been told, I would have been inclined to discount the value of what you say. Now that I know that you are factoring in your own thoughts, I give more consideration to what you offer."

Made sense.

"Thus?" Conner inquired.

"Thus nothing. You were the one who said that I was less than fully attentive and gave less than full love. I'd like to know why you think this is true."

"Do you mind if I ask you something?" Conner ventured.

God smiled, nodding his head.

"The Bible points to at least one time when you turned your back on Israel. Isn't that a demonstration of your not giving all of your attention to us?"

"Well said."

Conner began to feel a bit smug. If he was really God, had he not thought about this?

"Do you have children?"

That was a question out of left field. "No."

"Well, for the sake of this discussion, imagine that you do have children."

"Okay," Conner agreed.

"Do you think that it would be important to step back from them for their own sake?"

"You mean give them space?"

"Yes."

Conner thought about it. "Yes. Of course." Conner was getting the point. "I see what you're saying," he conceded.

They were silent for a moment. Conner wanted time to process this a bit more. God sat there impassively. Conner wouldn't have been surprised if a bird had alit upon his shoulder. None did. God continued to look at Conner but not with an I-won-the-point look. Instead, it was with an I-support-your-thinking-about-this look. He wasn't rushing Conner and didn't make him feel as though they were in a debate.

Conner conceded the issue about attentiveness, at least for the moment. "What about the lack of love?" It was more a question than a challenge, although it came out somewhat more aggressively than intended.

"What about it?" God asked.

"There were a few instances recounted in the Bible that struck me as your being pretty darn mad."

"I was. To which are you referring?"

"Remember the flood? Remember Ananias and Sapphira? Remember Sodom and Gomorrah? Remember that fellow who touched the ark?"

That was when Conner ran out of remember whens.

"Do you know what omniscient means?"

Oh, no. Here we go again. "It means that you are all knowing," Conner answered.

"All knowing," God highlighted. There was silence. Conner backtracked to understand why he had been asked that question. Was God trying to throw him off track? After a moment, Conner realized the purpose. Conner could now see God's point.

"Okay, you *do* remember these instances." He emphasized 'do' for God's sake.

"Would you ever punish your children?" God asked. No challenge, no smugness, nothing other than what seemed to be an innocent inquiry. It quickly crossed Conner's mind that he would not want to play poker with God. Then the word omniscient popped back into his head and it provided a second reason to avoiding gambling with him. Conner's brain smiled as he thought of playing someone who knew what was going on in your head and didn't betray any of it with his outward facial appearance. Man, if he had those characteristics, he could really clean up.

Conner snapped back to reality. Would he ever punish his children?

"Of course. But you already knew my answer," he added playfully, even daring to toss in a wink. "However, I would never spank them."

Silence.

"Okay, maybe I would do it once, but only if they really, really deserved it."

More silence.

"...and maybe I would do it a second time, if the situation called for it."

Silence. God was encouraging Conner to work this out in his own head rather than being instructed. Conner gave himself a little time to think about it.

A great argument raced into his head: "There's a whole lot of difference between spanking someone and killing them," Conner said.

"And you base this on...?" God didn't finish his sentence, thus inviting Conner to complete it.

"You don't think that there is a difference between a spanking and death?" Conner was louder and more challenging than he had intended.

"It's not polite to answer a question with a question," God commented, then added "I do it, too."

God continued. "If you walked up to a house – let's say that it's a large house – and looked in through one window, what would you see? Let's also say that there are no curtains, blinds or other obstructions to prevent you from looking into the house."

"What? What has this got to do with death?"

"Just humor me. Answer the question."

"It would depend on what was in the house. I guess that I would see whatever was in that room. Is that what you're looking for?"

"Good. Now, let's suppose that I asked you to describe what was in the rest of the house without allowing you to look in through any other windows. In fact, I wouldn't allow you to walk around the house or make other investigations. What would be your answer?"

"I don't know. How would I know?" Conner tried to envision the situation. "Are there individual rooms or is it one big space, sort of like an auditorium?" He figured that maybe this was a trick. If so, he was going to demonstrate his keen mind.

God smiled. It was a kind smile, not one of frustration. "There's no trickery involved here. It's a house with seven rooms, each with walls and whatever one finds in a typical house."

"Well, in that case, I wouldn't know for sure. Maybe I could guess but it would feed off the information that I got from the only room I was able to observe. Only trouble is, if it were a bedroom, that wouldn't tell me much about the kitchen or the rest of the house." Conner thought a bit more about it. "And if it was the kitchen, that also wouldn't be too informative. Actually, it would be virtually impossible."

"That's my point."

"What point?" Conner asked.

"That you don't know all the rooms."

This was going a bit deeper than Conner had wished, although he sort of sensed where the road led through this dense fog.

"You're saying…" His thoughts trailed off.

"Keep going," God encouraged.

"…that I'm judging our world by only looking into one room. Is that what you mean?"

"Bingo," God said with a warm smile.

"Wow. That's a lot to think about. I'm not certain that I can get my hands around that, at least not right now."

"No rush," he offered. "You've got plenty of time to think about it."

"But I want answers right now," Conner semi-demanded. He replayed what he had just said, how he had just said it and to whom he had just said it. Whoops.

Reading Conner's thoughts, God said: "I equipped the human mind to address these issues. Faith is not necessary where certainty resides. Remember that. You have plenty of time to develop your thoughts on this and a myriad of other things. That's why you have life."

Another 'wow' ran through Conner's head. "This is a laboratory?" was all he could think to ask.

God slightly tilted his head as though pondering what had just been asked. Then he smiled. "Yes. That's one way to put it."

"I'd like to schedule another get together." One of Conner's professional strengths was also one of his greatest shortcomings, that of project managing his life.

"It doesn't work that way but I'll be back." God said the last part exactly like Arnold Schwarzenegger had delivered it in *The Terminator*.

Conner looked at him, not knowing whether to laugh or read something deeper into his imitation.

"One of my favorite movies," God offered.

"But I have loads and loads of questions," Conner pleaded.

"Of course. That's why you have the ability to use your senses in concert with your brains. This gives my children opportunities to conceptualize and to consider. In case you didn't notice, there are some differences between humans and the rest of the inhabitants on this planet."

Conner firmly brought his lips together. He nodded his head, looked away to gather his thoughts. When he looked back, God was gone...in a manner of speaking. But, in a larger sense, he was still there. Conner almost heard him say "Gather what you may from as many sources as you have available. Then, and only then, make up your own mind."

Conner leaned over and picked up his Bible. Although well-worn from study, it hadn't been intimately visited in a while. No time like the present to spend time with a friend.

Chapter 7

Two days later, Conner went into the kitchen and found God sitting there. God smiled. Conner smiled. God's smile was natural, Conner's awkward.

"Are you always this chipper in the morning?"

"The time of day makes no difference to me."

"It doesn't?"

"Nope. I don't sleep. I don't need to sleep. In fact, here's a news flash for you."

"What?"

"I don't need anything. Nuthin', nada, zippo, zero, goose eggs."

Conner thought about it. Yeah, God wouldn't have needs. Lucky stiff. Man, if that was me, I'd be doing some serious enjoyment.

"You wouldn't like it," God responded to Conner's thoughts.

"Oh, yeah? Give me a chance to find out."

"Trust me, you wouldn't like it. If you knew that you could have as much of anything you wanted, you'd be begging to be human again."

Conner didn't say anything. His intellectual side understood this logic. His emotional side wanted to experience it.

Smiling, God said: "There was a really great *Twilight Zone* about a rotten guy who died and got everything that he wanted. Early on, he asked why he qualified for heaven. He came to find out that he was not in heaven and that personal fulfillment requires uncertainty. It was really good."

"You watch television?"

"Oh, yeah. Great idea. Great invention. And there have been some really good shows. *I Love Lucy* was super. I should have kept her alive longer. *The Honeymooners* with Jackie Gleason and *Mission Impossible* were good, too. And then there was *Gunsmoke*. And how about *Hawaii 5-0*? 'Book 'em, Dano.' Oh, yeah. I loved that line."

Conner started to ask when he had time to watch TV, then thought better of it.

"So?"

"So what?"

"So have you figured out what you are going to do to spread the Word?" God asked.

After an extended silence, during which Conner was not interrupted, he answered: "No."

"It's not easy, is it?"

Conner grunted, conceding the point.

"I could have told you that two days ago. I just wanted you to have time to consider it a bit more deeply."

"I have, although trying to get my arms around how to bring others to the Lord…er, to you, is challenging, to say the least. When you tell me to reach *everyone*, I'm ready to quit before I begin."

"Have I ever left one of my chosen out there by him or herself?"

"I don't know."

God laughed. "Good one," he said. "Well, take my word for it. I've never chosen someone for a task, any task, and not effectively equipped him or her."

"Has anyone ever failed?"

"Of course."

"What do you mean 'of course'?"

"Anytime I choose someone, they may or may not succeed. However, it won't be because I didn't enable them to succeed. It will be because they lost faith."

"Like Peter getting out of the boat and walking on water."

"Bingo. He could have walked all over that lake had he maintained his faith."

Conner nodded.

"Good thing that he could swim," God added with a huge grin.

Both were quiet.

"I have decided to equip you with certain special skills that you will need to fulfill your destiny." Pause. "If you want to, that is," he added.

"I have a choice?"

"As I said before, people have free will. This is yours to undertake or dismiss."

"Yes," Conner replied. "Definitely."

"Excellent. Now, remember to use these skills wisely, not to show them off but not to ignore them either."

"Yes, sir."

"Good deal. And don't tell people that you and I have been chatting."

"Why not?"

"Because they won't believe you."

"Oh. Okay. I understand."

They looked at each other. Conner didn't know what to say. Apparently, God had nothing else to say.

"Ta ta," God said with a big smile.

"Wait a minute!" Conner whined, like a kindergartner being dropped off for his first day at school.

"What?" God asked.

"What are the skills?"

"Oh, you'll learn what they are in due time. Your assignment will be to determine how best to use them."

"Oh, for…" Conner began to say for God's sake, then thought better of it. "Come on!"

"Listen, if this was a paint-by-numbers assignment, I'd substitute a robot."

He's got a point. "Okay but will you be there, actively, to help me?"

"I'll be there," was all that God was willing to allow.

Conner looked at him.

"Faith is not necessary where certainty resides," he reminded Conner.

Then he was gone. Poof!

"Great!" Conner said dejectedly out loud.

After looking himself over, including naked in the full-length mirror in the bathroom, Conner concluded that he couldn't identify any changes. No physical changes were obvious. He didn't feel different. What could God have equipped him with?

He went to bed that night running an inventory of possibilities through his head.

The next morning Conner woke up, sat straight up in his bed and wondered if his conversations with the Lord had simply been a well-remembered dream. He decided that it had been real.

Nothing happened differently that day. He wasn't smarter, didn't have Superman-like vision, couldn't squeeze sand into a diamond and was not able to listen to conversations beyond a normal range of hearing. Each time he used the bathroom, he took an extra bit of time looking at himself in the mirror. Nope, nothing that he could see.

At the end of the day, he decided to go work out at the gym. He got on the stationary cycle, somewhat wondering if his gift would be increased cardio.

Absolutely not, he concluded shortly after starting. He completed his warm-up ride and moved into the weight room.

He wondered if he would have extraordinary strength. Nope. The weights were just as heavy as they had been the last time. Maybe heavier. After completing some barbell curls, Pete Carlyle, one of his gym-rat buddies, popped his head into the weight room.

"Hey, Conner, we need one more for some three-on-three hoops. Come on." It wasn't a question, only an expectation.

Conner started to protest, then decided to join him. "Okay. Be right there."

Conner relaced his sneakers, retied his shorts, returned the weights and went onto the basketball court. Five guys were shooting two balls, obviously waiting for the sixth player. Pete bounced a ball to him so that he could shoot a few. He went from air balls to rim shots and then made one from just inside the foul line, although it rattled around before falling through.

"Okay, he's ready," Pete said, not conferring with his friend. Conner considered protesting but changed his mind. If he were given a lifetime, his shot would not materially improve. He determined to play good defense and enjoy the exercise.

"What are the sides?" Pete asked.

Conner was about six feet tall but couldn't jump over a pebble. Pete was the same height and could dunk. All of the others were 6'5" or better, one probably closer to 6'8". From the way each of the others seemed to handle the ball, they had all played organized hoops before. Other than hockey (Conner could barely stand up on skates), this was the worst of what he would call the main sports for him. Aside from Pete, he didn't know any of the other guys. What had he gotten into here? He reiterated encouragement to himself with advice to play as well as he could and to enjoy himself.

The tall guy pointed to Pete and said that he and Conner would be on one team while the remaining three would be on the other. From what little Conner had seen, this looked like they were about to get a butt whipping.

"Enjoy yourself," he whispered to himself as he took off his sweatshirt and walked onto the floor.

"You guard the little guy," Pete said. Conner looked at him like he was crazy. Pete had pointed to what looked like the playmaker. At least that's what Conner thought about this guy's skills, having seen him dribble the ball without paying even the least attention to it during the warm up.

Mr. Playmaker came over and extended his hand. "Jordan," he said.

"Conner."

Great, he was going to guard a guy named Jordan. He's nearly half a foot taller, played organized ball and can probably leap over defenders with the greatest of ease. Conner took a deep breath and came back to his words of personal encouragement.

"Your ball," Jordan told Pete, suggesting that this slight advantage would not make any difference. Intuitively, Conner tended to agree with him.

Pete inbounded to the team's third player, Bob. He pump faked a shot, but it didn't faze the man guarding him. Conner came around the top of the key and Bob passed it to him. It went right through Conner's hands and out of bounds.

"Sorry."

"No problem," Pete responded. "Okay, good D," he barked.

The ball was inbounded by their team to a player and then passed to Jordan. Conner got into a low crouch to maximize his limited ability to stay with the ball. Bad idea. Jordan lifted straight up, seemed to stay there for half an hour, and calmly drained his jump shot, the ball not even touching the rim as it went through.

The game called for the scorers to take the ball out each time. Again the ball came to Jordan. This time, Conner crouched less, got closer and determined to make it more difficult for Jordan to take an uncontested jump shot. Good concept. Poor tactic. Just as soon as Conner stepped closer, Jordan was past him and dunking the ball with both hands before Conner could even turn around.

The other team shared high fives. Conner looked at Pete who smiled, understanding the mismatch.

The next five points were made by Jordan's threesome, Pete's team not even earning any chance to get the ball. Seven nothing and Conner's team had touched the ball on offense once, when they first took it out.

"Ya wanna play to eleven or switch sides?" Jordan asked.

Now this was insulting, to say the least. In effect, he was asking if Pete's team wanted to give up and try to balance the distribution of players on the court in another game. In other words, he was saying that Pete's team stunk. From what had transpired, he wasn't all that wrong.

"Nah, let's finish it," Pete said.

Pete's team got a little better, losing 11 to 1, having gotten the ball two other times. By the end of the game, the other team barely had broken a sweat.

"Water break," Pete said. The other team just stayed on the floor to continue shooting. Bob, Pete and Conner walked across the floor to the water fountain.

"They're good," Bob said, in one of lifetime's great understatements.

"Uh, yeah," Pete said sarcastically.

"Should we switch sides?" Bob asked. Understanding that this might be less than politically correct, he added "I'm good either way." He didn't mean it. Nobody likes to get drilled, especially by a bunch of cocky competitors.

"Let's try it one more time," Pete suggested.

Conner raised his eyebrows. Bob said nothing.

"You okay with that?" Pete asked.

"Yeah, I guess so," Conner responded.

"I'm good," Bob courageously offered.

"Let me go make a whiz and then we'll give 'em the what for," Pete said, scooting off to the locker room.

Bob joined the other three to take a few shots and Conner sat down in the bleachers. Man, I could have had a good workout inside with the weights but had to get suckered into coming in here, he thought. Okay, quit complaining. Just finish it off and do the best you can, Conner admonished himself. All you can do is the best you can do. After that, you can finish your workout.

Before getting up, he offered a little prayer. "Lord, I'm ready for you to show me what my unique skill is. If I don't know it, I'll have a heck of a time using it effectively for the purpose you intended. How about showing it to me after this game, or at least giving me a hint?"

Conner sat a little longer, then added "Seriously, though, Lord, thank you for giving me the ability to be here and to play basketball with these guys. I need to think more about what you have given me rather than what I believe I am missing."

Conner returned to the floor.

----- ----- -----

"You want me to guard him?" Pete asked, referring to Jordan.

"No. Let me take another try."

Pete didn't say anything and Conner took that to be reluctant agreement.

Conner happened to look over to the bleachers and saw an elderly man with a cane take a seat on the bottom row. The man moved gingerly, almost falling into a seated position. Conner wondered what he was doing in the gym. He figured that the man might be the grandfather of one of the other five or maybe he was just waiting for one of his grandchildren...or great grandchildren. After that observation and momentary reflection, Conner returned to the game at hand.

"You take it out," Jordan said, this time more dismissively.

Conner figured that this might be somewhat boring for Jordan. Better competition would be more challenging for him. Conner also figured that this game would be their last.

Bob inbounded to Pete who threw it to Conner. He returned the pass to Bob who sank a hook shot.

Wow, we're leading, Conner said to himself.

Bob inbounded to Conner who passed it to Pete. Not being guarded very closely, Pete chose to launch a jump shot. It hit the front rim and was easily rebounded by the tallest guy on the other team. His arms seemed to reach the ceiling. He could have stood there with the ball over his head and Conner could not have reached it, maybe not even with a chair.

The rebounder passed it to Jordan who caught it with ease. Conner crouched with a little less intensity but also closed the distance between them. Jordan took that as an invitation to drive toward the basket. When he put the ball down, Conner took a wild swipe at it and knocked it across the gym floor.

"Way to go!" Pete chirped. "Good hands."

Conner smiled, knowing that it was pure luck.

One of their team retrieved the ball and dribbled it back to the half court line. He inbounded from there. Once again, it wound up in Jordan's hands. Conner took the same stance at the same distance.

Jordan decided to rectify his mistake on the previous play, probably that of being too casual with the ball. He began another drive toward the basket. Once again, Conner took a wild slap at the ball and, much to his and everyone else's surprise, knocked it back across the gym.

"Yeah, that's what I'm talkin' 'bout," Pete said.

Conner smiled, deciding that he had been lucky twice in a row. However, somewhere deep inside, he sensed that luck hadn't been such a large part of those two defensive plays. Both had been wild swings, somehow hoping to get a small piece of the ball and both had resulted in his hitting the ball dead center. Conner wondered if it was luck or if slowing down might mean that he could steal the ball instead of batting it across the gym. He decided to find out.

He looked at Jordan who appeared to be annoyed more than concerned. Conner was certain that luck was all Jordan would attribute it to. "Let's go, little man," Jordan barked at Conner.

That's not the type of putdown that one likes to hear anywhere, least of all on a basketball court. Conner said nothing. Conner didn't have the ammunition to trash talk with him. He just determined to do as well as he could.

Two passes and Jordan had the ball again. Once more, Jordan was determined to prove that he owned his defender on the court. He faked a jump shot. Conner didn't bite. He faked it again. Same response. Then he chose to drive to Conner's left, instead of to his right. Conner kept his composure and, instead of swiping at the ball, tried to focus on its center. In an odd sort of way, everything around him slowed down. Thus, it was easy for him to reach out and take the ball in the middle of Jordan's dribble. Once done, he immediately passed it to Bob.

"Quick hands," Pete said.

Bob passed it back to Conner. At that moment, it was clear to everyone on the court that Jordan was determined to put Conner in his place. He stepped closer and continued to inch in. Conner stepped to his right and Jordan started to cut off his path. Once again, everything slowed down. Conner returned to his original stance and headed off to his left while Jordan's entire weight was still going toward Conner's right. That left the entire floor open. Conner made a layup off the backboard as easily as if he was the only person on the floor. Jordan was still at the foul line by the time that the ball went in.

"Kick A!" Pete yelled. "What woke you up?"

Conner smiled, realizing that something strange was going on.

For the next three plays, it was mano-y-mano between Jordan and Conner. The other four players were leaving them alone, understanding that this had to be settled between the two combatants. But now it was no match. Had Conner wanted to do so, he could have dribbled between Jordan's legs. Conner chose not to embarrass Jordan, only to do his best.

On the next play, Pete took a jump shot that missed. The tall guy on the other team rebounded the ball. When he went to pass it to the third player, he brought it to his chest. He did this in such slow motion that it was not a challenge for Conner to almost walk over and take it away. When Conner had possession of the ball, play returned to normal motion, the tall guy having a dumbfounded look on his face.

Conner happened to look over to the old man in the stands. He was smiling and tapping his cane in obvious delight. He was clearly enjoying this turn of events.

Pete's team won that game 11 to 0, the scores mostly coming from Bob and Pete because Conner was getting double and triple teamed on each play. Once he had the ball, it was easy passing it to one of his teammates, especially since the defenders were reacting in slow motion. Had Conner actually wanted to do so, he could have driven around all three on each play and scored on a layup himself.

Pete loved this result and couldn't wait to say "Ya wanna switch sides?" to the other team.

The irritated silence communicated that the others were not willing to concede being overmatched. A third game was played with Pete's team winning again in a shutout. All through it, the other players moved at a normal pace until Conner needed them to slow down. Then they would slow down and it became like Conner was an NBA veteran playing against elementary school kids.

"Gotta go," Jordan said, without even a high five or other salutation. The other two reluctantly said "Good game" and followed their star out the door. Pete and Bob stood with Conner.

"Where did that come from?" Pete asked.

"Yeah, man," Bob added.

"I don't know," Conner said. And then he did. The old man in the stands was gone.

"Hey, I need to get home. Thanks a lot, guys. Nice meeting you Bob. Good seeing you again, Pete." He waved as he ran toward the exit.

"Conner, wait a second," Pete said.

Conner stopped.

"Bob and I play on a regular team. Full court. It's great. We play tomorrow. We can add you to the roster. Can you play?"

"Well…" Conner said and then paused. "This was a fluke," he confessed.

"It sure was different than any other game you brought to the floor," Pete said with a wide grin. "But you'll never know if you can back it up unless you test it out again."

He was right, of course.

"What time?"

"It starts at 6:30. We get the floor at 6:00. We play right here."

"Okay, see ya then," Conner said.

Conner didn't see them exchanging high fives as he exited.

A little to his surprise, nobody was home when he arrived there.

Chapter 8

The next day literally flew by. Uncharacteristically, he was particularly well focused on whatever he was doing, almost as though he had consumed some potent caffeine. When he had a free moment, he daydreamed about the three-on-three game the night before. Had it been a fluke? He also spent time wondering about the old man who had watched him play and had then disappeared. Was that the G-Man in another body or just a coincidence? There were justifications for both. And, not to be forgotten, Conner nursed his aches and pains from the half-court game the day before.

At 5:15 P.M., Conner went to the gym, stopping to get a smoothie for some quick energy. From the way that it hit his stomach, it was clear that he hadn't taken the time to eat wisely all day. Not a good idea. Daydreaming was one thing, starving another. He got to the gym at 5:45 and decided to ride the bike for about fifteen minutes to warm up. He hadn't been playing basketball that often and, after all, he wasn't a teenager anymore.

He got on the bike and rode. It wasn't the exercise kind of ride that he did at home or in the gym. Instead, it was a warm-up-the-old-muscles rotation. He chose the stationary bike that had the moving handle bars so he could warm up both his upper and lower body. When he was finished, he stretched.

Just after 6:00, Pete looked down the locker row and said "Hey, man, I'm glad that you're here. Did you bring your A game?"

"As much as ever."

"Then we're in great shape," he said. "If you play anywhere near like yesterday, we'll be competitive."

"And if not?"

"This team will kill us. Everyone on this team played Division I basketball, a couple even pro ball overseas."

"Oh, great," Conner said. "Listen, Pete, yesterday had to be a fluke. I never played like that before. Not even close."

"Yeah, yeah," he said. "See ya on the floor. Hustle it up. We only have a few minutes to get warmed up."

Before Conner could better prepare Pete for the letdown that he fully expected, his friend was gone.

"Great. Just great."

Conner finished lacing up his sneakers and stood up, ready to take the floor and probably be faked out of his shorts and sneakers by whomever he guarded. His heart started racing. Maybe I could have a heart attack and skip the embarrassment, he thought. Stupid idea, of course. Who would wish for a heart attack, much less in order not to play in a basketball game? Dope.

He bowed his head, bringing his hands together between his knees. "Lord," he began, then realized that he didn't really know what to say. He paused for a few seconds. "Lord, allow me to understand your purpose and to rise to it, that I keep your objectives above my pride and that I model how all men should behave. Thank you for this opportunity. Thank you for everything, Lord, especially salvation, the one gift that transcends all others. I ask this all in the name of Jesus. Amen."

Conner stood up, took a deep breath and went into the gym. Here goes, he said to himself.

There were seven players shooting baskets to the left, including both Pete and Bob. There were eight players shooting baskets to the right. Those eight looked like behemoths, part man and part bear, with the dominating part being the bear. They wore expensive uniforms. Even their sneakers matched. They must have a sponsor, Conner figured. They were neatly organized into drill formations working on layups. Then they broke into an organized semicircle and took jump shots. It was a precise, well-orchestrated use of time. Pete's team looked incredibly ragged by comparison. On top of all that, the other team had an actual rooting section. There were more than twenty people cheering for them, virtually all of them wearing team colors. Two of the women even had pompoms. Talk about overkill.

Conner stood at the door for a good minute before Pete hollered to him to come over.

As he approached, Pete tossed him a jersey. Like those jerseys being worn by his teammates, this one was well-worn. It had the number seven on it. "Go get 'em, tiger," Pete said. "I'm not gonna start you. That will give you a chance to see what we're up against. We'll find an opportunity to get you in. Don't worry about that."

Conner didn't worry about *not getting* in. He worried about *getting* in.

Before he could further embellish his anticipated defeat, he distinctly heard a voice, although he realized that it was in his head.

"With God, all things are possible. Remember Goliath?" the voice concluded.

"I do," he said aloud as he donned his jersey.

"What?" Pete asked.

"Nothing," Conner said. "Let's do this."

Pete introduced Conner to the rest of the team. Bob winked at him as Pete introduced each of the other five. "Good to have ya," was the gist of what most said, although not with much enthusiasm. They looked like a bunch of lovable losers painted by Norman Rockwell.

Before the team broke, Conner stepped into the huddle and said "All things are possible with God."

"Yeah, right," was the only comment made. Briefly, Conner thought about Joshua and Caleb entering Canaan. This was very different and yet very much similar.

Thank you, Lord, Conner said to himself, knowing that God was with him and that this was but a step on the journey to what God wanted him to do on a bigger stage. Conner just wasn't sure how this gift, if he still had it, would tie into God's purpose. He relaxed knowing that God would show him.

The whistle blew and each team brought out its players. Aside from Bob, the other team's five players towered over Pete's team. Bob jumped center. He was not only three or four inches shorter than the man he was jumping against but probably fifty or sixty pounds lighter.

The other team won the jump ball and scored with two passes and a dunk in five seconds. Pete's team had an impossible time inbounding the ball against the other team's full-court press. Out of five tries, twice they threw it away and twice they had the pass intercepted. On the other try, the team's guard double dribbled when he was caught in the corner. It was 18-2 after four minutes and ten seconds.

All this time, the other team's rooting section had created a deafening noise, even for such a small number of people. With hardly any other folks in the stands, the sounds reverberated off the walls. Conner wished to muzzle them, especially one particularly loud woman, who really didn't seem to have her priorities in life all that straight. Then Conner reprimanded himself, thinking that she might well be perfectly adjusted, just the type of person who gave 100% to whatever she did. Probably not, but he was willing to give her the benefit of the doubt.

After Pete's team threw the ball away again, Pete called time out. "Worse things have happened in life," he said.

"Like getting run over by a cement truck?" one of the players said dejectedly.

Everyone laughed, although the illustration didn't seem all that unconnected.

"Conner," Pete said, "you go in for Drew."

"Thank goodness," Drew said. "Rotsa ruck," he added sarcastically, happily heading to the water cooler, not even waiting to hear if Pete had any instructions.

They put their hands together as Pete said "One, two, break" and everyone less than enthusiastically joined on the last word.

When they took the floor, they saw that the other team had made changes to its lineup. The three inside players were replaced. They hadn't sacrificed any size in doing so. The two guards remained. Conner was told to defend one of the guards, number eighteen.

The other team inbounded comfortably as Pete's team didn't press them at all. Eighteen held two fingers up signaling a play. He never paid any attention to the ball. It could have been tucked up under his arm as though he was walking on the street with it. Yet, he kept his dribble alive as he proceeded toward the top of the key.

Okay, Conner said to himself. Just relax.

In the middle of his dribble, Eighteen took the ball and casually threw it toward his center who had broken free under the basket. Conner had no problem stepping to his left and intercepting the pass. He also had no problem beating everyone down the floor for a layup.

"Nice, Seven," an opposing player said. "You better remember that," he added. "It'll be your only positive memory of the day."

Conner smiled, not cocky, just remembering the passage from Mark that had gone through his head before the game. He tried not to judge Eighteen. After all, trash talk had become part of basketball culture.

Eighteen inbounded the ball and his mate brought it up the court. When he went to pass it to Eighteen, Conner was easily able to step into its path and take it to the basket for another layup. The scoreboard now read 18-6.

Once more, the ball was inbounded to Eighteen. Conner decided to pick him up at three-quarters court. Eighteen smirked and waved his partner across the court, fully confident that he could dazzle Conner just as he had probably done to others all his life. He put the ball in his left hand and started to dribble between his legs as he walked forward, clearly intent on humiliating his defender.

Eighteen did that for three paces before Conner stepped in and simply tapped the ball back between his legs, trotted over to pick it up and made yet another layup. When he turned to go back up court, it was obvious that Eighteen was none too happy. Perhaps sensing this, their team captain on the bench called for a time out.

When Pete's team huddled up, there was surprise on the faces of Conner's teammates. Drew, the guy Conner had replaced, said "Nice going. Really. Nice going."

"Thanks."

"Yeah, really," he added. "I didn't expect us to get eight points the whole game. We've reached that and it's still the first half."

"All things are possible with God," Conner repeated.

"I guess so," he replied. "But let's see how long God sticks around when they make their adjustments."

Conner stopped talking. He who has eyes will watch and he who has ears will listen. As for the others, well, God gives us choices.

Pete chimed up "Let's clog the middle. Good boxing out. Let's leave Piper and Conner to take care of the outside. Our focus has to be one and done each time they bring the ball up. I'll talk to the ref about keeping after them about three seconds in the lane."

After being silent for a few minutes, the other team's cheerleading squad returned in full force. Obviously, to everyone associated with their team, what had happened was simply a fluke, nothing more. The rest of the game would proceed as the game had begun, in a rout.

Eighteen loudly proclaimed "I've got Seven," looking at Conner defiantly. In other words, this was going to be him against Conner and he had no intention of anything surprising happening.

Pete, Bob and the other forward bottled up the lane. Piper, a good playground hoopster but not someone who had played beyond high school, did his best to assume the pose, that of a good defender against their other guard. The other guard passed it to Eighteen who, seeing Conner step forward, immediately passed it back.

Was he intimidated?

The other guard caught the ball and when Piper crouched defensively, he got off a jump shot that went in without a rattle. The referee held up three fingers. The scoreboard read 21-8.

As Piper and Conner walked to the end line to inbound the ball, it was clear that the other team planned to resume its full-court press, something that had caused problems early in the game.

Conner told him to throw the ball where he was not. Piper looked at Conner quizzically. "What?" he asked.

"They're good defenders. Throw it to where I'm not."

"Okay," he replied compliantly.

"Look one way and throw it another," Conner confirmed.

"Gotcha," Piper said, still confused.

Piper picked up the ball and proceeded to look to his right. The man guarding him shaded in that direction. Conner stood pretty much at the foul line with Eighteen guarding him to the side of where Piper was looking. Then, without tipping it off, Piper threw the ball to his left. Without a problem, Conner trotted over and picked it up.

When he turned to go up court, Eighteen was down in his best defensive posture. "You and me," he challenged. "You and me, buddy boy."

Conner wanted to say something, then thought otherwise. The quote from Proverbs bounced into his head: *Pride goes before destruction, a haughty spirit before a fall.* That had always been a favorite passage of his. Besides, he admitted, this isn't me, only my body. Conner was supposed to spread the Good News, not show his individual supremacy. Conner smiled at Eighteen, trying to project warmth and caring.

Conner's regular speed against slow motion, something that only came into play when it needed to be present, created a clear mismatch. Conner dribbled as though he was going left and Eighteen tried to respond, figuring to beat him to the spot and draw a charge. Conner changed directions and Eighteen tried to shift his center of gravity. This caused him to lose balance, although not completely. Just before he regained his balance to head off in the correct direction for the second move, Conner changed direction again and, this time, Eighteen could do nothing but fall down on his rump, his heels slightly off the floor. It looked pretty funny, more like a Keystone Kops sort of thing than a basketball move, but it definitely didn't draw laughter from any of the spectators rooting for them.

Once past Eighteen, Conner slowed down to draw their other players toward him. All four took at least one step toward Conner. As they did so, he passed the ball to Pete in the corner who hit a three-pointer. About five minutes remained in the first half.

As Conner went up court, he told Piper to take away the outside shot from the man he was guarding. "If he beats you on a drive, make it be toward the center of the court and whatever happens will be on me. Okay?"

"Okay," Piper said and did exactly as he was asked. The man he was guarding saw the overplay and drove past him. Conner stepped in and the guy with the ball figured that there was an open pass to Eighteen. When he released it, Conner intercepted the pass and scored on another easy layup. He tried to stay within himself. This was not about his greatness but, instead, about what God could do through him. It was a bit of a struggle for Conner because he was not used to anything near this level of success. Nevertheless, he managed to keep his ego in check.

The next time, Piper's opponent decided to drive but not to pass the ball. Conner took it at the bottom of his dribble and passed it to Piper for an easy breakaway layup. Next time, not willing to concede to this, the same guard tried a jump shot. However, Piper was close enough to him that he didn't really have a good look at the basket. Instead, it was an off-balance shot that resulted in an easy defensive rebound for Bob. Piper brought the ball up the court.

Conner wove behind Piper and took the ball. Both guards double teamed him. Piper saw that, went toward the basket and Conner easily fed him the ball for a layup. After stealing their inbound pass, Pete's team set up offensively. Conner did the same thing as before, getting the ball from behind Piper, the two guards even more aggressively guarding him. Conner jumped up and passed the ball to Piper. Their large center came to block him and Piper was able to easily pass it to Bob who made a two-handed dunk.

Again, the other team called time out.

Pete and Bob were beaming, the other players half smiling and half stunned.

Drew asked "What are you doing in a recreation league? Where did you play college ball?"

"I didn't play sports in college."

"You didn't?" he said incredulously. "Why not?"

"I wasn't good enough."

"You weren't good enough? Who else was on that team, Michael Jordan and Julius Irving?"

Conner laughed "I just wasn't good enough."

Drew just shook his head. "Can I be your agent?" he asked, half joking, half serious.

"I have help." Conner said.

"Huh?"

"Do you believe in Jesus Christ?"

Trying to be cute, he answered "I will if you want me to."

Conner didn't respond but suddenly began to realize how well he was positioned to influence others. I get it, he thought. I get it.

Conner reminded himself that he wasn't on a mission to destroy. He had what he felt was an obligation to make the evening meaningful for both teams, a chore that was not going to be easy. Thus, he focused on defense.

Piper continued to hound one guard while Conner loosely watched Eighteen, all the time observing that his opponent's level of frustration was rising. If one of their forwards took a shot, then Conner let him do so, not intending to run all over the court. If they made those shots, good for them. However, they only made a shade over a third of them. Pete, Bob and the other forward controlled the defensive boards.

On offense, Conner handled the ball long enough to spot one of his teammates who was open. Lots of times Conner would start driving to the basket, draw in the defenders and then pass it to someone who was free for an uncontested jump shot or layup.

By the end of the first half, Pete's team led 36-24. The other team's cheering section was silent, more stunned than anything else. Both teams huddled under opposite baskets to adjust their strategies. Pete's team was the more relaxed of the two. Whenever Conner happened to glance down to the other end of the court, he could see two or three of them glaring back. One of the glarers was always Eighteen. This was not what the other team had expected and the players were not happy about it.

----- ----- -----

Although Pete wanted Conner to start the second half, he declined. First, he wasn't used to this much basketball. Even though he could move somewhat casually and still be appreciably quicker than anyone else, these were movements that he didn't normally do, like zigzagging back and forth. Second, he was still the newbie on the team and he wanted to appropriately respect his teammates. With a twelve-point lead, Pete replaced Conner.

The other team was surprised not to see Conner playing. Since they had won the opening tap, Pete's team got to inbound the ball in the second half. Much as they had done early in the first half, the inbounding process was botched four straight times. By then, the lead was down to three points. The other team's cheerleading vocalists were back in full voice.

Pete called time out and everyone agreed that Conner had to go back in.

As before, Piper looked one way and inbounded another. Conner grabbed the ball and dribbled through the slow-motion defense for an uncontested layup.

"Come on!" yelled Eighteen. "We agreed," he added.

Agreed what? Conner wondered. He was soon to find out.

After stealing the ball, Conner passed it to Piper and stood close to the half court line, more out of range than anything else in order to allow the others to have their hand at trying to score. Really, he was just an observer.

Then, wham, he caught a forearm in the chest and went down in a heap. It was no love tap, more like a sucker punch in a boxing ring. When he looked up, Eighteen was glaring down at him. Eighteen didn't need to say anything. His intention was clear, as was his lack of sportsmanship.

The ref blew his whistle and put his hand on Eighteen's chest, pushing him toward his team's bench. "There's no need for that, Eighteen," he said. "One more like that and you'll be tossed out of the league, not just out of this game. There's no room for behavior like that." Then the ref signaled a technical on Eighteen.

Conner sat on the floor trying to regroup while Eighteen showed zero remorse. Instead, he continued to glare. To him, this was war and you did what you needed to do. In this case, it was cold conk the other team's difference maker.

Conner's teammates came around as Pete helped him up. "You want payback?" he asked. "We can give them payback, you know," he added for emphasis.

"Absolutely not," Conner said. "He's hurting worse than I am."

Conner wondered where this wisdom came from. Then he smiled as he realized its source.

"Don't tell me," Drew chimed in. "This is the turn-the-other-cheek part of you."

"Matthew 5:39," Conner cited, no longer amazed at his Bible recall.

"Figured as much," Drew said.

Conner looked over to Eighteen. There was no concern and certainly no apology associated with Eighteen's countenance. Had Eighteen been the one hit, Conner could have understood his look. It was difficult to understand under the current conditions. Conner strove to see this through his eyes. After a moment, he saw some light.

"Listen, guys," Conner said. "Let's give him a second chance. Please."

Conner saw varying responses in his teammates.

"Please?" he repeated.

Four of the seven replied with an audible yes. Two nodded their heads. One did not reply. Pete said "No."

He turned to Pete. "I'm asking you to ignore what Eighteen did. Don't try to pay him or any of them back. All I want you to do is to make certain that you don't make yourself vulnerable. Can I count on you?" he asked. Pete didn't respond. "Pete, I'm *asking* you," emphasizing the word 'asking' in order to suggest that alternatives were not available. Again he added "Please."

Pete looked up. Conner smiled. Finally, Pete smiled back. "Okay," he said, "but if that happens again, all bets are off."

Conner walked to the foul line. All the other players were behind him. This was a technical foul that he would be shooting. Whether he made it or not, Pete's team would inbound the ball.

Before receiving the ball from the ref, he was surprised to hear Eighteen say "Sorry about that." It wasn't genuine but at least he had said something.

Conner turned to face him but not defiantly. "Hey, heat of the battle," he responded, patting Eighteen on the arm. Eighteen appeared surprised by Conner's gesture. "I'll probably pay for it more tomorrow when I wake up than I will tonight. I'm not as young as I like to think. Thanks for saying something."

Then Conner stepped to the foul line. There was a certain amount of tension in the air. Conner unintentionally released an air ball, drawing neither iron nor backboard. Following that, he said "Whoops." Everyone laughed, even Eighteen.

From that point on, everyone played the game, no shenanigans from either side. Conner played enough to ensure his team's victory by ten points but stepped back enough to allow everyone else to feel involved, on both teams. When the final buzzer sounded, Pete's team huddled before shaking hands with the other team.

"Be gracious," Conner requested.

The players lined up and exchanged handshakes. When Eighteen and Conner were face to face, Eighteen said "Hey, sorry about that. Good game." Then he gave Conner a hug.

"No problem," Conner said. "Thanks for the apology. You're a good man and you will be a good role model for others. And you're one heck of a basketball player."

They smiled at one another.

"Backatcha," Eighteen replied and then they moved along.

Chapter 9

Another two teams had taken the floor, warming up for the next game. Pete's team walked to a corner of the gym.

"How 'bout some pizza?" Pete suggested. "After all, we gotta celebrate Michael Jordan's evening."

"Michael Jordan? It's more like the Angel Michael," Piper corrected.

For Conner, this was a bit embarrassing. However, he was beginning to see its importance.

"Are we all comfortable with my offering a prayer?" he asked.

"Yeah," "Sure" and "Who cares?" were the responses.

"Thank you, Lord, for this opportunity to play. We ask that you keep us, our families and friends under your protective hand. We ask that you provide us all with opportunities to spread the Word about the Good News. And we ask this all in your son's precious name. Amen."

All but one of the players said Amen. Piper said "Shalom."

"Shalom?" Conner asked.

"I'm Jewish," he answered.

Conner smiled. "Interesting."

Piper smiled. "Don't tell me," Piper said, "I don't look Jewish."

"No, no," Conner responded quickly. "That's not at all what I meant. I was wondering if I had insulted you with that prayer."

"Why would you think that?" he asked.

"The reference to Jesus."

Piper looked down a bit and smiled. "Hey, each to his own. I chose to pick out of that prayer what I wanted, not necessarily what you gave."

Conner made an I-get-it face, ready to move on. However, something inside him suggested that he pursue this a bit further.

"Well, maybe there's something in the part that you omitted that might have value to you."

"Oh, no," Piper said with just a hint of irritation. "Is this gonna become the Come-to-Jesus speech?"

"Not intentionally."

Piper said "You take your path and I'll take mine. Okay?"

They were both uncomfortably quiet for a moment.

"Piper," Conner began. "Are you secure in your beliefs?"

"What?" came the challenging question.

"For example, do you feel threatened when someone talks about Christ?"

"Listen, it's not my favorite topic of conversation but I can handle it."

"Would you do me a favor?"

"Depends...if you ever finish this whatever you're doing."

"All it requires is your reading something."

"I can't wait to find out what that will be," he said with moderate sarcasm.

"I'll even buy you the book."

"This is getting intriguing. What's the book?"

Conner smiled. Before he could continue, Piper stepped back and said "Oh, I get it. You want to preach to me, right?"

"Nope."

"What then?"

"It does involve the Bible but I won't say a word. All I want you to read is the first four books."

"Four books?" he exclaimed. "I don't read four comic books in a year and now you want me to read four full books?"

"Whoa. Time out," Conner jumped in. "Have you ever read the Old Testament?"

"*My* Bible?" he asked.

Conner smiled. "Yeah, *your* Bible."

"No more than I had to for my Bar Mitzvah."

"It's a great book. Really interesting."

"Too many uses of 'thou' and 'shall' for my taste.

"I have a solution for that," Conner offered.

"I can't wait to hear what it is."

"Christianity has added books to the Old Testament to make a more complete Bible."

"Yeah, that's what I heard. Twice as much boredom." He looked around for support but found the other six riveted to the seriousness of this conversation.

"Actually not," Conner corrected. "For one thing, there are now many versions of the Bible, including ones that present it in today's language. For another, in my opinion, it's easier to relate to most of the New Testament than to much of the Old Testament."

Bob couldn't contain himself. "I agree. I absolutely agree."

Conner looked up at Bob, somewhat startled.

"For me," Bob offered, "the telling of what took place, the parables and the epistles are easier to read than all the 'begats' in the Old Testament. I like both but my favorites are from the New Testament."

There was silence among everyone on the team, time enough to let Conner reflect on what Bob had just said. Conner appreciated his confirmation but understood that this was not the time to discuss it further.

Piper's next question brought him back to their conversation.

"What do you want me to read?" he asked.

"The first four books of the New Testament are called..."

"The Gospels," Piper finished.

Conner smiled at him. "Correct," he affirmed, pleasantly surprised.

"And you want me to read the Gospels?" Piper asked.

"That's it."

"For what purpose?" he asked. "So that I convert? So that we can call our team something like the Christian Brothers?"

Conner smiled, trying to sidestep potential land mines.

"Those four books are interesting reading," he began. "They read more like a novel than like a history book. With the right selection of a Bible version, you won't think of this as reading the Bible."

"And you're gonna get me that book?"

"Yeah," Conner answered.

"I never heard of a Jew who would turn down a free book," he offered, somewhat to break the seriousness of our conversation.

Everyone smiled, perhaps to ease the growing tension.

"The first four books are Matthew, Mark, Luke and John. I believe that when you get to John, you will value having read the Gospels, regardless of whatever spiritual decisions you make. Knowing what takes place in the Gospels will make you a more complete person."

"Fair enough," Piper said. "You buy the book and I'll try to read the Gospels. But no promises," he added.

"All I ask is that you try. I'm guessing that you'll get hooked and read more than the four."

"I doubt it but we'll see," Piper responded.

Jeff, one of the quieter members of the team, chimed in: "Hey, are we gonna get pizza or stand here proselytizing all night? My stomach is talkin' to me."

"Point taken," Pete said. "Sal's is a block north of here and it's good. Let's go."

Before they left, Conner and Piper shook hands.

Conner stayed with the team for about an hour, enjoyed the camaraderie and loved the pizza. Before they left, Pete got Conner to confirm that he would be available for their next game in a week. When Conner said yes, their celebration seemed to take on a new level of energy. Feeling wanted like this was magnificent. Conner reminded himself of the source of his influence. And don't forget it, he told himself.

Chapter 10

It didn't surprise Conner to find God waiting for him when he got home.

"See the game tonight?" he queried, immediately thinking how silly that question was.

"You did well," God said.

"No, *you* did well," Conner corrected.

"I gave you that additional skill set but your use of it was what impressed me."

Conner didn't say anything.

"You were selective in your use of your newfound abilities. A lesser man would have exploited that occasion for personal aggrandizement."

"Aggrandizement?"

"Personal pride," he defined.

"I know what that means. I'm just surprised to hear you use it. What happened with the 'I speak in the language most familiar to the person with whom I am speaking' speech?"

God chuckled. "I do…and did."

Conner realized that use of the word 'aggrandizement' was comfortably within his regular vocabulary.

"Point taken."

"I was also impressed with your taking the opportunity to encourage your teammates after the game."

"Thank you," Conner replied, not knowing what else to say.

Both of them were silent for a few moments.

"Keep up the good work," he instructed.

Then Conner was alone again in his kitchen.

----- ----- -----

Pete and Conner were finally able to coordinate their schedules to go bowling. They had a fun time, although Pete beat Conner by more than 30 pins each time. For the most part they talked about everything but the last basketball game. It was almost as though Pete was avoiding it. Conner didn't say anything either.

Finally, Pete spoke up. "Hey, Conner, I gotta ask you something."

Conner predicted his question: "How did I all of a sudden get this good at basketball?"

"Yeah. Exactly."

"It's tough to answer," Conner replied. "Well, not *that* tough to answer," he corrected, "but tough for someone like you to comprehend."

"What the heck does that mean?" Pete challenged.

"Tough for *anyone* to comprehend," Conner corrected.

"Try me," Pete said.

"God gave me certain powers." He paused. "This is gonna take a bit of explaining. Make that a lot of explaining."

Pete interjected "Now you're gonna tell me that you had a chummy little chat with God and he decided that you needed to become a better basketball player."

Conner smiled, one because of the reference to a 'chummy little chat' and two because it was way beyond being good at a sport. Conner dove into the conversation. "You're right about the former and sort of close to being right about the latter."

Pete stared at him with a look unlike one Conner had seen on his face before. It was half tell-me-more and half I-need-to-have-you-committed.

"Look, Pete, it's hard for me to understand and even harder to explain. But, based on our friendship, I'll try." Pause. "Just remember one thing."

"What?"

"Remember that the kind of improvement I have shown in basketball is…" He was at a loss for the right word.

"…a miracle," Pete finished.

"Yeah, it *is* a miracle. And it's such a miracle that it should make everything else that I am going to tell you believable."

Pete waited silently.

"Well," he began with some hesitation, "I ran into God a few times before he gave me these new powers."

Pete's face was totally expressionless.

"A few weeks ago during a rough spell, I was trying to decide what I should pray for. My thoughts centered on the word 'abundance' and I couldn't quite get a handle on what I wanted. Through a series of meetings…"

"Where?"

"The first was in an office building. The rest were in my kitchen."

"Your kitchen?" Pete exclaimed. "I thought that you were going to tell me that he spoke to you from a burning bush or a pillar of fire or a cloud or something like that."

"Nope. Most of the time it was in my kitchen, although I think that I saw him at one of our basketball games."

"And what does he look like?"

"It's often different. Mostly, he's a nice old guy."

"Nice old guy, eh?" Pete said, struggling to subdue his sarcasm.

"Listen," Conner said. "You asked and I'm telling. If you don't want to hear the explanation, then I'll save my breath."

"Don't get all huffy," Pete replied. "So why did he give *you* these skills?"

"To spread the Gospel."

"Excuse me?"

"To spread the Gospel. He wants me to spread the Gospel."

"By playing basketball?"

"Yes. I think that he believes that something like this will get a pretty large audience."

"Get a pretty large audience," Pete repeated.

"Yeah."

"And he selected you," Pete said, seeking confirmation.

"Yes."

"Great," Pete said. "Let me recap what I just heard. God picks you out of the population."

Conner interrupted. "Just remember that virtually every prophet or special person that he chose, including Moses, King David and Ruth, were men and women *without* a lengthy list of extraordinary personal gifts. I don't take his selection of me as some sort of anointing because of what I've done. Let's get that straight."

"Okay," Pete continued. "He picks you. Then he speaks to you face to face, something that the Bible says he would not do because it would kill a person."

"Yeah." Conner thought about the glow that Moses had on his face after he had spoken with God on Mount Sinai.

"Let's assume that he changed his mind about burning up anyone who looked at him."

"He's changed his mind a few times," Conner said. His thoughts went to the several notes he had made in his Bible of individuals seemingly successful in negotiating with God.

"He picks you. He speaks with you. In your kitchen, no less." Conner was nodding his head with each point. "He gives you basketball skills that are phenomenal, way beyond anything that you have shown to even be a possibility. And he wants you to spread the Gospel."

Pete looked at Conner for confirmation. Expressionless, Conner looked back at him. Then, after reflecting on it for a bit, Conner said "That about sums it up."

"Just how do you plan to do this spreading?"

"I think that I first have to get people's attention. That should come from my playing basketball."

"You think that you're good enough to get a large audience from how you play basketball? Hey, it's one thing to beat some guys in a gym game but quite another to get an opportunity to have the skills against, say, a good college team."

"I was thinking more about the NBA," Conner commented, not even knowing where this confidence came from.

"The NBA? Are you nuts!!!"

"Could be," Conner said. "I'm supposed to appeal to a really large audience."

"Maybe he wants you to be the first pebble into the water and let the ripples reach out to others."

"Could be," Conner said. "I'm certainly not going to predict it. I'll wait for his direction."

"Conner," Pete began hesitantly. "Could I meet God?"

The question seemed almost silly. "You can speak with him anytime," Conner answered with a smile.

"I know, I know," he said. "But I'd like to hear *him* speak back to me, maybe even see him like you've done."

Conner smiled. "That, my friend, is up to him, not you or me. If he is going to include you in this project, then it's his call, if you know what I mean."

"Yeah, I know what you mean. But when you speak with him next time, could you ask if I could be included?"

"Will do. But I don't know when, or if, that will be."

"Keep it on your list."

"Okay," Conner said, concluding their conversation.

They settled up the bill and went their individual ways. Conner hoped to find God at home when he arrived.

Chapter 11

Conner burst through the door of his apartment and raced into the kitchen, half expecting God to be there. He wasn't. Conner didn't deny himself feeling a little disappointed. Conner didn't see him for the rest of the week.

Eventually, their next basketball game came around. On the one hand, he looked forward to it. On the other, he feared that he would no longer have the extraordinary skills that had brought him to this point. Before exiting his car to enter the gym, he closed his eyes and prayed out loud, wanting to both hear and feel what he was about to say.

"Lord, thank you for my experience thus far. It has been marvelous. Truth be told, I have only treated it as a gift that glorifies me more than it exalts You. If You choose to continue using me as Your vehicle, may I grow in maturity such that I suppress my ego in favor of effectively fulfilling Your intentions. May I be a billboard for You. May I draw others to You. May I be a steppingstone for their passage to the Kingdom of God. And I ask all this in Your precious Son's name. Amen."

He found an empty locker, tossed in whatever he wasn't taking into the gym, placed his combination lock into the hole that secured the locker, spun the dial clockwise a few times to ensure its integrity and, with several delightfully childish skips, went bounding into the gym.

There were considerably more people in the stands than he remembered from his previous game. He wondered why. He walked toward his team and was greeted warmly by Pete who came out to meet him.

"You ready?" came his greeting.

"I plan to give it my best," Conner replied. "How 'bout you?"

"Oh, yeah," he said. "We're all ready. Let's take 'em apart," he added.

"Let's have fun," Conner corrected. "We can play hard, play competitively and still have everyone leave tonight feeling good about himself and others."

Conner wondered who, from inside his body and through his mouth, was talking.

"I take it that you've been speaking with him."

"Who?" Conner asked.

"You know. Him. The BIG him."

Conner caught his message and smiled. "Actually not."

"Really?" Pete asked incredulously.

"Really," he responded.

"Did he drop you and move on to someone else?"

"I guess that we'll find out," Conner answered, surprisingly not fearful either way.

"I hope not," Pete concluded. "I hope not," he added, as though a second saying might ensure that Conner's skills were still intact for this game.

Piper bounced Conner a ball and he shot it, hitting the front of the rim. Not bad, he thought. Normally, he would shoot one or two air balls, seeking to have the ball go through the rim without touching it. After a couple of those, his next shot typically would be way too strong. He didn't worry about it. He realized that his skills were not centered in a newfound ability to shoot from the court, the bench, the stands or even the rafters. They came forward in his ability to move faster than others during critical times of the game, especially on defense. And they came from his ability to anticipate decisions by his opponents.

More importantly, if God wanted him to continue with this, he would do so. If not, he would not do so, regardless of how much Conner wished to be gifted with basketball skills. Again he noted how calm he was about this.

He took a few more shots, fed others the ball from caroms that came his way, and generally did more socializing than basketball preparing. In a few minutes, a loud buzzer rang, signaling the end to the warm up. Players from the two teams either trotted or lumbered to their respective benches, both on the same side of the court, separated by the officials' table. The two referees with their gray shirts and black shorts came onto the court with the game ball. One was clearly more senior than the other. He motioned to Pete and to the other team's captain to come forward. Doing this, they received appropriate and predictable instructions. Pete and the other team captain shook hands. Pete returned to their huddle.

"Ready, guys?" he asked.

"After a prayer, if you're all okay with it," Conner offered.

"Go for it," came the refrain, as though they had discussed and prepared for this request. A little bit of laughter following the chorus semi-confirmed his suspicion.

"Lord, thank You for this opportunity to glorify You as well as to share fellowship, friendship and positive competition with the other team. May we be successful in reaching others with Your message such that they will not only want to be on Your team but also help spread the Word. Thank You for all Your gifts. May we play today's game in the safety and enjoyment of Your hand. Naturally, though, may we win the game handily," he included with a smile.

"And we ask this all in Your precious Son's name. Amen."

With some laughter, everyone said "Amen." He was a little surprised that Piper participated in the prayer, knowing that it would be given to and through Jesus. He would not have been taken aback had Piper walked away, not in denouncement of what they were doing but, instead, to respect his Jewish heritage. Conner was even more amazed that Piper energetically participated in saying Amen. Conner was happy for that but he gave it no particular thought beyond what was on the surface.

The Colts sported the well-used uniforms that they had worn when they played last time. Conner had washed his jersey, good old number seven, and had put it on over his gray t-shirt. Although their jerseys matched, their shorts and sneakers did not. Each player wore whatever he had in his closet. That was not the case for the other team. Once again, as with the team that they had played the week before, this team had new jerseys, matching shorts, insignia sneakers and a whole bunch of fans in the stands.

What surprised Conner was the number of spectators that didn't seem to be there in allegiance to either team. If there were sixty-ish fans in the bleachers, thirty were clearly the other team's, five were there for the Colts and the rest seemed to be unaffiliated. Conner suspected that they were either leftovers from the previous game or in attendance early for the next game.

Apparently, that was an incorrect conclusion. He also noticed that quite a few of them were either looking or pointing at him. Someone hollered "Let's see what you got, Seven." Conner looked over to the other team's bench and saw that all their players had jerseys with double digits. In other words, he was referring to Conner. He looked back at the man and smiled awkwardly.

"Oh, boy," he said quietly to himself. "Lord," he started, then stopped. No reason to ask for extraordinary skills. "Thy will be done," he concluded, trying to remember his place in this series of events.

The five of them walked onto the court, Conner chosen to start this game. The other team was already there. Each player walked around and touched fists, the quicker way to shake hands. "You're the one, huh?" Eleven asked Conner. "Don't look like nuthin'," he added.

"Good luck," Conner replied with a smile. "Let's enjoy ourselves."

"I plan to," he said contemptuously. Then he turned to Fourteen and said 'Nuthin'," obviously to reaffirm to his playing partner that they had nothing to fear.

Conner chose not to respond, either in word or gesture. He and Piper walked to their guard positions. Bob jumped center and the two forwards, Andy and Pete, defended their basket. Everyone was in place.

"Let's have a good, clean game," the head referee said as he walked to the center jump spot. He looked at the scorer's table, got their ready signal, turned back to the two who were looking to tap the ball to their team and tossed it up. Bob got the better of the other center and the Colts took control.

Piper brought the ball up court, passed to Andy who dished to Bob underneath for an easy layup. Good start.

They chose to play zone in the beginning. The other team kept the ball on the right side of the basket while Conner played on top to the left. After a little bit of movement, Fourteen hit a three pointer.

This went back and forth for a while with the score being 11-5 in the other team's favor. Time out was called. Conner still hadn't touched the ball, either on offense or defense. In fact, the ball seemed to live on the opposite side of the court. Conner wasn't sure if it was intentional or not but it worked.

"Hey, Seven," the spectator who had spoken to Conner before the game chirped, "how about getting into the game? I didn't come here to watch you take the night off."

Conner looked at him with the kind of quizzical look that someone has in place of saying "Are you nuts?" He wanted to say something but knew that he should just keep his mouth shut, which he somehow managed to do.

He looked at some of those folks who were sitting around this chirper, not recognizing any of them. One man was looking at Conner and he was hard pressed to look away. Conner saw him slightly nod his head up and down, then take his right hand and make a sort of circular motion away from his body, the kind that tells the recipient to pick up the pace. There was something very familiar about that face but Conner was certain that he had not seen it before.

However, he did come to think that his purpose here would not be maximized if he played too much of a behind-the-scenes role. As they huddled, Conner suggested "Let's play a one-two-two." That meant that there would be one chasing guard and four others in more or less of a box. Nobody objected and it was a given that Conner would be the chaser.

Eleven inbounded to Fourteen. They strolled down the court, talking and laughing as though they were walking through a park. Conner stepped forward as they crossed the half court line. "Oh, here we go," Fourteen said and Eleven laughed. Before he had barely gotten two steps across the timeline, he started dribbling between his legs, more Harlem Globetrotter than schoolyard ballplayer. Conner didn't move.

Apparently, the rest of the Colts were being entertained with this player's dribbling and did not pay attention to the fact that one of their players was unguarded under the basket. At the top of his dribble, Fourteen took the ball and fired it toward his unguarded teammate. In regular circumstances, that would have been an uncontested easy layup. In these circumstances, Conner stepped to his right and caught the ball, dribbling past the stunned passer for two points.

After the layup, Conner could tell that Fourteen was dismissing the play as pure luck. Thus, he walked to half court and, without doing anything overt, indicated that he would be dribbling it past Conner. He signaled Eleven to go forward. He was getting ready to show the gym some of his Magic Johnson.

When he got closer to Conner, he stepped to his right. To Conner, it all happened in slow motion. When Conner determined that he was going to crossover, he stepped to his right (the other player's left) and forced Fourteen to dribble into him, earning himself a charge. Both players fell down, Conner more to lessen the supernatural powers that he didn't think should be too highlighted.

"Praise the Lord," Conner said as they fell to the floor.

"Amen," Fourteen said. You could have knocked Conner over with a feather. That was probably the very last thing that Conner expected him to say. He would not have been surprised to have seen Fourteen jump up to protest the call, try to elbow Conner on the way up, curse or do any number of other destructive things. Yet he had simply affirmed Conner's praise.

Both players stood up. Conner reached out his hand and they had a nice handshake, their eyes sharing good thoughts for each other. Pretty much everyone in the stands, no matter their allegiance, broke into applause.

Conner stole the ball on their next three times up the floor and the Colts were now in the lead. They took another time out. As they were walking to their respective benches, Fourteen and Conner passed each other. Conner smiled at him.

"It's true, ain't it?"

"What?" Conner asked, not having any idea of what he was talking about.

"You're special."

"We're all special," he responded, trying not to be condescending.

"I mean playing basketball."

"Yeah, sort of."

"You always been like this?"

"No, just recently."

"Why?"

"Kind of a long story."

"I got time after the game," he said.

"You're on," Conner said. "Let's meet up there," he said, pointing to a particular spot at the top of the bleachers.

Fourteen turned and left. To everyone else, it could have been a pleasant or a taunting exchange. Nobody knew but everyone who had seen it wondered to what Conner had been pointing.

"What was that about?" Pete asked.

"Nothing. He and I are gonna talk after the game."

"Did he threaten you or something?" Bob asked, puffing up a bit.

Conner smiled. "No, no, not at all. We're just gonna talk."

"You're okay?" Bob asked for reassurance.

"Fine. Perfectly fine."

Chapter 12

The game went as expected. Conner only got involved in order to keep his team ahead. Otherwise, especially on offense, he didn't do much. His thing was shutting them down, not wowing them with dazzling moves, especially since he didn't have any. The Colts won 64-51. Afterwards, they huddled and prayed. There were two interesting things about that. For one thing, the rest of his team was waiting for him to lead them in prayer. That felt great. And three of the other team joined, including both Eleven and Fourteen. Conner was delighted with that, not because what it meant for him but because of the encouragement that it provided.

Afterwards, Conner collected his stuff from the locker room, told the guys that he couldn't join them for pizza and made his way to the top of the stands, to exactly where he had pointed during that one conversation on court. Fourteen was already there.

"Conner," he said, sticking out his hand.

"Dwayne," he replied, offering a warm handshake.

There was an awkward moment during which both were silent. Then they started to talk at exactly the same time…and with exactly the same words.

"I didn't…"

They both laughed.

"Jinx," Conner said.

"What?"

"Jinx," he repeated.

"What's jinx?"

Conner was surprised that this was not universally understood. "When two people say exactly the same thing at exactly the same time, the first to call jinx gets to keep the other silent for some amount of time." He smiled.

"Why?"

He didn't have a prepared answer. "Just for fun."

"Weird," he said. "Can I call jinx anytime?"

"No. Of course not. It's only when we say the same thing at the same time. Otherwise, we'd be silencing each other all the time."

"Not a bad idea," he said.

Conner thought about it. "With some limits, that might be a very good thing."

They fell silent again.

"What were you going to say when we jinxed?" Conner asked.

"I was going to say that I didn't think you were going to be as good as you are on the court."

"Thanks," he said, acknowledging the compliment.

"What were you going to say?"

"I was going to say that I didn't expect you to say amen when I praised the Lord."

"Why?"

"Why what?"

"Why would you think that? Do I look like someone who would or wouldn't be prayerful?"

Conner felt terribly uncomfortable. What a dreadful piece of stereotyping he had just committed.

"I'm really sorry," he apologized.

"I'm not looking for an apology, just an explanation," he continued.

Conner shuffled his body, trying to get more comfortable, trying to find the words to complete his apology without it coming across as a pathetic excuse.

Finally, he blurted out "Busted!"

Fourteen looked at him but said nothing.

"I believe that all of us do some stereotyping. It can be beneficial, such as when you see someone in a crowd and it sends off warning signals to you. It can also be harmful, such as this very moment. Truth is, I put you in a category that totally discounted you. I'm really sorry."

Dwayne wasn't about to let go. "What category?"

Oh, gosh, I wish he would let this go, Conner thought. Okay, here goes. "I saw you as a black, street hoopster who had nothing better to do than show off his skills in the gym." Conner wanted to crawl under the stands.

Dwayne let that explanation sit for a while, then replied "I am."

Conner said nothing. He continued. "I am black, I love basketball, I've hooped it up in the playgrounds since I was a little kid and I like competing in the gym. You're right about those. But why would you think that I wouldn't be right with the Lord?"

"I didn't say that you weren't right," Conner defended.

"Come on. Yes, you did. Listen, you've been honest up to now. Why are you going somewhere else with this?"

Conner was silent again. "Busted," came his tried and true defense.

"Darn sure," he said. "If I was a cop, I'd haul your little white backside into jail and throw away the key." He smiled. Conner returned the smile. Conner appreciated the foot coming off his neck. It was a moment of genuine sharing.

"Okay, where to from here?" Conner asked.

"I'm curious where you got your skills and where your faith fits into this."

Dealing with that line of inquiry would be a lot easier than the corner he had gotten into.

Conner shifted again and then decided to jump right in. Either Dwayne would consider him nuts or, if Conner was lucky, he'd want to know more. Without spending loads of time, Conner silently asked God to help him out.

Matthew 10:19 came to mind: *But when they arrest you, do not worry about what to say or how to say it. At that time, you will be given what to say, for it will not be you speaking, but the Spirit of your Father, speaking through you.* That passage always gave Conner comfort. Although he was not being arrested, he was in a place that called for help. Maybe it was a bit of a stretch but he always found it to work, at least when he thought to ask for the help.

"God has chosen me for a mission," Conner started. Dwayne said nothing. Conner could see that he was going to collect information before interacting. Conner appreciated his approach.

"He came to me in the form of different men," he continued, somewhat waiting for Dwayne to respond sarcastically. Nothing.

"He gave me extraordinary basketball skills to spread the Gospel. I'm just getting started." Still nothing.

"And that's it," Conner concluded.

"That's it?" he said. "You met God, you were chosen to be a prophet and you have incredible skills."

Conner nodded.

"How long have you been nuts?"

"What?"

"How long have you been delusional?" he pressed.

"Dwayne…" Conner implored, as though double crossed. "You asked me to tell you my story and there you have it."

He chuckled a bit. "When was the last time that God worked through someone like this?"

"I don't know," Conner replied, more whiney than he wanted to sound.

"When was the last time that *you* heard he worked through someone like this?" Dwayne continued.

"How the heck should I know?"

"I said that *you* heard about it."

"I never heard about it."

"Or read about it?" he inquired.

"In the Bible."

"That's a couple of thousand years ago, right?"

"Yeah."

"And now you believe that he's decided to do it again?"

Conner said nothing.

"And through you?"

Conner said nothing.

"Come on, Seven, this just doesn't make sense."

Conner decided to participate. Otherwise, this would be a sad one-sided conversation. "I'm guessing that he has done this a bunch of times in the last two thousand years."

"Have you heard any reports that confirm your suspicion?"

"No," he said, hanging his head dejectedly.

"You're darn tootin' you haven't," he continued.

"You don't think that this has happened since the end of the Bible?" Conner inquired.

"Of course it has," he said.

"Then why are you pushing me this hard?"

"Because I don't think that God wants you to explain it that way."

"Why?" Conner asked.

"If he wanted you to be his spokesman, why would he give you these skills instead of just making you eloquent, rich, famous or whatever?"

Conner searched for an answer. "Maybe because he wants me to appeal to a certain class of people."

"Like those in the hood?" Dwayne challenged.

Oh, gosh, here I go again, Conner thought, back into the corner. "Maybe," he said feebly.

"Wrong!"

Conner wondered why Dwayne was being this firm in his stance.

"I'm sure that he wants you to lead people through your example, not through telling them that you were chosen."

"And you know this how?" Conner asked, wondering how Dwayne had the nerve to be so certain.

Dwayne smiled. Then, as Conner looked at him, his face changed into the various faces God had worn during Conner's interactions with him, including that one guy in the stands who had implored him to pick up the pace. This high-speed photo gallery, for lack of a better term, took a fraction of a second. He now sat before Conner as Dwayne.

"Oh, gosh. I must have sounded stupid."

He didn't release Conner too quickly. "It's okay. I just wanted you to think a little more about how you go about this. It's not really to our benefit for you to talk about conversing with God and suggesting that I spoke back to you, much less that you've seen me. Does that make sense?"

"Yes...and no."

"I'll accept the yes but why the no?"

"You did it in the Bible."

"I did. And..." he prompted.

"And it didn't work out too well."

"Yeah, that was then and this is now."

"I still think that your making an appearance now would go a long way toward getting everyone lined up."

"I don't want them lined up. You're familiar with the concept of free will?" he asked.

"Yeah, yeah, I get it. Okay, I can't argue with you."

"You can but it doesn't work."

"You want me to do this thing but without telling folks that I am getting direct orders from you. Is that it?"

"In a manner of speaking," he said. "I want to encourage them but without demanding them. Demanding hasn't worked out too well in the past." Conner could see that he was probably reflecting on thousands of years. "That was then and this is now," he repeated.

"You're the boss," Conner said, not with anger or frustration, more with determination. "I guess that means that you don't want to meet Pete," he said, assuming that God was aware of that conversation.

"You got that right."

"I figured," Conner said.

"Now go get 'em, son."

With that, Fourteen vanished. Conner looked around the gym to determine if anyone had seen him disappear. Everyone was riveted to the next two teams playing on the court.

Chapter 13

Fourteen was actually God. Or was he? Maybe Fourteen was a real person and God had just borrowed his body for a little while. Or maybe Fourteen had a good walk but God cloned him to meet with Conner. Or maybe…

What's the difference?

Suddenly inspired, Conner grabbed his stuff and
raced to the locker room, hoping to catch Fourteen
and see if he knew what was going on. A few
members of the other team were around but
Dwayne was nowhere to be found.

"Hey, guys. Nice game tonight."

"Yeah, you too."

"Anyone see Fourteen?"

"Fourteen who?" one of the players asked.

"Hey, aren't you Eleven?"

"Yeah, I'm Eleven. Who's Fourteen?"

"Your back-court mate. The other guard."

"You mean Dwight?"

"Dwayne."

"I don't know any Dwayne."

"Okay, Dwight. Where is he? Did he leave
already?"

"No."

"Great. Where is he?"

"He's at home with pneumonia."

"Pneumonia? He's at home?"

"What are you, some sort of echo? Yeah, he's at
home. He's been home for a week."

"Who was the other guard?"

"Hey, man, weren't you out there tonight? Didn't
you steal like a million passes from us?"

He waited. Conner waited. He continued.

"The other guard was number twenty-one. His
name is Mark but we call him Carrot Head 'cause of
his red hair."

Conner was beginning to see what had
happened...or not happened.

"Do you have anyone with the number fourteen on it?"

"What you askin' for?" Eleven challenged.

Conner pushed for an answer. "Do you?"

"D.J. Anderson used to play for us. He wore number fourteen. He got killed in a drive-by shooting nearly a year ago. We don't use his number no more. This little patch…" He pulled out his jersey and pointed to a patch over the heart. "…is in his memory." He looked at Conner. "Now, is that all?"

"Yeah. Sorry. Good game."

"Yeah. Good game."

Conner headed home. Life is becoming more and more adventurous, he thought.

----- ----- -----

The next morning, Conner was sipping his tea, thinking about where he was and where he wanted to be. He determined to map out a plan rather than just go with the tide. His challenge was to spread the Word. The question was how could he best do so? At this rate, he might reach a handful of people. That would be good but how could he make his pebble create a larger ripple? Bigger stage, he thought. Perhaps the NBA was a little ambitious but playing college ball wouldn't be out of the question. If he was good enough, then that would give him a larger platform. And why shouldn't I be good enough? he wondered. I was doing okay without making too much of an effort. Although the players in Division I would be better, they wouldn't be like

100% better. Even if they were, I should still be able to at least hold my own.

He hoped.

Conner thought about the colleges where he lived. Which ones would be high profile? He wanted to go for a big-name school but he didn't want to move too far away. "California would be fun, though," he said out loud as he stood up to get more hot water for another cup of tea.

"It would, wouldn't it?" came the voice.

Conner dropped his mug and it shattered all over the kitchen floor. Fortunately, he had not poured the hot water into it.

"Shoot, man," he hollered. "Quit doing that."

"Sorry," he said. "Sometimes I forget."

"Yeah," Conner said, accepting his apology while he found a broom and dustpan to pick up the pieces.

"What's the matter with going to California?"

"How could I?"

"Or Florida, North Carolina, Connecticut or anywhere, for that matter?" He seemed oblivious to Conner's question.

"I'm in my mid-thirties, I have very little savings, I don't know very many people outside of Illinois and I wouldn't even know what to study, much less if I would even be eligible to play, having already graduated college."

"Not too old, money isn't an issue, you'll meet people, Bible Studies, and yes, you'd be able to play at least one year," he said in answer to all the expressed concerns.

Conner couldn't help but smile, just one step short of laughing. "You're amazing," an expression he didn't often use.

"Thank you," God replied, seemingly genuine in his appreciation of the compliment.

"You're saying that I should up and quit my job, apply to some school, make its basketball team, relocate and use that to spread the Word?"

"If you get some coach's attention before you apply, you could probably get a scholarship."

"Hmmm. Good point. Where do you think that I should apply?"

The conversation had turned to a father-and-son-type discussion of where the boy might go to school. Father and son in the secular world, that is.

"This doesn't work out as well if I tell you each step."

"Yeah, I guess so," Conner said, disappointed in that not being the process. On the other hand, that made his world open up quite a bit.

Conner leaned back against the counter and daydreamed for a few long, thoughtful minutes.

"And you're where?" God interrupted.

Conner snapped back to the present. "Just contemplating options."

"And what have you come down to?"

"Well, it's a little bit early but I'm thinking Stanford, Duke, Michigan or Florida."

"All high-visibility powerhouses," he commented. "You follow basketball?"

"College," he said. "Pro ball is too last minute for me."

Conner laughed, thinking about there never being any suspense in God's world. Then he thought harder about it.

"Don't you always know who will win?"

"Lots of time. I do if I want some particular outcome to result from the game. Like encouragement for a player, a lesson for a coach, or something like that."

"You mean that you don't know the outcome for some of them?"

"Right. I'm as much a fan as you of a really good game."

Conner smiled. Holy cow. God not knowing the outcome of something was, well, amazing. It was sort of ungodlike.

"You seem stunned."

"I am. I mean, I thought that you knew everything. Isn't that what omniscient means?"

"It does."

"So?"

"Actually, the word omniscient isn't really the right word to use."

"What is?"

"There isn't a word that has been coined yet that, in point of fact, defines the reality."

"And just what is the reality?"

"Well, it's sort of like a spectrum. Think of the color spectrum, for example."

Conner pictured the continuum of colors, from one extreme to another. "Okay," he said.

"My knowledge is like that. If I wish, I can determine everything. However, if I also wish, I can let things unfold, then direct them on an as-needed basis."

"Even go back and change what happened?"

"I can," he said.

"Is that where we get déjà vu?" he asked, unexpectedly curious.

"Son, you're asking for things that I have determined are not for your knowledge."

"Oh, come on," Conner begged.

God smiled, the message becoming quite clear that Conner wouldn't be getting the answer to that particular question in the near future, if at all.

"I think that the easiest way for a mortal to think about this is with me as the director of a play. It has a script but I encourage the actors to be somewhat impromptu when they feel the urge. I won't change what they do unless I have a particular purpose. If such turns out to be the case, I can back everything up to where they went off the track, give them a little boost in the right direction and continue the play."

"Oh," Conner said, kinda understanding and kinda lost. He chose not to continue the conversation. At the very least, he wanted to noodle this a bit more.

"If you're interested, the closest I've seen anyone come to the correct explanation comes from Dorothy Sayers in *The Mind of the Maker*. Good book. Whew, does she ever have a vocabulary."

"You're impressed with someone's vocabulary?" Conner asked, again surprised.

"Now, where were we?" God inquired, totally ignoring Conner's question.

"You don't know?" Conner stuttered, amazed that he would have lost the thread of their conversation.

"It's just an expression, a way to get back on track. Of course I know."

Conner wasn't sure that he believed the response. "Okay, where were we?"

"Oh for earth's sake!" God exclaimed.

"Earth's sake?"

"It's a stupid expression, sort of like your 'oh for heaven's sake' that makes as much sense.

Conner returned to their discussion. "Do you remember or not?" he challenged.

"You're challenging God?" he asked.

Oops. Maybe not such a good idea. But, what the heck. "Yeah. You don't remember, do you?" That may have been a little too bold.

God smiled, then repeated their conversation word for word from 'You seemed stunned' right through 'give them a little boost in the right direction and continue the play.' He even used their own voices and included every inflection.

Conner felt kind of stupid. Fix that: He felt very stupid. People in the Bible who challenged God often ended up destined for an unpleasant eternity. Conner wondered about that.

"How come you don't kill me?" he asked, the question flowing from the idea of what happened in the Bible.

"Because you dared to challenge me?" he asked.

"Yeah," he said, less than eloquently.

"It's about attitude," God said. "*Why* someone does something is a lot more important to me than *what* he or she in point of fact does."

Conner smiled. "I love that answer," he blurted out. "That is exactly what I had hoped was the case."

"Makes sense, doesn't it?" God asked.

"Absolutely."

"Good," God concluded. "Now give more thought to the university thing and we'll talk."

"But…" Conner called.

Too late. He was gone.

-----, ----- -----

Conner kept playing one saying over and over again in his head: "If God brings you to it, he will bring you through it." Thus, within reason, Conner could go forward without concern for secular constraints. If something needed amending, God would do it.

One of the first things to fly into his head was audience size. Maybe I should seek a team that always has large audiences, both live and on television. And has lots of other media coverage, he thought.

He also thought about travel. If I was on one coast or the other, playing good teams on the other coast would be a traveling nightmare, something he did not relish doing.

He thought about education. Should I even be concerned about my own education if my primary purpose is to spread the Word?

Should he go to a smart school, like an Ivy League institution, in order to show the public that he was neither nuts nor mentally challenged?

What about tuition, living accommodations and spending money? What about scholarships, loans and grants? Should I only go to a school that will give me a free ride?

Would it make sense for me to go to a faith-based school? Notre Dame and Holy Cross popped into his mind but he wasn't too excited about going to a Catholic institution. He couldn't think of any basketball powerhouse that was evangelical Protestant. Maybe Baylor, but he wasn't too sure about its affiliation. Besides, years back, they had experienced a major embarrassment on their basketball team.

Okay, he finally decided, here are the parameters: A noted basketball history; not immediately on the coast; limited concern for his own education; a respected but not dramatically academic institution; full scholarship; and not necessarily faith based.

Conner called Pete. "Hey, man, do you have a few minutes?" He did and they settled on meeting at Joshua's Java, a local coffee shop. Conner thought that there was something special about meeting there. Cain's Coffee or Balaam's Beans just wouldn't have worked.

Conner told Pete what he was thinking of doing. He was careful to steer away from the God-spoke-to-me approach that he had been reminded not to use. Pete made no reference to their earlier conversation about Conner's mission, perhaps because he had forgotten it or possibly because God had intervened. Conner let that sleeping dog lie.

Pete's immediate response was: "What? Are you nuts? You're gonna drop everything to return to college and try to play in a five-star basketball program? And all this because you showed up a bunch of gym rats? Why don't you go down to Houston and ask NASA if you can ride on the outside of an intergalactic rocket? You're tweeties. Certifiable, at best."

Conner wasn't too terribly surprised by the response. Now that he had asked his friend, it was too late to come at him from a hypothetical approach. Conner could have told him that he was writing a book, that he wanted to play a farfetched mind game with him or something equivalent. Here he had fulfilled the textbook description of ready-fire-aim. Well, 20/20 hindsight aside, he smiled and asked Pete to consider it anyhow. With a shake of his head for emphasis, Pete worked with him from that point forward. After an hour of discussion, they agreed that Conner should apply first to Kansas and then to Kentucky.

"Fair enough," Conner concluded. "Now comes my getting in touch with the coaching staff."

"Go for it, my friend," Pete said. "There's no time like today."

Chapter 14

After doing some research, Conner composed his introductory email letter.

.

Coach:

Two requests: First, please read this all the way through, regardless of what conclusions you reach before the end. I will keep this correspondence short. My second request will be forthcoming.

My name is Conner Ramsey. I am thirty-four years old and I am a college graduate. I never played sports in college; my eligibility is still intact. For reasons that you will learn when we get together, I can play basketball on any team in the country. Also for good reasons, I have chosen the University of Kansas.

I understand that it is farfetched to believe that someone my age has not yet been discovered. Again, there are good reasons for this. I ask one favor. I will travel on my own nickel to show you these skills. Thus, my second request is to have ten minutes of time to play during one of your practices. I will take the worst player on your team and beat the best two players in a two-on-two.

This is not a gimmick or some sort of trick. If you cannot invest ten minutes to see if this is real, I will go to the next school on my list until I find a coach who has ten minutes. My cell phone number and e-mail address follow. I will wait two days for your response.

I hope to hear from you.
Sincerely,

With the appropriate contact information included, Conner sent it off. Today was Monday. He would give this coach until 5:00 PM on Wednesday. If he didn't hear from the coach by then, he would call once before moving to the next coach on the list.

After sending the e-mail, he lost a little confidence. What coach in his right mind is going to let a crackpot like me even come into the gym, much less scrimmage with his team? If he did that for one person, he'd be getting nutsy letters every week.

What would Conner do if he were the coach? Would he be willing to take a shot at someone so convinced that he could make the team that he would come to the university to try on his own nickel? If I was the famous coach of a basketball powerhouse, probably not, thought Conner.

Of course, Conner had the odds-favoring effect of a higher power. With that thought in tow, he pretty much put the whole thing out of his mind and devoted himself to other matters, one of which was more reading of the Bible.

Conner remained very busy for the next two days. He was in bed and soundly asleep early each evening. By the time that he came home on Wednesday, he had actually forgotten about the e-mail. It wasn't until he had eaten something for dinner that he remembered this to be the cutoff date. He took one more bite and hustled into the other room where his computer sat patiently by. He powered it on, signed onto his service provider and checked for messages.

Holy cow! It looked as though he had one from the University of Kansas. Excitedly, he opened it up, then allowing the thought to come into his mind that it might possibly be the equivalent of a rejection letter. He didn't dwell on that thought too long.

Dear Mr. Ramsey:

I am writing on behalf of Coach Diehl.

Thank you for your correspondence. As much as we appreciate your energy and confidence, there are too many factors that preclude us taking you up on your offer. As you might imagine, we get many letters like this and cannot accommodate each one. Beyond that, the semester is about to begin and we have already been working out together as a team. In addition, there is the matter of your limited eligibility; the number of scholarships we are allowed to issue; and the number of players we can have on our roster.

We wish you every success in your endeavor.

Sincerely,

Danielle Armbruster

Public Relations Department

Conner was disappointed but also determined. He understood this response. Now he had to show his determination. Who is next on my list? he asked himself. He sent his next e-mail to the coach of the University of Kentucky. Two days later, he received an e-mail, astonishingly similar to that which he had received from Kansas.

Deciding not to waste more time, he sent a flurry of e-mails to Connecticut, Duke, Florida, Indiana, Michigan State, North Carolina and UCLA. He got back similar e-mails from Duke, Michigan State and

UCLA. Florida, Indiana and North Carolina did not write back.

What now? Conner asked himself. One more barrage of e-mails and then I'll take a different approach. Off went e-mails to Iowa, Missouri, Nevada, Ohio State, Oklahoma, Texas and Wisconsin. Same thing: No thanks. Best of luck.

More than a week gone and not anything to show for it. Should he continue with NCAA Division I schools or move to a lower tier? Or forget about it entirely? Forgetting about it was out of the question. Time to come up with another list.

On Conner's new list were still good basketball schools but not ones expected to draw significant regional, much less national attention. Conner decided that if he waited for an opportunity with a major power, he might miss his window.

The parable of the loaned money came to mind (Matthew 25:15). It told of a man who gave three servants various amounts of money with instructions to invest it for him while he was gone. Upon his return, two servants returned double the amounts given them. *Well done, my good and faithful servant*, each was told. The third servant had buried his money and returned the same to his master. He was summarily thrown out of the house. *To those who use well what they are given, even more will be a given.* Conner could not bury the talents that God had given him until a more convenient time. He had to act now.

Conner sat down at his computer to research other schools. Two hours later, he had two lists. List 1 contained recognized schools, ones that could at least be imagined making the NCAA Tournament, although not likely going further than the first or second round. List 2 consisted of other institutions. He would write to all the schools on the two lists. If none responded, he would pursue another avenue.

Each e-mail was personally addressed and embedded the school's name in the text. In that manner, as he had done with all his correspondence, each coach would feel that the e-mail had been constructed for him personally. In another two hours, all the e-mails had been sent. One by one, he received the thanks-but-no-thanks responses or no response at all. Finally, though, he received a note from the coach at Brantley University, in nearby Elgin, Illinois. It read:

Dear Conner:

I have gotten some whacky requests in my time but yours goes straight to the top of that list. I didn't know whether to wad it up and use it as a litter basketball, to frame it for entertainment, to report you to the police or to see if you are for real.

I guess that my curiosity got the best of me. I want you to know that we have limited scholarship support. However, if you can come by the gym at 8:00 AM on Monday, I will have a few members of the team available to see what you can do.

As you mentioned, what harm can ten minutes do?

I look forward to your arrival.

Sincerely,

Jason Wright

Head Basketball Coach

Brantley University

Conner sat there with a grin that stretched from ear to ear. Holy cow, he thought. I am going to take another step toward this goal, he thought. How could that be? This is great. This is…

Immediately, he realized that he was an idiot. Why was he astonished that he was getting an opportunity? He took his hands off the computer keyboard, put them together and laid his head in them. "Thank you, Lord. May I remember that these are Your talents, Your inspiration and Your purposes. May I do my best to fulfill them without allowing my ego to create any kind of interference. And I ask for Your blessings in so doing. I pray this in Your Son's precious and holy name. Amen."

His heart was beating like he had just run a sprint.

"Holy cow," he said out loud. "Holy cow," he repeated.

Aside from rereading 1 Thessalonians, 2 Thessalonians and Titus, he spent Saturday simply relaxing. He ate well, watched some college sports, took a bath (something he very rarely did), watched two movies and took a nap. He shut off his phone and only once checked e-mail. The man was in his cave.

The next day, he went to church, worked out lightly, ate well and got plenty of sleep, including a nap. He expected it to be tough to fall asleep that night but such was not the case. After setting his alarm clock, he closed his eyes and was out for the night. It was another restful night's sleep.

He woke up at 5:30 and shut off the bedside alarm. Conner had two eggs and toast, skipping any sort of meat. Right now, he needed to have a totally settled stomach.

----- ----- -----

The gym had a few cars sitting alongside. Conner parked his amongst them, grabbed his bag and headed to the closest door. It was 7:30. As he entered, a security guard turned his attention from watching the practice to Conner's entry.

"No one but the team allowed," he said, assuming a posture that suggested Conner not even consider debating the point.

"I'm expected."

Assuming a little bit different posture, the guard took his clipboard. "Name?" he inquired.

"Ramsey. Conner Ramsey."

He looked back down at his clipboard, apparently saw Conner's name on it, checked his watch and made an entry on the page. "Coach said for you to go to the locker room, take locker number 765 and be on the court by the south basket no later than 8:00 AM."

After learning how to get to the locker room downstairs and which was the south basket, Conner took off. He found the locker, tossed his stuff into it, slapped on a lock that he had fortunately brought along and headed back up to the gym.

Then he moseyed over to the south basket and plunked himself down in the first row of the stands.

The entire team – or so it appeared – was running drills. They were just finishing two lines of layups, virtually each player dunking with one or two hands. Man, were they ever big and athletic.

Then they switched to an organized form of jump shooting. Everyone seemed to know exactly what he was to do. Student managers helped the process while the coaches stood huddled discussing something. Conner recognized the head coach from pictures. At ten 'til, the coach blew his whistle and sent everyone to the bench. Then he walked over to Conner who immediately stood up.

"I take it that you're Ramsey," he said.

"Yes, sir," Conner replied, extending his hand. The coach took it and then stepped back to look at Conner. What the coach saw was a less-than-impressive specimen, wearing a blue t-shirt, grey shorts, white low cuts and half-high socks. Conner was dramatically undersized in comparison with this team and was easily old enough to be the assistant coach, if not the head coach. The coach smiled and just shook his head.

"I guess that we've both come this far," he said.

Conner smiled, knowing what he meant. "Yes, sir."

"Okay, come on the floor. Let's see what you've got."

Conner walked with him to the foul key. "Let me see you make ten of ten from the line."

"Sir…," Conner began, hesitantly.

The coach looked at Conner, probably expecting an excuse.

"I'm not a good shot."

"What?" he said, not totally surprised, at least not by the inflection of his voice.

"My thing is defense."

"You're in your thirties, you're barely six feet and you can't shoot a basketball." He turned to face his team and assistant coaches, all sitting there politely. Apparently, he had shared the story with the players. They could all hear the conversation. The coach must have rolled his eyes because a few of them started to giggle. Eventually, it became infectious, as laughter has a tendency to do, and the entire bench was rollicking.

Conner was halfway toward laughing with them or crying in embarrassment. He took a deep breath. God is with me, he thought. Even so, his heart was beating mercilessly, almost exiting from his body.

"Coach," he said forcefully. "Give me less than ten minutes to play a two-on-two. If you don't see something worthwhile, I'll leave."

The coach turned back to Conner, once again looking him over. The silence seemed to last for an hour, although it was truly only momentary. Then he turned back to the players.

"Walker and Obumje," he called out. The two stood up. "You're on one team. You're skins." Then he looked along the bench, finally settling on the player sitting at the very end. "Harris," he hollered. The young man stood up unsurely. Conner could only imagine what must have been going through the head of this player selected to team with him.

"You're with Ramsey." Harris trotted out and Conner reached out his hand. Hesitantly, he took it.

"This won't be painful," Conner said, smiling. Like a man who has lost both his sense of taste as well as of smell, Harris had no appreciation for what was just said if, indeed, he had even heard it. He was more like a man headed toward the gallows than toward a game of two on two.

The four players walked onto the court. "You two," the coach pointed at Conner and Harris, "will inbound. It's half court, loser's ball, first to ten. Any questions?"

Meanwhile, the players on the bench were barely paying attention. It was more like they were at the movies waiting for the lights to be dimmed and the show to begin. In one-on-one conversations, they were chattering about different topics.

Before the coach could throw in the ball, Conner held up his hand and got closer to Harris. "Listen," he said, "this may feel like it's a mismatch but it's not. I want you to relax and enjoy this. God is on our side."

Conner believed that, had his hair been on fire, his eyes been twirling, his ears flapping and his nose twitching that he would still not have seen any reaction from Harris. Conner was clearly neither Knute Rockne nor Vince Lombardi. He decided to let it go, figuring that the proof would be in the pudding.

Conner was pumped up but Harris was close to catatonic. When Harris inbounded, he threw the ball way over Conner's head and straight to Walker under the basket. It was a no-brainer layup for them.

"That's one," coach hollered. Walker and Obumje started to inbound but the coach whistled them to a stop with "Losers' out," he said.

Once again, Harris was going to inbound. Walker called over to him. "Hey, Harris, I'm right here." The bench erupted into laughter.

Conner felt bad for Harris and walked over to him, privately saying "Listen, you can lose looking like you're in a panic or lose like a man. You choose."

Something inside of Harris must have clicked because he inbounded the ball like he was ready to go. Perhaps it was the wisecrack from Walker that had snapped him back into the moment or maybe it was what Conner had said. Either way, it seemed obvious that he was going to do his best. I'll go down fighting, seemed to be his new attitude.

Conner tossed it back to Harris who gave it back once more. Okay, Conner thought, I'm not here for my shooting skills but I guess that I'll have to make them work for at least a little while. Obumje guarded Conner while Walker loafed around where Harris stood. Conner waved Harris to the corner. That gesture brought out a burst of laughter from the bench. So be it. Harris drifted to the corner and Walker took a couple of steps in that direction.

Conner started dribbling, not too effectively, mind you, and started off to his right. In true defensive fashion, Obumje moved in that direction without crossing his feet. Halfway between the defender bringing his right foot toward his left and shifting his body weight to his left, Conner changed direction and started off to his left. In trying to stop his momentum, Obumje stumbled off to his left and an easy layup resulted, Walker totally not expecting this to result.

"Nice D," someone chided Obumje good naturedly from the bench.

"One all," the coach hollered.

Conner winked at Harris. He was in shock, possibly surprised that they had even scored one point. Conner motioned him over while the bench continued to ride Obumje.

"Which of the two can you guard better?"

Harris shrugged. Conner said "You guard him," he said, pointing to Walker. "Don't give him a jumper. Make him drive toward the center. I'll get him from there. Okay?"

Harris nodded, noticeably swallowing with difficulty.

"Don't hurt yourself," one player said from the bench, referring to Obumje.

"Very funny," he said, looking right into the face of the cynic. "Ten – one," he added, meaning that they would beat the newcomer by that score.

"You're on," he received in reply. "Dinner at Cornwall's," came the prize.

"Get your wallet," Obumje said, looking at Walker. Walker nodded his head with exaggeration.

Obumje inbounded the ball to Walker who tossed it back to Obumje. Conner easily stepped in and stole the pass, much to everyone's surprise. Obumje crouched, ready to put him in his place. Conner faked a pass to Harris. It was clear that Conner's mate didn't want it but he did move to the corner again. Walker moved a little with him but, remembering what had happened last time, stayed in the vicinity of the basket in order to defend against another drive.

Instead of faking one way, Conner stepped past Obumje and drove toward the basket. Walker started in to defend but, even though Conner slowed down, Walker had no chance of catching up with the shooter. The ball was banked in for a score.

"Cornwall's" the heckler called out. "Dee-lish-ous," he said, accentuating each syllable. It brought a bit of tension to the floor that had not been there before.

"Two-one," called out the coach.

The next time, Obumje inbounded and Walker was more attentive. Both of them were now intent on doing what they had to do to right this ship. Walker held the ball in his two hands with his elbows sticking out to each side. Then he dropped his right hand and palmed the ball in his left.

"Press left," Conner reminded Harris. Harris stepped forward to take away the outside shot and force Walker to go past him on his right. "Good," Conner encouraged.

That was pretty much what Walker had hoped would happen because it was obvious to most everyone that he wanted to make an ostentatious dunk in comparison with Conner's childish off-the-backboard layups. And he probably wanted to do it with his off hand, that being his left hand, just for the additional flash factor.

Walker was past his man and headed to the hoops. On his second dribble, as the ball was just above the floor, Conner stepped in and took it away. Then he passed it to Harris and calmly said "Shoot!"

Walker was hardly recovered from his run without the ball when Harris nailed his jumper. Obumje had just been a spectator for all that time.

Harris and Conner slapped high fives. For the first time since the teams were selected, Conner could see that Harris was beginning to relax.

"Three-one," called out the coach dispassionately.

Conner didn't have much time to think about what must be going through Harris' mind but it probably would have been interesting.

It was now obvious that neither Walker nor Obumje was happy. The bench, to its credit, was totally silent, stunned into it most likely. For the moment, the wisecracks had been stored.

"You inbound," Obumje said. You could see that Walker did not like that instruction but he did so. Had this been playground ball, the two would have had words.

Harris stayed off of Walker for the inbound but Conner got a little closer to Obumje. Walker faked an inbounds pass but did nothing. Then, anticipating no challenge, Walker bounced the ball to his teammate. It never got there. Conner stepped in, stole the pass and rifled it to Harris who had drifted toward the basket. He made an uncontested layup.

"Four-one," called out the coach. More silence from the bench.

Obumje inbounded the next pass to Walker. "Press," Conner reminded his teammate. Harris closed the distance between himself and Walker, favoring the side that would make Walker drive toward the middle of the court. Walker stepped to his left, then tried to reverse sides and get to the left side of Harris, the side that was furthest from Conner. However, Harris had planted himself there and Walker bowled him over. Walker and Harris both went down.

The coach blew his whistle. "Shirt ball," he said, acknowledging the charge. Harris jumped up and tried to help Walker arise. Walker wanted no part of it. He was definitely miffed. One could easily see his competitive nature. And he didn't like being embarrassed by an old nobody and a freshman bench hugger.

Harris, to his credit, had relaxed. When shirked by Walker, he had looked over to Conner with a grin and a wink. Suddenly, he and Conner were fast friends. When they came together for a high five before starting the next play, Conner said "After inbounding, just find a place where you're comfortable hitting jumpers."

"Whatever you say, boss" he replied with a smile.

Harris inbounded and Conner found himself staring into the unfriendly face of Walker, crouched into a really serious defensive stance. "Come on, old man," Walker taunted.

"Respect your elders," Conner replied with a smile. Walker didn't think it too amusing.

Just for fun, in normal speed, Conner planted his left foot and stepped with his right to Walker's left. That gave the defender time to shift over there. Then Conner crossed over and stepped with his right to the defender's right. Again, Conner gave him time to shift to cover that. Then Conner revved it up a bit and did the same thing. Like his teammate earlier, Walker couldn't recover quick enough and tumbled to the ground. Conner drove past him, past an immobile Obumje and made yet another layup.

"Five-one," called out the coach, somewhat disgustedly. "Time out," he added. The four players came to him. He turned to Walker and Obumje, crossed his arms and said "You guys wanna play or goof around?"

Obumje looked down. Walker acted like he hadn't been listening. "Sixth man and all conference," the coach said. "Could have fooled me." Obumje continued to show contriteness, Walker disdain.

"Skins ball," the coach concluded, dropping the ball. Walker dribbled it to half court, then carefully inbounded to Obumje. Conner stepped back to the top of the key. Obumje took a jump shot from two feet behind the key, quite a distance, and swished it. He was all grins. Walker didn't even acknowledge it.

"Five-two," hollered the coach, somewhat relieved, no doubt.

As Harris walked past Conner to inbound the ball, Conner whispered "Toss it toward the basket, not to where I'm standing. Let me run to it."

Harris raised his eyebrows, signaling a combination of 'I don't get it' and 'Why?' with one look. To his credit, he did as he was asked.

Conner knew that Walker would be guarding him closely, expecting to steal the inbounds pass. Obumje was a couple of feet off of Harris for the inbound. Following instructions, Harris tossed the ball over both Walker's and Conner's heads toward the basket. Conner had quickly rotated to get between Walker and the ball. Then it was the matter of another simple layup.

"Shoot!" Walker yelled out, except that he used another word.

That drew the coach's whistle. "Take a seat," he instructed his angry player. Walker grabbed a towel that was offered as he returned to the bench. He walked all the way to the end and took the seat that Harris had originally occupied. "Kline," the coach called. Up jumped another guard, this one a player that Conner recognized. He remembered reading about the young man who was known Kenny Threes, although his actual name was Kenny Kline. He had been an All-American high school player who had seriously hurt his leg in a car wreck. After that, the major colleges didn't want to take a chance on him and he had ended up at Brantley University. He could still shoot the ball accurately from literally anywhere. Now a junior, he was on the verge of breaking virtually all the school scoring records, including points; field goal percentage (surprising, especially for a guard); three-point attempts, field goals and percentage; and free throw percentage.

"What's the score?" asked the coach, this time not happily.

"Six-two," Harris responded.

Harris and Conner walked toward each other. "Who do you want?"

"Kline will kill me," Harris responded.

"Not if you play him the same way. Take away the jumper, force him toward the middle and keep him away from the basket. Can you do that?"

"I can try," Harris said. "Hey, what's your name again?" he added.

"Ramsey. Conner Ramsey."

"Shedrick Harris," he replied. They touched fists.

Kline inbounded. Shedrick did as promised, staying close to him, keeping him away from the basket. Obumje held the ball. His confidence had somewhat eroded, although he was doing the best he could to maintain a self-assured posture. Kline came out for the ball and Conner intercepted Obumje's attempt to get it to him.

"Come on!" Kline said, then clamped his mouth close.

Conner handed the ball off to Harris and got away from him. In just a few minutes, Conner's teammate had evolved from looking like a scared rabbit to a much more confident player. This time, he waved his teammate away, Conner moving to the corner. Kline followed him. Harris stepped as though he was going to drive, then jumped up and shot before Obumje could respond. Swish.

"Seven-two," the coach called out.

Conner took a peek at the remaining players and coaches on the bench. Everyone was riveted to what was taking place on the court, several mouths literally hanging open. There were no side conversations and no daydreaming. All but Walker were watching the play intently. Walker sat aloof at the end of the bench.

Obumje inbounded to Kline. Harris crowded him as promised. In spite of that, Kline went straight up and nailed what would have been a three pointer. Shedrick looked over and shrugged. That was returned with a thumbs up signal, letting him know that he had done well and that not every instance ends the way that is desired. Harris smiled back and winked once more. He had understood the message.

"Seven-three," the coach called.

Shedrick passed Conner the ball who again went through his left-right move. Kline, like the others, wound up on his bum while Conner drove toward the basket. He slowed down to let Obumje come over, then passed to Harris in the corner. His jump shot hit the rim and bounded away. Conner retrieved it before Obumje could turn or Kline could stand back up.

"Nice hustle," the coach said sarcastically to no one and everyone at the same time.

With both Obumje and Kline still having their momentum coming toward the ball that Conner had already retrieved, it was easy to pass the ball to Harris. He took it and, with one step, launched up for a two-handed dunk. Then, for effect, he held onto the rim for a second, before letting go. In a regular game, he might have gotten a technical foul. Here, nobody made a comment.

"Eight-three," came the score from the coach.

Obumje inbounded to Kline. This time Harris crowded him even more. Kline decided to shoot but he was clearly forcing it. The rebound came back toward the shooter and was harmlessly corralled by Harris who had kept Kline behind him. Harris brought the ball back past the foul line, as is the rule in half-court games. He fired a pass to Conner who dribbled for a moment with his back to the basket. Obumje was guarding him but Kline came over to double team him. Conner launched a somewhat wild hook shot that hit the backboard, then the rim and rose high above outside the imaginary cylinder. As it came down, Harris had timed his leap. He caught it and flushed it through for another two-handed dunk. This time, he did not hang on the rim.

When he landed, his feet were spread wider than his shoulders and he started to beat his chest, then stopped. Conner was glad to see that his teammate had thought better of that. Instead, Harris looked over to Conner and pointed up, apparently glorifying God.

"Nine-three."

Kline inbounded but Conner stole the ball from Obumje on the first bounce of his dribble. He fired it to Harris who went up for another dunk. This time, though, Kline would have none of it. In a foul that would have gotten a player ejected and probably suspended had it been in a game, Kline ran into Shedrick's shins and totally flipped him over, the revolution driving Harris to the floor, his shoulder hitting first with his head not far behind. The thud was loud and clearly terrible. There was no question that a serious injury had just taken place.

Everyone stood up at once. Conner was at Shedrick's side in a flash, the coach joining immediately. The rest of the bench followed, players and coaches alike.

Chapter 15

Shedrick did not move. There was much talking going on but no action. The trainer was not present so there was no medical support. As the seconds ticked away, the conversations grew more numerous, more frantic and louder.

"Quiet!" Conner shouted. The gym grew silent.

"You," he pointed to one of the assistant coaches. "Call 9-1-1." The man remained in his spot, looking at Shedrick, at Conner and then at the coach. "Now!" Conner added vigorously, prompting the man to leave running.

"Everyone else, please stay put…quietly." Conner then provided everyone with instructions. "For those who care to join me, please bow your head." All heads lowered, although nobody consciously realized what Conner was about to do.

"Father," Conner began. "Please bring our brother, Shedrick, through this. Please show everyone here, everyone who wishes to see what You can do, that You are a God of mercy and might. Please allow us to have this moment together with our brother and Your son. And we ask this in Your Son's name. Amen."

From what Conner could tell, everyone said Amen.

Five seconds later, Shedrick slowly opened his eyes. He then rolled over onto his back and brought his right wrist to his forehead.

"Wow," he said. "What happened?"

Spontaneous applause erupted from the team. Tears flowed from Kline's eyes. He was not the only one both relieved and moved.

In a few moments, Harris brought his feet to his backside so that he had his knees raised. "Help me up," he requested.

Some of the team started to help while others instructed them to let him be for a minute. In the end, Shedrick grabbed two outstretched hands and was helped up. The players backed up to give him room. He stood a bit wobbly but not apparently much worse for the wear. There was silence. With his infectious grin, he said "Was that a shooting foul?" and the entire gym exploded into loud and relieved laughter. Kline was the first to step forward and simply say "Sorry." He hugged Shedrick in a way that he wouldn't have approached doing in the past. He realized how close he had come to seriously, if not fatally, injuring his teammate. Competition was one thing, idiocy another. Kline had stepped across the line and he had been granted a reprieve. It was God's mercy at its finest, perhaps most obvious.

Kline turned to Conner with a look of question. "Who are you, man?" he asked. Everyone listened.

"One of the believers," Conner answered, more appropriate and eloquent than if he had relied on his own devices to concoct an answer.

"That's all?" Kline asked and everyone knew what he meant.

"That's it," Conner said. "And who are you?" Conner inquired of him, trying to maximize the moment.

"A lot different now," Kline said.

Shedrick turned to Conner. He pointed up and said "Let's finish this."

"No way," the coach interjected. "You guys have demonstrated your worth. This game ends ten-three in your favor." He pointed to Shedrick when he gave that score. Everyone except Walker energetically applauded. He just walked away from the huddle. The coach started to reprimand him but then thought better of it.

"Ramsey," he instructed, "to my office. The rest of you, see you tonight for our second practice."

Conner turned to Shedrick. "You gonna be okay?"

"Okay?" he exclaimed. "I just had the best day of my life. I'm gonna be fine. Super fine."

They smiled at each other.

"I'll wait here and see you after you speak with the coach," he said.

"Not if you're my friend," Conner replied.

"Huh?" he grunted, a confused look on his face.

"You smell worse than me. Go shower. Besides, you deserve the accolades they will give you for your play today."

It was clear that Shedrick did not know what to say. Conner saved him the trouble of searching for it. "Go!" he instructed. Harris obeyed and started to walk toward the locker room. "See ya here nice and clean after that," Conner said.

Harris turned, smiled and replied "You got it!" and double timed his footsteps out of the gym. Concurrent with his exit, Conner headed to the coach's office, having figured out its location from his exit path, entirely different from the players' exit path.

As he was leaving the court, the assistant coach and a 9-1-1 team arrived. Seeing the floor empty, they stopped.

"Where is he?" the assistant coach asked.

"He recovered," Conner replied.

"Recovered?" came the question from the assistant coach, sounding somewhat like a challenge.

"Remarkable, eh?"

"When I left, he was colder than an ice cube," commented the assistant coach.

"He was, indeed," Conner agreed.

"Where is he now?"

"In the locker room, I believe."

"Let's take a look at him," the EMT said. Without waiting for confirmation, the 9-1-1 team took off toward the locker room.

With a quick look at Conner, the assistant coach followed.

Conner was already enjoying what he could imagine would be the conversation. He turned and resumed his walk to the coach's office. For no particular reason, other than a feeling of exhilaration, he began trotting instead of walking. How cool, he thought.

Suddenly, he was brought back to reality. He stopped in his tracks and silently chided himself. What was I thinking? he wondered. Still on the court, Conner stopped, bowed his head and brought his hands together.

"Thank You, Lord," he said aloud. He didn't know where to go from there. It was overwhelming. "You are amazing." There it was again. Amazing. Nothing else came. He was silent for several seconds. "Thank You, Lord," he said again, ending with "Amen."

He looked up, took a deep breath and was just about to resume his walk when he heard "You're welcome." Conner looked around the gym. It was entirely empty. He didn't contest the discrepancy.

Chapter 16

It wasn't too difficult to find the coach's office. A huge sign over the door: JASON WRIGHT, HEAD COACH. If you missed that sign, you would have had to be either totally oblivious or blind. Conner entered. Off to the left sat the coach behind his desk. He had a pencil that he was tapping on a mostly-empty sports drink container. He was fairly expressionless. He sat there for a few moments while he looked at his visitor and continued to drum the pencil. Conner wasn't sure what to do. The coach wasn't that much older than Conner. They were more contemporaries than teacher-student. Yet

Conner was there for a coach-player relationship. He waited.

"Sit down," the coach said.

More drumming. Then he stopped and leaned forward. "What the heck happened out there?"

"Sir?"

"Don't sir me. What the heck was that?"

"Which part?"

"Both parts!" he said vehemently. "Both parts," he repeated, this time a little more casually.

Conner didn't know where to start. He began with the basketball scrimmage. "Well, sir…er, not sir. Shedrick is a fine player and we just beat them to the ball. Maybe they weren't taking us seriously enough."

"The heck they weren't!" he said. "What do you think Kline was doing on that last play?"

Conner had several thoughts to share but chose to hold his tongue. C.S. Lewis liked to say something along the order of 'People are in favor of forgiveness until they have to give it.' Although Conner was angry about that cheap shot Kline had given Shedrick, he thought that not commenting about it made more sense.

"Well?" the coach asked somewhat impatiently.

"Listen, coach, I told you that I could play. You gave me a chance. If you want me to play on your team, I will enroll at Brantley and play. If not, I will seek an opportunity elsewhere."

"Heck, Ramsey, of course I want you to play. I'm just trying to figure out why you never played ball before."

"Me, too, sir." Oops, Conner didn't mean to add the 'sir' part but chose not to try to undo it.

"Nobody goes from being nothing to finding his game in his thirties."

Conner remained silent. Since he was not going to explain the circumstances, he had nothing to offer.

"Say something, man," the coach ordered.

"Michael Jordan," Conner said, trying to come up with someone who had blossomed later in life.

"He was cut in eighth grade. By the time he got to college, he was ready to go," the coach countered.

"Albert Einstein."

Coach Wright smiled, understanding now that Conner was playing with him. "Okay. I get it. There is no explanation. But are you sure that you never played in college?"

"Yes, sir. I mean, no, sir. What I mean is that I did not play."

"Where did you go to college?"

"Ohio University."

"Really?"

"Yeah."

"My sister went there. I almost did, too."

"Small world."

"And you didn't go out for the basketball team?"

"Nope."

"Why not?"

"Because I could barely walk, dribble and chew gum at the same time. I'm still not good at dribbling."

"Looked pretty good to me today. Wasn't pretty but it got the job done."

"Thanks."

"You made the others look like they were running in taffy."

Conner laughed. The image was funny. He didn't say anything.

"To what do you attribute your newfound skills?"

"I am trying to learn their purpose, sir."

"If you call me 'sir' one more time, I will brain you. Call me 'coach' when you address me."

"Will do, coach," Conner responded, hoping to have sidestepped his question.

"And what was that other part out there?" he asked, less certain of himself.

"Are you a man of faith?" Conner asked.

The coach hemmed and hawed a bit, then responded with "We go to church…when we can."

It was funny how his eyes turned away when he answered. When it came to something he knew, like basketball, he was an in-your-face person. For something like this, he was an elementary school kid.

"Like most people, I guess," Conner commented.

"I think so."

"I would venture to say that everyone out there, after that foul, was prayerful for Shedrick's health."

"Absolutely," he said.

"Personally, I would credit his recovery to the power of prayer."

"Oh, come on!" Coach Wright said, tossing down the pencil. "You can't be serious."

"I am," Conner countered. They sat there for a few moments. Then Conner asked "Why do you dismiss that possibility?"

"Prayer doesn't work that way."

"What way?"

"Bing, bang, bong," he said.

"We're just not used to it working that way. We look to discount it before we accept it. Answered prayers happen all the time."

"How do you know?" he questioned.

"Good point. I can only say how it impacts my life, although the Bible is full of examples of answered prayers."

Judging from his body language, the coach was starting to get his underwear in a bunch. Conner backed off. "Okay, sure," he concluded.

This was followed by several moments of awkward silence.

"What are you expecting?" the coach asked.

Conner didn't know how brassy to be but decided to go for the whole enchilada. "Scholarship - tuition, books, room and board."

The coach sat back and put his feet up on his desk, although not defiantly in front Conner, more off to the side. His team was going to be average this year, maybe below average, depending on how mobile Kline could be and how hotheaded Walker would behave.

"How do I know you can perform like that all year?"

Conner said nothing because anything that he would say would only diminish what the coach had seen on court. The coach respected his silence.

"Yeah," he said, "words don't make a difference."

More silence.

"One more thing, coach."

"What?" he barked more than asked.

"I'd like to be partnered up with Shedrick when we're out there." Oh, boy, where did that come from?

"Oh, now you want to coach, too?" he said.

"No, sir, I don't. It's not a demand or a condition. It's a request. He has a good heart and we connect."

"I'll consider it. But remember, *I* make the decisions around here."

"I understand," Conner replied. "Thanks for considering it. What now?"

"I'll connect you with Coach Murphy and he'll get you through the application process. Get back for practice tonight. I'll present you to the team, although I doubt that you'll need an introduction."

"Great!"

Conner's smile must have been huge because the coach said "Wipe that dopey grin off your face and let's see what you can do on an ongoing basis."

Conner stood up. The coach looked him over, like a farmer considering buying a cow.

"For one thing, we need to get you in condition. A guy your age who is a bit overweight is an accident waiting to happen."

"I'm not overweight," Conner replied.

"Yeah, right," the coach said sarcastically.

"Not much overweight."

The coach ignored this defense, changing subjects. "And you never played ball in school…high school or college?"

"Nope, not even junior high."

"You better be telling me the truth."

"I am."

"I'll be darned."

Chapter 17

The rest of the day was crazy. Coach Murphy was younger than Conner, somewhat green (what lots of people call a new soul) and determined to do whatever Coach Wright instructed. He felt like the luckiest guy in the world to be on the coach's staff. Truth is, Coach Wright only wanted him around as a gopher, tossing him bones from time to time.

"Murph," he said, taking the assistant aside, "this guy might be the real deal. We need to get him admitted and squared away. I'm taking a chance and giving him a scholarship. What do you think?"

"Oh, yeah, coach. He's the real deal. Did you see...?"

"Yeah, Murph, we're in agreement. Now, do you think that you can get him situated? I need him admitted, registered, given a dorm room and everything. I'd like him paired up with Harris. Do you think that you can handle that? It's really important to our program, Murph."

"Sure, coach. Sure thing. I'll do it. Don't you worry about it. I'll do it."

Thus charged up, Assistant Coach Taylor Murphy got Conner through everything...and that means everything. By the time the noon hour had rolled around, Conner was a Brantley University graduate student, had his schedule, had his books, had checked into the athletes' dorm and was headed to lunch with the team. If Coach Wright wanted something, he obviously got it.

"Got it done, Coach," Murphy proudly exclaimed as he and Conner walked into the section of the dining room designated for the men's basketball team. Coach Wright, with a mouthful of something, simply winked at him and gave him a thumbs-up sign. No eloquent speech would have been more meaningful to the assistant coach. Murphy felt like a trusted confidant.

Conner waited for the coach to swallow as he had indicated with a stop sign signal with his right hand. He gulped some water, stood up and spoke to those sitting around. "Some of you met Conner Ramsey on the court this morning." A few people nodded; others kept eating. "He'll be joining us. Please welcome him."

"All right!" came a holler from one of the seats furthest from the coach. Conner recognized it instantly as Shedrick's voice. He smiled. The rest of those seated applauded, although it wasn't a you're-our-savior appreciation, more a child's response to a parent's instruction. No matter. Conner appreciated the opportunity.

"Now go get some food and find a seat somewhere," the coach told Conner as he resumed eating. "Oh, and make sure that you get him to practice tonight, Murph," he instructed the new player's apparent chaperone. Coach Murphy smiled and enthusiastically nodded his head.

Conner turned to go and get something to eat when Shedrick stepped forward and gave him a hug.

It was a little awkward but Conner didn't want to embarrass him so he hugged Harris back.

"How's the noggin'?" Conner asked?

"Bruised but unbent."

"Must be made of concrete," Conner said with a smile.

Both stood silently for a moment, sharing the experience.

"Thanks," Shedrick said. "Thanks a lot."

Conner didn't know if he meant about the basketball or the prayer, although he assumed it was about the latter. Since he didn't have anything to do with either, he didn't feel the need to respond.

"Come on. I'll show you the food rituals," Shedrick said, only too happy to guide Conner along the chow line. Conner followed him.

It turned out to be a good thing that Conner had him as his tour guide. With all this food, Conner was confused as to what to take as well as how much to take. Constantly chattering, sometimes with important information and sometimes with just noise, Shedrick explained the coach's philosophy about eating, digesting, exercising, stretching, studying and relaxing. Had Conner shown more than a modicum of interest beyond the food, he was confident that he also would have heard about the coach's philosophy about going to the bathroom, showering, shaving, dressing, dating and everything else. As it turned out, Conner managed to return to the table with a tray full of appealing food, something he would not have expected from a university cafeteria.

Shedrick guided Conner to his table. It was a little
bit sad because he sort of sat isolated from the
others. Being able to pal with Conner clearly meant a
lot to him. Walker, Obumje and Kline were seated
up near the coach's table. None of the three made
any effort to welcome Conner.

"Did they get you admitted, registered and into
the dorm?" Shedrick asked.

"Yeah, yeah."

"Well…"

Conner held up his hand. "God first," he said.

"Yeah, yeah, sure," Shedrick said and bowed his
head. Conner offered thanks to the Father for his
many blessings, past, present and future. He asked
for his continuing guidance and for opportunities to
further his message. Shedrick and Conner both said
"Amen" at the same time. As Conner opened his
eyes and looked up, he saw that some of the team
had been staring at him. He didn't know if they had
prayed alongside or just been curious. Either way, he
was glad.

"What room are you in?" Shedrick blurted out
after the prayer, giving Conner almost no time to
catch his breath. What a barrel of energy, Conner
thought.

"Er…" He couldn't remember the dorm name or
room number but fished the key out of his pants.
Reading it, he said "Conlan, Room 260."

"Yes!" Harris said, slapping the table.

Conner looked at him, wondering about the
significance of what he had just reported.

Shedrick looked back. Seeing nothing, he said "We're roommates. Isn't that great?"

Conner smiled back at him. If he's always like this, Conner thought, I will need to take drugs to survive. "That's terrific," Conner replied. "I'm delighted."

"You know what they're calling you?"

"They?"

"The rest of the team," he explained.

"No, what?"

"J.C.," he said.

"Oh, no," Conner replied, knowing to whom they were referring.

"You know what they're calling me?"

"I can't wait to find out."

"Lazarus. Isn't that cool? You're J.C. and I'm Lazarus. That's sooo cool, don't you think?"

"No."

"No? Why no?"

"Because there's only one Jesus and it's not me."

Shedrick's face was a little deflated but he didn't let it throw him off stride. "Oh, they don't mean any harm."

"The road to hell is paved…" Conner let the quote go uncompleted.

Shedrick chose not to say anything further about it. That allowed Conner to get some food into his hungry body. Halfway through his platter, Shedrick started eating, too, accordingly allowing them to finish at roughly the same time. They took their trays to the conveyer belt and left for the dorm. Virtually all the team and coaches had already departed. Assistant Coach Murphy continued to work at the mound of food he had gotten, including two different pies for dessert and a huge drink. Soda, no doubt. He was not responsible for conditioning. Good thing, too.

Chapter 18

When they got to the dorm, they took the stairs up to the second floor. Shedrick held out his key for Conner to read. 'Conlan 260.' "See?" he said. "We're roomies."

"I never doubted it," Conner replied, although it seemed strange that a key should have such a clear identifier on it. If it fell into the wrong hands, it was an invitation to steal from that room. Having seen recent TV reports on this being done with valuable trophies, it doubled Conner's concern. Fortunately, he didn't have anything worth stealing. At least nothing tangible.

Conlan 260 had two rooms and a common area. Each room had a bed, a desk and a closet. The rooms were exactly the same size. Shedrick's was to the left, Conner's straight ahead. Both had windows, although the one on the left looked out on the quadrangle while the other stared off across a parking lot. Conner's stuff, what little he had brought along from the apartment, lay strewn across his bed, along the floor and on his desk. It wouldn't take long to put away the few things that he had brought along.

As for his job, hopeful to have been correct in committing to this adventure, Conner was fortunate to have been given an unpaid leave of absence.

Although his boss thought that he was nuts to pursue a full-time graduate degree, he did appreciate Conner's work and work ethic. "We'll find something for you, if you return in a year," was all he said. And, with that, Conner was out the door.

"Is that all you brought?"

It was a fairly meager pile. "Yup."

"How come?"

"I wasn't sure that I would be staying." Conner's apartment lease still had another two months on it. He wanted to keep it and had enough money saved up to afford the cost.

"Huh? You weren't sure that you would be staying. What does that mean?"

Conner considered how best to answer this question. "Well, I came up here to see whether there was a fit between the university and me."

"Oh," he responded. "I guess that there is."

"It would appear so."

"What kind of fit?"

"I wanted to see if I could make the team and if there would be a good relationship with the coach."

"Well, you definitely made the team. But you did irritate a few players."

"We did it together," Conner emphasized. "Remember?"

"I was lucky. You were good."

"We were both good."

Shedrick was silent for a couple of moments while Conner started putting his clothing into drawers or hanging them up. Then Shedrick said "Why would you want to play basketball at your age?" Suddenly uncomfortable with his question, he tried to correct the clumsy wording. "I mean, you're good and all but don't you, like, have a job, a home and a family and that sort of stuff?"

Conner smiled. Shedrick had hit the heart of the matter. Now committed to not explaining the origin of his mission, Conner stopped what he was doing and looked up at his newfound friend and teammate. "I can be flexible right now. When I was younger, maybe about your age, there were things that I wanted to do, things that I thought I might be able to do."

"Yeah," Shedrick listened attentively.

"But I never did them. Either I didn't act in time to do so, I chickened out or I decided that other things were more important."

"Okay."

"I'm at a point in my life now that allows me to try some of those things."

"Like basketball," he added.

"Yeah, like basketball."

"But didn't I hear that you never played organized ball before?"

"You heard right."

"Then what suddenly turned on the light for you? I mean, how did you, out of the blue, decide that you were good enough to play on a team like this and that you should do so?"

"You know, Shedrick, that's a great question. I'm glad that you asked it. And I think that you are one of the few people who I know who might understand why."

It seemed as though Shedrick stood a little taller, buoyed by this compliment. He said nothing.

"It's really a combination of doing what I hadn't done before, pursuing a personal dream, and following what I hear God telling me in my heart to do."

Conner stopped to see his roommate's reaction. Shedrick was nodding and obviously processing it. He had stopped looking at Conner and was staring at a vacant spot on the floor. "God was telling you to play basketball?"

Conner smiled. "In a manner of speaking."

"Why?"

"You're a man of faith, right?"

"You bet," Shedrick responded firmly.

"Do we always know his purpose?"

Shedrick thought briefly and then responded "No."

"Well, I hear what I hear. I think that it has something to do with spreading the Word." That was as far as Conner was willing to take it in this conversation.

"Wow." Shedrick paused. Then he added "How?"

"I'm not sure. Maybe if we distinguish ourselves on the basketball court, others will take notice and we can help at least some of them become saints."

"Saints," he echoed, then asked it in a question "Saints?"

Conner looked at him. It appeared that they had differing definitions of what a saint was and was not.

"You mean like Saint Thomas, Saint Paul and like that?"

Conner smiled. "In my church, every Christian is called a saint. One doesn't have to go through some human process to get recognized. When you accept Christ, you're a saint. You're one of his soldiers."

"Ohhh," Shedrick said contemplatively. "I never thought about it much before. I just figured that you had to be sainted, like being knighted" He thought for a moment more, then added "But I like your definition. It makes more sense to me."

"Good. Anyhow, that's what I will try to do."

"Didn't you already graduate college?"

"Yeah. I'm taking graduate classes."

"Interesting," he commented, not really interested.

Conner returned to putting things away.

"How are we gonna spread the Word?"

Conner loved his use of 'we' in asking that question.

"Play hard, study hard, walk the talk and invite others to join us...or we them."

"I like it," he said. "I'm in," he added.

"And I'm glad that you are. We're an army of two." After a momentary pause, he added "Make that three...for the time being."

Then Shedrick turned and headed into his bathroom. In a manner of speaking, the voyage had begun in earnest. When the door closed, Conner said out loud. "This should be interesting, Lord. It's all up to you."

He didn't get any overt response but felt peaceful inside.

Chapter 19

Conner had no idea what kind of student he would be, especially after having been out of school for such a long time. However, the fact that he would be pursuing a Master of Arts in Biblical Studies degree would track well with what he was doing outside of class. He was excited about virtually every aspect of being at Brantley.

Conner looked over the books he had gotten for his classes. Oh, my gosh, he thought. This is not going to be easy. He pulled out his schedule to see which classes he had and when they were scheduled during the week. The first would be *Heroes of the Old Testament*. It would meet Tuesday and Thursday mornings from 10:00 to 11:30. He found the printed syllabus and confirmed that the three books required were in his possession, although well down in the tall stack he had brought into the room. After checking to see which one would be the first assigned, he pulled it out from under the others. He read the jacket and opened to the introduction. Somewhere right after doing those two things, he fell asleep.

"Hey, we gotta get ready," Shedrick said, banging on the open door.

"Yikes! Have a heart, man. I'm an old guy. You wanna kill me?"

"Sorry," he said. "I wanted to give you time to wake up before heading to the gym."

Conner looked at his watch and realized that he had slept for a full two hours. Wow, I needed that, he thought. He rolled off his bed and did a few pushups to get the blood flowing.

"Don't burn all your energy," Shedrick said, coming into the room. "The evening practices are always tougher than the morning ones."

Conner stood up, found his windbreaker, laced his sneakers and joined Shedrick in exiting the room. He had his car keys, room keys and phone. Picking up the cell phone triggered him to realize that he hadn't called anyone, not even thought about it. Weird, he reflected. Maybe later.

They got to the gym and went directly to the locker room. The attendant there greeted Shedrick and said to Conner "You're the new guy, right?"

"Conner Ramsey," he said, extending his hand.

He moved some towels he was holding over to his left arm, allowing him to shake hands. "Glad to meet you," he said. "Jake Crumpler but most folks just call me Eagle Eye...for obvious reasons." Jake's handshake was like being enveloped in a bear hug. Although it was not painful, one could quickly understand that this was an enormously powerful man.

"Glad to meet you, too. Eagle Eye, huh?"

"Yeah, it works for all of us. You got a number preference?" he asked.

"Which are available? Actually, all other things being equal, I'd love to have number seven, if it hasn't either been retired or is being worn by someone else."

Jake looked at his clipboard that was sitting on the locker room bench. "Nope, you're in luck. I'm surprised that it's available."

"I'll take it!" Conner said, closing the deal.

"Wait here," Jake instructed and disappeared for about two minutes. When he returned, he brought back a large stack of stuff, mostly clothes. "When you're done with each practice, just toss your clothes in there." He pointed to a large bin on wheels. "They'll be ready for the next practice. Same for game clothes. This other stuff is for your locker. If you need anything else, let me know and I'll see what I can do."

"Thanks," Conner said appreciatively.

"What size shoe do you wear?" he asked.

"Eleven and a half."

"Be right back," he said and returned with two new pairs of top-of-the-line sneakers.

"Wow. I didn't expect this much."

"Eagles basketball," Jake replied. "You get it done on the court, stay out of trouble, do well enough in your classes and the rest is taken care of for you."

"Apparently so. Thanks."

"Don't mention it."

Shedrick was already suited up for the practice. It took Conner a few minutes to get ready. His roomie went on ahead.

"Don't be late," Shedrick said. "Coach makes all of us pay for the sins of each. Good way to get on everyone's wrong side is to get the rest in trouble."

"Got it. Thanks."

Conner got dressed, careful to put everything he didn't need neatly in the locker, which was very spacious, indeed. Compared to lockers he had used, this was a mansion. It was floor to ceiling and roughly two and a half to three times wider than a traditional locker. It had shelves, hangers and a mess of other things, mostly hygiene products. The sneakers fit fine and he finished lacing them. As he started to stand up, he realized that someone was towering over him. He looked up to see a person very much emulating a California Redwood tree, the very top reaching into the clouds. This tree had on a practice uniform. Conner reckoned him to be one of his teammates, although Conner hadn't seen him at this morning's practice.

"Name's Clyde Forrester," he started. "I go by 'Enforcer,' just so you know. That's an on-the-court and off-the-court title. You're the new guy, although you're obviously not new." Very funny, thought Conner but chose not to say anything. "Some of the guys said you've got game from this morning. Some of them said that you were lucky. Some of them said that you're a religious freak. I don't really care which. My job is to remind you to play your role, whatever it is, and not get any of us in trouble off the court. You follow?"

"Clearly," Conner said, not yet standing up.

"Good. It starts with being on time. Now get out there."

"You got it," Conner said, slamming his locker closed and darting past the skyscraper. Conner could hear the Enforcer's heavy footsteps following.

A larger squad than this morning was there. Everyone was stretching. There were no basketballs on the court. Conner joined them, realizing that his flexibility was something well short of theirs. Most of them were able to sit down, extend both legs and hold the soles of their feet. If Conner bounced, he could just about touch his toes. He pretended to move to something else, bringing one foot behind him as he sat there and supposedly worked on his quads. He had just switched feet when the coach came into the gym.

Immediately, everyone jumped up. Conner followed suit. Each player grabbed a seat in the bleachers, not on the bench. They took the first four rows and were in a tighter span than they would have been on the bench. Conner understood the rationale and thought it quite wise. This way everyone could see and hear the coach. Makes sense to me, he thought.

The coach conferred with two of his assistant coaches, one of them scurrying off on an assignment. Then he turned to the players. "Gentlemen, we have our first game on Thursday evening. It's a home game. We won't have to worry too much about logistics. I'll post who suits up by noon Wednesday. Whether you suit up, play or not, I'll want everyone there. For those of you who don't suit up, I'll want you taking notes. Coach Markham will have clipboards and templates. Turn them into him before you leave the game. Your notes are important for us and they are important learning opportunities for you, as well, especially if you have visions of coaching in the future, which I know many of you do."

Nobody said a word, although one could probably have picked out those who had no worry about playing from those who knew they would be handling a clipboard just by their body language. Conner stole a glance at Shedrick and, had he not known otherwise, would have put him in the don't-suit-up category. Conner didn't know where he would be put but intended to make the decision easy for the coach by playing well in practice.

"Ramsey, stand up." He did so. "This old guy, Conner Ramsey, wants to play for us. He showed me something at our morning workout. We'll see over the long run. Try to be nice to him. He's probably old enough to be father to some of you. However, that doesn't mean that I want you to baby him. If he's not good enough for the Eagles, it's adios to him. Got it?"

A chorus of yes, sirs came out loud and clear. Not bad, Conner thought.

"Okay, let's run some burns." A huge groan came from the team. "Five sets in groups of eight."

Conner had no idea what he was talking about. He looked over to Shedrick who made a motion suggesting that he would explain. They all got up and walked down to the floor. The first eight included Kline, Walker, Forrester and Obumje. Conner took it that the other four were at the top of the food chain, as well.

On his whistle, they took off, running hard, stopping, touching the ground, changing direction, running backwards and doing a number of other things that made Conner nauseous just watching. One could see that they were competing with one another. At the end, it lasting for what looked like an eternity, the first one back under the backboard was

Walker. "Two seventeen," barked out the assistant coach who had timed this. Oh my goodness, Conner thought. I am going to die right here.

The next and then the next groups went with 2:30 and 2:37 times respectively. Then it was the final group. There were just seven in this group. Conner suspected this was the lowest end of the food chain...and he was on it. With the whistle, they took off. Aside from trying to watch what everyone else did, Conner couldn't begin to keep up with them. About a third of the way through, he was winded. He fought through it. Halfway home, he felt like puking. By the time he finished, a full forty-five seconds after the slowest guy, he was truly ready to puke. Instead of sitting down like everyone else, he hustled to the bathroom where he did make a stomach deposit into the toilet. Yech! He wished that he had brought gum. No quitter in him, he returned to the floor.

"Nice," Walker said sarcastically. Conner said nothing, still trying to normalize his body.

"Again," said the coach. Another refrain of groans, this time good naturedly accompanied by some boos. "Let's go," he said, clapping his hands.

Same thing. Three groups of eight and his group of seven. This time, Conner determined to stay within himself and disregard any need to keep up with the others. He just wanted to finish in one piece. He did, a full minute after the last guy. He caught a bunch of grief from the other players. He now looked every bit the equal of Coach Murphy,

the Pillsbury Dough Boy. However, this time he
didn't have to run to the bathroom.

"Impressive," Coach Wright said looking straight
at Conner. "Some of you gentlemen won't be much
help to us in the fourth quarter, now will you?"
Nobody responded, least of all Conner. "Layups,"
he called out.

Everyone again knew where to go, some to the
north basket, others to the south basket. Conner
went with Shedrick, standing behind him on one of
the two lines. One line was the shooters and the
other the rebounders. But this wasn't the casual
layup drill that one watches before a game. No, this
was jam it down time and serious rebounding. They
did three full rounds of this and Conner looked like
a junior high schooler compared to everyone,
Shedrick included. At least Shedrick had some hops.
Had there been a book on the floor, Conner may
not have been able to jump over it. The good news
was that he made two of three layups.

The coach blew his whistle. Everyone assembled
into a semicircle. Once again, he looked straight at
Conner and said "Impressive. Next time, try not
hanging onto the rim that long." That broke
everyone up. Conner noticed that Kline and Walker
took the laughter a little too far. Conner started to
think the 'payback is hell' thought but caught himself
in time. I'm not here to defeat or alienate, he
thought. I'm here to encourage, support and invite.
He let his personal ego go and refocused. "Foul
shooting," the coach called out.

Again, everyone knew where to go. This time, the team broke up into six groups, each one shooting at one of the six baskets that were available. The other baskets had five players per grouping; Conner's had six.

Each player took five shots, then rotated to the end of his line. After his fifth shot, the shooter called out how many he had made. Everyone called out fours and fives. Wow. This was one fine foul-shooting team. Conner's first foul shot was an air ball. He made one of the next four. "One," he called out, much less loudly than anyone else.

"What did you say, Ramsey?" the coach hollered.

"One," he responded loudly.

"Take a lap and next time let me hear you proudly call out your score."

Conner said nothing, did the lap and returned to his place in line. The second time he was able to claim two shots with all at least hitting the rim. The third time was even better – three. One of them, though, was a horrible bank shot. He had no idea how it went in.

"Bleachers," the coach called out. Everyone returned to their original positions in the stands. The coach crossed his arms and looked out at the team. "Ramsey," he said, "you were a half day slower than your teammates in the burns, you were ESPN blooper material during the layups and you proudly claimed six of fifteen foul shots."

Some covered laughter erupted. The coach looked in the direction of those making it. Silence ensued.

"Are you sure that you should be here?"

"Yes, sir…er, coach."

"Well, let's find out if you can do something during a scrimmage. You eight," he said numbering off eight players, "are with Wilcox." The eight dashed off behind the assistant coach. "You eight," he said pointing out the next eight, Shedrick and Conner included, "are with Bromberg. You're yellow," meaning that this team would don a yellow singlet over its warm up tee shirts in order to distinguish one team from another. "The rest of you grab some pine." The remaining fifteen players went into the stands, some of them clearly disappointed not to have been chosen.

The other team had Kline, Walker, Obumje, Forrester (the giant from the locker room) and four other mountains. Conner's yellow team had two gangly-looking beanpoles and six players in the 6'0" to 6'2" range. It was a slaughter ready to happen.

Chapter 20

Assistant Coach Bromberg called his guys together. "You two," he said, pointing to the beanpoles, "are inside. We'll play a three-two. You three," he said, pointing to Shedrick, another guy and Conner, "are outside. Make it good."

'Make it good'? What kind of coaching is that, Conner thought to himself. That was like 'Try not to get killed' or something equivalently eloquent.

The other team was still huddled up with Assistant Coach Wilcox. They were laughing, somewhat to the obvious displeasure of the head coach. A little more of that and they would have paid for it. Perhaps sensing his growing anger, they wisely or luckily throttled back. Wilcox barked out five names and those players started walking to mid court.

Conner called the other four to him. "Listen," he said, "this looks like a mismatch. However, we have God on our side."

"Not again," Gary Dixon, one of the beanpoles said. "Let's just play basketball and not get all religious here."

"Fair enough," Conner said. "At least let me suggest how we play."

Gary crossed his arms in defiance but Shedrick popped in with "Give him a chance. If it doesn't work, we can change it up. It's not like we're favored going into this."

Gary uncrossed his arms and made a conciliatory face, understanding that they were mismatched anyhow. "Okay," he said much more nicely.

"Great," Conner started. "Let's play the three-two the way that the coach wants. However, you two," he said, pointing at Gary and the other beanpole, have one major assignment – one and done. We get every defensive and as many offensive rebounds as possible. Otherwise, just enjoy yourselves."

The two looked at him like he was crazy. "Trust me," Conner said.

"Shedrick," he turned to the remaining two, "you and…"

"Chris Shaffer," the other player said.

"You and Chris take away the outside shots. Gary and…"

"Wes Harmon," beanpole number two said.

"Gary, Wes and I will take care of underneath. Okay?"

"Whatever," Gary said, totally unconvinced.

"Teamwork beats cockiness," Conner said. "Let's just give it a try. We've got nothing to lose, only lots to win." He looked around. Responses ranged from energetic by Shedrick to you're crazy by Gary. "Hands in." All joined and Conner said "Score on three. One, two, score." Only Shedrick joined Conner with the final word.

Once on the floor, nobody shook hands or wished anyone else good luck. For Wilcox's team, this was just a warm up. For Bromberg's team, this was being led to slaughter. Forrester jumped against Gary and easily won the ball for his team. Gary and Wes backed down low, Shedrick pressured the ball, Chris sort of dawdled and Conner stood at the top of the key. Walker brought the ball up and passed to Kline. Chris did not press him so Kline drilled a three pointer.

"What are we playing to?" Walker asked, almost bored.

"Just play," Coach Wright said. "Don't get too full of yourself."

Walker just smiled and skipped backwards towards his position.

Shedrick brought the ball up and passed to Chris. Immediately, Chris took an ill-advised, off-balance shot that barely caught the rim. Team Wilcox came back up the floor. Already, Walker was laughing. Coach Wright, visibly annoyed, held his tongue.

"Get him," he said quietly to himself, hoping that Conner's magic could be duplicated from this morning.

Walker passed the ball to Kline who, again uncontested, drilled a three pointer.

Coach Wright blew his whistle and walked onto the court. He called Chris over and said "You want to play on this team?"

Chris looked at him and responded "Yes, Coach."

"Then you better start playing both ends of the court. You get my drift?"

"Yes, Coach," Chris answered.

"Each five is a team. Offense and defense. Anyone who doesn't understand that," he turned to make certain that everyone could hear, "will not be with us to enjoy the fruits of our work. Do you understand?" The question was almost shouted.

"Yes, Coach," came the loud response from everyone. The coach walked off the court and play resumed.

Chris inbounded to Shedrick who brought the ball past the timeline. The ball went from Shedrick to Conner to Chris, back to Conner and into Gary who looked to shoot, drew Forrester and nicely passed the ball to Wes for an easy two.

"Well done," Conner called out as everyone hustled back. "Now let's get serious," he added.

"Hey, serious this, old man," Walker said, obviously challenging him to a little one on one. Conner said nothing.

Kline and Forrester understood Walker's intentions and established picks for Walker to use.

The others on Team Bromberg kept their positions. Just before Walker went into his take-it-to-the-rim attitude, Conner offered a silent prayer: This would be a good time, Lord, he said to himself.

Two dribbles and Walker was ready to go. On the next dribble, Conner stepped forward and took the ball away. So surprised was Walker that his hand looked to still be dribbling an invisible ball. Like a flash, Shedrick was running with Conner who bounced a lead pass to him allowing the freshman to slam home a two-handed dunk.

"Yeah, that's what I'm talkin' 'bout," Shedrick said as he landed.

Only Obumje had pursued the breakaway, Kline too dumbfounded to do anything, Walker too annoyed. The other two on their team had been too far away to do anything.

The scoreboard read six-four. Coach Wright now sat on his chair leaning forward with both feet on the floor, instead of leaning back with his legs crossed. Nobody said anything, assuming the steal to have been an aberration.

When Team Wilcox got into its offense, the beanpoles kept their big men out of the paint, effectively handling the larger men that they guarded. One could see that they were maintaining inside position in order to control rebounds. Chris, newly charged, bodied up on Kline. Shedrick closed on Walker who was now on his side of the court and Conner studied Obumje. The ball came around to Obumje who tried to bounce it into Forrester. Conner saw the pass and stole it midair. As Team

Bromberg took to the offense, Chris and the other team's forward got tangled up, both falling onto the hardwood.

Coach Wright blew his whistle. As the two players started to get up, the coach said "Start it over. Yellow ball."

"Sorry," their forward said to Chris.

"No prob," Chris responded as they both headed down court.

Meanwhile, Conner had grabbed Shedrick and instructed him to play point. "Why?" Shedrick had asked.

"So you can break if I steal the ball."

"Whatever you say, boss," he responded with a smile. "Whatever you say," he repeated with a wink.

"You're such a turkey," Conner laughed.

For the next several plays, Shedrick showed his dribbling and passing skills, Conner backed off on the offensive plays and the other three took on a more serious attitude about winning. Conner, Shedrick and Chris shut down the outside shooting of the other team's guards, forcing play to focus on the four big men. That led to some serious shoving being exchanged. Eventually, it turned mean as Forrester threw Wes to the ground. He stood over him. Conner immediately stepped in and helped Wes up. "You okay?" he asked.

"Yeah," he said, touching his lip to see if it was bleeding, which it was not. "I'm okay."

"Yellow ball," Coach Wright hollered out. Forrester didn't argue, knowing that he had instigated the contact and foul.

At the end of five minutes, Conner's team held the lead, 18-14. Conner did not dominate, only stepping in periodically to keep his team ahead. Shedrick had 12 of their team's 18 points, all but two on breakaway dunks.

"Huddle up," Coach Wright hollered. Everyone assumed the semicircle. "Notice anything?" he asked. Nobody said anything. Everyone knew that speaking up at this time would be a mistake. When silence prevailed, the coach said "An average team playing together can beat a good team playing like individuals."

Kline and Walker, in particular, were looking down. Forrester and Obumje were looking at the coach. The fifth player on their team was doing a little of both. "Now which do you think you are…Walker?"

Walker looked up. He was clearly peeved but said nothing.

"I asked you a question, Walker," the coach persisted.

"We're losing," he said.

"Glad you noticed. Think you can improve that score?"

"In a heartbeat," he responded. "Even a blind squirrel can find an acorn once in a while." Instead of looking at the coach, he directed his stare at Shedrick. It was intentionally intimidating. Shedrick said nothing, although the challenge was clearly there.

The coach continued. He looked up to the scoreboard and said "18-14. Let's make it 30 wins. Losers run burns. Got it?"

Grunts from the other team demonstrated their agreement and determination. "Yes, coach," from all the players on the yellow team confirmed their understanding.

"Wilcox and Bromberg. You've moved from coaches to refs. Let 'em play up to a point."

"Yes, coach," each responded. They drew their whistles out of their pockets and draped them around their necks.

"Purple ball," Wilcox said as he walked the ball to underneath the inbounding basket.

Conner's team huddled. "Let's play man-to-man." He assigned each person to an opponent. Let's get to 30. How about 'thirty' on three?" He looked around. Everyone was into this. "One, two, thirty" and all five of them hollered it out. The other team did not even huddle up.

Obumje inbounded to Walker who made a long pass to Kline. Underneath, Chris was banging with Forrester and Wes was holding his own with the other forward. The semi-casualness of the scrimmage had definitely taken on a different complexion. The fun and games were gone. To those on the floor, this was as important as a conference game.

Shedrick was chasing their point guard, Walker. Chris stuck to Obumje. Conner had Kline. Walker and Obumje kept passing between themselves waiting for an open shot. Shedrick and Chris played good two-man defense, switching when they had to. Eventually, Kline drifted to the top of the key for a pass, expecting to have an open look at the basket. Walker's pass was easily intercepted by Conner who dribbled the length of the court for an uncontested layup. It was Conner's first two points.

"Nice pass," Kline said to Walker. To his credit, Walker said nothing, although had this been a game in which the coaches were not involved, there would have been some exchanges between the two.

A good bit of competition followed. When 30 had been reached by Conner's team, the other five had only put up 22 points.

"Take your burns," Coach Wright said to the other team. Even the three who hardly played had to take that medicine. While they were doing that, Chris came over to Conner who was standing watching the burns with Shedrick.

"Hey," he said. Conner looked up. "Nice," he offered.

"You, too," Conner said and they exchanged light fist touches.

The remainder of the practice allowed the other players to become involved but Conner did not scrimmage any further. After telling his assistants what to do, Coach Wright called Conner over and they walked to a secluded section of the gym.

"Listen," he said, "I don't know what it is about you but three things seem obvious to me. One, you've got talent, although you look as awkward as hell when you have the ball. Two, you don't seem to be playing hard on every play, especially on offense. And, three, what the heck are you doing here?"

"Playing basketball and bringing others to Christ."

"What!?!" he burst out. "You're a basketball-playing evangelist?"

Conner laughed. "Yeah, I guess that you could say so."

"I don't know what to make of that," the coach said.

"You don't have to make anything out of it," Conner advised. "I'll play and help the team. You just give me a fair break, that's all."

Coach Wright leaned back as if to adjust his view of Conner. "You are one strange bird. But I'll give you a fair break. But nothing more."

"Fair enough," Conner said.

Without anything further, Coach Wright walked back to the practice. Conner hopped up and trotted back to where Shedrick was working on some drill. When he arrived, the coach blew his whistle and everyone got back into the semicircle.

"Good practice. Make that *interesting* practice. I've been coaching for a long time now and I've seen good teams and I've seen dogs. This puppy…" he let it sink in, "has the potential to be really good. That will only happen if we work as a team, each man playing his role. If anyone is too concerned with his stats or his ego, he will get plenty of time catching splinters. But, if all of you men think about the team's greater good, we have some thin air to grab. And I mean very thin air."

He looked around. All of them were intently looking back at him, even Kline and Walker.

"Good. Shower up," he instructed and everyone broke for the lockers.

Shedrick and Conner walked to the other side of the gym and knelt down. Chris Dixon, Gary Shaffer and Wes Harmon followed, not exactly knowing why. When they saw the two others kneeling, Chris, Gary and Wes followed suit. The coaches all looked across the gym, not used to seeing something like that. However, they made no effort to join in or break it up.

"Father," Conner said, "thank You for this opportunity to glorify You. Thank You for the skills and the modeling You provide us. We have what we need. Now it is our job to use these talents in a way that brings glory to You and brings others to Your doorstep. May everyone look forward to hearing *Welcome, my good and faithful servant.* And may we serve You in a way that maximizes the number of people who will hear those words. We ask this in Your Son's name. Amen."

All five said "Amen."

Chapter 21

Walker was waiting for Conner as he entered the locker room. He got right up in his face and said "Cocky son of a bitch. We ain't got time for you, old man."

Conner was beyond shocked. He stammered for a moment, then asked "Why do you say that?" It wasn't meeting confrontation with force but it also wasn't Caspar Milquetoast in nature. Shedrick started to step in but was restrained by Conner. He stepped back and listened.

"Pretty boy comes here and is lucky a few times, then rubs our face in it. Not here, pretty boy. Not here." His words were as attacking as they could be. There was no seeking understanding or compromise in them.

Conner looked down, then back up. "What would you like me to do?" he asked Walker. The question was neither threatening nor condescending. It was simply worded with the intent to see if there was a solution.

"Go back to your silver spoon home and leave this to those of us who need it."

"Need what?" Conner asked.

"Need our tomorrows. You've already had a lot of yours. Leave ours alone."

Conner looked at him for a moment. Then, as he began to say something, Walker turned away.

"Hey, wait a minute!" Conner called out. Walker ignored him and walked to the next row of lockers. Conner followed him.

"Listen, Walker, a man at least gives the courtesy of his ear to someone he has just called out. I deserve that."

Walker looked around. A few of the other players were overhearing the conversation. Somewhat trapped, Walker said dismissively "What?"

"In the first place, I don't come from a silver spoon. I live a very modest life. In the second place, I have nephews and nieces who I encourage to follow their dreams. I have a purpose here and I am following my dream. Third, my dream doesn't conflict with yours. If you're good enough to succeed, then you should be able to do it with all comers. In fact, my dream and your dream have more in common with each other than you are willing to consider. Fourth, you have potential to be a leader but you can kiss that off if your primary motivator is intimidation and self-interest. People don't follow others for very long when they are browbeaten. The greatest leaders draw their populations. Chasing someone away doesn't make for charismatic leadership."

Conner paused for a moment, then continued. "Now, you can keep going along with a chip on your shoulder or be proud of the people who are on this team. If you continue the former, you're on your own, in more ways than you know. If you become part of this team, a real part of it, then you've got an army to support you. I can tell you one thing."

"What's that?" Walker asked, not quite so belligerently.

"It's a lot more fun feeling like a teammate than like a lone coyote."

The two men looked at each other. Walker refused to soften. Conner extended his hand. Walker did not reciprocate, instead saying "Yeah," and turned away to his locker. After a moment, Conner went back around to his locker. Nobody who had observed the conversation said anything.

Conner and Shedrick headed out together.

"Good going," Shedrick said. "That jerk has a major chip on his shoulder. He's a senior. Last year, Kline joined the team and Walker was no longer the go-to guy. I figure that he's afraid of falling even further."

"I can understand that."

"That's on him, though," Shedrick said. "Coach won't tolerate it too long. I've heard stories of how he brings down the high and mighty."

"I hope that he won't have to do that."

It started to sprinkle so they held onto their conversation and ran the rest of the way back.

Chapter 22

"Hello, Pete?" Conner said into the phone to his friend from home.

"Yeah?"

"Conner here."

"Hey, man. How are you?" Pause. "Where are you?"

"Well, I'm on the Brantley University basketball team."

"What do you mean you're on it?"

"The coach gave me a tryout and I made the team."

"And you're going to school there?"

"Yup."

Silence.

"Golly," Pete said.

"More than golly," Conner replied.

"Did God follow you up there?" Then he realized how that sounded and said "You know what I mean."

Conner chuckled. "I know what you mean. He's definitely with me."

"How's it going?"

"A few of us have started to pray. That's a bit different."

"Great," Pete said with little enthusiasm. "How's the competition?"

Although slightly disappointed that Pete wasn't interested in the spiritual aspects of what was taking place, Conner understood. He decided not to push the issue.

"Well, everyone is really good. Thus far, I've pretty much held my own."

"Do you room by yourself or with others?"

"My roomie is a freshman named Shedrick Harris…"

"I know him," Pete interrupted. "…or of him, anyhow."

Conner waited to hear what Pete had to say.

"He was high school All State in Illinois during his junior year, then lost his parents in a drunk driver accident over that summer. He chose not to play his senior year in honor of them."

Conner didn't say anything.

"Strange, eh?" Pete offered.

"How did you know this?" Conner inquired.

"It's kinda odd, actually. Harris' older sister married a good friend of my brother. One day, I was playing hoops with a bunch of them and the story came up. Then I saw a human-interest report in the paper later that week. It just struck a chord."

"I can imagine."

"He's playing there?"

"He is. I guess that his reputation earned him a shot on the team."

"Nice guy, huh?"

"Super guy," Conner confirmed.

"Is he a starter?"

Conner smiled to himself. "No. At least not yet. There are a lot of really good players on this team."

"Yeah, I can imagine."

"We'll see," Conner said. "It all takes place on the court."

"You're gonna freak."

"About what?" Conner asked.

"When you play games. Real games. The crowds will be just a little larger than the recreation game crowds for the Colts."

Conner smiled. "I suspect so."

"What are your plans? And how can I help?"

Conner appreciated his friend encouraging and supporting him. "Just by looking out for my apartment. I don't have any plants or anything but just make sure that it doesn't burn down."

"Burn down? Not much I could do if it did."

"You know what I mean."

"How is your family taking this rebirth?" He referred to Conner's brother and sister. Conner's parents had both died when he had been in college, his mom from cancer and his dad from a heart attack.

"Laura has always been a live-and-let-live type. She's happy for me if I'm happy. Danny is intrigued. I always thought that he would play college ball but he chose to do otherwise. When we used to play one on one, even when he was young, he would beat me like a drum. I loved watching him play hoops in high school. He was good, really good. I speak with them occasionally. If things stick, I'll see about getting Danny up here for at least a weekend. He'd probably get a kick out of it. Of course, my playing college basketball might be too much for him, remembering how we were as kids."

"Great," Pete said. "I was wondering what I would have thought had my brother done what you're doing."

"What do you think?" Conner asked, interested in the answer.

"I guess that I would have been jealous, especially since, like Danny, I was the better athlete growing up."

They both reflected on that a bit.

"Hey, need to run. We got our first Colts game tonight without our star. Sure that you can't get back just for it?"

"I'd love to, Pete."

"Just kidding. Just kidding. You've got your hands full up there. Do well. Let me know when I can come observe. And…" There was a pause.

Conner could sense that Pete was struggling with something that he wanted to say. "Yeah?" he encouraged.

A little more silence. "Good luck with your mission."

Conner got a bit choked up by Pete's well wishes. "Thanks, man. That means a lot to me."

A little more silence and Pete said "Later."

"Blessings to you, Pete."

"Yeah, bless you, too."

They hung up. Conner savored the conversation a little longer.

----- ----- -----

Later that night, Conner lay awake on his bed. His body was tired but his mind was racing. He thought about many things, those that related to his personal world and those that related to his mission. Both, of course, involved basketball. His mind jumped between the two streams of consciousness.

He felt that his immediate mission was to involve the entire team in becoming more faith-based. If he could do that, he would look to the next larger circle of people, then to the next and the next. Eat an elephant one bite at a time, he thought to himself.

"You can't swallow the ocean in one gulp" came another's voice.

Conner looked up as though someone had shocked him with a few volts of electricity. There, at the end of his bed, sat a fiftyish man, somewhat goofy, with a Brantley University singlet worn over a long-sleeve shirt. He looked like a front-row fan, one of the team's rabid rooters. Every college and professional basketball team has its zealous fans, either few or many. Brantley did, as well. It was the athletic director's job to make certain that none of that enthusiasm spilled over into competition violations. Getting caught in a breach of NCAA rules could mean serious sanctions regarding scholarships and post-season play, the latter of which was a significant fund-raising source for most institution.

Conner immediately realized who this person must be.

"Shoot," Conner said. "You scared the…" He didn't finish, not knowing what he could insert without offending his visitor.

"…bejesus out of me?" the man completed.

"Yeah, but isn't that kind of non-Ten Commandments'ish?"

God chortled, then responded. "Rules are made for exceptions," he said.

Conner just shook his head. Life's complicated enough, he thought, without God playfully changing the rules.

"What were you thinking?" God asked.

Conner did their sort-of-agreed-upon tilt, it meaning 'Come on. That's a dumb question.'

God said "I ask you to say things out loud so that you can both crystallize your thinking and, more importantly, hear what it sounds like. It's astonishing how different something said comes across from something simply thought or read."

Conner nodded his head in agreement. He definitely knew that to be true. He often read out loud what he had written in order to edit it. This always made a difference.

"I have a lot of thoughts. On the mission side…" Conner waited to see if God would want him to change the title of his undertaking from mission to something else. No comments were forthcoming. He proceeded. "On the mission side," he repeated, "I am beginning with the team and intending to expand from there."

"Good" was the only response he received.

"On the personal side, I'm only being good enough to win, not to razzle dazzle anyone."

Here he waited for a bit more guidance. None was offered.

"That's it? No corrections? No advice? No nuthin'?" Conner asked.

"You need to find your path. If I wanted to do everything, I'd have either stepped in or created a robot. This still falls under the free will umbrella."

Again, Conner tilted his head.

"…sort of," God added.

Both smiled.

"I take it that I can count on you to be in the front row for our games?" Conner asked, slightly changing subjects.

"I'm always in the front row," he answered.

"I mean literally," Conner appended.

"Possibly. It depends."

"On…?" Conner invited.

"On a whole bunch of things. Man, are you ever controlling. I'm glad that you're not me."

"Me, too," Conner added.

This time, both laughed.

"I tried that before," God said.

"Tried what?"

"Letting someone be God, sort of like that great TV program *Queen for a Day*." Conner could see God thinking about it.

"What happened?"

"You didn't see the movie?" he answered.

"The movie?" Conner was confused. *The Ten Commandments* with Charlton Heston flashed through his mind.

"No, no," God corrected his thinking. "*Oh, God* with George Burns."

"That was real?"

"Not the movie but the idea. The real thing didn't work out quite as well."

"How come?"

"I'll have to…"

"…kill me," Conner finished the sentence.

"Right on that," God confirmed. Then he held up his hand. "Okay, enough about this. You have some sleep to catch up on and exciting things coming up. I just wanted to check in with you."

Conner thought that pretty funny. God checking in with him. He chose not to say anything.

God continued. "You've got the right idea. Love your mission, go after it deliberately but don't let its pace be too slow. Although I have all the time in the world, you don't."

"What does that mean?" Conner shot back, half lightheartedly and half seriously.

"Ta ta," God said and then the rabid rooter was gone.

Conner slept well that night.

Chapter 23

The next day was to be the last before classes began on Tuesday. Conner awoke early, said his morning prayers, mostly focusing on the blessings that he and everyone received each day, then included something along the lines of 'Thy will be done' and hit the floor. He opened his bedroom door and found Shedrick already up and at 'em.

"Wow, aren't you the eager beaver," Conner commented.

"Yeah, I do early, not late. Never could sleep in."

"I'm not much different. How early does the cafeteria open?"

Shedrick looked at his watch, then said "In fifteen minutes. We can be first."

"Sounds like a deal to me." Conner was happy that this nice young man was also a morning person. Otherwise, the mismatch would have been difficult to handle, although certainly not impossible.

"Let me jump in the shower, throw on some duds and then we can go over there," Conner said.

"Roger that," came the reply. "I'll use the time to get my books lined up for classes tomorrow."

Conner promised to inquire about Shedrick's studies. Not only did Conner want to do well on the basketball court and in the classroom, he wanted Shedrick to succeed, as well. This was particularly important to him now that he had heard from Pete about his roommate's family life. He figured that eventually the two would get around to sharing backgrounds with one another. No rush, he thought.

Practice that morning was more individual than competitive and not overly taxing from a physical perspective. It focused on foul shooting, inbounding, last-second plays and when to foul, other than when it was just in the heat of play.

When it came to foul shooting, Conner wanted to improve his marksmanship. When he had gotten to his locker this morning, a computer-printed certificate was taped to it. "Team's Best Fowl Shooter" it read, mocking the word. This was not a distinction he wished to possess.

During that segment of this practice, players were divided up, this time randomly by numbers, and assigned to different baskets. They rotated through, each player taking his five shots. When he was done, he shouted out the number he had made. If he missed his last shot, he shouted out the number and then ran around the outside of the court. Any shortcuts resulted in at least one more lap.

Conner had increased his focus and was able to consistently make three or four baskets. More importantly, he thought, he was not missing the final shot. Thus, he was not required to run the lap. He noticed, too, that very few players were running the lap.

He thought about this, then understanding the rationale. The coach wanted them to be able to hit their free shots, especially when it counted during crunch time. Doing this typically meant deeper concentration. This exercise helped the players achieve that greater level. Impressive, he thought. Subtle, but effective.

As it turned out, through the random-numbering assignments, he was in the same group as Obumje. Of the elite players, Obumje seemed to be the nicest, certainly the most cordial.

"Conner Ramsey," Conner said, offering his hand in a traditional handshake manner.

Obumje looked at him, somewhat in surprise, then broke into a broad smile. "Injujai Obumje" he said, taking Conner's hand warmly. "I am glad that you are here." He spoke in what Conner guessed was a slightly African accent, although his English was excellent.

"Me, too," Conner said. "Thanks for the welcome," he added.

"I am sorry that some of the 'stars'," here he rolled his eyes and artificially emphasized the word, "are having a little trouble with you."

"I think that I understand," Conner responded.

"It used to happen each year. It was a rite of passage. Last year's star or stars who did not graduate or leave early, found themselves staring at their new competition. The pack has to find its own water level," he said, mixing metaphors. Conner understood. "You came in after the water level was thought to have been established. Those who are acting challenged do not view the good of the team as of paramount importance. I suspect that Coach Wright will become involved when he has to."

"Does Clyde Forrester fall into that group?" Conner asked, referring to the Enforcer he had met in the locker room.

Obumje squinted his eyes, trying to discern the reason for this question. Then, thinking that he understood, broke into another beautiful smile. His white teeth contrasted markedly with his dark skin.

"Ha, ha," he laughed. "You want to be certain that the forest doesn't fall on you, eh?" he asked.

"Exactly," Conner replied.

"No, he has control of his ego," Obumje said. "His interests are strictly for the welfare of the team. I think that you know the two or three who might have problems."

"I do, indeed," Conner said. "Thanks."

"You are welcome," came the reply, as Obumje took his turn at the foul line.

At the end of the practice, the coach blew his whistle and pointed everyone to the stands. They all hustled over there.

"Foul shooting is getting better," he began. "Inbounding still needs work. If the other team sees that we are weak in this area, they will exploit it. Not being able to inbound is a tremendously demoralizing thing for a team. Besides, it can change the score in a heartbeat."

He looked around. Nobody dared say anything. Conner liked the iron hand exhibited by the coach. Too much discipline was far better than too little.

"In most situations, the bench, especially the assistant coaches, will help you with fouls. We foul hard but we foul clean." Here he looked over at Kline, reminding everyone who had seen it that this was the kind of play that would not be tolerated. Kline bowed his head.

"Any questions?"

None were offered.

"This afternoon will be physical. See ya then."

Everyone stood up and hustled back to the locker room, including Shedrick and Conner, although they didn't run. The coaches remained on the floor to cover some additional topics.

After showering, the roommates agreed to take a walk through campus before lunch. Shedrick obviously knew more about the campus than did Conner but the two also visited some buildings that were new to both of them. It was a nice, comfortable walk with no agenda in mind by either.

Eventually, during this walk, the topic got around to family. Shedrick was interested in Conner's family and sorry to hear about his parents. Conner, in turn, was interested in Shedrick's journey, especially over the last three years.

"I just didn't want to play," Shedrick said of his self-imposed withdrawal from the sport. "Nobody understood, especially not the coach. But I heard what I heard and that's what I went with."

"What do you mean by 'I heard what I heard'?" Conner asked.

"There weren't voices or complete sentences, if that's what you mean. I'm not that cuckoo, you know. I didn't see an apparition or have a visit from an angel. It was all inside. Just a feeling, that's all."

Conner thought about this and wondered what Shedrick would do if God suddenly appeared to them. He'd be singing a different tune, that's for sure. On the other hand, Conner wouldn't have said anything much different from Shedrick before he began having his in-person kitchen visits.

"I really admire that, Shedrick," Conner said. "It's hard to make some decisions and then stick with them, particularly in light of critical feedback."

"I know. But, as I look back on it, I'm glad that I took the year off. Now, I'm ready to play again."

"How did you pick Brantley University and, if you don't mind my asking, why did they give you a scholarship? You didn't play for an entire year and you're an out-of-stater. That doesn't suggest the formula that Coach Wright would seek."

"You think that a guy with your profile would be likely to play for the Eagles?" he asked with just a tinge of sarcasm.

Conner smiled and shook his head. "No. Not at all. But, then again, I challenged him with a letter and he took the gamble."

"My high school principal knew Coach Wright from college. He made an introduction for me and I worked out up here in June, just after graduation. I had stayed in great shape, working particularly hard because I wasn't playing on a team, and it showed. The coach welcomed me right away."

"I'm glad that he did," Conner added. "Do you have any siblings?"

Here, he could see, he had touched a nerve. "My younger brother died in the accident. My older sister has her own family. In a funny sort of way, we don't see each other because it brings back bad memories. Oh, we do somewhat, especially during the holidays but, otherwise, we live in two different worlds."

"Must be tough, eh?"

"Yeah but who doesn't have a little rain in their world?"

"Amen to that, roomie."

"Let's go chow. We don't want to leave any food unconsumed. After all, we have to go undefeated this year."

"Undefeated?"

"Under feet," he said, pointing to the bottom of his moccasins.

Conner smiled and the two went into the cafeteria, taking trays and pursuing their food desires...within the guidelines administered by the team.

Chapter 24

The afternoon practice wasn't anything spectacular, other than being grueling. Coach Wright had them do extensive stretching, reiterating time and again how important this was to the player and, naturally, to the entire team. "If you get hurt, you hurt us all. If you get hurt diving for a ball, we will love you for it. If you get hurt because of lack of conditioning, we will not appreciate it. Especially me. Especially me," he repeated for emphasis.

Then the team did three sets of burns. Full speed. After that, it was defensive drills, especially running back on defense after a missed shot.

"Run hard just past midcourt and then turn, coming to your position as quickly as possible. I will not tolerate anyone not hustling back on defense. If we cannot beat the other team with our shooting, which sometimes will be the case, I want to beat them with defense, which should always be the case."

He looked around at everyone. The coach had a good way of making everyone feel as though he was acutely aware of what each person was thinking. He did this in many ways, not the least of which included these kinds of pauses.

He concluded with the guards working on weaves and the big men working on picks. Everyone was totally exhausted at the end. All the players had been wearing gray Brantley tee shirts and there wasn't a dry one to be seen. Conditioning was obviously important. It and defense could win games that would otherwise be lost.

That evening, Conner decided to read ahead for his class coming up the next day. It was a religious studies course entitled *Heroes of the Old Testament*. Naturally, the Bible was one of the required texts. In addition, he had two other reference books, each looking more academic (i.e., boring) than the other. In spite of this, he expected the course to be a good one.

He accessed the syllabus online and printed it out. He highlighted the key points, those having to do with grading, absences, both excused and not, tests, papers and presentations. Then he opened each of the two academic textbooks and compared their tables of content, especially interested in learning who each author thought should be described as a hero. Most of these heroes, as Conner expected, were similar. However, there were a few that were highlighted in one text that were not listed in the other and vice versa.

Conner looked over the ones that were similar and reflected on a few of these. The Patriarchs, of course. They were in a section all to themselves in both books. Then, in alphabetic order, there was a list that included Daniel, David, Elijah, Esther, Job, Joshua, Moses, Noah and a few others.

One of the books, not limited to the Old Testament, highlighted Barnabas, a Conner favorite. Conner was also happy to see that one author had included Mordecai, Esther's cousin. To Conner, Mordecai was more deserving of heroic status than was Esther but he knew that his was the minority position. Having a noted author sort of agree with him, at least on the basis of his table of contents, was cool.

On the other side of the coin, he was surprised to see that one of the authors classified Jonah as heroic. Epic, maybe. Heroic? I reason not, thought Conner. He would be interested in reading the author's justification. But not just now.

Instead, Conner opened to the book of Job. Intent as he was in wanting to reread this book of the Bible, he didn't last very long. Between early wake up, breakfast, the easier workout, the walk around campus, lunch, and the harder workout, he rested his head on his arms and fell asleep. When he awoke, he got up to use the restroom, then looked for his roomie to see what Shedrick wished to do. He, too, was sleeping soundly at his desk, using the book as his pillow, unlike Conner's use of his arms.

Shedrick's arms rested on his thighs, his head seemingly supporting the full weight of his upper body.

Conner looked at his watch, decided that it was time for them to eat, and woke up Shedrick with a pat on the back. Shedrick groaned "Thanks a lot. You just ruined a wonderful dream. A terrific dream. I was about to set an NCAA Tournament scoring record."

"Yeah, right," offered Conner. "Let's go eat something. I want to turn in early tonight."

"Good idea," Shedrick concurred, dismissing the dream.

After Shedrick used the restroom, they both headed back to the cafeteria. This will become a well-worn path, Conner thought. It could be worse, he added. A lot worse.

Chapter 25

Up early the next morning, Conner sat on the edge of his bed. He had a few 'interesting' things ahead of him. In order to be successful, he needed to stay focused. His mission was to spread the Word. He must stay single-minded concerning that. He also needed to be ready to participate when it came his turn on the basketball court. If he did not do well there, then his ministry would not have a platform. And he needed to do well at school. There was the issue of remaining basketball eligible but there was also the opportunity to develop his walk with the Lord, especially wanting to take advantage of the courses for which he was registered. If they were anywhere near as good in reality as the titles appeared, he was in for a treat. He felt very lucky that Brantley offered a master's degree in Biblical Studies.

Right now, the mission took center stage. Although he would have liked God to be there to help him think this through, he believed that he understood the free will concept and, more crucially, he fully believed that God was watching over his every action. He took great solace in that.

Step one for his ministry would be somehow getting the team to be more prayerful. If he could do that, the team could be a model for the fans. That would be substantial. And if the fans got into it, then some television and radio networks might give it visibility. It might not be a story that would capture the headlines for very long but, then again, it might. Conner decided to let God handle tomorrow as he had plenty to handle today.

He thought about the quote from Matthew 6:34 concerning worry. Like many others, it was a favorite. *So don't worry about tomorrow, for tomorrow will bring its own worries. Today's trouble is enough for today.*

----- ----- -----

"Today, gentlemen, after going through a good warm up, we are going to scrimmage. From what the coaches see this morning and this afternoon, we will decide who will play front line, who will play second line and, overall, who will suit up. We have fifteen seats on the bench. Obviously, we have more than that on our squad."

The coach looked around at those sitting shoulder to shoulder on the bleachers. It was as though he looked at each young man with enough time to make him feel as though he was personalizing the message. Coach Wright was not a man to deliver speeches. He was a man who gave instructions to an audience.

"My…*our* criteria will be teamwork first, talent second. No matter how talented any player is, he won't smell the floor if he doesn't hold up his twenty percent of the entire game. I'm talking about defense and hustle, not just scoring."

Here he made certain to look directly at Walker and Kline. Walker looked like he could care less. Kline looked directly back at the coach, although not defiantly. Conner was not surprised at this, nor was he surprised to see Obumje and Forrester totally into what the coach was saying. Naturally, Harris was riveted to the coach's every word.

"We are bigger, faster and better than the team we play Thursday evening. They are not in our class. Even believing this, the game is played on the floor, not in a coach's head. If we don't play well, we will lose. I can point to dozens upon dozens of illustrations when David slew Goliath on a basketball court." Here he looked at Conner.

"But assuming things go according to form, I should be able to see, learn and adjust without jeopardizing the outcome. I certainly don't want to lose to this team but I am not out to beat them by a hundred points. That doesn't do anything for anybody, us or them. What I want to see is our playing at a high level."

Again he looked around.

"Any questions?"

Conner raised his hand. There was nearly an audible gasp from the upperclassmen. Asking questions after an instruction set was breaking an unwritten rule. Nobody had ever done it from this group, seniors noting that for all four years, and now the newcomer was defying tradition. All heads went from noting Conner's raised hand to immediately looking for the coach's reaction. There was a certain tennis symmetry to the head movements, as though everyone was following the play on a tennis court.

"What, Ramsey?" asked the coach, not exhibiting undue frustration but a little surprised. Apparently, this don't-ask-a-question tradition was more in the minds of others than an expectation from the coach.

"Sir...er, coach," he corrected, "would you have any objection if, before we started practice, after we finished practice, before we started a game and after we finished a game those of us who wished to pray gathered for it briefly?"

As soon as it was out of his mouth, Conner wanted to stomp all over his tongue. Had this been a cartoon, it would have been Elmer Fudd or some character like that yanking out his tongue, throwing it on the ground, and jumping up and down on it, great clouds of dust rising as he did so. This was not something that should have been asked. Permission should not have been sought. Instead, the activity should have been grassroots in nature. Those who wanted to do it, should have done it. Then, if it met with disagreement, they could have dealt with that conflict. Now, if the coach denied the request, taking action would be difficult, very difficult.

Also, as soon as Conner asked his question, someone from the group said, quite clearly, "Get that Jesus freak out of here." Surprisingly, it wasn't Walker but, instead, one of the guys sitting on the cusp line of being allowed to suit up. His name was Brandon Wilson. Immediately, the coach turned to that player.

"Stand up, son," he said in a quiet but very strong voice.

The player did as he was told. It was pretty obvious that he wished he had not said what he did.

"Brandon, do you know where you are?"

"Excuse me, coach?"

"I said, 'Do you know where you are?'"

"Right here, coach," he responded, trying to be a little bit funny and looking around for support. None was given. He returned his look to the coach.

"Have you heard about the home of the free and the brave?"

"Yes, coach." He wanted to say more but knew that he had enough of his sneaker already stuck in his mouth.

"And what does that mean to you, young man?"

"That we tolerate…er, accept all kinds, coach."

"Brandon, we don't just tolerate them, we encourage and support them."

"Yes, coach."

"…even if they are foolish, inappropriate or contradictory to our own views."

"Yes, coach."

"Do you believe in a supreme being, son?"

"Coach?"

"Do you believe in God?"

After a truly uncomfortable pause, feeling like hours, Wilson said "Sort of."

"Sort of? What does that mean?"

"Well, coach, I go to church with my parents when I'm home."

"You think that's an answer to my question?"

In that huge gym, you could have heard a pin drop.

"I'm sorry, coach. What's the question again?"

Without becoming outwardly exasperated, the coach repeated his question: "Do you believe in God?"

"Yes, coach."

"If that is the case, why would you have a problem with someone else asking to observe his faith if it did not infringe on anyone else's time or rights?"

"I don't, coach."

"Then why did you offer such a challenge to it?"

"Well, coach..."

"Spit it out, Wilson. You opened this can of worms. Now that it turns out to be a can of something else, let's clean up this mess."

"Coach?"

"Answer my question. Listen, if you can't stay focused here, how can you handle adversity on the court or in other facets of your life?"

Although it would have been natural for most people to follow this dialogue by looking from one participant to the other, depending on who was speaking, most of the players looked at the floor. They felt badly for Wilson and they didn't want to be selected as the next victim. Look down, be quiet and let this storm pass, most thought.

"Why did you offer such a challenge to it?" the coach repeated much more loudly.

"I'm sorry, coach. It was a stupid thing to say. I'm having challenges in my spiritual life and I lashed out unfairly." Then he turned to Conner and said "I'm sorry. I shouldn't have said that."

"Thanks," was all Conner said, feeling badly for Wilson but very appreciative of what the coach was doing. In another country...

"Sit down, Wilson. You showed courage in making that apology."

Wilson sat down and Coach Wright waited another moment before he resumed speaking.

"Gentlemen, if we don't live, eat, get along and play basketball together, we won't get anywhere. Have you seen what the papers have been writing about us?"

All heads nodded.

"Nobody expects us to do anything. *A kingdom at war with itself will collapse. A home divided against itself is doomed.*"

Conner almost fell off the bleachers. Here was the coach quoting the Bible, somewhere in Mark, Conner believed. He remembered their discussion in the coach's office that first day. "Are you a man of faith?" Conner had asked and the coach had

responded with "We go to church…when we can."
And now he was quoting the Bible?

Perhaps aware of what he had done, the coach
added "United we stand, divided we fall. Does
anyone know where that comes from?"

Someone chimed up with "Lincoln?" but he
didn't say it very confidently.

"Actually not," answered the coach. "It goes a
long way back before Lincoln. A long way," he
added. "But the point is, whether we listen to quotes
or just make up our own, we have to stick together."

All at once, Conner could see the coach spinning
this back to the team. The freedom of speech,
religious liberties issues were no longer in the
forefront. They were replaced with a how-does-this-
help-the-team spotlight. Conner was a little
disappointed in this but could appreciate what the
coach was doing and why.

"Do I make myself clear?"

About a third of the team answered halfheartedly
"Yes, coach."

"Do I make myself clear?" Coach Wright
repeated.

"Yes, coach!" came the loud and universal chorus,
much like a marine unit might respond to an
officer."

The coach turned to Conner.

"Ramsey," he said, "you are one of the most
perplexing people I have ever met. You are five
hundred years old…"

Laughter exploded, the release of tensions from the earlier exchange with Wilson. The coach held up his hand and everyone quieted down.

"You are five hundred years old," he repeated, "and you are acting like an angel or something."

Conner did not respond.

"As long as your shenanigans don't disrupt the team, you can pray before, after, during or whenever you wish."

Conner nodded his appreciation, thankful that it had turned out well. He knew enough not to say anything.

"Just don't pray in place of playing defense."

Again, the team burst into laughter. Even sullen-faced Walker had to laugh at that. Surprisingly, the coach even chuckled, a sight he did not often share in front of the team. After a moment, he held up his hand and the team quieted down.

"Coach Murphy has a list of who is going to be on which team for this scrimmage. If you're not on the floor, stay in the game mentally. Heaven help you if you aren't paying attention. Nobody is too big for this team. Nobody. When everyone has heard his name, go grab an appropriately-colored singlet. Yellow goes to the south end, red to the north end and blue sits right here."

With that, Coach Wright stepped back and was replaced by Coach Murphy who read off the names and team colors. Predictably, the expected first team was kept together. They wore yellow. Thereafter, talent seemed to be evenly divided among the red and blue teams. Conner and Shedrick were on the red team.

As the coach had promised, after warming up, all they did for both practices was play against one another. Conner and Shedrick had gotten their heads together before the red team began warming up. They were joined at the foul line by two others. The rest of the players on the red team weren't interested. Conner said a brief prayer and then they went about their business.

Conner spent as much time as he could encouraging his teammates, congratulating his opponents and playing just slightly above his competition. Eventually, the yellow and blue teams decided to drive outside the lane or shoot from the outside. Trying to drive inside the lane usually ended up with Conner taking it away. Shooting from the outside meant doing it with someone's hand in your face.

The red team won the round-robin scrimmage, even against the first team. Afterwards, the coach had everyone sit back in the bleachers.

"Gentlemen, that was good. I got solid looks at a number of players. Some of you surprised me. Both positively and negatively. I also see some natural partnerships. However, I don't want to get too locked into them since they might possibly end with injuries and then we'd have mismatched playing mates. But that's my problem."

As was his custom, he looked around. "Any questions?" He looked at Conner who smiled at the coach but offered no other gesture or word. "Good. See ya back here for our next practice."

As everyone stood, Conner stepped up on the bleacher seat and said, without yelling, "Anyone who wants to join us for prayer, we'll meet at the foul line."

Shedrick, Conner and the two red team members proceeded to that spot. They were joined by four others, two each from the yellow and blue teams, although none of the high-profile players. Unexpectedly, as they got to center court and knelt down, Obumje came and knelt beside Conner, placing his hand on Conner's shoulder. Conner was delighted to have him join.

"Father, thank You for these wonderful talents that You give us. May we use them in ways that multiply their stand-alone value and in ways that encourage others to come to You. For those who have already made that commitment, may they experience Your support such that they feel empowered to help others. Thank You for salvation, mercy and grace. Amen"

And all said "Amen." Then they stood. Each of them felt just a little bit better having shared this moment. None said anything else as they headed to the locker room.

Chapter 26

Conner had his first class, *Heroes of the Old Testament,* at 10:00 AM. He arrived there at 9:45 and grabbed a seat in the back of the room. Eight other students were there, five of whom were female.

Seven of the eight looked very young to Conner. The other person looked appreciably older than Conner. He must be near retirement, thought Conner. Interesting age diversity, he noted. Young, old, no matter. Education is always in fashion, he thought to himself.

He opened his spiral notebook, the one on whose cover he had written the course number, name, time and location. He put today's date on the top of the first page. Then, like everyone else, he waited. Nobody else in the room seemed to know one another and there was no conversation taking place. Everyone seemed just to be biding time for the professor.

Finally, at two minutes after the hour, as defined by the clock on the wall, Conner said "Hey, everybody." He waited for them to turn around. They did.

"Let's introduce ourselves. My name is Conner Ramsey. I am from southwest Illinois and I am very much looking forward to this class. It's been a while since I've been in school, as you can imagine from looking at me, but I am here solely because I wish to be."

He finished and looked to the woman next to him. She introduced herself in like fashion and the introductions went counterclockwise around the room until they ended with the older man. Up to that point in time, everyone had used Conner's template to provide information.

The older man stood up and said "I am Professor Reginald Cook. Studying people is what I enjoy doing. That is why I like to teach this course. Even though I am not a contemporary of these heroes, I have gotten to know them pretty personally. In fact, when I get to heaven, I don't think that I will be all that surprised when I speak with any of them."

He took his books with him from the back row as he walked to the desk at the front of the room. He was quite short, not much over 5'6". He walked like a man who had confidence in who he was. He had a kind face with a mostly-gray beard. His hair was thinning but neatly kept. He didn't have one of those comb overs that make people look awkward. He wore a white shirt, dark slacks and a sports jacket. He had a tastefully selected dark tie that matched well with his primarily-brown outfit.

Once to the front of the room, he removed the lectern from on top of the desk and set it on the floor near the window. Then he sat down on the desk. Well, maybe it was more of a hop and plop, since he couldn't just sit down on the desk because he was too short to do so. Once there, he resumed speaking.

"We will have a semester to get to know some of the truly shining figures in the Old Testament." He looked at one young lady and said "Who is your hero?"

"My dad," she said with a smile.

"Very good," he laughed. "I meant from the Bible."

"Oh, I am sorry, Professor. Jesus," she answered.

"Well, I can see that I will be a dentist with you, young lady," he said.

"Sir?" she said.

"I will be pulling teeth," he explained. Everyone at least smiled. "Now," he continued, "who is your hero from the *Old* Testament?" He emphasized the world 'Old" so that she could provide a name that was within this universe.

"I don't know," she said, scrunching her face in order to squeeze a name out of her brain.

"I know that you don't know. But, off the top of your head, who would you choose if you had to choose but one person?"

She sighed and then said "Moses," her eyes widening to see the Professor's reaction.

"Good," he said. "Now, without repeating any name given, who is yours?" He pointed to a second female and she said "Noah." They went around the room with Conner going last. The other six named David, Daniel, Solomon, Joshua, Esther and Elijah.

"Well, sir," Conner said when it was his turn, "I think from the remaining hundreds, I would select Mordecai, Esther's cousin."

"Interesting," the professor said. "I don't believe that Mordecai has ever bubbled to the top of the list, certainly when such names as Job, Shadrach, Meshach, Abednego and others remained available. But," he paused, "good choice. Good choices to everyone. Now, let's see if we can't meet them more up close and personal, as the saying goes."

That was the beginning of the class and the entire ninety minutes flew by. Conner was disappointed when the Professor pointed to the clock on the wall and said "Time's up. Your syllabus explains what you are to read, what you are supposed to do and how you are supposed to submit it. Don't be late!" And, with that, he grabbed his books and headed to the door.

"Young man," he said, pointing to the other male in the class, "please return the lectern to the desk. Thank you!" Then he was gone.

What fun, thought Conner. This is gonna be great. He couldn't wait to get back to the dorm room to begin studying.

Chapter 27

When Conner arrived back at his room, Shedrick was already there, sprawled across the common room's sofa. "What took you so long?" he asked.

"I had class," Conner responded.

"Me, too. We were out in fifteen minutes."

"I guess that's the difference between undergraduate and graduate courses."

"Remind me never to go for a graduate degree."

"You, my friend," Conner said, "are gonna have your hands full with what you're taking."

"No foolin', fool," he said, à la Muhammad Ali or Mr. T.

"Good," commented Conner on the impression. "That's the best Winston Churchill I've ever heard."

Shedrick made a face, then smiled.

"Let's grab lunch before everyone else takes all the good stuff."

"Lead away, my good man. Lead away."

"When's your next class, Conner?"

"I have one at 2:00. How about you?"

"Same."

"What are you taking?"

"Hermeneutics."

"Herman who? Is he the teacher?"

"Hermeneutics. It's the study of the interpretation of written texts."

"Meaning?"

"Meaning that we look at different books in the Bible and interpret readings from them. I think that's it. At least I'm guessing that's it. I suspect that I will find out at 2:00 PM today."

"Not on an empty stomach."

"Wouldn't want that," Conner agreed. "What do you have at 2:00?"

"*American History up to the Civil War.*"

"Sounds interesting."

"Yeah, like Herman whatever his name is."

"Hermeneutics. You're such a turkey."

"Call me Tom."

"I'll call you whatever you want if you'll just walk a little faster. I'm starving!"

----- ----- -----

Conner got to class at 1:45 and, once again, found a seat in the back of the room. He was glad that this was in a different building. It would have been monotonous to meet too long in the very same classroom. There were nine students in this class and, from what Conner could tell, none of them sitting around there had the profile of a professor.

At five minutes to the hour, in came a curiously interesting looking person, presumably the professor. His clothes were disheveled and his hair was blown all about. He wore glasses that one could see were smudged even from ten feet away and they had white tape where, apparently, they had broken. His sports jacket looked as though he had used it as a seat cushion just before coming to class. His shoes were thoroughly scuffed, the heels worn down to the leather, if that's what it was. They had probably never been shined. Conner didn't get a look at the soles but he would have guessed that there were holes in them, as well. His books, too, mirrored his personal style. They were old, with what appeared to be notes inefficiently jammed into a variety of pages. Even his notebook was in disrepair.

Thus, Conner's first impression, and that of his classmates, was not at all positive.

"I am Professor Ving, David Ving" he said. "You can call me Professor Ving." He looked up, expecting to see laughter. Seeing none, he looked back down. Then he took attendance and began his lecture. And lecture it was. For the next eighty-two minutes, he was the only one to speak. Ramsey and his classmates wrote fast and furiously, not quite certain what to write.

At 3:25, Professor Ving stopped and, finally, looked up, something he had not done for the entire period of his monologue. "Any questions?"

Nobody asked anything, not because there was a dearth of questions but because everyone wanted to get out of there, Conner included. Asking a question would be tantamount to another dissertation and each student's capacity for the day had already been met.

"Excellent," the professor concluded. "Your assignments are in the syllabus. I will see you next time." With that, he gathered his material and escaped to the door.

As Conner looked around the room, he saw the same look of puzzlement on each student's face. He stood up. "Can you all wait just a couple of minutes? I'll make this quick," he implored to his classmates. In one form or another, the other eight committed their willingness to remain. Conner went over and closed the door.

"Obviously, this is going to be difficult," he began.

That understatement was met with laughter and a few sarcastic but good-natured statements.

"If we – at least if I – If we are to get anything out of this class except the in-one-ear-and-out-the-other academic crap, pardon my French, I think that we will have to work together."

Nobody else offered anything. Conner continued.

"For one thing, I believe that we should begin each class with questions because it does not appear that the professor will leave us time for questions at the end."

There was general approval to this suggestion.

"Also, I think that we need to have the courage to interrupt him on questions that come up for us during his…his whatever that was."

"…boring," finished a young man on the other side of the room. Everyone laughed.

"I was very excited about this class when I signed up for it."

Everyone nodded.

"I expected to learn loads from it."

Again silent affirmation.

"We still can. Let's not fall into the trap of taking this for a grade and leaving with very little. We are the ones who can make this course memorable." Conner looked around. Everyone was looking at him, appreciating his attitude. "Let's do it!" he concluded.

"Amen," one student responded. "Amen" added most of the others as they gathered their books and stood up.

Conner collected his text and notebook. One student passing by patted his shoulder and said "Good job." Conner looked up and said "Thanks." After that, everyone went on his or her own way.

----- ----- -----

When Conner walked into his dorm room, Shedrick was again waiting. "How was your class?" he inquired of his young friend.

"The guy kept us for nearly an hour," Shedrick complained.

"Oh, poor baby," Conner said mockingly. "College is gonna be tough for you if you're expected to learn something."

"Very funny. Very funny."

Conner put down his books.

"How was your class?" Shedrick asked.

"Ninety minutes of monotonic delivery," he answered. "We saw the professor's eyes twice, once when he walked in and once when he walked out."

"Oh, my. That sounds like it'll be a great course."

"I like why we're there and what we're supposed to cover. Otherwise, this will be painful."

"Sounds like it."

"Well, we'll see. Maybe things will change."

"Yeah, right. And just what Scriptural reference do you have to support such a bold statement?"

Almost to Conner's disbelief, he said "Matthew 17."

Shedrick waited for the quote, much less surprised than Conner that one would be delivered.

"*If you have faith as small as a mustard seed, you can move mountains.* That's not quite it but you get the idea."

"Yeah. Well, you better go to the spice store and get yourself some mustard seed because that old boy sounds like a mountain."

Conner laughed. "Good one," he complimented.

Shedrick looked at his watch and, semi-urgently, said "Practice today is at 4:00. We'd better hustle."

Conner looked at his watch and silently agreed. They ran into their respective rooms and were running to the gym less than two minutes later. They arrived in time to change and be on the floor three minutes before the bewitching hour.

"Let's see who wants to pray," Conner said. He looked around and saw the players in various forms of activity and non-activity. None of the coaches had yet arrived. "Prayer at the foul line," he called out. Most of the team just looked at him. A total of five others joined them. Conner made it a simple prayer, one that was encouraging, and one that was short.

He always wanted to pray as though he was speaking to God, not as though he was repeating a mantra. Chants were the ways that little children learned to pray. *God is great. God is good. Let us thank him for our food. Amen.* Older kids and adults should speak to the Lord. He wanted to model this kind of prayer.

After Conner's prayer, the seven then went to get ready for the practice just as the coaches entered the gym.

At the end of the practice session, which wasn't too exhausting because of the upcoming game the day after tomorrow, the same seven convened at center court. This time, Conner asked if someone else was willing to offer the prayer. Shedrick jumped in and delivered. It was a nice change of pace.

Chapter 28

Conner had one class on Wednesday while Shedrick had two. Once again, they had been strategically chosen and scheduled to accommodate team practices or shoot arounds, the latter taking place on game days.

Conner's third class, *Comparative Religions*, was another he very much looked forward to taking. He had decided to take twelve credit hours, a bit more than required in order for him to maintain full-time status. However, along with his mission, he definitely wanted to see if he could develop his knowledge, thus better positioning himself as an apologist. Each of his three courses was four credit hours.

When he arrived, fifteen minutes before the start of the 10:00 AM class, the room was packed. There were at least twenty-five students in there. Two chairs remained vacant, both in the front of the room. Conner took one, although he preferred sitting in the back. At precisely 10:00 AM, the door opened and in walked a tall, very dark, African-looking, well-dressed man. Unlike Professor Ving, this man was straight out of a fashion magazine. Crisp shirt, snappy bowtie, sports jacket with elbow patches, sharp creases in his trousers and shiny, laced shoes. Conner judged him to be in his mid to late forties. He put his materials on the desk as everyone grew silent.

"My name is Bartholomew Andrew Greene, Greene with an 'e' at the end. My friends call me Bags because of my initials." He looked around and then added "But you can't." Everyone laughed.

"Let me tell you about myself, at least what is important to this course. I was born in Africa, raised in Europe and have lived my entire adult life in the United States. I have traveled greatly. I have a bachelor's degree in European history from this institution, a master's degree in Biblical Studies from Cambridge, a master's degree in Greek from Stanford and a Ph.D. in Theology from Duke. I am also an ordained Presbyterian minister." He paused to look around to see if anyone had any questions. None were asked.

"Thus, I am academically sound. My passion is studying all the major religions of the world in order to develop my understanding of that one to which I subscribe, it obviously being Christianity. However, this is not a course in which I will try to convince you to become a Christian if you are not. That decision is up to you. Most Christians believe that God chooses us, not the other way around. If you subscribe to that, then, when it's your time, you will either accept or decline his invitation. I can neither manage Jesus' time schedule nor talk you into accepting that summons. However, if you wish to explore this further, it happens outside of this class. Inside, neither I nor you will be proselytizing. That goes for Christians, Jews or any religious persuasion. Understood?"

He waited while everyone either said yes or nodded his or her head. Then he continued.

"My purpose here is to have you teach yourself. In a manner of speaking, this is a self-teaching course." Here, again, he stopped. "But it is not a self-grading course." That brought laughter and a few quick remarks from the class.

"By the time that you leave, I expect you to be able to fundamentally understand and knowledgeably discuss all the major religions of the world. You will practice understanding them and discussing them in this class. This course is divided into two parts — our class sessions and your homework. I expect you to participate and grow during our discussions. I expect you to learn the facts during your out-of-class research work. Am I making myself clear?"

Again, everyone affirmatively responded to the professor's question.

"You will deliver three presentations. One will be an individual presentation on a religion or an aspect of a religion. It will be delivered to your small group. I will be dividing you into these groups. A second presentation will also be an individual presentation but it will be to the entire class. It, too, will be on a religion or aspect of a religion, but on a different topic from the first one you cover. The third presentation will be a small-team effort on a controversial topic. It will be delivered to the class. You will have one-page papers each week and a final paper due at the end. All of those will be graded. Otherwise, the grading will consist of class participation. I want quality, not quantity. Therefore, if you've got an Energizer Bunny mouth, take it somewhere else."

Again the laughter shared everyone's appreciation of how Professor Greene was introducing this course.

"If you don't think that knowing your religion and that of others is important, then you should not be in this class. I tell that to you for your own good. For those of you who are agnostics or atheists, I welcome you as warmly as I do anyone else. Your journey through this course should be a fascinating one for you. Any questions?" None were raised. "Let me take attendance, assign you groups, give you the assignments for this week, both reading and papers, and turn you loose."

He looked around the room, then continued. "I want to be certain to give you some good advice: Anyone who waits to get started will not finish this sprint. I also want to tell you that I am a fair grader. I have no problem giving A's and no problem giving F's. If you keep your head in the game, you will do well. If not, then Friendless Flora Flockingham will visit your transcript. Are we clear?"

Again, there were smiles and agreement. Professor Greene completed his groupings and assignments, then pleasantly told all the students "Now, get out of here." Everyone packed up and left, two students coming up to the professor to either brown nose or ask a question. Conner considered shaking the professor's hand, then decided not to go up front. He left with the mass exodus.

As he walked out the door, he was rereading the textbook jacket cover and bumped into someone. He looked up to see a woman who, apparently, had been doing the same thing. "Sorry," they both said at the same time.

"Jinx," she said.

Conner lit up. "Whenever I say that, nobody seems to understand it. I'm really glad to hear someone else use it."

She smiled. Conner couldn't help notice that she didn't have a wedding ring, although she was a bit older than the rest of the students. Well, he could have helped notice but he chose to look. They continued out of the class into the hallway.

"Esther," she said.

"Wow. *For just such a time as this,*" he quoted from the Bible book of the same name.

"Four fourteen," she said, citing the chapter and verse.

"Yeah, I guess that you've heard that line before."

"Not as a pick up line," she said.

Conner stopped and looked at her. Direct, isn't she? he commented to himself. "Wait a minute," he began.

She cut him off. "Just kidding. It seemed like perfect timing so I just tossed it out there."

"No, no. It was great. It's just…" It was clear that Conner was at a loss as to what to say.

She laughed. "And your name is…?"

"Oh, sorry. Conner. Conner Ramsey."

"Esther Conrad," she completed her name.

"Nice to meet you," they again said at the same time. "Jinx," they also both said at the same time. They laughed.

"Okay, here's my line," Conner began. "I'm way behind in my Hermeneutics course. During class today, I heard you say that you had already taken it. Could I get some tutoring?"

"You're already behind? How is that even possible?"

"Okay, I'm expecting to fall behind."

She laughed lightly and nodded her head. "We'll see," she said.

"I was wondering if lunch today might be a possibility?" he boldly inquired. "That is, of course, if you are available and interested."

"I am and I am," she said.

"You're God?" he asked.

"What?" she responded.

"Well, you said that you are I am and that means that you are God, doesn't it?"

She shook her head playfully. "Maybe we should skip lunch," she teased.

"Not on your life. You already said yes."

"Well, doesn't a girl have the right to change her mind?"

"No, not when it involves a lunch date with me."

"Good enough. Where would you like to go? Would you like to meet there?"

Conner thought about it and decided that he shouldn't be too pushy. From his limited knowledge of what restaurants were around campus, he chose one and offered a time.

"See you there at noon," she said turning to go.

"Yeah," he responded, simply standing there and watching her walk off. "Wow," he added quietly. "Double wow."

----- ----- -----

This time Conner got back to the room first. Shedrick arrived at 11:25. This had given Conner a few minutes to begin reading the assignment given by Professor Greene. When the door opened, Shedrick seemed to slink into the room.

"What's the matter?" Conner asked.

"What isn't the matter," Shedrick commented. "Talk about horrendous professors. I stupidly signed up for a *Primer on Religions* course and the professor is…unbelievably bad."

"Oh, sorry about that. I've got one like him. Is it a him or a her?"

"Him."

"What's his name?"

"Ving."

Conner started laughing, almost convulsing as he thought of Shedrick sitting in that class suffering through the monotonic delivery of Professor Ving.

"What the heck is so funny?" Shedrick asked, almost annoyed at the joy his roomie was taking in his suffering. "I wish that you had to take this course from him."

"I do."

"Huh?"

"I've got him for a graduate class and it is the kiss of death. At least you got out early."

"I'm not gonna survive him for an entire semester," Shedrick whined.

"Your choice," Conner said. "It sounds like a good topic, though."

"Topic, schmopic," he said. "What difference does that make if I can't tolerate the professor?"

Conner chose to say nothing.

"Trouble is," Shedrick continued, "there's nothing else open at that time and I need to take something on Wednesday mornings. Ohhh my!" he wailed.

Conner chuckled. "You'll live," he said.

"Yeah, you're right." Shedrick seemed to don a happier face. "Let's go to lunch."

"Can't."

"Can't?"

"Can't."

"Why?"

"I'm going to lunch with someone from class."

"Oh, no. Female?"

"Yes."

"Already?"

"She's just a classmate, that's all."

"She's just a classmate, that's all," mocked Shedrick. "When ya gettin' married?"

"Okay, Mr. Funny. I'll see you this afternoon."

"Where ya going?"

"No way, José. You'll come and scope her out. Forget it."

"Good buddy you are. Find out if she has a gorgeous young friend…or daughter…or granddaughter," he teased.

"You're so funny," Conner said as he left.

----- ----- -----

"How did it go?" Shedrick asked immediately after Conner came back to the room, not even allowing him time to close the dorm door. It was as though Shedrick had been sitting in exactly the same spot just waiting for his roomie to return.

"Fine" was all Conner said.

"Fine? Fine? That's it? I want to hear the whole gory story. You know, where you profess your love and she tells you that her heart belongs to another and you fall down to implore her to take you instead and…"

"Okay, okay. Enough already. You should be studying for Professor Ving's class."

"Ring a ding Ving," Shedrick commented.

Conner laughed.

"This guy is gonna kill me," he whined.

"Hey, Shedrick, remember when you first walked onto the court with me against Walker?"

"Yeah, Walker and Obumje. And your point?"

"Remember what you thought?"

"Yeah."

"What? What were you thinking at the time?"

"Why me? We're gonna get creamed."

"And what happened?"

"We won."

"Get it?" Conner asked.

"No."

"First you thought that you were going to lose, maybe even get skunked. Next you thought that we could be competitive. Finally, you were hotdogging dunks."

Shedrick smiled in remembrance.

"Maybe the same thing will happen with this course. You'll hate it, open up to it and wind up loving it."

"Not!" Shedrick concluded.

"Maybe," Conner amended.

"This is your tactic for not answering my question about Mrs. Ramsey?" he said, kiddingly referring to Conner's lunch date.

"You got it. However, as of the moment, you can be best man."

"Yes!" Shedrick said with a Tiger-like up and down fist pump.

"Gotta study. Later." Conner headed to his room to do some reading. He had a few hours before the next practice.

"I, on the other hand, have another class," Shedrick said morosely.

"Enjoy!" Conner said, closing his door.

----- ----- -----

After practice, Coach Wright had them sit in the bleachers. All the players fell into place. "Gentlemen, we've got our first game tomorrow evening. Coach Murphy will read the names of those who will suit up. The order in which he reads them will not indicate who is starting or anything else. For those of you not asked to suit up, you will each receive a ticket and be able to sit behind the bench. I expect you to wear a nice shirt, tie and sports jacket, as though we were traveling for an away game. No jeans, no sneakers or flip flops. Wear socks. The group that is named for tomorrow's game will be changing as the season progresses. You can earn a spot on or off the team. Nothing is written in concrete until the conference tournament. Any questions?"

None were offered.

"We have a morning shoot around tomorrow, then nothing until two hours before the game. Be dressed and in the locker room at that time. We'll go on the floor for warm ups, come off prior to the game, I'll speak with you and then we'll enter as one. Good luck."

The coach turned and left the floor while Coach Murphy read off the names. Both Conner and Shedrick were included on the list. Others were not this fortunate and Conner could see disappointment on many faces, especially those who thought that they had a good chance. When the list was completed, everyone stood up.

Conner called out "Prayer" and his stalwart band went to center circle. As it turned out, all of them were going to suit up. Conner asked for prayer and one of the more soft-spoken players offered to lead them. After concluding, he spontaneously put his hand in the middle and it was joined by everyone else's. "One, two, three, prayer," he said, much like one would do at the end of a huddle. And that's just what they did. On the count of three, everyone said the word Prayer to conclude the brief prayer session.

----- ----- -----

"Made it," Shedrick said on the way back to the dorm. He had contained his excitement in the locker room. For one thing, he didn't want to seem bush league. Making the dressing squad was not equal to playing. For another, he hadn't wanted to hurt anyone else's feelings when they were all together.

"Yeah. That's good," commented Conner without too much enthusiasm.

"Oh, you were gonna make it. You knew that."

"I don't know. Yeah, probably. Let's not forget to pray."

"Your prayers have been answered. Mine, too," Shedrick concluded.

"Are you serious?" Conner challenged him. "Mine have miles to go before I sleep."

"Robert Frost," cited Shedrick.

"Very good."

"Believe it or not, we touched on that poem yesterday during class."

"See? Goes to show you that you're learning valuable stuff already."

Shedrick scrunched his face in answer.

"What do you mean that you have miles to go? To the nationals?"

Conner snorted a laugh. "No, my friend. My goal is larger than that."

"What is it?"

"To spread the Word."

"What?" Shedrick asked, half inquisitively and half unbelievingly. "How ya gonna do that?"

"One bite at a time, my friend. One bite at a time."

"What does that mean?"

"It means that I want to start with prayer for ourselves and then include more and more people."

"And you intend to do that how?"

"First with your help, which you have already started to give me."

"I did?"

"Absolutely. You have taken an active role in thanking the Lord and in demonstrating it to the rest of the team. Because of you, we have a band of seven prayer pilgrims."

"Yeah, I guess that's right," Shedrick said, "but they're participating because of you, not me."

"I don't think so but let's not quibble. If we remain encouraging and have good fortune on the court, we can at least get people's attention. That's one step in the right direction. If they will at least open their ears, their minds and their hearts, then God's invitation has a chance to be welcomed by them. That's my mission."

"For whom?"

"For everyone."

"No, really. For whom?"

"I'm as real as real gets, Shedrick. A man's reach should exceed his grasp. We need to set ambitious goals."

"Robert Browning."

"You're a regular reference source," he said to Shedrick.

"We covered that one, too, in class yesterday."

Conner smiled. "Lucky I'm giving you the right quotes. And the prof didn't even call to tell me to test you."

Shedrick smiled. "Seriously, Conner, who's your audience?"

"I am serious, Shedrick. If we do this right, we can reach, reach, reach the stars."

"Who's we?"

Here Conner stopped and considered his choices. Without too much lapse, he said "You, me and God, for starters. And the three of us are unbeatable."

"Well, he is, anyhow."

"And we might as well join the right team."

"Little did I ever think that I was going to room with a cross between Michael Jordan and Billy Graham."

Conner smiled.

"…and Methuselah" he added.

Conner laughed. "Respect your elders."

"Yes, oh mighty one."

Now it was Conner's moment to scrunch his face and shake his head. "You're hopeless," he said.

They were both silent for a few moments.

"I'm in," Shedrick said.

"Meaning?"

"Meaning that if you think we can make a difference to this kingdom's inhabitants for the next, I'm in."

"We can and I'm glad. Beyond glad."

They walked toward each other, clasped hands and hugged.

"And it also means that I'm starved."

"I'll buy," Conner said, "at the cafeteria."

"Very generous of you," Shedrick responded, knowing that their food was covered as part of their scholarship.

Off the roomies went to dinner. Once out the dorm door, Shedrick said "Now tell me about this femme fatale who got you to buy her lunch."

"You're too young to hear stories about romance."

They both laughed and double stepped down the stairwell.

Chapter 29

Thursday finally arrived. It was the first game, first home game and the fans' first look at this year's team. The programs had long since been printed. As a result, Conner's name was nowhere to be found within them. He didn't worry about that. In fact, he thought, it might work to his advantage, much like a groundswell movement for a candidate. Sometimes the energy associated with something like that can be more powerful than something that has been in the hopper for a long time.

The team had a light, more or less informal shoot around for its morning session. The coach didn't speak to the team as a whole. He just wandered around the floor and spoke with various individuals. All he said to Conner in passing was "Ya ready, grandpa?" Conner laughed.

Afterwards, Conner attended his two Tuesday/Thursday classes. Professor Cook was tremendously thought provoking. He taught in the Socratic style, wanting his students to discover answers rather than be given them. What a great class, thought Conner.

Lunch was just a salad by himself and was followed by Professor Ving's class. It was as predictable and yawning as had been the first one. Oh my word, thought Conner. How could this class be so different from the other two? Doesn't anyone monitor or evaluate these professors? If they do, they definitely skipped Professor Ving. Using up all ninety minutes, Conner finally got to return to his room. Shedrick hadn't yet returned.

Conner kicked off his loafers, closed his door, took one of his texts, stretched out and began reading. He didn't get through half of a page before he was asleep, the book resting on his chest. He dreamed about steam trains passing in opposite directions on adjacent tracks. The passengers were throwing yellow tennis balls back and forth as the trains sped by. He was sitting on the limb of a tree just watching what took place. A short while later, two other trains did the same thing and the passengers threw yellow tennis balls back and forth, as well. When Conner woke up, he remembered the dream but couldn't put it into any meaningful context.

He heard Shedrick return but chose not to get up or call out. Let him think that I'm sleeping, he thought to himself. Then he reached over and got his Bible. He thought about which prophet he should read, then settled on Habakkuk. He liked this one a lot. It was encouraging and it was short. He could read the entire thing at one sitting without pretending that he was taking a speed-reading course. The Book of Habakkuk reminded the reader that God is in control and that he despises evil. When Conner got into the third chapter, he stopped to read and reread the second verse. This was a favorite of his, especially now. It was well marked up in his Bible.

I have heard all about you, Lord... Conner thought that he had done more than hear about the Lord. He had met him. Face to face. Several times.

...and I am filled with awe by the amazing things you have done. God truly is amazing, he thought. He savored this passage, words not forming to do it justice.

In this time of need, begin again to help us, as you did in years gone by. He felt a little bit guilty describing this as a time of need but, when he rethought the phrase, need does not have to mean desperation. He certainly felt in need of help for his mission. Heck, he thought, we're always in need. All of us. It's just that some recognize it, while others don't. And some keep it in their thinking, while others let the realization slip from time to time. He, Conner, recognized it but, truth be told, he let it slip from time to time. He needed to do better. He felt as though he was getting better.

He finished Habakkuk, set the Bible on his chest and closed his eyes again. This time, though, he didn't fall asleep. Instead, he thought about what a wonderful world this was. Yes, he was both happy and scared with his King David-like mission. But even that aside, life was super. And what made it even more super was that the next life offered something infinitely better. Like most Christians, he didn't want to move to the next life just yet but, at the same time, couldn't wait. Quite a dilemma.

After lying there for another half hour, he rolled onto his feet and went into the common room. Shedrick was sitting on the sofa. Well, he wasn't exactly sitting. The sofa was against one wall. Shedrick had his stocking feet against the wall, his rump on the cushions and his upper body on the floor.

"What in heaven's name are you doing?"

"Waiting for you, of course."

"Oh, give me a break."

"I was just going to get something to eat. Care to join me?"

"Let's do it."

Once again, they headed off to the cafeteria. This time, though, because of the upcoming game that evening, they were instructed to eat very wisely. They followed directions. Afterwards, they went back to their dorm room and relaxed.

"Is Miss Wonderful coming to the game?"
Shedrick asked.

"I don't know."

"You don't know? How can you not know?"

"I didn't invite her."

"Why not?"

"I didn't tell her that I was on the team."

"Why not?"

"Why yes?"

"Because people tell other people that they're on
the team, that's why yes."

"You're nuts."

"A little."

They were silent for a bit, then Conner said
"Shedrick…"

"Yeah?"

"I really appreciate you."

"Hey, man, I appreciate you. You've turned my
life around," Shedrick said. This surprised Conner a
bit.

"Not really," Conner observed, not knowing what
else to say. He kicked himself for being so
inadequate.

"Yes, really."

"Well, thanks. As for you, I particularly appreciate
how you've joined me as a prayer pilgrim."

"How could I not when they tell me you saved
my life through prayer."

"I was wondering if anyone had said something.
You never mentioned it before."

"I didn't know what to say."

"I think that it was because God saw that I need you and this mission needs you."

"Well, he got me."

"Good. I'm feeling a little bit uncomfortable about asking our group to go out on the floor for a pre-game prayer. I know that I shouldn't feel worried about it but I do, nonetheless."

"Yeah, I can understand that." After a brief silence, Shedrick added "We do what we feel is right and we let God take care of the rest."

Conner smiled. "Exactly."

"Exactly," Shedrick echoed.

"Thanks."

"You're welcome."

Chapter 30

When they got to the gym, Eagle Eye, aka Jake Crumpler, the chief attendant, was decked out in his Brantley colors. He wore them for every home game. Thus far, his winning percentage when wearing them was well over eighty percent. "Don't change" three head coaches had been telling him. He wasn't about to.

Some of the players were already there, others were drifting in. Aside from hey-how-ya-doin' salutations, there wasn't much conversation. Several of the players were getting taped, others massaged. There was a quiet seriousness that Conner had not seen before.

Conner and Shedrick were talking about something when one of the prayer pilgrims, Gary Dixon, came over. "Are we going to pray tonight?"

he asked. He was a sophomore and a pretty good player. He needed a bit more weight to bang underneath with the others. He never complained and always tried his best.

"Of course," Conner said confidently. "We'd be lost without him, wouldn't we?"

"That's what I was hoping you'd say. When are we going to get together?"

"I'd like to do it twice, once before we play and once after."

"Okay."

"Gary…"

"Yeah?"

"Thanks for being part of this prayer team. It means a lot. Your leadership and encouragement are really critical. We still have a bigger audience to reach."

Dixon looked a bit confused, then seemed to either understand or dismiss it. "Yeah, sure," he said and returned to his locker row.

"It's good to have guys like that," Shedrick reflected.

"Sure is."

They finished getting on their warm ups and headed to the floor. When they got there, Gary was already stretching. He, Conner and Shedrick rounded up the others and they went to the foul line. It was still the same group. They stood in a circle and bowed their heads. "Gary?" Conner invited. Although a little surprised, Gary stepped right up to it and offered a touching prayer. It was genuine and wonderfully phrased.

"That was great," Conner said after the prayer session had concluded.

Gary just smiled and nodded his head.

The warm up was easy. Aside from vendors and other people working in Carlson Fieldhouse, there were maybe a few dozen people in the stands. The first game of the year was called Eagles Red Day and every fan was expected to wear as much red as possible. Everyone already in the stands was wearing at least a red shirt, if not also a red hat. Several had red pants and skirts on, as well. This evening was definitely going to be a sea of red.

The other team, Kansas Northern, also warming up, wore their visitor green colors. Their mascot, an American Bullfrog, was boldly displayed on their jerseys. It had the look of a determined reptile, much like the University of Maryland's Diamondback Terrapin. Knowing which team was which would not be a problem.

The warm up went well and the teams ran off the floor just as the fans started streaming in. Conner could begin hearing the noise level rise. This place will be loud, he thought.

Coaches Murphy, Bromberg and Wilcox were in the locker room when the players returned. They instructed everyone to get their game uniforms on and to be seated in the meeting area in ten minutes. When the ten minutes rolled around, everyone was dressed and ready. That's when Coach Wright walked in.

He was dressed in a suit. It was the first time that Conner had seen him in anything but a golf shirt that sported an Eagles logo. Red, blue, white and even yellow. Always that style shirt. Now he looked like a tier-one coach.

"Gentlemen, I can point to dozens of times when a sports program like ours was upset by a school nobody had ever heard of before. It wasn't because that team was too cocky. It wasn't because that team was overmatched. And it wasn't because they were outcoached. Each and every time that has happened, it was because the losing team was slow in getting focused.

"That will not be us tonight. They may hit their first fifteen half-court shots and be leading by twenty but I don't want it to be because we are not focused. I am not worried about the score. I am only concerned about your being focused. Are we clear on this?"

Everyone shouted "Yes, coach!"

"When you are out there on the court, I want you to play like a team, not like five individuals who don't know each other. I want crisp passes. I want as many second chances as you can get and I don't want them getting offensive rebounds.

"Most of all, I want you to play top-of-the-line defense. Anyone who doesn't play hard defense will have a good seat for the rest of this game. Are we clear on this?"

Again, everyone shouted "Yes, coach!"

"Okay, here's the starting lineup. Kline, Walker, Forrester, Obumje and Harmon. I'll substitute as I see necessary. Remember that we're one team. Are we clear on this?"

"Yes, coach!"

"Okay, let's welcome these folks to our house."

Everyone stood and moved to the exits. In a few minutes, they would be out on the floor. Conner was curious what it would look like with fans filling all the seats. He soon found out. As expected, it was a total sea of red. Conner had never asked what the seating capacity for Carlson Fieldhouse was but now, seeing all these people, he realized how truly large it was. He told himself to find out after the game.

When the Eagles were led onto the floor by their captain, Clyde Forrester, the eruption of cheers was deafening. Although Conner and Shedrick were at the back of the line and, therefore, well into the tunnel leading from the locker room, they could still hear the reverberation. For both of them, this was a first, although Shedrick had played in front of some pretty large crowds during the high school playoffs. But nothing like this.

"Wow," said Shedrick.

"Double wow," said Conner.

When they hit the floor with the tail end of the team, they were almost bowled over by the color, the noise and the overall atmosphere. Stay within yourself, Conner told himself. You're here representing something far more important.

The Eagles huddled, got a few last-minute go get 'ems from the coach, and then broke to run drills. This created a bit of an awkward situation for Conner, now angry with himself for not having thought this through. Up to this point in time, he did not have occasion to gather his prayer pilgrims for

the pre-game prayer, other than the one that they
had given during the warm up. Now it was a bit too
late. They ran their layup drills followed by their
outside shots. Then the warning horn blew and
everyone returned to their respective benches.

Conner grabbed Shedrick who grabbed Dixon
and so on until all seven were together. They walked
to the foul line on the side of the court where their
team would be shooting. A hush came over the
crowd as everyone tried to figure out what they were
doing. It was particularly strange since not everyone
on the team was huddled there. They formed a circle
and Conner led them in a brief prayer. Then they
broke and returned to the huddle. The buzz around
Carlson Fieldhouse was interesting, much of it
related to questions surrounding that group. Many
variations of explanation were given but nobody was
sure. The coach, a little perturbed with the timing of
this prayer, chose to let it go.

Everyone put their hands together and gave an
"Eagles" yell. Then all but Kline, Walker, Forrester,
Obumje and Harmon sat down. As the newbies,
Conner and Shedrick sat at the end of the bench.

Conner bowed his head and asked for God's
guidance. The noise in there made it difficult for
Conner to even hear himself think. Nevertheless, he
was able to block out the racket and deliver his
thanks and prayer. "It's in Your hands, Lord," he
concluded. "Amen," said Shedrick who somehow
had heard this last sentence that Conner had offered
out loud. "Amen" said Conner and affectionately
slapped Shedrick's thigh.

The visiting team was tall, possibly two or three inches on average above the Eagles' starting lineup. Overall, though, the Eagles were tall throughout, Conner being the shortest. The other team's bench had a couple of players at 5'10" or less. If necessary, thought Conner, our second team will dominate.

The visitors won the tip and immediately hit a three. If nothing else, they could say that they were leading at one point in time. Kline missed a quick three and the defenders rebounded. They look well coached, thought Conner, although he realized that it was a bit early to draw any conclusions.

Again, shortly after crossing half-court, the same player dropped in another three. Six zip stood the score. This was beginning to look like what the coach had said might happen with the other team draining threes.

The next time across the midline, Walker threw away a pass underneath to Obumje. Even this early into the game, the crowd was becoming restless. Maybe they should switch jerseys, one fan said to his buddy. I hope not was the reply. If that becomes necessary, it's going to be a very long season.

The visitors from Kansas continued to move the ball well and either hit very long threes, well above fifty percent shooting, or had open drives from the spread defense. At 15-6, Coach Wright called time. All the bench players stood up as the starters, thus far unsubstituted for, sat down.

"Six turnovers and not one offensive rebound," he said. The players were looking down, all but Forrester and Obumje. "Ramsey," he called out, "you're in for Walker. Harris, you're in for Kline. Dixon, you go in for Harmon. Forrester and Obumje, you stay." The three checked in at the scorer's table.

When Walker heard that he had been taken out, he grabbed his towel and moved away from the huddle, not interested in hearing what the coach would instruct to the rest of the team. Kline and Harmon stayed in the huddle.

The announcer told the crowd of the substitutes, mentioning that Ramsey, number seven, was not listed in the program. Another buzz seemed to move along the crowd. Some stemmed from curiosity about this unlisted player. Some stemmed from those who recognized them as part of the group who had circled the foul line before the game started.

"Hey, old man," yelled a visiting team heckler at Conner. "This ain't the AARP."

Conner laughed and winked at him. That somewhat threw the heckler out of rhythm and he was silent for a few moments. Then he started up again with "Don't forget your walker" and "I've got some Geritol for you." It continued on like that for a while with Conner rather enjoying it.

Shedrick was getting irritated by the taunting and started to turn around. Conner, sensing this, grabbed his arm and said "This is why we're here. Don't confuse our mission. Just enjoy it."

Shedrick relaxed.

"Remember, if they press and there's nowhere to pass, look one way and throw it the other. I'll get it."

The horn sounded again and the players returned to the court. The clock showed 12:16 remaining in the twenty-minute half. Surprisingly, the other team was showing a bit of swagger. A little early for that, thought Conner.

They chose not to press and Shedrick inbounded to Conner who immediately gave it back. Conner knew that he would look awkward dribbling all the way up court. At midcourt, the other team picked up the ball and closed on Shedrick. He passed it off to Conner who gave a touch pass to Dixon for an easy two.

A big cheer went up.

"Now that's what I'm talkin' 'bout," a man dressed in red with his face painted the same color yelled. "Go Seven," he added.

Shedrick and Conner retreated to the guard positions, while Forrester, Dixon and Obumje were working to keep the other team's big players out of the box. Shedrick knew to press his player and to force him toward the middle if he decided to drive, which he did. Once there, Conner stepped in and took the ball in mid dribble. Knowing what would happen, Shedrick was already down court. Conner's pass resulted in a two-handed dunk.

Aside from one very distant outside three, the visitors were blanked for the next three minutes. Either Conner stole the ball for a Shedrick dunk or the Eagles' big three got a rebound. There were no second chance points for the visitors. With 8:50 remaining, the score was 22-18 in favor of the Eagles. Conner had four steals and no points.

Shedrick had ten points. Obumje had two, Forrester had two and Dixon had two. The crowd was jubilant again. Time out visitors.

The visiting heckler was not deterred as Conner came to the huddle. "The ambulance will be here soon to take you back to the home," he shouted. Conner smiled at him and meant it to be a warm smile. He was not certain how the fan had taken it but he didn't worry about its reception. He could only control what he did.

The coach substituted five players, putting Kline, Walker and Harmon back in along with two other players who had not yet gotten in. As they sat down, Forrester and Obumje high fived the other three. "We make a good group," Forrester said. "Amen to that," Conner responded.

From that point forward, the Eagles took control, winning by a final score of 84-68. Neither Conner nor Shedrick got more playing time. Toward the end of the game, some of the fans started shouting in a rhythmic cadence "Seven, Seven, Seven," clearly saying that they wanted Conner back in. It didn't work.

After the final buzzer, the teams shook hands. Conner and his pilgrims went back to the foul line and formed their circle. Interestingly, Forrester joined. Conner offered a prayer of appreciation. Although the fans were beginning to move toward the exits, quite a few stopped to again look at this small circle of players standing with their heads bowed at the foul line. By that point in time, it was obvious that they were praying.

When they broke, Conner took Forrester's arm. "Thanks for joining us. That means a lot. You have the power to influence many. Your connecting with us sends a strong message to other members of the team and to the audience."

Forrester was clearly uncomfortable with recognition about this. "It was nothing," he said. "There's something about it that looks right."

"I'm glad," was all Conner added. Then they all headed into the tunnel, slapping hands with whichever fans were leaning over the railing and whom they could reach.

One young fan yelled "Seven, can I have your jersey?" Conner, not knowing what to do, kept moving without saying anything other than smiling at the young man. Maybe he looked like an easy mark for the souvenir-collecting youngster. Maybe it was something else.

Once in the locker, the team sat in the meeting area before they went to shower and dress. Coach Wright, flanked by his assistant coaches, said "Good game. Slow start but good intensity. Nice job by Harris, Ramsey and Dixon getting us on track. After that, we began to flow. That's why this is a team effort. I want to see us get jump starts from anyone on the team, not just from our headliners.

"Instead of the Fab Five, that's our Faithful Five," offered Wilson, the same player who had made the disparaging remark and been reprimanded by the coach a number of days ago. This time, though, it wasn't an insult but more of a compliment.

"Faithful Five, eh?" asked the coach. "Fair enough. Nice game. We'll look at film tomorrow."

Everyone stood up and moved toward their lockers. Good start, thought Conner. Really good start.

Chapter 31

Once he got back to the dorm, he told Shedrick that he was going to read and would see him in the morning. "Nice game," he said. "Ten points, eh? You may wind up leading the team in scoring."

"Hardly," he said. "Besides, all of them came from you."

"It was your instincts that got you going ahead of them."

"Okay, I won't argue it. We know the reason but if you want to deflect any credit, I'm happy to take it."

"You deserve it."

"Thanks."

"Night."

"Night."

Hardly had he closed his door when his cell phone rang.

"Nice game," said the voice on the other end.

"Come again?" he asked.

"Nice game," the female voice repeated.

"Esther?" he asked.

"Very good," she answered.

"I didn't know that you were there or that you even liked basketball. Actually, maybe you don't," he added quickly.

"I love basketball. My dad was a high school basketball coach and I played at a small college in Iowa."

"Oh. Interesting."

"I didn't know that you were even on the team. I can tell you that I was very surprised to hear your name and see you come in. And then you did really well. Was that your roommate that you were telling me about? And why didn't they put you back in? You were the one who changed the game's momentum."

"I didn't do anything," Conner corrected. It's a five-man game and the others just needed a breather. I was lucky to get in and lucky to make some plays. By the way, yes, that's Shedrick, my roomie. Pretty good, isn't he?"

"He definitely has the hops. I know that it's late, Conner, but can I ask you something?"

"Fire away. I don't have class tomorrow and the coach doesn't schedule morning workouts after a previous night's game."

"Oh, you'll sleep until noon."

"Not so. I always get up early."

"My question is this: Before and after the game, you and some of the players went to the foul line. Was that to pray?"

"It was indeed."

"I've never seen that done before a game. I'm surprised that the coach didn't get mad."

"I sensed that he wasn't pleased all that much but we did sort of have his blessing."

"Blessing. That's funny."

"Yeah."

"I'm glad that you did that."

"It's what's important," Conner said matter of factly.

"Yes, it is," she said. "Can I ask you one more question?"

"You just did."

"Corny," she commented.

"Fire away."

"Can I return the favor and buy you lunch tomorrow?"

"You're on. I love free lunches."

"There's no such thing as a free lunch."

"Great. Now I'm going to lunch with Miss Quotation of the Year."

She laughed. "It's not that bad. I'll meet you outside the south entrance to Carlson Fieldhouse at 11:30. I'll drive. I've got a place that I want to take you."

"Free lunch and limo service, too. See ya then."

"Bye."

"Bye."

He hung up. What a magnificent evening this had been. As he washed up and got into bed, he slowed himself down, both mentally and emotionally. At the same time, he reminded himself that the credit went to God, not to him. Then his very favorite quote rolled into his head, it being Colossians 3:23. *Work hard and cheerfully at whatever you do, as though you were working for the Lord rather than for people.* He wondered if he had done this and, if so, whether to his maximal ability.

He closed his eyes and prayed. "What a wonderful experience, Lord. Thank You so much for the opportunity to have this ministry. I will try my hardest to make it both successful and far reaching. But I know that it will only achieve what it achieves through and with You. Keep my head focused on my responsibilities and my role. Please help me to stay humble. And, if I may request, please come back and visit…in person. Thank You for everything, Lord. In Your precious Son's name I pray. Amen."

Then he rolled over. He fell asleep immediately and slept very peacefully.

----- ----- -----

His phone rang pretty early and Conner kicked himself for not shutting it down before he went to bed. He glanced over to his clock and realized that it was already 7:00 AM, somewhat later than he normally awoke. He adjusted his eyes to look at the small number on his phone but did not recognize it. The area code was local. He decided to answer.

"Hello. My name is Richard Means."

The caller paused as though waiting for a response. Conner had none and remained silent.

"I am the chief sports reporter for the *Sentinel*."

Again, Conner waited politely.

"I'd like to do a piece on you."

Conner thought about it and then said "Well, Mr. Means…"

"Richard. You're old enough to call me Richard," he laughed more than spoke his correction.

"Okay, Richard. I am flattered and I would love to do that. However, I am new to the team and I don't know what the coach's policy is regarding our doing interviews."

"Oh, it's okay," he said. "The coach won't mind."

"I'm sure that you're right but I feel compelled to ask the coach first."

"How about if we have the interview and then, if he says no, I'll toss it?"

"I don't think so," Conner answered, becoming a bit suspicious. Although he had never dealt with journalists, he knew that the story always came first, often at the expense of the participants. Besides, he knew nothing about the *Sentinel,* whether it was reputable or sleazy, large or small, pro-university or a muckraker, middle of the road or extreme. He needed to learn about it, as well.

"Can we set something up and then we won't have to do that when the coach says that it's okay?"

"When did you have in mind?"

"How about late this afternoon, perhaps following your afternoon practice?"

Conner had learned that Friday practices were open to the press and this reporter's request seemed reasonable.

"Sounds logical," he replied. "If the coach says it's okay, I'll see you after the practice. How will I recognize you?"

The reporter laughed. "I'll recognize you."

"Good. Thanks for calling."

"Bye."

Before Conner could offer his goodbye, the reporter had disconnected the call. "Cold," Conner said. He decided to get up. His stomach was already talking to him. He hoped that Shedrick would be awake but, if not, he was going to the cafeteria for breakfast by himself. Turns out that Shedrick was awake and hoping to do the same. They both threw on walk-around-the-campus garb and headed for breakfast.

Once they had exited the dorm building, Conner was surprised to see a great deal of hustle and bustle on the campus. Then he remembered that it was still a school day. He suspected that there were plenty of early-morning classes.

He was glad that he had his classes limited to Monday through Thursday. Coach Wright had been insistent about this in order for players to be able to travel with minimal conflict on Friday, if necessary. The coach wanted his student athletes to miss as few classes as possible. He also wanted them to stay eligible to play. That is why he had dedicated tutors available for his players.

Not very long after they had left the dorm, someone from a group of three students came over to the two of them and said "Great game, Harris. If the coach had left you in there longer, you would have had 30." Then he looked over to Conner and said "Nice game, too," but without too much enthusiasm.

"Thanks," Conner said.

"Why thank you," Shedrick said, with a big smile. "The coach knows what he's doing. We have lots of good players on the team. I'm just ready to chip in where necessary."

It was Shedrick's first 'interview' as an Eagle, even though it was just a conversation with another student. Conner could tell, though, that Shedrick was somewhat practiced at this, probably having done many in high school.

"Good luck this season," the student said as he returned to his two buddies.

"Thanks," they both said.

Neither Conner nor Shedrick said anything while the young man departed.

"Let me ask you something, Shedrick," Conner began.

"Fire away," responded the new celebrity.

"Did the coach ever say anything about interviews?"

Shedrick thought for a second, then said "He's got a policy on dealing with the press, outside supporters, potential agents and pretty much anyone else not on the team."

"What's his policy on speaking with reporters."

"It's firm. Don't do it unless you clear it with him first."

"Yeah, that's what I thought."

"Why do you ask?"

"Some reporter called this morning…"

"Already?"

"Yeah. And he wanted to do a story. I told him that I needed to get clearance from the coach but he wanted me to answer some questions anyhow. He said that he wouldn't print anything if the coach didn't say it was okay."

"Richard Means from the *Sentinel*," Shedrick guessed with more than a wild shot.

"Yeah. How did you know?"

"I never met him but the coach singled him out as the most aggressive one. Apparently, the guy is good, is pro-Brantley and is relentless."

"Well, do we give him our attention or not?"

"Not without the coach's okay."

"Gotcha. Thanks." He paused. "I'm not used to giving interviews. Any advice for a newbie?"

Shedrick stepped away from Conner and looked at him as though trying to identify his roommate. "Newbie? How about Oldbie?" he asked.

"Very funny."

For the rest of the few minutes' walk, Shedrick shared unprepared suggestions for handling interviews.

----- ----- -----

Conner decided to use the quiet time after breakfast and while Shedrick had a class to study. Even though he only had three courses, he had loads of reading to do. He even had a few papers due early the following week. Having been out of school for quite a number of years, he would be rusty at best. In other words, he needed to get in front of his studies.

As he sat down to study, Conner closed his eyes and bowed his head.

"You can tell me in person," came the invitation.

Conner, once again totally surprised, looked up while knocking over the cup that held his pens, pencils and highlighters.

"You scared the…"

"Bejesus," the young man reminded him.

"…out of me," Conner finished.

The young man sat there smiling. He didn't recognize the child, maybe aged ten, but instantly knew who it was. The opening line by his visitor was not that of a normal ten-year-old.

"Why a child?" he asked.

"Why not?"

"Do you always answer a question with a question?"

"Do you?"

"Come on," said Conner, finding it a smidgen difficult to have an adult conversation with someone who looked this young.

"Besides," said the boy, "I'm at least partly Jewish."

"Is that what Jews do?"

"What do you think?" came the humorous retort.

"Very funny."

"And how come you're always male?"

"What is this, *Twenty Questions*?" He paused, then continued. "I began as a man that you could possibly envision as God in human form."

"You already did that with Jesus."

Ignoring Conner's flat attempt at humor, God continued. "Then I began giving you a little variety. Since this is a men's dorm, I didn't figure coming here as Marilyn Monroe would be a good idea."

"Why? Nobody ever sees you."

"Oh, but they do. They may not when I'm in your kitchen or your dorm room, but they sure as shootin' do when I'm on the street. Do you think that I was invisible when we met originally in that office building? Or what about when we had coffee together at that café?"

Conner realized he was right.

"Of course I'm right," the young man said in response to Conner's thought.

"What's your point?" Conner challenged. "Sometimes you're visible and sometimes you're invisible. What's the point?" he repeated.

"The point is, as you've often mentioned yourself in your prayers, if people tried to see God in others and acted accordingly, this place would be a whole lot better off. Instead, most people see others as either obstacles or means to an end."

"Wait a minute," Conner challenged.

"Wait a minute nothing. How are you doing in seeing God in others?"

Conner reflected on this and, with much less volume, responded "Not well."

"Not well, indeed," God punctuated. "And you're one of the better ones."

"Point taken."

"Thank you," God said without sounding as though he meant it.

After a moment of silence, Conner asked "Why are you here?"

"Well, I happened to be in Illinois and figured that I might as well drop in…"

"Very funny. Very funny."

"I've never figured out why people, especially men, repeat things."

Conner looked at him, waiting for an explanation.

"You just said 'Very funny. Very funny.' Why did you repeat it?"

Conner couldn't answer.

"Like when the dog runs off and the owner yells 'Get him. Get him.' Why repeat it?"

Conner was becoming increasingly confused.

"Or the baseball player who settles under a fly ball and yells 'Mine. Mine.' twice. Once should do. Or, if not, why not three times?"

Conner was now totally perplexed.

"Never mind," the boy said, totally dismissing it.

Talk about tangential thinking!

All Conner could think to say was "I don't know." Pause. "But it would seem that *you* might have an answer." He sarcastically emphasized that one word.

"I do but…"

"I'd have to kill you," Conner said, completing the sentence.

The boy laughed.

"So, Mr. Ramsey, what was going to be your prayer?"

The subject had changed suddenly. Conner tried to return to the moment just before God had appeared.

"I was going to thank you for your splendor, appreciate your mercy and grace, thank you for your greatest gift of salvation, ask for continued strength and for success in this mission."

"Got it."

"What do you mean?"

"I got it. Thanks."

Conner tilted his head. Before he realigned it to his spine, the boy was gone.

After shaking his head in disbelief, all the while smiling, Conner debated whether or not to offer the prayer he had been about to give, then realized that it would only be repetitive. He turned to his studies.

Chapter 32

Lunch with Esther was enjoyable. She had taken him to one of her favorite out-of-the-way spots. It was on a hill and overlooked a lake. At this time of year, it was probably at its most beautiful.

She had lots of questions, some of which were difficult to answer. They came in three groups. The first related to why he was at Brantley University: Why had he returned to school? What was his prime focus while at school? What was he studying? Why was he playing basketball? Why hadn't he played when he was younger?

The second group related to his past: Where was home? Where was his family? What did his family think about what he was doing?

The third consisted of but one question: "What do you want to do when you graduate?"

Interestingly, she didn't ask one question about the prayer circle at the game. Perhaps she had forgotten about it, didn't understand it or didn't know what to say. After a while, the avalanche of questions made him feel as though he was experiencing an interrogation. He told her so.

"Oh, gosh, you're right," she said. "I don't know what came over me. You're just so interesting and different that I'm fascinated. But I'm sorry. I'll stop asking questions now."

Conner laughed. "No, questions are okay. I don't have all the answers and I'm interested in learning a little about you, as well."

Esther looked down, rather shyly, but said nothing.

From that point on, they had a delightful, two-way conversation. Conner did not feel quite up to sharing his mission with her. Not just yet. Location, location, location, he thought, when it came to setting up a restaurant. Timing, timing, timing, he said to himself, when it came to enlisting others. For this, the timing did not feel quite right. He went with his gut.

----- ----- -----

After she dropped him off, Conner decided to go see the coach. The door was closed and he knocked. "Come in!" came the instruction. "It's unlocked."

He opened the door to see the coach in his traditional Eagles golfing shirt. "Mr. Ramsey," came the salutation.

"Coach."

"To what do I owe the honor of this visit?"

"Well, coach, I came to ask you a question but now I have two."

"One at a time, son. Oops, I guess that you're too old for that moniker." He smiled.

"I guess so," Conner acknowledged. "I'd like to know your policy concerning interviews. I had a call this morning and put off scheduling something until

I checked with you. Shedrick said that we had to clear all interviews with you. Is that correct, coach?"

"Yup."

"It was a call from Richard…"

"…Means with the *Sentinel*, right?"

"Exactly."

"What did he want?"

"An interview. I didn't engage him in enough of a conversation to find out his approach."

"His angle, actually." The coach took a deep breath and sat back in his chair. He didn't invite Conner to sit. "I think that you're okay to speak with him. Are you comfortable doing so?"

Conner nodded.

"Stick to facts. Don't offer conjecture on the team. And definitely don't speak about anyone on the team, other than, perhaps, his excellence on the court. The last thing that I want is some internal strife. Make sense?"

"Yes, coach."

"What was the other question?"

"How come you didn't put at least Shedrick back in the game?"

"At least?"

"Well, me too, I suppose."

The coach laughed. "Because I'm the coach. Now, any other questions?"

"No, coach. Thanks."

"Our next game is tomorrow night. It's also a home game. This one will be a lot tougher."

"Yes, coach."

Conner turned and left. At least he had an answer to the interview question. He would speak with Richard Means after the practice. Stick to the facts, he told himself. On the other hand, this could be a wonderful vehicle for him to fan the fires of his mission.

One thing that crossed his mind was that he was promoting prayer, not necessarily spreading the Word. Were they the same? He wondered if he was going about this the right way. He pondered that all the way back to the dorm, oblivious to everyone else on the path.

When he got back to the dorm, he opened his Bible looking for the passage on the Great Commission. He knew that it was in Matthew but he couldn't quite remember where. His Bible was well marked up with his notes and he remembered that he had put a great big asterisk next to that passage. He started thumbing through Matthew. Finally, at Matthew 24:14, he found what he was looking for. *And this gospel of the kingdom will be preached in the whole world as a testimony to all nations, and then the end will come.*

Remembering that there was another passage on this same topic, he racked his brain to remember where it was. Something inside of him suggested Acts and he opened to it. Fortunately, Acts 1:8 was that location. *When the Holy Spirit has come upon you, you will receive power and will tell people about me everywhere…to the ends of the earth.*

Maybe prayer was or was not the same thing as spreading the Word. If so, he was on the right track.

If not, it was a natural first step toward the same thing. Maybe it was even more than a single step. Maybe it was many steps along the way.

He felt good about what he was doing but impatient with his progress. He determined to continue his efforts without creating the belief in others that he was fanatic in any other manner than healthy dedication.

----- ----- -----

Later that day, the coach focused on defense, defensive rebounding ("I want everyone boxing out his man") and a show of energy to the other team, it being the University of Texas at Mesquite. At the conclusion, he had everyone grab a seat on the bleachers. By now, they had their usual seats, almost as if they were assigned, although they were not.

The bleachers, from the twentieth row and up, was littered with journalists and others covering the team. This was the day that was reserved for them to observe. However, they were not allowed to come below the twentieth row all around the court. Only the school photographers and those with special passes were permitted closer access. A firm but customer service-oriented security force made certain these rules were enforced.

As he walked to the bleachers, Conner looked about, wondering which one was Richard Means. He had no way of knowing. "I'll recognize you," the reporter had said. Good enough, thought Conner. Right now, he needed to pay attention to the coach.

"Kansas Northern played us close. I expected something like that, although I thought that we would pull away by more in the second half. We limited ourselves by being tense. Now that's past us. I expect us to flow from the get-go, play ruthless defense and controlled offense. Any questions?"

None.

"Be smart in what you do tonight and what you eat before the ballgame. Anybody who doesn't take care of himself and his team will be buying tickets to get in here. Got it?"

"Yes, coach!"

"See you tomorrow evening. You know the time."

Shedrick asked Conner if he was headed back to the dorm. "First I'm gonna speak with that reporter."

"Richard Means," Shedrick confirmed.

"Yup."

"Be smart."

Conner smiled. "Maybe I can make a celebrity out of you," he kidded his roomie.

"You're the one who needs help," Shedrick kidded back. "Lots of it."

Conner began walking up the bleachers until a thin, middle-aged man approached. "Conner, I'm Richard Means." His handshake was surprisingly firm for such a body frame. "Let's go up there to get a little privacy." He pointed to a spot where nobody was sitting. They walked there together without saying anything. Conner sat down and Means joined him. The reporter had a notepad and a recorder.

"I hope that you don't mind my taping this. I want to get my facts straight."

"Fine by me."

"Tell me about yourself. Give me a little background."

"How about if you tell me what you know and I'll either correct or embellish it?"

Means looked at Conner in a way that conveyed this was not proper protocol. However, he was willing to play along.

"You're thirty-four." He stopped and looked for confirmation.

"Look, if you're going to stop before getting my okay on each thing, we'll be here for a bloody long time," Conner said. "I'll correct you if anything is inaccurate. Fair enough?" He wasn't nasty, only efficient.

Means nodded. "You were brought up in southwest Illinois. You did not play basketball in either high school or college. You were not recruited but now have a full scholarship. Nobody ever heard of you, especially not your basketball skills. Now you have decided to return to college, are taking graduate classes in Biblical Studies, I think, and have made the team."

Means looked at Conner. Conner looked back, telling himself not to laugh, not even to smile.

"Do you mind telling me how the heck you did that...made the team, that is? After that, I'd like to know why. I'll tell you, my friend, this makes absolutely no sense."

"Because it never happened before?"

"Because people don't just all of a sudden get basketball skills that allow them to play on a team like Brantley at thirty-four years old."

"Probably not," Conner said.

"Come on, man, tell me what's going on."

Conner did smile. He knew that this whole thing was very improbable. Make that impossible…without God's help. But he had been counseled not to try to deal with it by delivering a close encounter explanation.

"Here's the thing, Richard…"

Means leaned forward.

"I can't explain it myself."

One could almost hear the air come out of a balloon as Means exhaled.

"Well give me a little background. What inspired you to give this whole thing a try? I mean, weren't you working, well past college sports and otherwise occupied?"

"I was. I just felt something inside telling me to give this a try."

"And you simply jumped up and came to the university?"

Conner smiled again. "Not exactly. First, I tried out my skills in a recreation league."

"A recreation league? You went from a recreation league to college basketball?"

"That's what happened."

"That's impossible!" Means paused momentarily. "Okay, let's assume that it's true. What did you do after that?"

"I wrote to a bunch of coaches and asked for a tryout."

"What happened?"

"I got turned down left and right."

"What teams wouldn't give you a tryout?"

"You name it, I pretty much tried it."

"Big name schools?"

"Kansas, Duke, UCLA and Connecticut, to name just a few."

"And none of them told you to come up?"

"Nope."

"Hmmm. How did you wind up here at Brantley?"

"Coach Wright was willing to give it a try."

"Interesting. Of course, I don't buy into it."

"Listen, Richard, I'm telling you what happened." Conner started to stand up. "If you're not interested or if you don't believe it or if you can't write about it or if anything, then we're through. Everything you and I said is true. Now, is that it?" By then, Conner was standing.

Means jumped up. "Sit down. Sit down. Don't get so huffy. This is an improbable story and I need to check it out. You gotta admit that it's improbable."

Conner laughed to himself. "I admit that."

"Were you hit with gamma rays, did you drink some magic potion, were you touched by an angel or did aliens invade your body? Did any of those happen?"

"Not that I experienced." Here Conner felt bad about not saying something about the angel. Then, again, he wasn't touched by an angel. He decided that his denial was acceptable.

"This is an incredible story," Means said. "I'd like to introduce it as part of an ongoing human-interest series and develop it throughout the season. Would you work with me on this?"

"Provided you focus on the right things."

"And what are they, may I ask?"

"My faith."

"Your faith? Hey, this isn't a Christian publication. It's a secular, for-the-people newspaper."

"I'm not telling you what to write or how to angle it. I'm just telling you that the most important thing in my life is my faith and I don't want an article or a series misrepresenting that."

"Okay. I understand. No, I'll keep your priorities straight…or try to. Fair enough?"

"Fair enough."

"One quick question."

"Shoot."

"Why is it important that your faith be highlighted as your leading characteristic?"

"Because it is what drives me to be who I am and do what I do."

"Remarkable. Okay. We're on. Thanks. Bye."

Before Conner could respond, the reporter was up and gone. Conner remained seated, wondering if he was approaching this correctly.

Chapter 33

Saturday morning Conner made a special point of getting the *Sentinel* and seeing if there was a piece on him. There was. It was on the third page of the sports section, one column for the length of the page. The headline read "Faith in Basketball."

Conner thought that pretty clever since there were several ways to interpret it. It began with 'A 34-year-old playing basketball would evoke thoughts of someone nearing the end of his NBA career. Not when it comes to Conner Ramsey.' It went on to talk about the improbable story of his being on this team. Mostly, it set the stage for the series Means planned to run. True to his word, the reporter wrote of Conner's commitment to his faith. Although not lengthy in description, it did accurately put faith as his number one priority.

"Movie star," Shedrick said, when he had read it.

"Yeah, right. Russell Crowe has been asked to star as me in the Conner Ramsey Story. Crowe was delighted and said that he would do it for nothing."

"Greeeat," Shedrick said sarcastically. "Can I have a role in the movie, too?"

"Absolutely. How about the cashier at the Eagles Nest?"

"Very funny. Very funny."

Conner laughed to himself thinking about what God had said about men saying things in pairs. They were both silent the rest of the way over to the cafeteria. They went their separate ways to get breakfast. Shedrick liked a hot breakfast – omelet, meat, hash browns and toast. Conner liked a cold breakfast – cereal and fruit. Conner was done first and selected an available table. Shedrick came over and sat down. They were about to give thanks when someone who neither knew came over. He was clearly a student and a bit uncomfortable at being there.

Conner regrouped and looked up.

"Oh, I'm sorry. Were you about to pray?" he asked.

"We were," Shedrick responded.

"I can wait," he said.

"No, no," Conner insisted. "Would you like to pray with us?" he asked, pushing out a chair and inviting the young man to join them.

Shedrick, to his credit, let his grimace only be seen by Conner. Conner offered a prayer, adding a piece that could relate to this visitor, it dealing with success in studies. When the prayer was done, Conner asked "What can I do for you…or did you come to speak with my more famous friend, Shedrick Harris?"

The young man looked once to Shedrick, then back to Conner. "Actually," he said hesitantly, "I wanted to ask you a question."

Conner slid his seat back from the table to face the young man and invitingly said "Fire away."

"Well, this is a bit embarrassing."

He fidgeted uncomfortably. Conner looked at Shedrick who raised his eyebrows as if to say 'I have no idea what he wants.' Conner waited patiently.

"Can we speak somewhere privately?" he finally asked.

Conner was about to pull out a Sherlock Holmes line and say that Dr. Watson shares in all his work, then thought better of it.

"I guess," he said, trying not to be negative, although a bit disappointed to watch his cereal go soggy in his bowl. "Why don't we go over here?" he asked. "Excuse us, Shedrick," he said and the two went to the more secluded table at the other end of the cafeteria.

"What can I do for you?" Conner asked as pleasantly as he could.

"Well, you are an inspiration to me and to some of my friends."

"Wow," Conner said, somewhat taken aback but pleased with what he had just heard. "I'm flattered. Thank you. In what regard, may I ask?"

"Your faith."

"Great," Conner said, truly delighted with that being the reason. "But why are you embarrassed?"

After a few seconds of additional discomfort, he answered. "My name is Jeremy Wingman. My friends just call me Winger."

"Nice to meet you. My name is…" Conner said as he offered his hand.

"Oh, I know who you are." Conner said nothing. Another moment or two of hesitancy. "Anyhow, we have a fellowship group that has been meeting for two years. Pretty much all of us are juniors. It meets twice a month."

"That's wonderful, actually," Conner said, waiting to hear why this had to be a private conversation.

"Yeah, I know. We've all really grown from it."

"I'll bet. Go on."

"Well, some of us would like you to either join or at least speak with us at a future session."

"Why only some of you?" Conner studied Winger a bit more closely. "Is that the problem?"

Jeremy looked down, confirming that Conner had hit the nail on the head.

"Jeremy…" Conner said and waited. After a couple of seconds, Jeremy looked up. "Listen, I won't be hurt no matter what you say. Okay?"

Jeremy nodded.

"Let's take this thorn out and we'll all feel better."

Jeremy smiled. "Okay," he began, "but this is by far the minority."

Conner waited.

"Some of them think that you are the Antichrist."

"Antichrist?" Conner exclaimed. "Me?" It seemed preposterous. It was preposterous. He was stunned.

"I'm sorry," Jeremy said as he began to get up to leave.

"Jeremy," Conner said in his softest voice. "Please don't leave. I would love to visit with your fellowship group. I don't know how but maybe I could dispel their beliefs…for those who think that I am the Antichrist, that is. I guess that we'll never know unless we deal with it. Besides, as you probably well know, when we speak for the Lord, he gives us what we need to say."

More confident now, Jeremy worked with Conner to set a date for the visit. At the conclusion, Conner asked "Can you tell me why they feel this way?"

"You're sort of too good to be true."

Conner was truly stunned. Too good to be true? Me? Yikes. Double yikes.

"We'll be able to take care of that, I can assure you," Conner commented.

"I hope so. You're an inspiration to most of us but there's still this small minority."

"Don't worry, Jeremy. I am guessing that their motives are pure."

"They are!" Winger blurted out. "They're really good guys but…but they've got this bee in their bonnet about the Rapture, the Tribulation and all that. And, as you know, the Antichrist plays a big role."

"Actually, I believe that the Word tells us that there will be multiple antichrists."

Jeremy didn't say anything.

Conner stood up. Jeremy jumped up, as well. "I'll see you then." They shook hands and Jeremy hustled out of the cafeteria.

"Antichrist," Conner muttered as he returned to his milk-soaked cereal.

"What was that?" Shedrick asked.

"He was uncomfortable treating me like a celebrity and wanted me to come to one of his fellowship sessions. We set a time for it."

Shedrick just shook his head and went about eating, not saying anything. Conner turned to his unappealing breakfast, finally abandoning it after two bites.

The rest of the day was spent studying and writing the first of many papers for his courses. Since he had brought his laptop from home, he was able to write and save his work. Printing it was another situation. He had not brought his printer along. Shedrick's was temporarily on the fritz. Therefore, Conner had to save his work and take it to the computer lab to be printed. Not a huge problem but somewhat inconvenient.

----- ----- -----

At 3:00, his cell phone rang. It was Esther.

"Are you excited?" she asked.

"You mean about the game?"

"About the game and also about the article in the *Sentinel*."

"Yes and no. Yes about the game and we'll see about the article."

"You're strange."

"You're only just finding this out now?"

She laughed.

"Listen, Esther, here's the thing. I love basketball and playing here is very exciting. But – and this is what I am trying to keep in front of me – it is a means to an end. Nothing replaces my faith and my faith is leading me to model Christianity for others. If I can touch one person in a positive way, I will be glad. If I can touch more, that will be even better."

"You're giving me the updated version of the parable of the talents, aren't you?"

"Yeah, I guess. Whatever. I'm just doing my best."

"You definitely are strange."

"Thanks for the compliment."

Now they both laughed.

"Hey, are you coming to the game tonight?"

"Of course."

"Would you consider getting a milkshake or something after the game?"

"With whom?" she teased.

"Very funny," he said.

"Of course."

"Great." They set a place to meet in the gym afterwards. If she wasn't permitted to remain in the gym while he showered because the cleaning crew would be tidying it up, they determined a place to meet outside. If all else failed, he would call her on her cell phone.

"Good luck tonight, Mr. Seven."

He smiled. "Good luck tonight to you, too, Mrs. Seven." As soon as he said it, he regretted the implication. He didn't know whether to say 'sorry' or let it ride. He chose the latter. She didn't comment about it either, although, without telling him, she liked the way it sounded.

Chapter 34

The pre-game warm-up was the same as it had been last time. Stretching, layups, outside shooting and free throws. Conner made seven of his ten from the line and was well pleased with that. Wouldn't it be great if I could hit nine or even ten? he thought. UT/Mesquite looked big but there was more to this game than just size. When the horn blew, both teams retreated to their locker rooms to change into their game jerseys and hear last-minute instructions from their coaches.

Conner donned his number seven and thought about his exchange with Esther. Mr. Seven, he thought. I like it.

Once they were dressed, they were called into the adjacent meeting room. The coach was standing at the front. Everyone was quick to grab a seat and be quiet. When the last player was seated, the coach began.

"I looked at their statistics. They average three full inches taller than us and more than fifty pounds heavier." He looked around. "We'd be in trouble if this was sumo wrestling. But it isn't. Although size makes a difference, it's not the differentiator. You've heard it before: It's not the size of the dog in the fight, it's the…" he waited for them to finish it.

"…size of the fight in the dog," everyone shouted.

"You got it, boys. We'll start the same five as last time. Again, I'm looking for energy from the get go. I'm using this game to gauge where we are. It's still early in the season. We've got loads more wins before we're done."

A big cheer when up from the team. "Final Four. Final Four. Final Four" they chanted. The coach held up his hand.

"We can't make the Final Four with five players. It takes a team. Remember that. Okay, let's go."

They hustled out onto the court that had been darkened for effect, not something done for Thursday's game. Spotlights led each player to the bench. Each was called by name. It was pretty chilling stuff. When the coach's name was announced, everyone had already been introduced. Then the lights went on. The UT/Mesquite Coyotes were already on the court, tolerating the Eagle fanfare. Just part of basketball, they thought. "It doesn't change the score, men," the Coyotes' coach had reminded them. "Just endure it and then let's put it to them."

Unlike the previous game, Conner had decided to assemble his prayer pilgrims before the start of the actual game instead of before the start of the warm up. He reasoned that there would be more spectators in their seats and, thus, potentially more individuals to positively influence. The prayer group now comfortably included Obumje and Forrester. One additional player jogged over before they had formed their circle. Seemingly out of respect, the crowd grew quiet. It wasn't a total silence but the decibel level had definitely gone down. Conner prayed for Kline and Walker. He prayed for safety. He prayed that they may be an example to all who watched them. And he prayed for success. When he was done, all said "Amen" in a way that could be heard by those at courtside. When they turned to go back to the bench, many in the crowd applauded. It was a small victory but it was one nevertheless.

Once the game started, putting it to them is exactly what UT/Mesquite did. Apparently, their game plan was to bang from the outset, willing to trade fouls for effect. Forrester was able to give as well as he got but he soon had three fouls in the first twelve minutes. Obumje avoided the banging but lost much of his aggression. Walker was slippery but Kline got hammered several times. Eventually, on a contested layup, the other player inadvertently drove his knee into Kline's thigh, an excruciatingly painful injury. They called it a deep bruise and Kline had to be carried from the court. By that time, the fans were livid. For safety's sake, during one timeout, additional police were called and positioned themselves behind the Coyotes bench.

Coach Wright had been riding the referees almost immediately. At first it was polite: "This is basketball! They're going to hurt our players. We have an entire season. You have to take control."

After Kline got hurt, the coach became infuriated, something he was not prone to do. His actions got him one technical and his assistant coaches had to step between him and the referees to avoid a second which would have been an immediate ejection.

When Coach Wright turned back to his bench, he called "Ramsey, you're in." Conner jumped up, checked in and came to the huddle. "You're fast. Now I want you to be really fast. You take out their speedy guard with the hardest foul he's ever felt. You got that?"

All eyes turned to Conner.

"I can't do that, coach."

"What? What do you mean you can't do that?"

"I can't try to hurt someone in a game, coach."

"What? Are you a pansy? Don't you care about our team? I want you to lay him out. Now are you going to do that?"

"No, coach."

Coach Wright was fit to be tied. From the arguments with the referees and the realization that his star player would probably be out for a couple of weeks, he was madder than a bunch of riled hornets. Consequently, he wasn't thinking straight.

"Then get the hell out of here. Go ahead. Leave. Get gone, you pussy. You won't fight for your team. You're a disgrace. I don't need you. We don't need you. We've got plenty of real men on this team. We don't need a senior citizen. Get lost." The coach started to walk towards Conner as though instigating a fight. Conner stood his ground, his hands at his side. Coach Murphy stepped in. "Let him go, coach. Let it go." He was right on both counts.

Before Conner turned to go, he said "Coach…"

Coach Wright, who was now facing the team, turned back to him, a look of defiance on his face. "What!" he shouted.

"Don't fight them. It's not good for the university, the team, the players on both teams and the game." Then Conner turned and left. The coach said nothing but it was significant that he didn't get in the last word.

As Conner headed to the tunnel, he saw Esther. She had a puzzled look on her face, not understanding why he was going to the locker room. Was he hurt? He just shrugged. He seemed to be okay. She just waited. She did turn on her phone, though, just in case.

When he got to the locker room, he took off his singlet and was about to undress more fully when Coach Murphy came running in. "Listen, Conner, don't change just yet. Hang around here, please. I think that you made your point with the coach but he needs time to process it. He might ask you back out there."

"Thanks, Taylor. I appreciate what you did and what you're doing but I'm done for the night. If he is going after an eye for an eye, that's not something that I can do."

"But he's not. That's just it. He's a proud man but he's a reasonable man, too. Right after you left, he seemed to calm down and cancelled the hit on their guard. Then he went after the refs again. Maybe they'll get control of this game."

Conner thought about it and said "Let me pray about it. I'll either be here or not when you come back."

Coach Murphy wanted to debate this further but realized the futility of doing so. He nodded his understanding and left. Conner sat down at his locker. He heard someone in the next row of lockers. "That you, Eagle Eye?" he asked.

"Nope," came the reply and around the corner came a Catholic priest, a conclusion Conner surmised by seeing the collar the visitor wore.

"Sorry, father," he said.

"In more ways than one."

"What? I don't understand."

"In more ways than one. What, are you deaf, too?"

Conner was a little bit taken aback by such an aggressive response. "No, sir. I just didn't understand what you meant by that."

"In more ways than one. I'm father because of my collar but I'm also father because of my son."

"Aren't you a priest?"

"At the moment."

"At the moment?" Conner echoed, completely lost.

"But I am also your father," he added.

Conner was about to protest when he understood. God was visiting him.

"You're nuts," he said, not smiling.

The priest laughed. "Takes one to know one," he said in a totally childish rhythm.

Conner thought for a second, then asked "Did I do wrong?"

"No," came the unequivocal answer.

"Then what are you doing here?"

"Just offering a bit of unsolicited encouragement. I'm proud of what you did. You are modeling the best that man can model. Keep it up."

Conner didn't know what to say. Finally, he managed to get out a "Thanks."

"Don't mention it, my son," he said.

Just then, Eagle Eye appeared. Seeing the priest, he said "Father, I'm sorry, but you're not allowed in here."

"I was just taking confession from this young man," he said, pointing to Conner.

"Confession? Here?" Jake thought about it, then said "Well, you can't do it here. I'll get fired."

"You'll get fired if I take confession?"

Eagle Eye thought about it, clearly confused. "Yeah, I guess so," but it was clear that he was not certain.

"How about if I give him his last rites?" the priest playfully asked.

Conner jumped in. "Father," he said, leading him toward the exit, "I will stop by your parish later to confess and get last rites, if that's okay with you."

The attendant continued to stare at the two, perplexed about the priest and wondering why Conner was in the locker room, uninjured, during the game, much less being administered last rites. He said nothing.

Finally, with a wink, the priest left. Conner just shook his head and smiled. What a card, he thought. Conner didn't ponder very much longer as to whether to stay or leave. He felt he should wait for at least a little while.

The game on the local radio station was piped into the locker room. He sat and listened. After another hard foul, this one on Walker, the crowd erupted, as did Coach Wright. Conner was afraid that he would assign a hit man, much like the Temple coach had done years before and gotten into serious problems because of it. The game was halted while Walker, usually able to avoid such hits, remained down. The announcer said that he was conscious from the hit but that his shoulder appeared injured. From what Conner could make out, Walker had gone up for a rebound and been pounded by one of their players, much like a football end getting hit at the height of his jump as he tried to catch a pass. In fact, that was pretty much the explanation that the announcer gave. Eventually, Walker arose to the roar of the crowd and walked off. He was taken for x-rays. Conner could imagine the coach going ballistic after this. His two star players were not only out of this game but also out for weeks, maybe longer. Conner envisioned Coach Wright either in the refs' faces or looking for revenge. Surprisingly, neither happened.

One thing that Conner thought about was the crowd. This was a riot about to happen, yet the fans were controlled. He found out, much to his surprise, that it was the coach's doing. Once Walker had exited, the coach took the public address announcer's microphone and asked for silence. In a few seconds, Carlson Fieldhouse quieted.

"Ladies and gentlemen, this is unfortunate." He couldn't continue because of lots of yelling and booing. He raised his hand again and the fans quieted once more. "The game takes place on the court. We love your vocal support. Nothing else is acceptable." Again, more yelling. The coach repeated. "Nothing else is acceptable. We are Brantley University." From that, there erupted wonderful cheering. He had effectively defused a very volatile situation. He had turned anger into more positive energy.

Apparently, the refs had gotten the message and were blowing their whistles more often. Once the refs took charge of the fouling, Brantley caught up from a twelve-point deficit. At halftime, the score was 42-42. That was all well and good but both Kline and Walker had been pretty seriously injured. Even if no bones were broken, those kinds of injuries prevented a player from even practicing.

When the players started coming into the locker room, Conner was torn between leaving and staying.

He chose to stay, partly based on Coach Murphy's urging. They came in chattering about the several dirty plays from the first half. Nobody seemed surprised to see Conner still sitting there. The coach's office did not require him or his staff to go through the players' locker room. None of the coaches came in with the players.

Shedrick came over and sat down. "I thought that you might still be here," he said. "It was brutal out there."

"I heard," Conner responded. "Are you okay?"

"Oh, yeah. The coach put me in just when the refs were taking over. I didn't score but I didn't lose my head."

Conner smiled.

"It's unbelievable when a team plays like that," Shedrick commented, almost to himself more than to Conner.

"It is. For a basketball game, that was bad."

They shared silence, both thinking about the previous twenty minutes of basketball.

"You gonna stay?"

"I'll go into the halftime meeting and see what the coach says."

"Good idea."

A little while later, Coach Murphy leaned in and told everyone to go to the meeting room. When they were seated, Coach Wright came in.

He looked around, stopping at Conner. "You're not here," he said, at the same time motioning him to stay in his seat. Then he gave a wonderful I'm-proud-of-you speech that included his poor judgment. He was told that Walker had dislocated his shoulder and would be out for a while. Kline had a deep thigh bruise and that would probably mean similar time missed from practices and games.

"We didn't expect to get through this season without injuries. We also didn't expect to get them either this way or this early. Because we didn't retaliate," and here he looked briefly at Conner, "we have gained the respect of many, well beyond the confines of this arena. It was an important opportunity that we capitalized upon." He paused, then restarted. "Let me be perfectly clear on one thing. I don't want a bunch of babies on my team. I won't tolerate them. But, more importantly, I want us to do what is right. Our legacy transcends the results of one game or one season. Don't get me wrong. I want to win this and every game we play. I want us to be known as a tough team. But, most of all, I want us to be known as great representatives of the game and the university."

He looked around. All eyes were on him.

"Do I make myself clear?"

"Yes, coach!" came the response, almost a cheer.

"Okay, you yokels, complete what you have to do and get out on the floor. We have some unfinished business to take care of."

The players stood up and went to the locker room.

"Ramsey!" called the coach. "My office," he tersely said. Conner followed him.

When they got there, the coach walked around to his side of the table and sat down, at the same time telling Conner to close the door. Conner did as he was told and sat down, too.

"I've got a problem," the coach began. "On the one hand, I can't have players telling me what to do or not do." He paused. "On the other hand, I have to admire your stance on this. I was somewhat out of control. Burning some extra energy on you put me back on the right path."

Conner said nothing.

"If I let you come back for the second half, I lose some of my sting. If I don't, I lose…" He let the rest just tail off. "What do you think I should do?" he surprisingly asked.

Conner tightened his lips, lifted his eyebrows and slightly shrugged his shoulders.

"Yeah, I shouldn't be asking you." He was quiet while he thought about what he wanted to do. "Okay, I think that it's right over might," he concluded. "Come join us," he finished. "Now get out of here."

Conner left smiling…and admiring the coach for making this difficult decision.

Chapter 35

The teams came out at roughly the same time, each through a different tunnel. As soon as the first Eagle hit the court, the fans applauded wildly. Some, still angry at the injuries, yelled for them to retaliate. Most, though, were appreciative of how they had behaved.

The coach of the Coyotes came over to Coach Wright as soon as the teams had come back into

Carlson Fieldhouse. They shook and held hands as the visiting coach said something to Coach Wright. The home coach didn't say anything, only nodding his head. At the end, both went back to their respective benches.

When Conner came back on the court, the first person he saw was Esther. She was ecstatic to see him. Like a little girl, she brought her hands to her chin, her arms pressed against her chest, her smile as big as Texas. Conner smiled at her. What a princess, he thought.

The next person he saw was Richard Means, the journalist. He looked like he had a big question mark on his face. He was wearing his press pass and he put out his arms, palms up, signifying 'What's going on?' Conner smiled at him, too.

And the third person he saw was Jeremy Wingman, aka Winger, from the fellowship group. Conner and he just exchanged looks, Conner ending it with a wink and a smile. Winger didn't know how to act, although he was dressed in avid fan attire.

Coach Wright huddled up the players. "Their coach came over and apologized for the injuries, saying that nothing had been intended. I didn't say anything to him. The league and public opinion will decide. That's not our business. Our business is winning and this game is a long way from over."

He looked over at Conner, then returned his attention to the team. "I reconsidered my actions regarding Ramsey. This will be the only time that I am wrong this entire season. Now that we have it out of the way, you can rely on me to make perfect decisions."

Everyone smiled.

"Enough about that. Same three starters plus Ramsey and Harris. Play hard, play clean. No second chances." Here he pointed to Forrester, Obumje and Dixon. They all nodded their understanding. "Let's go get 'em. Eagles on three."

Everyone put his hand into the huddle and broke with the refrain.

Shedrick walked over to Conner. "Same deal?" he asked. "Press the outside shot and force the inside drive?"

"Yeah, let's do it. And one other thing."

"What?"

"Watch yourself on breakaways. This isn't the cleanest team in the land. I don't want to have to pray over you again," he said smiling.

Shedrick just nodded.

There was no contrition on the face of the Coyotes. If their coach had really apologized to Coach Wright, it didn't look as though he had passed along a change of plans to his players. Conner looked at them. They were huge…in both directions.

The Eagles inbounded to start the second half and Shedrick brought the ball up. The cheerleaders near one of the baskets were chanting their inspiration. The crowd wasn't too loud, paying attention to how this new backcourt would do. They passed the ball around and Forrester, usually not a scorer, got an open look inside. He made the easy layup and got banged doing so. The crowd responded angrily, although it was a reasonable foul. Forrester's strength allowed him to sustain the hit and still sink the basket. He made the foul shot. 45-42.

Conner hadn't watched much of the first half. Therefore, he didn't know who was who on the Coyotes. He let Shedrick pick his man. Conner's man brought the ball up. Clearly, like virtually all major college guards, he was a good dribbler. As he crossed half court, Conner picked him up. The smirk on the guard's face was insulting. He began to hold his hand up to call a play when Conner stepped in, took the ball mid-bounce and dribbled for an uncontested layup. The crowd loved it. 47-42.

As might be expected, the same guard wanted to provide some payback. When he got the ball, he confidently signaled everyone to not only go forward but to park themselves on the right side of the court. He was going to handle this himself. Only Forrester did not go with his man, ready underneath to defend his basket.

Conner, not one for showboating, decided that this would be a good opportunity to show something special. Instead of waiting for the guard to reach half court, Conner picked him up at his foul line. This was going to be mano-a-mano. Conner decided not to steal the ball. Instead, he was going to pin the guard in the Coyotes side of the court, perhaps drawing a foul. Each time the guard tried to turn, Conner was there. It was as though the guard was being double or triple teamed. With no place to go and nobody on his team available, he drew a ten second violation. He slammed the ball down, thus drawing a technical on top of it. The crowd absolutely reveled in this. Shedrick made the foul, then inbounded to Conner, it not being contested by the other team. Conner got it to Obumje in the corner for a smooth three pointer. 51-42.

The Coyotes called time out. As Conner ran back to the bench, he did it with his head down, wanting to exhibit appropriate modesty. Also, he felt wonderful inside and he wanted to reflect on the moment. Everyone else stood up and shared high fives with the starters as they sat down. The crowd was now raucous, although in a good way. The noise was nearly deafening.

"Good," was all Coach Wright said. "Very good." Forrester had a huge smile on his face, as did Obumje. Shedrick was jamming to the music being played. "Harris!" called out the coach in not his most friendly tone. "If you want to try out for the cheerleading squad, be my guest. Otherwise, pay attention."

"Yes, coach," he said, hunching his shoulders a bit.

Conner stifled a laugh. Cheerleaders. He'd save that reminder for later.

"Hands in," was all the coach said, having nothing to add to the nine-zero start of the second half. Conner reminded his big men to box their big men out, allowing for no second looks. They all nodded, not insulted to be getting on-the-court advice from one of their own. Actually, they liked the way Conner stepped up to do this.

When they walked back out, the guard who had gotten a technical was nodding his head, looking at Conner. "We'll see," was all he said. "We'll see," he repeated.

Conner reminded himself of his mission.

The Coyotes brought the ball up and Conner picked him up at reasonable three-point range. He passed it to the other guard. Shedrick gave him no room to shoot. Back and forth it went between them before Conner stepped in. He intercepted the ball and, in what seemed like a single motion, fed Shedrick who had taken off like a jackrabbit. A beautiful two-handed dunk brought the advantage to eleven and the crowd to an even higher level of excitement.

Conner told himself not to look around. He didn't want this to be about him but, instead, about what he drew from a greater power. Looking around would have been ego driven. At least he thought that it might be seen as such, much like the players who pounded their chests after a big play, especially in basketball and football.

The next time that the visitors brought the ball up court, they decided to give the other guard an opportunity to turn the tide, such that it was. Shedrick closed off his outside shot. When he decided to drive, Shedrick forced him toward the center of the court. Conner again stole the ball and led Shedrick for another dunk, this one with plenty of showmanship as he spun around and dunked it over his head. Needless to say, the hootin' and hollerin' that this brought out of the crowd was stuff one would likely find in sports movies.

Not having scored in the half brought determination and frustration to the visitors. Once again, the other guard held the ball with Shedrick very nearly draped all over him. And, once again, he drove toward the center. This time, though, he figured that he could draw Conner and pass to the other guard. Conner saw it coming, took the pass and threw the ball softly down court. Shedrick was the only one who had a chance for it. Retrieving it at the foul line, he leaped without dribbling and slammed down a one-handed windmill dunk. Conner smiled and the crowd cheered like it was a slam dunk contest. The Eagles had scored fifteen unanswered points to begin the second half and the score was 57-42.

Conner was somewhat surprised that the Coyotes did not take a time out. Instead, the two guards walked up court talking with one another, one dribbling the ball. One was shaking his head until he was motioned away by the other, that being the one Conner guarded. At half court, he passed to his backcourt mate, then called for the ball back. Now he stood too far away to shoot but with the ability to dribble, if he wished. The ref did not count to five seconds because Conner had drawn back. For one thing, Conner figured he was too far out to shoot. For another, there was no longer any need for Conner to take over the game. The lead was now sufficient.

The other guard went to the opposite corner and motioned the other three Coyotes to him. They followed. The Eagles defenders, growing more confident in Conner, went over to the corner, as well. The crowd grew silent. Apparently, this guard still believed he could go one on one with Conner. However, instead of driving, the guard took a wild three-point shot. In fact, he was so far from the three-point line that the rules should have given him four points, had he made it. He didn't. It was an air ball all the way, taking one bounce in court and going into the front row.

"Air ball. Air ball," came the merciless chant. "Air ball. Air ball," they continued in mocking fashion.

The visiting team's coach called a time out just as someone in the stands tossed the ball back onto the court. Nine players had turned to go to their benches. The tenth player, the guard who had just shot the air ball and was being harassed mercilessly by the fans, caught the ball as it bounced toward center court. He then took it and, like a baseball player, threw it forward. Conner was now crossing the foul line, looking up for Esther to share a smile, when the ball hit him flush on the side of the face. He went down immediately.

Chapter 36

To his credit, the guard who threw the ball either didn't mean to do that or immediately regretted his action. No matter, the damage had been done. As soon as Conner hit the floor, the player ran over to him, kneeling at his side. When Shedrick turned to see Conner sprawled on the floor, he rushed over. Sensing that the other player had done something, but not having seen it, he moved him aside brusquely and took Conner's limp hand. An instantaneous silence had come over the crowd.

The trainer jumped out and, as luck would have it, the team's primary physician happened to be at ringside for this game. They both pushed their way into the circle of players that had formed around Conner. People in the stands were blocked from seeing anything because of the players. Esther watched, almost without breathing. She had seen the entire thing.

The player who had thrown the ball still remained nearby. However, when the players from the bench came on the floor, several of them witnessing what had happened, they shoved him away in no polite manner. It was a credit to them that one of them did not take a swing at him. The player made his way back to his team. The refs, meanwhile, were trying to determine what had happened and what was fitting action for them to take. They assembled and discussed it. One of the three had seen what had happened but was unsure if it was intentional. No matter, argued the head referee. Technical foul, ejection for the player and game warning to the team. One referee explained their decision to the scorer's table while the other two went to each coach.

The Coyotes coach was talking to his players, having already sent the problem maker to the locker room. On his way, he was pelted with soda, programs and language unfit for children. Fortunately, nobody threw anything more dangerous. When the head referee came to the coach, he stepped back from the team, listened and acknowledged the decision.

When the other referee tried to speak with Coach Wright, he probably wished that he had been given another assignment. Coach Wright, additionally frustrated at not being able to do anything for Conner, stood up and gave the referee an earful. And it was an elephant's ear.

"Had you been thinking about the game instead of yourself or what you were going to drink later on, you would have realized that this was out of hand from the get go. Now I have one player with a broken leg, another with a dislocated shoulder and the third lying here unconscious. What the heck were you thinking? What would it have taken to get you to manage this game? I can tell you that this is not the end of my complaints. The way I feel right now, I would seek to have the three of you banned from the sport. This is unforgivable, undeniably unforgivable."

To his credit, the referee said nothing, choosing not to defend their actions or to give the coach a technical foul for abusing the officials. He let the coach vent and then told him what the on-the-court decision had been regarding fouls.

"You think that will bring back these three players? And they're each a star on this team. You think that a technical and an ejection will suffice? You guys are morons, total morons." With that, the coach turned back to those who were taking care of Conner. The referee tried to say something, holding the coach's arm. Coach Wright shrugged the hand off of his arm and disregarded the referee. Again, to his credit, the referee decided to ignore the insult and returned to his two compatriots.

Conner still lay unconscious and a stretcher was rolled out. The crowd was silent, except for periodic moments when someone would yell something abusive to the visitors. Others would try to shhh the shouter, it sometimes working, sometimes not.

Coach Wright was sensing that something ugly might happen. Once again, he went to the scorer's table and took the microphone.

"Ladies and gentlemen," he began, not significantly having to wait until conversations had died down. "Thank you for your passion and your restraint. There's not a one of us who isn't boiling mad. However, I implore you *not* to take this out on our visitors or the referees. Let him who is without fault cast the first stone," he said, paraphrasing a Jesus quote. "Please contain yourself. I am certain that Conner would want your prayers, not your revenge. If you have it on your heart, please pray for him." Then he replaced the microphone and walked back to the circle of people standing around Conner. The fans applauded. Well, most of them did. A few still wanted to share their incensed opinions.

Shedrick, feeling a kaleidoscope of emotions, was a bundle of nerves and energy, particularly frustrated at not being able to do anything to help his friend. Finally, he stood up and motioned to the prayer pilgrims. He pointed to the foul circle and they started walking over there. When the other Eagles players saw what they were about to do, they joined as a show of team unity. Coach Wright and his assistants went over, as well.

Then, in an extremely surprising move, many of the Coyotes players, having heard about the team's ritual, joined the group. It was a large circle and many in the stands were crying, both for Conner but also for the display taking place right before them. It was a sight to behold. Still, some of the visiting players did not join, including their coaches.

Shedrick did not have Conner to conduct this prayer gathering. In respect to his friend, he led it. His prayer glorified the Lord, thanked the Lord and asked for health to be restored to his friend. His voice broke a couple of times but he managed to stumble through it. The way that the Eagles and Coyotes put their arms around one another to form the circle was somewhat of a miracle in and of itself. When he was done, the players returned to their benches.

By this time, Conner had been revived but was still lying prone on the ground. Everyone but those attending to him and the head coach had been instructed to move away and give him room. Thus, most of the fans could now see him.

For safety's sake, the doctor put his neck in a brace and then instructed the appropriate personnel to gently lift him onto the stretcher. Carlson Fieldhouse was completely silent as all eyes were trained on what was taking place with the injured player. Once on the stretcher, it was raised to rolling height and the medical personnel started to take it toward the exit.

As the stretcher reached the foul line, Conner raised his hand and gave a thumbs up. The explosion of love was palpable as was the roar from all. In a surprising display, fans started hugging. Most knew that they had just witnessed something special.

----- ----- -----

"You are extremely lucky," the doctor said, once Conner had been taken to the hospital, x-rayed and MRI'ed. "Getting a blow of that magnitude on the temple very likely could have killed you. As it is, you have a concussion." The only other person in the room was Coach Wright.

"How bad, doc?" Conner asked.

"Bad enough to prevent you from playing basketball for a while but likely not bad enough to have caused permanent damage. Quite frankly, from what I heard about what happened, I'm surprised that it isn't much worse. You're pretty lucky," he repeated.

"Maybe so," Conner said. "Maybe protected," he added.

The doctor either did not hear or chose to ignore his comment.

"What actually happened?" Conner asked. "All of a sudden I was looking at a bunch of folks standing over me. Did I pass out or…what?"

The coach answered. "One of their players threw the ball like a baseball and hit you flush on the side of the head. You went down like a sack of potatoes."

"He did what? Why?"

"He was frustrated."

"He meant to hit me with the ball while I wasn't looking?"

"We don't know his intent but we do know what happened."

"Surprising," Conner commented without malice.

The doctor jumped back in. "It's bed rest until your head doesn't throb. Then it's walking around. I want to see you in two days and hear from you earlier if your headaches are really bad. I am not giving you painkilling medicine. I don't want to mask anything. Your staying still will be the best thing you can do to minimize the discomfort. Any questions?"

"Just one, sir," he said. "Do I take it that I am free to leave now?"

"Good thing that you have a hard head," the doctor smiled when answering. "Yes, I think that it will be okay. Do you have someone who will be with you?"

"Well, my roomie will be available after the game."

The coach laughed. "Maybe your brain is scrambled," he said. It's 2:30 in the morning and the game has been over for a while."

"Did we win?"

"If you look at what happened to you, Kline and Walker, we lost. If you look at the score, we won by sixteen points."

"Well, that's the bright side," Conner said.

"Yeah, great," the coach said, with all the glee that was applicable for the moment. "Anyhow, Harris is outside and he'll be your babysitter for a while."

"Oh, lucky him."

Harris was signaled to come into the room.

"How ya doin', roomie?" he asked.

"I understand that we're off liquor shots and marijuana for a while."

Shedrick took a quick look at the coach and then at the doctor. Determining this all to be a joke, he joined in. "Yeah, but just for a little while."

Conner started to laugh, then grabbed his head. He realized that he was going to have some headache whoppers for a while, if this was representative of what was going to happen.

The doctor concluded with "I'll sign you out. Be certain to make an appointment with me in two days. And, remember, contact me immediately if you throw up or have any additional symptoms."

"Thanks, Doc," Conner said as the physician left.

Slowly, Conner struggled to sit up. Both Shedrick and the coach helped him. When he was sitting up, he realized that he was going to need help for more than the simplest things.

"Hey, Shedrick," he said.

"What?"

"I'm sorry."

"For what?"

"For what you're gonna have to do to tend to me."

"Listen, I don't change no diapers," he said with his gangster accent.

"Cagney."

"DeNiro," Shedrick corrected.

"Cagney by a mile."

The coach let them banter for a while, then looked at Shedrick: "Go get the car. I'll help with the checkout and bring him downstairs."

"Meet at the front? At the circular drive?"

"Yeah. That'll work."

After all was said and done, Shedrick and Conner arrived at their dorm room at 4:00 in the morning. Taped to the door was a note. Shedrick took it off the door and read it. "Call me, Mr. Seven. That's all it says."

Conner smiled. By 4:30 he was washed and in bed. His head pounded but he was in his own bed. "Ahhh," he said out loud and managed to fall asleep.

Chapter 37

Conner, normally a very early riser, didn't wake up until nearly 10:00 AM. He opened his eyes and sat up. Well, he tried to sit up. That's when he remembered that last night had not been a dream. In fact, it had been an episode in his life that he just as soon would have liked to skip. He sat on the edge of his bed and wished he had sunglasses.

He was finally able to stand up and make his way into the bathroom. When he was done, he opened the bathroom door and there, on his bed, sat Shedrick, Obumje and Dixon. Each one had a smile larger than the guy next to him.

"Ta da!!!" they exclaimed together.

"You look like a commercial for ugly teeth," Conner said.

"Nice to see you, too," Obumje said.

"I wish that I could attribute this headache to you, my friend. If I could, your leaving would make me feel a lot better."

They all laughed. It was obvious that Conner was in no position to be jostled around. They remained seated.

Dixon held up a section of the Sunday newspaper. It was the sports section of the *Sentinel* and blazoned across the front page was the headline 'Ugly Scene, Serious Injuries.'

Conner squinted at it, then started to amble across the room in baby steps to retrieve it.

"Just stay there," Dixon said. "We'll give you the Cliffs Notes."

"Maybe a better idea," Conner said, sitting down at his desk.

"The reporter called the game 'the worst reflection of sports' that he had ever seen." Dixon emphasized the part that he literally quoted.

"Wow," commented Conner.

"He really read the Coyotes team the riot act, especially lambasting the coach who could have put a stop to it early, even if he had been the one to come up with the 'rough and tumble' strategy. He goes on to offer a few choice words about the coach."

"I can imagine," Conner said.

"Then he gets into the player who threw the ball. In my mind, he spends far too much time wondering whether or not the action was intentional. The player did not come out for a post-game interview which the reporter says is 'unforgivable but expected from that team' but issues a written apology...written on what looked like a scrap piece of paper and read by their team captain. It was pretty lame."

"Did Means quote it?"

"Means?"

"The reporter."

"Oh, yeah. He does." Dixon said nothing, apparently silently reading it or some other part of the article.

"And?" Conner prompted.

"Oh. Sorry. Here it is. 'I apologize for my behavior. It came out of a moment of frustration. There is no excuse for it. I apologize to my coach, to my team, to the Brantley University Eagles and to their fans. Whatever the penalty determined by my University or the league, I fully accept it.' Here's the thing that riles me," Dixon said. "Nowhere does he either apologize to you or wish you well. What the blankety-blank was he thinking?"

"Blankety-blank?" Shedrick and Obumje said at the same time.

"Substitute whatever word you wish," Dixon responded. He continued. "The article goes on to skewer the other team, even suggesting that its basketball season should be cancelled."

"That's too harsh," Conner said. "They'll learn from it."

All three sets of eyes turned to Conner as though he had just said the craziest thing. To them, his compassion was misplaced.

"What are you talking about?" Shedrick asked. "They've ruined your and our season."

"Ever make a mistake?" Conner asked.

"Uh, oh. Here comes a sermon," Shedrick said good-humoredly.

Conner ignored him. "If God gives us mercy and grace, the least we can do is pass it along, don't you think?"

"Yes," Shedrick answered, "except to this guy and this team."

Conner started to shake his head, then recognized that doing this would not be a good idea. He stopped and tried to stay stock still.

"Listen, guys, I'm really not up to this discussion. I just ask that you pray for this player. I'm sure that he will suffer with what he did longer than me."

"Oh, for crying out loud," Shedrick said. "You're such a goody two shoes."

"And you're such a kill-'em-and-eat-'em person." Everyone laughed.

"I'll read the rest later. Thanks for bringing it up, though."

"Ya want us to bring you back something from the cafeteria?" Obumje inquired.

"I'm not really hungry," Conner said, "but thanks."

"Ya want *anything*?" Dixon asked.

"A new head."

"Too late. God only gives one to a person," Shedrick responded.

"Except in your case, roomie."

The other two athletes on the bed all leaned back as though hit by a wave and went "Whoa!!!"

"Guess you're feeling better, roomie," Shedrick said, glad to be insulted under these circumstances.

"I guess I do. Thanks for coming over," he said to Obumje and Dixon. "How are Kline and Walker?"

"Not too good, from what we hear. Kline's bruise is of the deep muscle variety, although he didn't break any bones. He is on crutches. Nobody is certain when he'll return but good money says that he won't even practice for two weeks. Walker has a shoulder separation with some associated tendon damage. He's cooked for weeks."

"Golly," Conner said. "What a mess. How's the coach doing? He was with me…with us until nearly 4:00 this morning when we got home. What a good guy. Tough exterior but he really cares, you know?"

The other three made various affirmations of that statement.

"Guess I'm not going to church this morning," Conner said.

"Guess not," Shedrick answered. "How can we fill your need?"

"Oh, that's okay."

"No, really. How can we fill your need?"

"Gee, that's really nice. Could we read something from Proverbs?"

"Which something did you have in mind?"

"Read today's date."

"What?"

"Today's date. There are thirty-one chapters in Proverbs. You can always read one. Read today's date."

"Oh, I get it," Dixon said. This being the sixth day of the month, he opened to Proverbs 6. Shedrick, Dixon and Obumje took turns reading it. Every once in a while, they would stop and discuss a verse or two. It took them about forty minutes to read through it. When they had finished, they all commented how much they enjoyed that.

"We should do it more frequently," Obumje said.

"Amen to that," Conner said. "Let's do it every Sunday, if not much more often."

Conner grabbed his head.

"You okay, roomie?"

"Yeah. Yeah. I think that I'll get some water and then lie back down."

"Good idea. We gotta go, anyhow." Obumje and Dixon stood up. "Call if you need anything. They looked at Conner, then at Shedrick. They touched fists and left.

"Holler if you need something," Shedrick said as he stood up.

"Thanks, my friend."

"Nuthin' to it."

----- ----- -----

"Esther? Conner."

"Oh, I'm glad to hear from you. I just walked in from church."

"I hope that you prayed for my headaches."

"I definitely prayed for your headaches…and all your other self, as well."

"Thanks."

"What's the verdict?"

"I got your note last night, er, this morning, but it was 4:00 AM and I didn't think a call would have been appreciated at that time."

"I would happily have awakened but I understand. How are you?"

"Concussion. Headaches. And I'm walking like a man who is 10,000 years old."

"That's pretty old."

"Maybe, but I now know how it feels."

They both laughed lightly.

"Are you able to get out, even go to classes?"

"I do plan to go to classes. At least to try. Otherwise, no basketball or anything else."

"I can imagine how you feel."

"Heck, I couldn't even play pool if I wanted."

"I know. I had a concussion once."

"You did?"

"I was a catcher on our high school softball team and a batter's follow through was exaggerated. She caught me toward the back of the helmet and totally knocked me out. It wasn't as bad as yours since I was wearing a helmet but I didn't feel too good for a couple of days."

"And…?"

"I recovered completely, as will you."

"Good. I need a positive prognosis."

"When do you go to the doctor?"

"I'll go tomorrow."

"Can I take you?"

"You'll make my roomie jealous."

"Tell him he can tag along as a chaperone."

"Nah."

She laughed and he smiled.

"I'll call you when I set the appointment. Is there a time that works best for you?"

"Afternoon, but I'm okay with skipping class if I have to."

"It's the beginning of classes! You can't start skipping already."

"Just watch me."

"I'll make sure that it's in the afternoon. That works better for me, too."

"Let me know. Now take it easy today. If you need something, just holler."

"I'll holler anyhow."

"Bye, Seven."

"Bye, Sevenette."

They both laughed, knowing the genealogy of that exchange.

Chapter 38

Conner propped his pillow up on his bed, took the *Sentinel* and gingerly settled down to read the entire article. Interestingly enough, it was a combination of news reporting and editorial. The reporting part told about the inspired play of the team, the injury to Kline, the different injury to Walker, and the inexcusable injury to Conner. 'Of all the players on the court,' it read, 'Ramsey was the one least deserving and, being in his thirties, least prepared.' After a few more lines, Means wrote 'This is deserving of a charge of assault and battery, as well as a personal lawsuit against both the player and the school. However, as I get to know Conner Ramsey, there is no way that he will be a party to either. It's more likely that he will say it was an accident and move on past it.'

Conner fished around until he found the business card for which he was looking. He dialed the number on it.

"*Sentinel.* Means."

"Conner Ramsey."

"Ramsey!" the reporter exploded. He had been sitting at his desk with his feet up. When he heard the name of the caller, he not only took his feet off the table but stood straight up. "How the heck are you?"

"I've got a Grade A headache but, other than that, I'm okay."

"I heard that it was much more than a headache. How about a concussion?"

"That's docspeak. To me, it's a headache."

"Did they say how long you'll be out?"

"No. I go to the doctor tomorrow. We'll see. Right now, even walking hurts. Listen, I just wanted to call to say thank you for the article. You are definitely painting me in too good of a light. But, of course, I appreciate it."

"I'm not sure that it's too good of a light. You seem to be doing all the right things."

"Lucky, I guess."

"Right," Means said sarcastically.

A brief bit of silence was shared.

"Can I come over and continue our dialogue?"

"Hey, I appreciate it and want to help but, right now, I'm not up for it. I was just calling to thank you for the article."

"Can I call or come by tomorrow?"

"Why don't you call me late afternoon tomorrow and I'll let you know how it's going. Fair enough?"

"Fair enough. And, if you need anything or think of something worthwhile, call me."

"I've got your number."

"Great. Feel better."

"Thanks. Bye."

"Bye."

Conner set his pillow flat on his bed and, again gingerly, moved his body in order to lie down. He turned off his phone and quickly fell asleep. His dream, which he remembered pretty well when he got up later, was of a swing in the sky. He was on it. The swing was not attached to anything but there was no fear of falling. The sky was a striking blue. The clouds were beautifully shaped and spaced.

People he knew would walk past him, seemingly on air, although it all felt perfectly natural. They would either say hello, as in a quick passing salutation, or stop and chat with him, although he did not remember any of the conversations, not even the topics. Those he remembered from the dream were in his current life but he also saw some from his past, including some of his relatives who were no longer living. Everybody was smiling. He wondered why his brother had not been among the passersby. Maybe Conner had missed seeing him.

Just before he awoke, toward what he later thought might have been the end of the dream, he was smiling at everyone when one rope on his swing broke. It happened so quickly that he didn't have a chance to hold onto the side that remained connected. He freefell for a while and then landed softly in the arms of someone but he could not see who it was. Whoever it was, he was not only large by people's standards but immense by any standards. He made the Lincoln Memorial statue seem small by comparison. This person's hands gently placed him on the ground and then this rescuer disappeared.

As Conner looked around, he realized that he was in an open-air arena and that there were thousands upon thousands of spectators, many more than at any sports or concert event. They were all quiet, waiting for him to speak. As he was about to address them, he woke up.

----- ----- -----

When Conner awoke, he dragged himself to his desk and began to read. At first, it was tough. The light was too bright. The print was too small. It was too warm in the room. His head hurt. And a number of other things were interfering. Conner stopped and bowed his head. He told the Lord that he was sorry about complaining and would will himself to do better. He apologized for the injury and hoped, actually expected, God to use it for better purposes. When he had finished praying, he felt considerably better and was able to accomplish quite a bit.

At 6:00 PM, Shedrick showed up with a tray of food for Conner. Not certain what his roomie might want or be able to eat, he had brought enough to feed an army. It included hot soup, salad, grilled chicken, mashed potatoes, broccoli, fish, boiled new potatoes, peas, bread and two types of dessert, peach pie and pistachio pudding.

"Here ya go!" he said as he set the overladen tray on Conner's desk.

"Are you nuts?" Conner asked. "Is half of this yours?"

"No, I ate. That wouldn't have been enough for me anyhow," he jested.

"What a comedian. You're a riot, Alice," he added, taking a line out of the *Honeymooners*, then remembering that it was one of the TV shows that The Man upstairs had indicated was a favorite of his.

"Hey, I didn't know what you wanted. I just tried to give you some choices."

Conner realized that he was acting like a spoiled brat. Here his roomie had gone out of his way to be nice and all Conner could do was kid him. He readjusted his attitude. "Hey, my friend, thanks a lot. You're really good to me and I'm sorry to be such a pain. I really appreciate you."

Shedrick stopped what he was doing, which, at the moment, was taking things from the tray and placing them around Conner's desk. Conner could see that Shedrick was visibly touched by the thanks. "You are more than welcome, my friend. I don't want anything happening to you, for loads of reasons."

"And those would be?" Conner asked jokingly.

"Well, you get me easy points on the court." Then he stopped and pretended to be deep in thought.

"Come on, come on," Conner humorously gigged him.

"And you get me easy points on the court," Shedrick repeated playfully.

"I guess that you've got at least one good reason, except that I won't be getting you easy points for a number of games to come."

"I'll wait," Shedrick said.

"If you're not nice to me…"

"Don't even go there. I can still poison you."

They both laughed. Later, they watched some TV in the common room before turning in.

"Sleep tight, my friend," Conner said.

"You, too. If you need anything, just holler."

"Gotcha," and they went their respective ways.

----- ----- -----

On Monday, Conner still had a pretty good headache. He drank a lot of water, thinking that it might help. As soon as he could do so, he called for an appointment with the doctor from the hospital. He was able to slide into a recently-vacated spot at 1:00 PM. Perfect timing, he thought to himself. Class, lunch and ample time to get there. He remembered, too, that Esther had volunteered to take him.

He wondered if he should go to the morning practice, just to offer support. However, by the time that he awoke, it would have been too late to get there for the beginning. He didn't want to break the momentum of the practice. He chose not to go. Maybe tomorrow.

Realizing that he still couldn't walk fast because the bouncing accentuated the pain in his head, he left very early to make it to his class. Even with that early departure, he barely made it in time. He wore dark sunglasses because the outside light really penetrated his eyes. He also wore a hat to further lessen the light.

When he walked into the room, the professor was already there and about to begin. Everyone turned to him and, spontaneously, broke into applause. Conner smiled, acknowledging this show of affection. "Thank you," he said softly and took a seat next to Esther, one that she had saved for him.

"And how are you feeling?" asked Professor Bags.

"Like someone hit me with a basketball when I wasn't looking."

Everyone laughed.

"...but I can't remember."

And everyone took their laughter to the next level.

"Just so we are clear," the professor said, "you are still responsible for all the work, remembering it or not."

"Oh, well. A guy can try, can't he?"

"Perhaps elsewhere," responded the professor, with a smile. Then he turned to the business at hand and the class session turned out to be very productive. Conner forgot about his ailments and spent the entire session engrossed in the professor's primary topic, fundamental Judaism. He found it fascinating, as did everyone else attending. The questions flowed energetically. Two of the students were Jewish, although reformed. Many of the questions were able to be answered by them. However, they couldn't answer some of the more complex questions that might only have been known by someone who was conservative or even orthodox. Where the questions went unanswered by the students, Professor Bags was able to provide the information. What everyone loved was the story-like way he provided the answers. He didn't just give facts. Instead, he painted beautiful word pictures, consequently allowing the students to not only 'see' the answers but more easily remember them.

After class, as Esther was walking with Conner – slowly – he said "That Professor Bags is really something. He's great, isn't he?"

"Definitely," she said, wanting to offer to carry his books but not wishing to insult him. She chose to remain silent about it. "He's really engaging. I just love the way that he tells stories about everything. It brings each topic to life, in many instances making me feel like I'm right there or that it happened just yesterday."

"Yeah, me too," Conner agreed as they made their way to the exit. Fortunately, this class was on the main floor. There were no elevators or stairs with which to contend. Conner hated elevators unless there were four or more flights going up or he was dressed up, which was virtually never the case.

"Are we going to head off to the doctor?" she asked.

"Head off, yes. Speed there, no."

"I knew that," she chided. "I wasn't exactly going to race you."

He smiled as they walked along. His headache seemed to be subsiding, although he wondered if the wonderful distraction of this attraction was more the cause. No matter. He was happy with the result.

"If it's okay with you, Esther, let's find his office and then eat something nearby."

"Sounds like a plan," she responded.

After much longer than it would have taken under normal circumstances, they made it to her car. She offered to help him in but he politely refused. "Esther, I really appreciate what you are doing. I just have some headaches. I'm okay and I'm getting better with each passing hour. If I need you, I won't hesitate to ask. Okay?"

"That's good for me, Conner. You let me know."

When they drove past the doctor's office, they were comfortable knowing their destination for 1:00 PM. Next came determining where to eat. They had about 45 minutes to grab a bite.

"I know just the place," she said, "if you are in the mood for pizza."

"If they can make it, I can eat it," he responded. "Paraphrasing Will Rogers, I never met a pizza that I didn't want to eat."

"Not very discerning, are we?" she countered.

"Not when it comes to pizza," he said. "I looove pizza."

"Apparently."

At that very moment, she pulled into a parking spot right in front of Bruno's Pizza.

"Is this the place?" he asked.

"No. I'd prefer to take you to Chung's Dry Cleaning," she said with good-natured mocking, pointing to the retail establishment next door.

"Yum. I looove Korean pizza," he offered, displaying a big smile.

"That's good, 'cause they'll clean your taste buds. Need help getting out?"

"Nope. I'm good to go. I'm just gonna follow my nose."

Once seated in Bruno's, his phone rang, although it was in vibrate mode. "Mind if I answer this? It's Shedrick."

"Go ahead," she said. "I'll use the washroom meanwhile."

He stood up as she arose. "Silly," she said to him, although she appreciated it.

"Hello?" Conner answered into his cell phone.

"Where are you?" Shedrick asked.

"In Bruno's Pizza, pretty close to the doctor's office."

"I thought that I was gonna take you to the doctor," Shedrick said, although without being accusatory.

"I'm sorry," Conner said genuinely. "I must have gotten my wires crossed. I thought that I had mentioned that Esther was going to take me. Maybe not. I really didn't mean to take you for granted...and don't want to do that ever."

To Shedrick's credit, he took the high road. "Maybe I missed that message. She's probably loads prettier, anyhow."

"That she is," Conner said with a smile into the phone, "but it doesn't justify my taking you for granted, which I didn't mean to do," he repeated.

"How's the pizza?" Shedrick asked, letting it go.

"We haven't ordered yet. I'll let you know."

"I hope that it's great. I looove good pizza."

"We are definitely roomies."

"Huh?"

"I'll tell you later. I'll see you after the doctor's appointment."

"Okay. I'll have my phone with me. Enjoy lunch. And enjoy Miss Lovely."

"Both, I hope."

As they went to prayer, Esther asked if she could offer it. Conner was delighted and she delivered a wonderful prayer, one that focused on God and asked for much more than just the world that impacted the two of them. He thanked Esther, telling her how touching that was. She shrugged her shoulders modestly.

The pizza was great. It was prepared New York style, just the way that Conner enjoyed. They got a medium with sausage and mushrooms. He ate like a man who hadn't eaten in days.

"Wow," she said. "I take it that you approve of my pizza suggestion."

"Nah," he said. "I'm just hungry." Then he winked at her and her infectious smile showed up. Although he hadn't known her for very long, there were things he was beginning to really cherish. One of them was her smile.

In between mouthfuls, Conner answered her questions about what he remembered on the court, what took place at the hospital, how he felt now and if he harbored any anger toward the player who had hit him with the ball. For the most part, he couldn't give her details because he didn't have more than vague memories. She filled in what she had observed. He said, with as much of a smile as he could muster with his mouth full of pizza, that he was feeling stronger "with each bite." As for whether or not he was angry at the other player, he gave that one considerably more thought.

"I'm sorry that he did it. I'm guessing that he feels terrible. Although I'll recover, he may keep the bad memory and, perhaps, receive repercussions that will last him appreciably longer. I guess that I'm not mad at him, per se. I can't believe that he would have done that on purpose. It was probably a moment of frustration that ended up much worse than he intended."

"I think that you're kinder than I would have been under these conditions."

"Maybe, but I doubt it. I think that you see the big picture. His act may have made for a better purpose."

She sat silent for a few moments, then said "Like Joseph."

"Joseph?" Conner asked, not understanding about whom she was speaking.

"Jacob's son," she clarified. "When he unveiled himself to his brothers."

"Oh, yeah. Right. He told them that they intended harm but God had good purpose in what transpired. Well, I hardly qualify to play the role of Joseph."

"Maybe, maybe not," was all she said.

He chose not to comment further.

They finished their pizza, consuming the entire thing, mostly through his doing. "I'm glad that you haven't lost your appetite."

"I looove pizza," he said again with a laugh. "If you ever want to know if I'm dead, get a pizza from this place and set it next to me. If I don't reach for it, I'm dead."

"That's good to know," she laughed her answer.

She insisted and he let her pay the bill. Then, after she had put more coins in the meter, they made their way over to the doctor's office, arriving right at 1:00. The receptionist had him complete some paperwork and then the nurse called him in. Esther wished him good luck. They squeezed hands as he stood up.

"Would your wife like to join you?" the nurse asked.

Conner and Esther looked at one another and smiled. "No, she'll wait here," he chose to say rather than correcting the mistake.

He was in with the doctor for about thirty minutes. When he came out, the doctor accompanied him. "You can do what you want short of playing ball. When you feel like you are ready to start more intensive physical activity, I want to see you again. Is that clear? No sports until I look at you again."

"Ya, Herr General," he said in his best German accent.

Both men smiled.

"Thank you, doctor. With those instructions, I hope to see you soon, not something most people say to a doctor, is it?"

"No, they don't, Conner. However, I want you to realize that you're at least one, if not two weeks from even beginning to play sports. Concussions are life-threatening events. If you don't let them heal, you are asking for big, big problems. And I mean very big."

"Message received," Conner acknowledged.

The doctor turned to Esther. "Do you understand that, Mrs. Ramsey?"

She looked at Conner, smiled and then said to the physician "Yes, I do, doctor. I'll take good care of him."

"Good. Now you two run along…er, walk along." The two men shook hands.

Chapter 39

The next week was full of commotion.

The *Sentinel* ran a daily series by Richard Means on the basketball team, focusing on the game in which the three players had been hurt, on the team's prognosis going forward and, especially, on Conner Ramsey. 'He's one of a kind' the reporter wrote, 'an older man playing a young man's game and excelling at it, all the while staying true to his faith.'

Conner received a lot of attention on campus, playfully being teased by those he knew as well as by those who were meeting him for the first time. In a manner of speaking, he had become something of a celebrity around campus.

The basketball team did not fare very well, however. Through the next weekend, they had away games with Pittsburgh and Nevada/Reno. They also had a home game against Iowa. They lost all three, getting totally demolished at Pittsburgh. With no one to run the backcourt, they could not capitalize on their big men. Turnovers were plenty and three pointers were few. After the destruction at Pitt, the coach tried to adjust by moving from an up-tempo game to one that was more ball control. It made the scores a little closer but it did not change the final outcomes.

Kline, Walker and Conner attended the practices and the home games. Walker traveled with the team. It was tough for the players who suited up to look over to the sidelines and see their teammates, their talented teammates, unable to help. It was even tougher for the injured threesome not to be able to make a difference.

----- ----- -----

Classes went well for Conner. He found himself able to effectively manage his time when he was healthy. Now that he was injured, he had even more time to attend to his studies. He loved all three courses, even nerdy Professor Ving. His favorite course, as one might suspect, was *Comparative Religions* with Professor Bags. That was partially thanks to the topic, partially thanks to the professor and partially thanks to his being able to sit next to Esther in class twice a week.

Out of class, Conner and Esther typically shared one meal per day together. Sometimes, too, they had study dates. Their favorite time, though, was fellowship. Whenever the weather permitted, they would take their Bibles and find a place to sit and discuss issues, passages or perceptions.

Shedrick and Conner continued to cultivate their friendship, even though they didn't spend quite as much time together as before Conner had gotten hurt. Shedrick was starting at guard but was having trouble scoring. That was because teams were favoring him and he did not get meaningful help from the other guard. He really missed Conner as his backcourt mate.

As far as Conner's health was concerned, the headaches were still there, although they were diminishing a little bit each day. When he started feeling a little spry, he would get down on the floor and do a few pushups. Just that rush of blood brought the headaches back and reminded Conner that the process was going to proceed slowly.

God did not visit Conner at all during this time. This was somewhat curious to Conner but he trusted that God was in control.

----- ----- -----

It was that Wednesday evening that Conner had been invited by Jeremy Wingman to share fellowship with his men's group. Considering that he had nothing better to do and had really wanted to learn more about this particular fellowship group, Conner gladly accepted. He joined them in one of the classrooms. Although the fellowship was typically six or seven students, there were twenty-seven there the evening that Conner joined them for the first time. Based on what Winger had said, Conner expected a half dozen people but he was delighted when he came into the room and there were many more, all of them students.

"Well, hello," he said.

Hello's were returned. As Conner looked around, he saw two of the students with Eagles singlets, both with number seven embroidered front and back. One was a home singlet, the other a traveling singlet. On the back of each was embroidered 'Ramsey' in large, clear lettering. Before letting it get out of hand, he checked his ego. It's you, Lord, he told himself.

He walked around the room shaking everyone's hand and introducing himself. It was a touch of class and the others appreciated his modesty. They introduced themselves, as well. Once everyone was seated in the rearranged classroom – it going from auditorium seating to horseshoe – Conner asked "Is there a topic that you were planning to discuss or maybe an excerpt from Scripture?" He looked around. Nobody said anything.

"Would you like me to suggest something?"

"How about Antichrist?" someone tossed out.

"That's interesting," Conner said. "I don't know much about it. I'm happy to learn what others think."

"What do you know about it?" the same questioner asked, a measure of challenge in his voice.

"Precious little," Conner responded, reminding himself to show constraint. Although the challenge was not justified, it could serve a purpose. "But I'll give it a try," he said after a slight pause.

"I don't think that there is any reference to it in the Old Testament," he began, then abruptly stopped. No one said anything. Conner looked around. Finally, he smiled. Nobody returned the smile. To an outsider, it looked very confusing. Conner didn't understand.

"Old Testament?" he repeated. Nothing. "Antichrist?" he prompted.

Finally, they got it. Of course there would be no reference to the Antichrist in the Old Testament since there was no explicit reference to Christ in it. When they did catch hold of the joke, most attending shared laughter.

Conner stood up. "Listen," he said, and everyone grew quiet. "Winger told me that some of you didn't want me here. He didn't tell me who felt that way and I wouldn't have wanted to know. He also told me that someone suggested that I was the Antichrist. All I can say is that I hope not. Otherwise, I am afraid because I would be in store for one heckuva hot eternity."

That brought out some additional laughter.

"I'll tell you what I understand but it's no better than what you understand, probably worse. And I'll not try to talk any of you out of thinking of me as anything. That's your prerogative. But for those of you interested, I am neither the Christ nor the Antichrist. I am simply a man who loves God. I

believe in God, his Son, salvation and eternity. I
want to live in God's beautiful kingdom after I die,
as I suspect that each of you wants to, as well.
Personally, I don't believe that the Antichrist would
be able to say that he loves God. And I also don't
believe that he would try to form or participate in
prayer groups. But maybe he's that good of a liar.
I'm not. I'll keep doing my thing and hope that you'll
see the real me."

A spontaneous round of applause broke out.
Winger was particularly pleased and applauded most
energetically.

"Okay, let's get to the Antichrist…in the New
Testament," he continued. His brief monologue and
subsequent reference to the New Testament seemed
to break the ice. From that point on, everyone
focused on the topic. It was a lively conversation and
Conner was glad that he was able to participate.
Although new to the group, he did most of the
facilitating. It may have been because of the topic,
the fact that he was the oldest, the fact that he was
the most well known or just that he liked to cultivate
discussions like this.

"When Winger mentioned the Antichrist, it made
me realize that I had no idea where the Scriptural
references could be found. I did a little research and
now understand that there are only two books that
use it – First and Second John. I made notes in my
Bible."

He opened his Bible to First John. Most of the
others did the same. "Look at First John 2:18.
Quote. *Dear children, the last hour is here. You have heard*

that the Antichrist is coming and many such antichrists have appeared. From this we know that the end of the world has come. Unquote. Pretty powerful stuff, eh?"

"Now look at First John 2:22. Quote. *And who is the great liar? The one who says that Jesus is not the Christ. Such people are antichrists, for they have denied the Father and the Son.* Unquote. Again, powerful stuff."

"Then there is a third reference in First John. Look at chapter four, verse three. Quote. *If a prophet does not acknowledge Jesus, that person is not from God. Such a person has the spirit of the Antichrist. You have heard that he is going to come into the world, and he is already here.* Unquote. Now, although that's also scary, there is some good news."

"What's that?" someone piped up.

"To me, the good news is that *a prophet does not acknowledge Jesus.* I'm not one hundred percent certain but it sort of suggests that the Antichrist, with a capital A, or the antichrists, with lower-case A's, cannot acknowledge Jesus. Since, like you, I want to recognize them when I run into them, perhaps that's one way to do so."

There was some around-the-room discussion about that before Conner continued. "There is also a reference in Second John. It's in chapter one, verse seven. Quote. *Many deceivers have gone out into the world. They do not believe that Jesus Christ came to earth in a real body. Such a person is a deceiver and an Antichrist.* Unquote."

Conner looked around. Everyone waited for his comments. "Those are the only four references. What do you think of them? Does this help us get a sense of who is the Antichrist with a capital A and who are the antichrists with lower-case A's? It does for me."

"There's one leader and a bunch of clones," someone said.

"That's my take on it," agreed Conner.

Someone else said "When he comes, we'll know that the real end has arrived."

"I'm not sure about that," said another. "I sort of remember other references in the Bible to either the end of time or Jesus returning that seemed imminent but turned out not to be."

There was some discussion about that. Without any conclusions concerning timing, another member of the group said "The Antichrist and his munchkin antichrists…" Everyone chuckled at the image. "…will deny God and Jesus." He looked directly at one of the members and said "I don't hear Conner doing that. In fact, it's quite the opposite."

From that, Conner had a pretty good idea who had labeled him the Antichrist within the group. He chose to take the high road. "No matter," he said. "We all form first impressions. But, just for the record, I believe in God, I believe in Jesus, I believe in the Trinity and I believe that the only way to the Kingdom of Heaven is through Jesus Christ." He paused. "I hope that this clears up what I believe."

Members around the room either applauded or banged their desks, including the person who apparently had been Conner's accuser.

"But let's get back to this topic. I think that there is more."

"What's that?" asked someone.

"We sort of dealt with it already. I believe that many people think that this Antichrist will suddenly appear and people will be smitten by him. He'll be good looking, resolve many world issues and say all the right things in the right ways."

"How do you know that he will be good looking?"

"He doesn't," Winger jumped in. "It's his impression of what the Antichrist will be. You have yours, I have mine and everyone who believes has his or hers. But Conner is probably right. I'm guessing that he will be John Kennedy handsome, Ronald Reagan articulate…"

"And Barack Obama athletic," someone finished for him. Everyone laughed.

The atmosphere had changed from one of some division to one where everyone felt much closer to one another, especially because they were focused on a common destination. Eventually, when the discussion about the Antichrist wore down, attendees began asking Conner about his injury, his abilities and a myriad of other things about the basketball team. Conner answered them as best he could, always giving credit to others when possible.

After almost two hours, the group broke up. Several members invited Conner back for the next one. "I'll come if I can. Thanks for inviting me. Keep up the good work."

"Good luck recovering," they generally said.

"Thanks a lot, guys," and Conner made his way back to his dorm, feeling particularly fulfilled. What a neat session it had been. He was very happy that he had attended.

Chapter 40

After another week, Conner was feeling lots better. He could do pushups without them escalating the pounding in his head. He could walk much faster, even managing to go up and down staircases. He even got a bee in his bonnet to start doing something athletic.

On Monday, following class, he went to see the doctor again.

"Doc, I'm ready to start working out," he began. "Otherwise, I'll need a lobotomy."

The doctor laughed. "You probably need a lobotomy for coming back to college to play basketball in the first place."

Conner joined in the laughter. "We each gotta do what we gotta do. This is my gotta do."

"I guess so. Okay, let's see if we can create a schedule for you to take baby steps on the way up to playing full out again."

Conner gave the doctor his full attention while they discussed an appropriate ramp up schedule for his physical activity. However, the doctor gave him two important instructions, emphasizing them twice and getting Conner's active commitment to them.

"One, concussions are dangerous things. You had a whopper. You're lucky that there isn't any permanent damage. That means that you have to be very, very careful about how you prepare your brain again. Since we know little about residual effects, you cannot experiment by returning to action too quickly."

Not only did the doctor ask for Conner's agreement, he made his patient restate it in his own words, much like a parent might do with a child. Conner did as he was told.

"Two, we believe that concussions can be cumulative. In other words, if you get another, it will be worse. That's why boxers deteriorate. That's why quarterbacks are in jeopardy. Do you understand that?"

Again, he made Conner rephrase the instruction.

"Okay, then," the doctor said. "You begin your regimen but you stop if you have problems. And I want to see you once a week for the next month, earlier if you are having any problems. And I mean *any* problems. Got it?"

"Got it, doc."

"Good. Now get out of here," he said with a smile.

They shook hands and he left. Esther, who had again taken Conner for this appointment, stood up when Conner returned to the waiting room.

"So?" she inquired.

"On the road to recovery," he answered with a smile and a thumbs-up sign. Conner couldn't wait to begin his re-conditioning.

----- ----- -----

The following week wasn't as positive as Conner would have liked. Starting off too energetically, he increased the frequency and intensity of his headaches. Thus, he had to slow down his routine.

As for spending time with the team, he attended but did not participate in all the practices and meetings. He even began going on some of the road trips. The one thing that he could do was lead his prayer pilgrims to the foul line before and after a practice or a game, then lead them in actual prayer.

Apparently, the prayers fell on deaf ears. Three more losses filled this week, all out of conference, to match the three they had lost the previous week. Coach Wright's plan to have a tough non-conference schedule turned out not to be a learning experience. Instead, it turned out to be a downer for all concerned — coaches, players, boosters, even cheerleaders. The only good thing was that Kline got to see some playing time and he hadn't lost his touch from outside. Had it not been for his shooting, the losses would have been much worse than they turned out to be. Even so, each was a double-digit loss, twenty-two to Wisconsin.

By the end of the following weekend, their record stood at 2-6. With a tough Conference schedule ahead, the prospects looked dim. Walker was scheduled to return the following week but there was no word on Conner. 'Ramsey Still Recouping' read the headline for one minor article. Otherwise, with Conner out of the spotlight, Means had decided to throttle back his focus on the thirty-four-year-old.

"We'll ramp it up when you're ready to suit up," he had said. "With you on the sideline, it's not hot news right now."

Personally, Conner had no problem with that. What he did have a problem with was not being able to move his mission forward. The only thing of substance that he was doing was meeting with Winger's fellowship group. Although he liked that and thought that it encouraged those who attended, an ever-growing population, he felt that it did not reach those most in need. He was frustrated by these setbacks, both his physical and spiritual ones. He wondered if maybe he should offer to give testimony or maybe speak at a church or related organization. Then he decided that his personal profile was not high enough for him to solicit these. If it was, organizations would be coming to him. His exasperation with this set of conditions grew.

On the positive side, Esther and he were enjoying each other's company. Both had other things to do but almost always spent part of the day together. Also, his studies were particularly rewarding. He loved the subjects and looked forward to both the class time as well as his out-of-class studies. He found himself growing in knowledge and understanding.

Sometimes, he thought that it would be nice if God would come visit him…and he prayed for that. But he was not visited and he trusted that it was for good reasons. When he thought about God being there, he envisioned asking him questions relating to his courses. How cool it would be to get the real scoop from the authority? he thought. Even if he couldn't share his source with his professors or his classmates, it would still be great.

The bottom line was that his healing took more time than he had wished; his faith and knowledge were nurtured; and his relationship with Esther continued to grow. However, the basketball team fell into an ever-widening chasm. The fans grew restless, and the schedule ahead appeared daunting. The *Sentinel* maintained its support, although papers across the country pretty much wrote the Eagles off. By the end of the next week, Walker started practicing with the team. Perhaps, with both Kline and Walker back, the tide might turn. Everyone associated with the team hoped for this outcome. Conner, too, felt stronger each day, although he realized that he was still probably at least a week away from any kind of scrimmage. He continued to see the doctor. They agreed that his progress was on schedule. "Remember the danger of going too fast," the doctor reminded him.

They lost three more, including their first conference game. They lost by 38 points to Iowa Central, the team most prognosticators picked to win both the regular season as well as the post-season tournament.

----- ----- -----

The third week of what seemed like this endless holding pattern was the most frustrating for Conner. He was beginning to feel well enough to play but heeded the doctor's instructions not to compete quite yet. He could shoot, run and lift moderate weights, but he could not compete on the floor. Since competition was the only thing that brought out his special skills, this was extremely maddening for Conner. Conner decided to focus on his foul shooting, vowing to make eight or nine out of ten.

When he practiced, one of the student assistants fed
him balls. After loosening up, Conner would say
"Okay, let's see how many of twenty I can make"
and ask the assistant to keep track. This made it a bit
more realistic but, of course, left out the game
distractions. For the most part, his foul shooting
percentage hovered just under ninety percent. Not
bad, he thought, for someone who used to hope to
at least hit the rim from the foul line.

The three games this week had both Kline and
Walker in the backcourt. That made things a little
better but did not materially stem the tide. They beat
Conway away, then lost to Wisconsin/Geneva at
home and Illinois Central away. They now had a
record of 3-11 overall, 1-3 in conference.

In the locker room after the game against Illinois
Central, Walker had uncharacteristically turned to
Conner and said "When you comin' back? We sure
could use you."

As the expression goes, you could have knocked
Conner over with a feather at that point in time.
Shedrick, who was standing next to Conner, almost
asked for clarification of Walker's question and
statement, then thought better of it.

"I'm trying. I'm trying," was all Conner could
think to say.

"Well, try harder," was Walker's concluding
comment, said without compassion.

Conner and Shedrick shared raised eyebrow looks
with one another when Walker turned and headed
into the showers. Later, when they returned to their
dorm room, they talked about the dramatic change

in attitude. "Apparently," Shedrick concluded, "he hates losing more than he hates being upstaged by you."

"Whatever the reason, I'm encouraged," Conner said.

"Well, try harder," mimicked Shedrick in Walker's distinctive raspy voice.

Both laughed.

Chapter 41

As Conner settled himself into bed, a voice in the room said "Give me a summary."

Conner switched on his light and sat up. There stood an Indian chief dressed in his war regalia. Conner immediately knew who it was. He was glad to see God, regardless of what people outfit he was wearing at the moment.

"Well, it's about time," he said, partially in humor, partially in total seriousness.

"I've been here all the time."

"Yeah, but I sure could have used some help, if only in deciding what to do."

"What did I tell you quite a while ago?"

"How many things am I supposed to remember in order to answer the one thing that you want me to acknowledge?"

"Oh, getting a little sassy, are we?" God asked and Conner realized how familiar he was acting in the presence of the creator of the universe.

"Sorry."

"I like pushback but I'm not crazy about disrespect. And I don't have a particularly sterling record when it comes to disobedience."

"Why the Indian outfit?" Conner asked, trying to move from the uncomfortable place they had been in.

"Why not?"

Conner smiled, remembering the answer-a-question-with-a-question discussion they had shared a while back. God also smiled.

"Give me a summary," God repeated.

"You know it all."

The Indian chief tilted his head, the headband almost falling off. He quickly brought his hand up to catch it. "Couldn't find one that fits," he said.

Now Conner tilted his head.

"Omniscient," Conner said, in effect asking why he was being required to provide a summary to someone who knew everything.

"Listen, we've already gone through that. I want you to hear yourself think. Most people don't realize that one of the greatest things about prayer is its time to reflect and hear oneself think."

"Sort of like a soundboard, eh?"

"Same universe," came the response.

"Sort of..."

"Hey," interrupted God, "are you going to answer the question or am I..."

"...gonna turn you into a pillar of salt?'

Both laughed.

"Okay. Let me see..." Conner thought about what would be most important to God. "First, I think that my ministry, if that's what one might call it, has come to a halt while I am on the sidelines."

"Not so, but continue."

Conner started to argue, then chose to follow instructions.

"I did feel that some progress was made with the fellowship group, the one I was invited to attend by Winger."

"Yes. Good stuff. Little pebble, bigger ripples," was all he said.

"In no particular order, I am enjoying my studies." He looked at the Indian chief for confirmation. Nothing was said.

"Do you agree?" Conner prompted.

"We're not grading your performance, you know."

"I know but you're commenting on everything else. How 'bout it?"

"Very nice," he said, total apathy dripping off his words.

Conner smiled but didn't pursue it.

"I am enjoying, maybe valuing would be a better word, my time with Esther."

"Okay, Romeo."

"Any comment?"

"I like that you're evenly yoked," he said, referring to the importance of common faith.

"That's pretty much it, I think," Conner concluded.

"Okay. Good summary. Now, your thoughts and plans."

"I need a power boost for the ministry, I'd like to expand the fellowship, I am pleased with the courses, I am delighted with Esther and I'd like to get healthy more rapidly."

"Good. Sounds like you're right on track."

"Right on track? I'm moving slower than a snail tethered to a tree."

God pointed to a picture that Conner had up on his wall. Normally, there was a photo of a waterfall with some inspiring message across the bottom. Now, there was a tree and, of course, a snail on a leash.

Conner started laughing. It was contagious enough that the Indian chief did the same. When Conner looked back, the waterfall had returned.

"You're funny," Conner said. "You have a much better sense of humor than most people think."

"That might be something to highlight," God said.

Conner thought about it, not certain if suggesting that God was a prankster would enhance or diminish his image. He leaned toward the latter.

"You're probably right," God said, responding to his thoughts.

"Isn't anything private?" Conner asked, challenging the lack of concealment when dealing with the Lord.

"Uhhh, no. And that might be something to remind everyone, as well. But be sure to emphasize that I'm not eavesdropping to catch them doing something wrong but, instead, to encourage them.

The you-can't-do-it messages come from you know who."

"All of 'em?"

"Lucifer is a negative-message-a-minute angel."

"Angel?"

"Oh, yeah. He's not a saint but he's still an angel. Of course, that will be changing in a while."

"A long while?"

"You know the rules."

"You'll have to kill me."

"Spot on."

"One question: Why did you let me get injured when it slowed down what you want to accomplish?"

"Who said it slowed things down?"

"Well, I'm not able to demonstrate my skills and get the kind of attention that I thought that we wanted to get."

"You're getting plenty of attention. You just think that it has to be in the newspaper?"

Conner hadn't really thought about that.

"Isn't there something that I could or should be doing to accelerate the process?"

"No, I don't think so."

"You don't *think* so?" he said, emphasizing the word 'think' in his question.

"No, I don't think so," God repeated, seemingly mulling it over.

"You are a piece of work," Conner commented.

"Actually, truth be told, you are the piece of work."

Conner realized that God was referring to the literal, he to the figurative.

"Okay, I get it," he said. "From dust to dust and all that."

"More or less," the Indian chief agreed without much animation.

"How come you're showing up right now? Is there something about to happen?"

"Absolutely," semi-whispered the chief.

Conner leaned forward.

"Tomorrow is coming," God said.

Conner didn't have to be a rocket scientist to realize that he was being teased. "Got it," he said in concession.

"Good. Keep up the good work. Gotta run!"

"Ohhh," Conner whined, then regrouped. "I'll be fine."

"I know. Ta ta."

"Bye Tigger," Conner said, acknowledging the Winnie the Pooh character whom God had portrayed with his salutation.

And then, of course, the room was empty once again.

Shedrick knocked on the door. "You okay?" he asked with a concerned voice.

"Fine. Just fine. Thanks. Night."

"Okay. Night."

Chapter 42

On Monday, Conner asked to participate in the practice.

"Did you get a clearance letter from the doctor?" Coach Wright asked.

"He told me that it was my decision."

"Maybe, but you don't practice without a note from him. Period."

Conner sighed and went to the foul line on the other end of the court to practice his free throws. The student assistant followed him and that was pretty much how the practice was spent for him, although he did join the team when they assembled to hear the coach give them instructions.

After the practice, he called the doctor's office to request the release letter.

"I'm sorry but the doctor is out of town. May I help you?"

Conner explained his circumstances and the receptionist said "I'll see what I can do. Can I have a call back number for you?"

Conner provided it and then headed off to class. Class was terrific, as it always was. Professor Bags was one of the best professors he had ever had. Not even one of the best. *The* best. He wanted his students to discover, not be told. "You can get loads of data these days. That's not a problem. You will differentiate yourself by what data you use and how you apply it."

After class, Conner got a return call from the receptionist. "The doctor will issue you the letter but, again, he cautions you to be smart."

"Yes, ma'am," Conner said. "May I pick it up this afternoon?"

"Yes. I will have the nurse sign it for him. When will you be here?"

They arranged for it to be ready shortly after lunch. Esther and he went to Bruno's.

"Are you sure that you're ready?" she asked, trying to balance concern with lack of meddling.

"I am. At least I think that I am. I've been running and lifting weights for a week now without any difficulties. However, if playing on the court causes problems, I'll back off."

"Promise?"

"No," he teased.

They didn't discuss it further. After lunch, he picked up the letter from the doctor. There would be a shoot-around and walk-through this evening, with a home game against Coleman the following evening. He hoped to do well in the practice and then be allowed to suit up. He suspected that the coach was aching for a win but also knew that the season extended well beyond this game. Conner saw how slowly the coach had inserted Kline and Walker back into the lineup. He figured on receiving the same, maybe even more cautious treatment.

When he returned to his room, he committed himself to studying but he found his mind wandering. He would start reading a passage, then think about the game, wondering if he had lost his skills. Then he would refocus, only to have his mind drift off to spreading the Word and the inadequate job that he felt he was doing. It was like this for several topics – Esther, Winger, Shedrick, even pondering how the player who had hit him in the head was doing. The result of all this was that he neither studied nor produced meaningful thought about any of the topics that interrupted his schoolwork.

He chose to take a nap. Once again, he dreamed about steam trains passing in opposite directions on adjacent tracks with passengers throwing yellow tennis balls back and forth as the trains sped by. Again, he was sitting on the limb of a tree watching what took place. A short while later, two other trains did the same thing and the passengers threw yellow tennis balls back and forth, as well. When he awoke, although he remembered the dream, he could not get closer to what it meant. He decided to write down as much as he could. When he was done, he set it aside.

----- ----- -----

Richard Means was doing a piece on Coach Wright for the *Sentinel*. As a result, he was given special permission to attend practices. As Means was a Brantley alum and devoted Eagles basketball fan, the coach was not worried about him spying for other schools. Still, he kept the reporter away from intimate contact with the squad during the practices. Means was relegated to anywhere above row 12, effectively the same as row 20 when the team had open practices.

Kline and Walker were still the number one guards. Coach Wright had Conner and Shedrick team up, a result that absolutely delighted the freshman. "This is great!" he seemingly shouted in a whisper, fearful that his enthusiasm might be misconstrued by others.

Conner just smiled. "As goofy as ever," he commented.

The coach showed the team a few new plays, had them walk through the formations and then had them do it full speed five-on-five. Fivesomes rotated between offense and defense in order to give everyone several chances to experience the patterns. After each team had been on offense four times, the coach told them to shoot, guards on one end of the court, big men on the other. They spent twenty minutes doing that before the coach called them back together.

"Men, we're pretty much back at full strength, depending on how Gimpy, Rotator Cuff and Head Banger are," he said pointing to Kline, Walker and Conner, respectively. "We've been pretty much written off by the regional media and we're not a confident favorite of the local media either. But they're not the ones who play the game. We are. And I think that we've got more game in us. What do you think?"

"Yes, coach!"

Coach Wright then turned to the stands and signaled Richard Means to come on over. The reporter did as he was told. When he arrived in front of the team, the coach put his arm around him.

"Mr. Means…"

"Yes, coach?"

"You are going to be up close and get to watch firsthand how this down and out lot of scrubs not only rebounded in the conference but made a national name for itself. And we are counting on you to document it and proclaim it loudly on our behalf. Can you do that?"

"I can do it if you can do it," he said with some confidence.

"We can do it." Then he turned to the team. "Can't we?"

"Yes, coach!" came the shout.

"There ya have it, Mr. Reporter. There ya have it."

Means smiled, took out his pad and pretended to start writing. Everyone laughed.

"Okay, men, go shower. Tomorrow we begin our journey back."

As everyone got up to leave, the coach called to Conner. "Ramsey, let me see you in my office before you shower."

"Yes, sir…er, coach."

Conner told Shedrick that he'd see him back in the room before dinner. Then he followed the coach to the office. Once there, the coach closed the door and motioned Conner to sit down. He went around to his large chair and sat down, as well.

"Ramsey, I want and you want…," he began. "We each need to make certain that we know what those things are and then decide how we will help each other achieve them. You following me?"

"Go on."

"I want to win. W-I-N," he spelled. "That's what makes everyone around me happier and what makes me happier. Understand?"

"Of course."

"Well, with this team, I can't win."

Conner looked at him strangely.

"Oh, I can win a few games but I can't win the big enchilada."

Conner continued to look but made no reaction.

"I'm talking about the conference and even the national championship."

Conner continued to wait.

"...unless you do your magic," he concluded.

Conner started to dispute that, more out of humility than anything else but he stopped, realizing that a debate would never be settled. "And so?" he asked.

"You want to win, too, but I can see that this isn't the most important thing in your life."

"No, coach, it's not. But it is a means to an end."

"Right. I want the team's victories to be your victories, as well."

Conner nodded.

"But I don't want to make a circus out of this. Are you getting my drift?"

Conner didn't envision a conflict and was therefore a bit confused as to why the coach wanted to have this conversation. After a moment of silence, he said "Actually, no, I don't get your drift." He said it very deliberately.

"You want to do your praying thing, play basketball and win...in that order."

Conner didn't dispute the sequence, although there were other things that he would have injected into this list.

"I want to win first and then accommodate anything else," the coach said, offering his list of priorities.

"Okay, coach, what's the problem?" Conner asked, still not at all certain where this was all headed.

"If praying and religion and stuff like that comes too much to the forefront, we will have a conflict."

"Why does there have to be a conflict?"

"There doesn't. That's what I'm saying. If you don't go beyond the prayer circle before and after the game, then we'll all be able to focus on what we need to accomplish."

"Fine, coach. That's all I was planning to do."

"Well, some fine folks, who happen to be boosters, are afraid that we will be thought of as a bunch of holy rollers and they're none too fond of the idea."

"Because we pray before and after a basketball game?"

"Something like that."

"Oh, come on, coach. This is silly."

"Ramsey, it's definitely not silly. If you knew how much money they contribute to both the university and to our basketball program, in particular, you wouldn't be calling it silly."

"Okay, it's not silly. But..."

"There are no buts about it, Ramsey. I want us to win but not at the expense of these boosters. You're here for one year and they're here for many years. You don't give us any money and they donate millions. You get my drift?" he asked, again using his pet phrase.

"Wow, coach, this comes totally out of left field. I don't see a conflict but you do. And now you want to muzzle me because of money."

They sat in silence for a minute.

"Let me ask you a question, coach."

"Go ahead."

Conner remembered their first conversation when he had asked the coach whether he was a man of faith. The coach had responded with "We go to church…when we can." Then they had discussed the power of prayer and the coach has dismissed it with "Prayer doesn't work that way…bing, bang, bong," he had said.

"If you had to choose between your faith and success as a coach, which would you choose?"

The coach remained silent for a few moments, then seemed to sense a way out of this tough question. "I don't have to choose."

"Let's say that you do."

"Listen, Ramsey, we don't have to be on opposite sides of this. As far as I am concerned…"

"Coach, answer my question – faith or coaching success." Conner was clear in his tone that he would not back off from getting an answer to his question.

"I'm not answering that."

"Fine. When it comes to basketball, coach, you're the expert and I'll follow your advice. When it comes to my faith, I've got a higher power to follow. I don't know what my actions will be beyond the prayer circles but I'm not going to put a cap on it for some worldly purpose. If that means that I can't play for you, then I will have to find another vehicle for what I want to accomplish."

"And just what is that?" the coach asked with a tinge of mockery.

"Spreading the Word of God. That's my primary purpose. This seems like a good way to do it."

"Listen, Ramsey..." the coach began, then stopped. He began again. "How about this as a solution?"

Conner waited silently.

"You keep playing and when you feel that you have to do something beyond the prayer circles, you and I have another conversation."

Conner took a deep breath in, then slowly exhaled. "I'm afraid not, coach. I need to know that there are no doors ahead of me as I pursue a course of action. I'm guessing that I will have plenty of obstacles that I don't know about without selecting a path that has difficult ones already in place."

The coach stood up and leaned across his desk. "You can't play anywhere else! You can't just up and go somewhere else. The league and I won't allow it!"

"I see," Conner said. "I'm sorry about this." He stood up, as well. "I wish you well, more for your soul than for your season. Don't make a pact with the devil, coach. It won't be worth it."

"Get out of here!" the coach yelled, "and take your holier-than-thou ways with you."

Conner, very disappointed but under control, left. When he got to the locker room, most everyone had left. He stripped off his clothes, jumped in the shower, dressed and decided to go for a walk. He was very disappointed, fearful that this unexpected setback would be monumental.

Chapter 43

The campus was very pretty and walking through it could be refreshing. However, he really didn't want to see people right now, especially those who might engage him in a conversation, probably about basketball. Well, maybe excepting Esther and he didn't feel like calling her. He walked downtown and got himself a smoothie at a local ice cream shop, then continued walking. He found himself at a modified park and sat down on one of the benches.

Perhaps it was coincidence, perhaps something else but the first person he saw was Esther. Of all the people to see right here, he was amazed that it was her. Apparently, they were meant to spend time together this evening.

"Esther!" he called. She stopped and looked around, not being able to locate the source of the voice.

"Over here," he said, waving his arms.

She tracked the voice back to where he was and broke into a huge smile. She began walking toward him as he walked toward her.

"Are you stalking me?"

"Yup, that's me, Mr. Stalker. First, I find someone I really like, then I spend quality time with them and, finally, I stalk them."

They both laughed.

"What in the world are you doing here?" they both asked at the same time.

"Jinx," he said, a fraction of a second before she uttered it.

"Rats!" she uttered.

"No penalty," he said, thinking back to his conversation with Dwayne, aka God, in the stands a while back.

"Thanks," she said appreciatively.

They walked along for a while. "Really, what are you doing here?"

"I visit the homebound for our church. A bunch of us do it. I was just visiting Mrs. Montague. And you?"

"Mine is not that simple."

"Wanna tell me about it?"

As he exhaled, he said "I guess."

"Let's go sit someplace," Esther suggested, sensing that Conner was struggling with something.

They walked along the street and came to a café. They sat outside. Both got tea. She got a sandwich. "I didn't have time for dinner," she confessed.

After getting the food and beverage, they prayed. Then she said "What's up?"

"I got kicked off the team."

"What?" she exclaimed with a full mouth of her chicken salad sandwich. Immediately, she raised her napkin to cover her mouth. "You were what?"

Conner told her what had taken place in the coach's office. All the while she listened, she did not take another bite or sip any of her tea. In fact, she sat there almost without swallowing, although she did have her mouth closed.

When he was done, she said "He can't do that."

"He can."

"It's wrong."

"That's not the issue."

"What can you do?"

"Find something else to pursue."

"You can't. You're a great basketball player and that's your ministry. You can't just quit."

"What do you suggest? Should I form a basketball team and barnstorm throughout the Conference?"

They both laughed at that, thinking of its absurdity.

"We could dress in old time clothes – really old time – and call ourselves the Five Apostles."

Esther started laughing at the visual and that got him to laughing, as well. Each made the other laugh even harder until they were sitting there with tears running down their eyes. In time, they slowed down, then stopped as the gravity of the moment returned to them.

"I'm sorry," she said. "I wish that there was something I could do."

"Me, too," he responded, taking her hand. "Me, too."

She finished eating, sharing the moments in silence. When she was done, he asked "Are you in a rush to get anywhere?"

"Nowhere whatsoever," she said.

"Great," he said. "Let's just sit here for a while."

"Fine by me," she concurred.

With that, they just enjoyed each other's company at that table, not saying much at all. Every so often, one or the other would offer something but it never developed into anything lengthy. They intentionally steered away from anything relating to the basketball situation.

"Can you find somewhere else to channel your energy?" she finally asked.

"To the best of my knowledge, basketball is the only thing that sets me apart. I wanted to use that special talent to see if I could draw more people to the Lord. Without basketball, I feel ill equipped to do anything."

"Now wait just a minute," she said with conviction. "That's just hogwash. A lot of great people did loads of thing for the Lord with a lot fewer tools than you have."

He nodded, knowing that he was just having a pity party.

"Need I continue?" she asked.

"Not really. I know. David, Moses, Noah…"

"Most everyone really," she said. "In fact, the one who seemed most well equipped…"

"Saul," Conner recognized.

"…did the lousiest job."

"Okay, okay. I surrender. Let me put on my armor of confidence."

"Excellent. Do you want to look at options?"

He sat back and looked at her. How was he this lucky to have someone like her in his life at right this very moment? Thank you, Lord, he silently said. He sat back up, this time with more self-assurance.

"You're right," he said. "Let's look at my options."

"Good."

Conner took one of the napkins on the table and used the pen that came with the bill. He wrote the number one. Next to it he wrote 'Play for Brantley.'

"That's pretty much out of my hands, though. If the coach puts those restrictions on me, I can't, in good faith, abide by them. As much as I don't admire his choice, I do admire his certainty."

Esther nodded but said nothing.

Then he wrote the number two. Next to it he wrote 'Play elsewhere.'

"I'm not sure that this is even a possibility. I wonder if I used up my year of eligibility playing here. I don't even know if I have more than one year available anyhow. Even so, transferring would mean losing next year, I think."

"I think that's right," she said.

Trying to set aside his discouragement, he continued. He wrote the number three. Here he paused for a moment, not certain what to write.

"Play in the NBA or overseas," she said.

"What?" he asked, not certain whether or not she was kidding.

"Go pro…or at least try. Are you good enough?"

He could have reached across the table and kissed her, less because of the fact that she was helping him through this than because she seemed to have such confidence in him.

"Barnabas," he said.

"Pardon?"

"Barnabas," he repeated.

"And you're using his name to…?" She invited him to complete the sentence.

"…to say how much I appreciate your encouragement."

She smiled, understanding the Biblical reference to the encourager.

"Thank you. That's a lovely compliment."

"Well deserved."

"So?"

"So what?"

"Are you good enough to play in the pros?"

He thought for a second, then said "Maybe. I'm not sure."

"Not being sure won't do it. You know that you have to believe it."

Conner nodded in agreement. "Let's pray."

She leaned across the table and took his hand. They both bowed their heads as he prayed. "Thank You, Lord for Your endless blessings. Even if we limit our appreciation to our five senses, we have much more than we deserve. When we expand beyond them, we can offer nothing but thanks. We most appreciate salvation, Your ultimate gift. While here, we appreciate Your mercy and grace. Thank You for each other."

At this point, he gave her hand a small squeeze and she returned the silent expression.

"May we find the best use of our talents and maximize them. Please continue to bless us, our loved ones and all those in need, especially spiritual need. And we ask this all in Your Son's name. Amen."

"Amen," she said.

They continued to add to the list they had started but, initially, nothing seemed to fit quite as well as the pro basketball option. One other possibility that they added was exploring his skills in other sports. "We can try," he said, "but I don't think that it's transferable." They agreed to at least explore this option, naming off a few other sports that might be possibilities. These included baseball ("I always liked it"), football ("I better not get hit"), hockey ("I can barely stand up on skates"), tennis ("Now there's a real possibility"), track and field ("Probably just the sprint events") and the martial arts ("That would feel like a contradiction to me").

Another option that they discussed was approaching the boosters who were against his ministry. "Nothing ventured, nothing gained," she had said. They agreed that this would be worth the effort. "After all, what worse can they do?" she had asked.

Most of the other things that they discussed fell somewhere into the list that they had already created.

"Let's prioritize them," she suggested.

He sat back and exaggerated a surprised face. "Aren't we the little organizer?" he said playfully but also with admiration.

She smiled and gestured with her hand for him to get going.

"Okay. What do you think?" he asked.

"It's not what I think, Seven. It's what you think. I'm just your Sancho Panza," she said, referring to Don Quixote's squire.

He smiled, knowing the reference. Smart girl, he thought to himself. Very smart girl.

"Okay, Sevenette, here's how I would rank them." He listed them in a one-to-five order, a number next to each. One was to get in contact with the boosters. Two was to explore other sports. Three was to go pro. Four was to give in and play for Brantley. Five was to play elsewhere. "There are other alternatives but I think that this is a good starter list. What do you think?"

"I like it," she said with a slight burst of energy.

"Then let's get started!" he said.

"If you don't mind, may I suggest something?"

"Of course."

"Let's look into numbers two through five before we explore going to the boosters."

"Why?"

"I just think that the coach and maybe the boosters need to stew in this a little. I'm guessing that you will get more cooperation down the road than you will right now."

"What if the team starts winning?"

"Then you won't be any worse off, will you?"

"No, I guess not. Good idea. Numbers two through five, here we come!"

Chapter 44

Esther was spot on when it came to her suggestion to hold off contacting the coach and/or

the boosters. Along with losing to Coleman, the
Eagles lost to Ohio Western away, Kingman at
home and Lupree State away. The first two losses
were understandable, the third very rare. Very rare
indeed. With it, the press had a field day, especially
with headlines. 'Wright is Wrong!' screamed one.
'Turgle Doesn't Work' suggested another, referring
to the Eagle turning into a turkey.

Their record now stood at 3-15, 1-7 with
conference play well underway. This was the worst it
had been since the team had joined the
conference…and well before that, too. Among other
suggestions, there were lots of rumblings about
changing the coach. Overall, the marquis sport for
the school was now the laughing joke of the region.
This did not make for happy times for anyone
associated with Brantley basketball. Some of the
papers made spirited suggestions that Brantley join
the junior college circuit.

While this calamity was taking place, Conner
continued to go to his classes and research the other
options that he and Esther had identified. He was
constantly besieged across campus with "When you
gettin' back into the lineup, Conner? They sure could
use you." He always responded with a noncommittal
"I just don't know," thus avoiding discussing the
reason for his not playing. Students, in particular,
were convinced that he was the difference, perhaps
elevating his worth as people are accustomed to
doing. Conner did not go to any of the practices or
chalkboard sessions. All his information came
through Shedrick who said that "There isn't an iota

of fun about being on this team these days."
Shedrick didn't hold anything against Conner. He
only missed his roomie's participation. However, he
understood Conner's position.

Conner wisely got Shedrick to promise not to say
anything to anyone about what had transpired with
the coach. "I don't want him thinking that I'm
talking behind his back."

Shedrick, like a stallion, was sometimes difficult to
rein. However, he stayed good to his promise and
avoided saying anything to the coach or to the other
players. It was tough but he managed.

Strangely enough, Shedrick's playing time
diminished, even though he was now clearly the
third best guard. Conner didn't say this out loud but
he surmised that it had something to do with the
two of them rooming together. In an odd sort of
way, he figured that the coach was getting back at
Conner by limiting the playing time of his
roommate. Maybe Conner was wrong but he
strongly doubted it.

Conner and Esther investigated the other sports
that they had identified. Each ended with a definite
conclusion that it was not the alternate skill set that
Conner possessed. They started with baseball and
went to a batting cage. Conner could barely hit even
the medium pitching. No, this wasn't it. It felt much
more awkward than when he had first played
recreation basketball, now seemingly eons ago.

Football was a bit more difficult to test. He got a
football and tried to kick it…unsuccessfully. Then,
when he tried to pass it, he thought his arm had

flown out of its socket. He wondered if his speed would make a difference but decided not to find out since it was likely that he would take at least one hit, if not many more, and his noggin was not prepared for it.

Next came hockey but that ended quickly, as well, when he laced on skates and proceeded to take a semi-serious spill, pretty nicely cutting his right elbow and forearm. No, that wouldn't do. Besides, like football, he was doomed to take some hits, clean or not. They agreed that contact was not the best thing for him.

Tennis had more promise. By coincidence, Shedrick and Conner roomed right next door to two guys on the tennis team. Conner asked if he could hit with one of them. He realized what a beginner he was from the start. Although he could somewhat make contact on the forehand side, he had no clue on how to hit a backhand. Serves, overheads and volleys ended his quest. He apologized to the neighbor for wasting his time.

Track and field made no sense. He was neither fast nor limber. He had already established that he couldn't jump. Good bye track and field. He didn't even try martial arts. Even if he was good at it, he didn't believe that it would be an appropriate vehicle for what he wanted to convey to the world. That, plus one blow to the head, might end it all for him.

Esther and he discussed, then dismissed a number of other things. In alphabetic order, they included archery, billiards, bowling, car racing, golf, lacrosse, ping pong, pistol and rifle shooting, snow skiing, swimming, water polo, water skiing and a number of others, as well.

It was going to be basketball or something not sports related. On the one hand, Conner was a little bit disappointed that he didn't have a sports option. On the other hand, he loved doing the research with Esther. She was tremendously positive all the way through.

----- ----- -----

Their first option had been to speak with the boosters. They had agreed to temporarily put that on the back burner. Their second option had been to find another sport. That turned out to be a dead end. Option number three was for Conner to go pro. To do so, he would have to do something like he had done with Coach Wright. His letter to the coach had gotten him the window he needed to show his stuff.

Doing the same with the pros would be an entirely different matter. They would be much less likely to even entertain such an idea. If someone was good enough to play in the pros, whether a college or high school player, every scout would know about him. Conner hadn't done enough to warrant their attention. Under these circumstances, his holding back full demonstration of his skills had backfired. Even so, he was happy to have acted the way he did.

"I'll bet that my dad would know someone," Esther had said. "If we could get him to call in a few favors, you might get that chance."

Conner thought about it. There was a lot of appeal to walking past college ball and getting on the NBA stage. If he made it there, then he would have a lot more freedom to speak his mind and he would have money to use for good purposes. It really enticed him. He asked Esther to explore the possibility of her dad making an introduction. "Chicago Bulls, please," he had requested. Then, before she called him, he told her to forget about a particular team. He figured that this would not be about his preferences but, instead, that of The Man upstairs.

Esther agreed with Conner about the fourth option, that of giving in and playing for Brantley. That was not something that he could do in good conscience. "Can't do it," was all he said. "Wouldn't want you to," she had responded. And, with that, this particular option was tossed out.

The fifth option was playing somewhere else. It, too, hit the recycle bin quickly. He couldn't afford to sit out this and maybe another year. No, it was not realistic.

In reviewing his options, the best ones were either talking with the boosters to change their demands or trying to get a shot with a professional team. The latter seemed to point more to the Harlem Globetrotters than the Los Angeles Wildcats. On second thought, not the Harlem Globetrotters. His ethnicity would redirect him to the Washington Generals, the persistent losers to the Globetrotters. That wouldn't work.

Concerning the boosters, Esther and he talked about how Conner might get an audience with them. They could research the names. In fact, Richard Means might help. Alternately, they could speak with the coach and ask if he would make the introductions. Going through the coach made sense. For one thing, maybe the coach had experienced a change of heart and this whole thing could be set aside. For another, circumventing the coach would be problematic, even if Conner was able to turn some or even all of the boosters around. The coach would resent the end-around. Yes, going to the coach first made sense.

Conner did not look forward to speaking with Coach Wright, especially since the ensuing time had included two games, both of which they lost, one to Indiana Northern and a second one to Iowa Central, 107-76 at home. Their overall record now stood at 3-17, 1-9. Now, without a doubt, everyone had written them off. Coach Wright knew that his reputation was becoming seriously tarnished and that this kind of record might well find him looking for another option, especially since he was in the last year of his contract. Most people would have agreed that a duffer getting a hole in one on a difficult par five had a better chance than the Eagles of winning their conference.

To his credit, Coach Wright correctly realized that he had the ingredients but that he was caught between the proverbial rock and hard spot…a stubborn Conner Ramsey and a wealthy group of my-way-or-the-highway boosters.

Chapter 45

Conner knocked on the open door. Coach Wright looked up and smiled. The coach hadn't expected anyone, especially not Conner.

"I'm glad that you're here, Ramsey," he said, immediately standing and offering his hand. Without hesitation, he slapped on his best used car salesman smile. "I was planning to get in touch with you. I think that we got off on the wrong foot with our last conversation. Can we talk about it, Conner?"

Already Conner knew that phoniness permeated the air. The coach never called his players by their first names. His behavior reeked of insincerity. Conner was disappointed but chose to say nothing. He wished for a miraculous change of heart but feared that he would be wishing for the improbable. Nevertheless, he waited.

The coach continued. "I think that we can work this out. Are you willing?"

"Coach, I didn't really come here to work this out with you." When he finished saying that, it sounded awfully negative to him. However, the coach didn't seem to pick up on the tone. At least he didn't give away his disappointment.

"Oh, gosh, let's at least try," he said with great affectation. "Nothing ventured, nothing gained."

Conner thought about Esther's use of that expression just a few days ago. How different it sounded now.

"Sure, coach." Let's see if a miracle might happen, he thought.

"We are at somewhat of an impasse. It's a tricky one, that's for sure."

Master of the obvious, thought Conner. Be polite and listen for common ground, he told himself, although not believing that the instruction was valuable, much like some children react to their parents' it's-in-your-best-interest advice. Yeah, right.

"Now, I respect how important your faith is to you. Although it doesn't play as large a part in my life as it does in yours, my faith is one of the more important elements in my life."

Oh, my gosh, thought Conner. This is like one of those cheap TV preachers who can change his expression at the drop of a hat, from elation to despair. I'm gonna be sick, he thought to himself.

"That's one side of the argument. Let's call it one position, instead. Okay?"

Oh, vomit, thought Conner.

"On the other side…er, the other position is that of some of our boosters. Money is their religion. They have lots of it and want to spend it on things that are important to them – like cars, vacations and Eagles basketball. Get the picture?" Coach Wright waited for Conner to actively acknowledge what he had been saying.

Conner obliged, just to get the dialogue moving. "Yes, coach, I get the picture."

"The question is: How do we find a happy middle ground for these two positions? Am I right up to this point?" Again, he waited for Conner to respond.

"Right as rain," Conner replied, a tinge of sarcasm creeping into his reply.

The coach looked quizzically at Conner, somewhat disordered by that nonsensical phrase. He pushed through it, not wanting to slow down. He took Conner's statement as affirmation.

"If I could get you to identify what you want to accomplish, maybe we could talk about it first and then decide what is or is not appropriate. And I promise..." Here he held his hand up as though he was being sworn in as a witness at a trial. "...that I will do what I can to further your interests."

The coach turned his head to the right and looked at Conner with his eyes all the way on the left. At the same time, he raised his eyebrows. It came across as an are-we-on-the-same-page-here question.

Conner had to think for a moment. Although he didn't want to compromise his position, he also didn't want to miss a chance at reconciliation, if it could be done without concession. Maybe this can work out, he thought.

"Coach..."

"We can do this!" Coach Wright said before Conner got started. It was clear that he wanted Conner to approach this with a can-do attitude rather than a more objective position. The coach was well aware that he needed to sell Conner on this. It was his do-or-die pitch.

"Coach, I didn't have some plan of attack, as it were, in coming here."

"Good, good," the coach said, more like the sheriff from *Dukes of Hazzard* than like the respected coach seen by the outside world.

"It's just that my primary mission, call it my ministry, is to spread the Word. I want to do that by example and encouragement. Frankly, I don't know where that will lead. But I do suspect, especially if we have success, that it will mean interviews and those will involve my professing my faith."

"How about if we put a moratorium on all interviews until the end of the season?" the coach wishfully tossed out there.

Conner simply tilted his head.

"Okay, that's not a good idea," he retreated. "How about if ..."

"Coach," Conner began. The coach stopped midsentence and waited.

"Coach, I think that the best idea would be if I met with the boosters one at a time, especially those who object to my faith."

"Nobody objects to your faith," the coach corrected. "It's when your faith is rubbed in their faces."

"I understand. Perhaps I can get them to be more open-minded, if you will. I'd like to meet with them one at a time," he repeated.

The coach was silent.

"If, at any time, it doesn't work out, I'll back off and we'll look at other options. Meanwhile, I'll rejoin the team...provided we start having these booster meetings right away."

That was Conner's position and he wasn't going to negotiate on it further. The ball was in the coach's corner. What Coach Wright did next would have monumental consequences.

By this time, the coach had sat back down. Now he sort of slumped in his chair.

"You're killing me, Ramsey, just killing me," he moaned.

"Not intentionally, coach."

"You're killing me just the same."

Both men sat in silence for about thirty seconds. As much as Conner wanted to toss in other thoughts to strengthen his position, he knew that this would not be a data-driven decision. He determined to wait. A moment later, Coach Wright sat forward.

"Here's what I'm willing to do," he began. "You join the team immediately and I introduce you to one of the boosters who objects. You prove to me that you're still the difference maker and you convert – ha, ha, get that? – the booster without pissing him off and I will continue to introduce you to boosters. Fair enough?"

Conner disliked the conditional phrase "You prove to me that you're still the difference maker…" but he realized that the agreement was a move in the right direction.

"Fair enough, coach," he said in agreement. "Who is the first booster?"

"Gordon McKenzie and his wife would be a good starting place. I will call them after you leave and set up a time for you to visit with them. If they are willing and available, I will let you know. Fair enough?" he again queried.

"And you will give me some background on the McKenzies, I presume." It wasn't a question, just a confirmation. "Others, too."

"Of course," replied the coach, now evermore the used car salesman.

"Then we've got a deal," Conner said, standing up and extending his hand.

Coach Wright also stood up and shook Conner's hand. "Good. Good," he said. "Now give me some of that difference making on the court. Can you still do that?"

"I'm hoping that's the case, coach."

With that response, the coach looked at Conner a little warily. He had wanted an overwhelmingly positive response, assuring himself that he had done well in this bargain. The more conservative response was a little disconcerting to him. Nevertheless, he brushed it aside, somewhat used to Conner's more humble demeanor.

"I know so, Ramsey. I know so."

Conner left, uplifted but not elated. This might work, Conner thought. Once outside, he called Esther to give her an update.

Chapter 46

When Conner returned to practice, he was greeted warmly by almost all the players, more modestly by Kline and Walker. Although the players were glad to have him back because of his basketball skills, they even more admired his strength of convictions. He was someone who distinguished between what was and was not important to him. Beyond that, though, he would not compromise where it mattered. They had a million questions for him but he asked them to hold off.

"Why don't those of you interested meet with me at the cafeteria for dinner?" he suggested. "Then I'll tell you what I can."

Most said that they could. A few had other commitments. At least it allowed everyone interested to satisfy his curiosity. It also allowed them to focus on the practice.

"Who has been leading the prayers in my absence?" Conner asked.

A whole bunch of heads bowed or looked away. From that, Conner could deduce that the prayer pilgrims had not continued praying in Conner's absence. Quick thoughts of Paul's Epistles ran through his head. He dismissed them quickly.

"Okay. Let's get back in practice."

Rather than embarrassing anyone, Conner walked to the foul line. Shedrick, Dixon and Obumje joined him immediately. Before anyone else had ventured forth, Walker said "Hey, man, haven't you given up on that stuff yet? Why don't you mumbo jumbo elsewhere?" It was a surprising turn from the Walker who just a few days ago had asked Conner to come back to the team. Perhaps he was beyond thinking that this could be a successful season.

Interestingly enough, it was Obumje who was most offended. He started to turn back to Walker but Conner caught his arm. "Not the kind of battle that wins the war or enlists soldiers for us," he said.

Obumje did not put up much of a fight. Instead, he refocused and continued his walk to the foul line.

Unexpectedly, a bass voice was the next to be heard, unmistakably Clyde Forrester's.

"You're an idiot," he said, clearly directing it to Walker. "If only to keep team harmony, why don't you shut your face!" It wasn't a question. It was an instruction. And it was given as only the Enforcer could do. To follow it up, Forrester joined the others at the foul line. This either emboldened or intimidated many of the others and all but four straightaway joined Forrester in heading to the foul line.

That left Walker, Kline and two reserves. After an additional brief hesitation, Kline and one of the reserves walked to the foul line.

Another hesitation and the final reserve joined.

Walker, still resolute, said "Whatever" in a derisive manner and turned his back on the lot.

Once in a circle at the foul line, arms around the adjacent two individuals, everyone who was going to join being there, Conner led them in a brief prayer. "Thank You, Lord. We strive to support each other, work as a team, enjoy this experience, invite others to join us and suffer the consequences of those who cannot see our purpose. May Your light eventually be seen by all and may we be instruments in helping that happen. We especially ask for prayers on behalf of our brother, Walker. In Your Son's name. Amen."

In a louder-than-expected response, those at the foul line said "Amen."

At that very same moment, Coach Wright and his assistant coaches walked onto the floor. It was obvious to the newcomers that Walker was, once again, the lone wolf...in a bad way. The head coach withheld commentary. "All up," he said, signifying that they were to assemble on the bleachers. The team was well familiar with the phrase and immediately found seats off the court.

"Gentlemen, we are back to full strength."

"Says who?" Walker spit out.

Coach Wright, noticeably red in the face from that outburst, stopped and, very deliberately, turned to face Walker, who had his arms on his thighs and was looking down, not unlike several other players. His physical posture did not give away his emotional posture. There was no question in anyone's mind who had been the player to interrupt and challenge the coach. There was now pointedly negative energy in the gym. Wright gathered himself before speaking. No player dared even breathe, Walker included. Walker realized that he had thrown down the gauntlet, not only at Conner but, with his comment, at the coach. He had unquestionably crossed the line.

"This has already been an interesting season," the coach began, more unhurriedly than normal. "In some people's minds, it has already been a lost season. Aside from the general public, that belief has reached the local media, some of our supporters and, apparently, even some of the players on this team." He had been looking around at the players as he spoke. Now he stopped and looked at Walker. The guard did not look up.

"Let me make one thing very, very clear to everyone here, players and coaches alike. There is no 'already' to this season. We are fully in control of our destiny. I plan to use our remaining conference games to get ourselves into better position for the conference tournament as well as for all that happens thereafter, including the NCAA playoffs."

Again he stopped and looked around.

"If anyone, including you, Mr. Walker, does not think that we should strive for that or that we cannot achieve those goals, I invite him or them to take their talents elsewhere. We have the talent to do this. What we need is the mental commitment to do this. We can win as a team but we cannot win as a group of guys, talented or not."

Everyone was silent.

"I am going to do something that is a little bit different. But I am just going to do it this one time. I am going to treat you as a democracy. You can choose to play toward those goals with the belief that we will achieve them or decide that you don't want to try. That choice is yours. Everyone who stays is an Eagles basketball player. Everyone who leaves is not. One at a time, I want you to tell me if you are in or out. It's your choice."

He looked around again.

"Anyone not understand that?"

Silence.

"Okay. Let's start over here," he said, pointing to Shedrick who sat on the first row to the left of the coach.

"I'm in, coach," he said with fervor.

"I'm in, coach," said Dixon.

"I'm definitely in, coach," said Forrester.

"I'm in, coach," said Obumje.

"I'm in, coach," said Conner.

Before the next person spoke, Walker stood up, got down from the bleachers and left the floor. The team was silent. Although the coach knew what had happened, he did not turn his head to acknowledge it. Instead, he kept his eyes on the next player to speak.

"Let's go," he said, wanting to get them back on track.

"I'm in, coach," said Kline.

And so it went throughout the team, everyone affirming his commitment to the team. When the last player had expressed his declaration, the coach nodded his head and put his hands on his hips.

"I'm not living in a fantasyland," he said. "We can do this. We can definitely do this. But do you think we can do it?"

"Yes, coach!!!" the team yelled as one.

"Good. Okay, let's get down to business. Guards over there and front-liners over there," he said, pointing to two parts of the gym floor. The assistant coaches had already been briefed. They knew where to go. Right now, everyone was focused on what he had to do.

The practice was one of the best they had run. They drilled like a team. They did not feel defeated, in spite of their abysmal record. They actually felt like winners. It was invigorating. Even the coaching staff took positive energy from the team instead of having to try injecting it into what had been a lethargic group.

By the time that the practice was over and every one of them had reassembled at the foul line for a closing prayer, joined by two of the assistant coaches, they were more positive than negative. Then they retired to the locker room. Walker was long gone.

"Wonder if he's coming back?" someone asked.

"Good riddance to bad rubbish," said another.

"He's a good player," someone said.

"Better than good," came the observation.

"This isn't a one-on-one sport," Forrester said.

And that ended the chatter.

Most of them went with Conner to the cafeteria to hear what he had been doing since the coach had given him an ultimatum and he had left the team. Within the realm of what he had promised God he would share, he told them what had taken place.

They loved it.

----- ----- -----

After dinner, Shedrick headed off to the library. When Conner got back to the room, he had a visitor. It was a middle-aged, extremely large, African-American woman, somewhat dowdy and, from what Conner judged by first impressions, not in a particularly splendid mood.

He stared at her, wondering why she was there. Was this another God outfit? Was it someone related to Shedrick? Was it someone who had gotten lost? Was it a nut job?

"May I help you?" he asked.

"Why would you want to, sonny boy?" she said with attitude.

He waited. She waited. He waited some more. She waited some more. He was not going to feed this fire.

Then she looked around and started laughing.

"Do you mind telling me what's so funny?" he asked.

"Why do you want to know?"

It only took a brief moment for Conner to put two and two together.

"Very funny, Lord. Very funny."

"How did you know?"

"You're the only one who consistently answers a question with a question."

"Doggone it. I have to learn to stop doing that."

"You have to learn something?"

"It's only an expression."

"Why do you answer questions with questions?"

"Habit."

"You mean to tell me that you have bad habits?"

"Why not?"

"Oh, here we go again," he said, rolling his eyes and holding his hands out, palms up.

The lady laughed, a lot of jiggling taking place along with it.

"Mind if I ask you something?"

"What?"

Conner giggled. "Once a God, always a God, eh?"

God smiled. "Predictability is good."

"Amen," Conner said.

"What's your question?"

"No insult intended but why did you pick a body like this?"

"What?"

"Why this body?"

"What's wrong with this body? Are you a bigot?"

"No! I'm not talking about skin color."

"Neither was I. Are you a fat-person or old-person bigot?"

Conner started to deny both, then didn't feel that he could do it in good conscience.

"Cat got your tongue?" God asked.

Conner made a facial expression like he didn't know exactly how to say what he knew he wanted to say.

"Just spit it out, sonny boy," she said. "You'll feel better."

"Jemima you ain't," he said.

God laughed. "You're too funny. I'll have you doing Improv when you get to heaven."

"They have things like Improv?"

God tilted his head and looked at Conner impatiently.

"I know. You'll have to kill me."

God nodded.

"Well, I guess that I am, shall we say, partial towards people who take care of themselves, whatever their ethnicity or age."

"Why?"

"Why what?"

"Quit buying time. My asking why is straightforward. Why are you partial to people who take care of themselves? Or, more relevant, why are you partial *against* people who look as though they don't take care of themselves?"

"It's unhealthy." Pause. "It's unattractive." Pause. "It's...it's...I don't know. It's a sign of slovenliness."

"Ooo. Four syllables. Good word."

"Come on. Really. Why don't you come around as a healthy person?"

"What makes you say that I'm not healthy?"

"All other things being equal, overweight ain't healthy."

"Overweight ain't healthy," God repeated, in exactly the same voice, pitch and intonation.

Hearing it made Conner realize that this lazy-speak did not do anything for him. He vowed to try to stop using it.

Conner continued with his thinking. "I don't know. I would be less inclined to trust myself or my loved ones to someone who doesn't have enough pride to take care of him or herself. That's all."

"What if I told you that I had a congenital proclivity toward gaining weight and that I couldn't do anything about it?"

"I wouldn't believe you."

"You wouldn't? That's incredible."

God using words like incredible seemed...well, incredible. How could anything be incredible to him?

"I like what I created," God said, reading Conner's mind. "I was happy in Genesis and I've been pretty happy since, especially since having my boy come back home."

Conner knew that he was referring to the resurrection of Jesus.

"But that begs the question. Why wouldn't you believe me?"

Keeping in touch with the main thread of the conversation was becoming increasingly difficult. However, Conner did remember that the question on the table asked why Conner could not excuse fat people from being fat.

"They may not become bodybuilders or swimsuit models but they can do better. Some portion of it is lack of discipline," Conner said.

"Poor boy," God said.

"Why?"

"Because you are intolerant. You judge people by how you act or think you would act. It doesn't work that way."

"I beg to differ. There are very few people who wouldn't agree with me."

"Wrong, bad breath. There are a lot of people who don't care."

"I find that hard to believe…unless they, too, are fat and out of shape."

"Believe what you want. I'm giving you the cow's moo."

"The expression is the cat's meow."

"Whatever."

"You're telling me that I should feel differently or can make myself feel differently?"

"Both."

"Is this a guilt trip?"

"You want one?"

"No."

"Then it's not."

"Thank God."

"You're welcome."

"You're nuts."

"Do you know what happened to the last person who said that to me?"

"Time out," Conner said, making a basketball timeout sign.

"What?"

"Am I saved?"

"Yes," God said like a little kid who just admitted that he took cookies from a cookie jar.

"Then I'm more relaxed. What happened to him...or her?"

"Nothing."

"How do you tolerate that?"

"I look into a person's heart."

"Then why did you kill that person who touched the tabernacle or convert Lot's wife into a salt pillar when she looked back or kill the couple who didn't give everything to the apostles?"

"You tell me."

Conner thought for a moment. "Because they weren't right in their hearts?"

"Bingo!"

Makes sense, Conner thought. "I'll bet at church that we can't tell who's right in his heart and who's not. Right?"

"Not right. If you're right in your heart, it's likely that you'll see others who are as well."

"But...?"

"But if you're not right in your heart, you won't have a clue."

Conner soaked it in.

"I don't really get you."

God laughed. It started as a smile, morphed into a giggle and then erupted into a huge belly laugh, tears and all. When she finally calmed down, she started to say something. Unable to articulate it, she started laughing again. A few iterations later, she said "Isaiah 55:8."

God quoting his Bible. Wow. Conner got out his Bible and rifled through it until he found the passage. God waited patiently. Conner read out loud.

For my thoughts are not your thoughts, neither are your ways my ways, declares the Lord. As the heavens are higher than the earth, so are my ways higher than your ways and my thoughts than your thoughts.

When Conner had finished reading, God asked "Get it?"

"The passage?"

"No. What you said."

Conner thought back but couldn't remember what he had said that God found this funny.

"You said 'I don't really get you.' Now how funny is that?"

Conner stared at him.

"You need help, son." And, with that, he disappeared.

Conner slumped back into bed.

"This whole thing is a dream, isn't it?" he asked no one.

"Nope. It's real," came the response from the otherwise empty room.

Chapter 47

When Conner awoke, he felt great. It was one of the best sleeps he had gotten in a long time. A very long time. He offered a morning prayer, focusing on a recommitment to his mission. All the other stuff – Shedrick, Esther, classes, popularity, even basketball – was good but leading others to Christ, well, that was beyond good. Way beyond good. Or, as he liked to say, waaay good.

He called Esther. "Ya comin' to the game?" he asked, although he knew the answer.

"No, I can't," she said, totally surprising him.

"You can't?" he whined. "Why not?"

"I have a date," she answered matter of factly.

He paused. Was this a joke? "With whom?" he asked, trying not to be possessive.

"You, of course, silly."

He breathed a sigh of relief. "Do not, under *any* circumstances, ever do that to me again. I'm an old man and you almost killed me."

"I'll come to your funeral."

"Don't bother."

She laughed. "Good luck."

"Thanks. See ya there."

"Bye."

"Bye."

----- ----- -----

"Ya ready?" Shedrick asked.

"I hope so," Conner answered.

"I'm really looking to wake up the crowd and change some opinions."

Conner nodded. "Anyone talk with Walker?"

"Nah. He's a moron. All that talent and no brains."

"See ya later," Conner said and left.

----- ----- -----

Conner knocked on the door. No answer. He knocked more loudly.

"What?" came the harsh salutation.

"It's Conner Ramsey. Can I speak with you for a minute?"

"No. I'm done talking," Walker said, but it didn't sound totally convincing.

"You don't have to say anything. I'll do all the talking and then I'll leave."

"It's open," Walker said and Conner went in.

The layout was similar to the one that Conner shared with Shedrick except that Walker got to live by himself. The room was actually neater than he had expected. As soon as he recognized his thoughts, he looked up and silently apologized, remembering his conversation with the Lord the previous night.

"What do you want?" Walker challenged. "Haven't you done enough already?"

Conner wanted to confront Walker. He hadn't done anything. Walker had done it entirely to himself. Instead, Conner took a breath before responding.

"Hey, I'm sorry for whatever role I played in that. I really am."

Walker said and did nothing. Conner continued.

"It never was my intention to displace or steal any glory from you. You're an incredible player. I'm good on defense and you're incredible on offense. But people come to watch offense."

Walker didn't say anything but his body language was just a bit more open.

"If I was the coach," he continued, "I'd have me play defense and you score 100 points."

Walker smiled thinking of scoring 100 points. The last person he knew who had scored 100 points was Wilt Chamberlain. That was in an NBA game.

"Also, basketball isn't what drives me, no pun intended."

Walker looked at him with a poker face. I wouldn't want to play cards with this guy, Conner thought.

"What drives you?" Walker asked, although somewhat contemptuously.

"My faith. If I can model it correctly, I feel as though I can make a difference for some people, perhaps many people. Basketball gives me a little bit of a platform to do that. If I wasn't on this team, nobody would pay attention to what I want to do. On this team, around well-known people like you, I get a little bit of your spotlight. Those who are open to it, then, might get encouragement. Make sense?"

Walker had started to nod in agreement. With the last question, he answered "Yeah. Sort of. I don't believe in God but I can sort of see where you're comin' from."

"Wow. That's great," Conner said, trying hard to exude excitement. "Only trouble is that with you gone, there's no spotlight. Besides, we seem not able to score without you."

Conner wondered if he had overdone it.

"You'll be fine," Walker said, starting to turn away.

"No, we won't," Conner replied. "The team needs you and I need you. Please come back."

"But the coach don't need me."

"He does but, well, he's a bit stubborn. Like you." Conner smiled.

Walker looked up. Then he smiled, too.

"You think he's gonna change his mind? I don't."

"If I talk with him and he is okay with it, will you come back?"

Walker held out for a little while, then said "Yeah."

"You'll probably have to apologize."

"I can apologize and then drop in 30," he responded, resorting to his natural cockiness.

"Will you be here for a while?" Conner asked.

"Yeah," said Walker. "Besides, here's my cell phone number." He held up his phone and Conner punched the number into his own phone. Then he attached a name to it.

"I'll return in a little while. Don't wander away."

----- ----- -----

"Coach," Conner began.

Coach Wright looked up. When he saw it was Conner, he smiled.

"Coach," Conner repeated. "I just spoke with Walker."

Wright's eyes opened in semi-amazement. He said nothing.

"He feels bad about how he acted and what he did."

"He should," the coach agreed.

"He wants to come back."

The coach wanted him back but didn't want to look bad.

"He's willing to apologize and not do that again."

Coach Wright was giving in to his wish to pull off his basketball miracle. "Well…"

"Can I tell him to join us for the game tonight?" Conner asked, much like a little kid asking to open just one Christmas present early.

"You sure that he will apologize?"

"I am."

The coach squinted his eyes as he looked at Conner. "How come you know all this? I thought that you two didn't like each other."

"We made up."

"Like heck you did."

"No, really. I went over there and we talked it through."

"That's even more of a miracle than that thing you did with Shedrick."

Conner smiled and waited.

The coach then completed talking himself into it. "Okay. Go get him. If he comes over now and talks with me – and is sincere with his apology – I'll let him play."

"Super, coach," Conner said and dashed out of the office, not wanting the coach to either change his mind or append any conditions to his statement.

----- ----- -----

"You still willing to apologize?" Conner began part two of the conversation with Walker.

"I am."

Every time Conner heard that statement (I am) he smiled. It was so…Biblical. The one that always stuck in his head was Exodus 3:14 when God was speaking with Moses. *I am who I am*, he had said. Those five words had been difficult for Conner to understand. The Lord's last conversation with him had shed a bit of light on it. God is different from us.

Conner flashed back to his surprise in class this semester when the professor had challenged the class to define everything that the Lord claimed to be. Conner's list had been lengthy. I am your shield, your reward, God almighty, the Lord, the first, the last, your husband, the living bread, the light of the world, the gate for the sheep, the good shepherd, the resurrection and the life, the way and the truth and the life, the father and the son and the holy spirit, and his list had gone on. He had been intrigued by this assignment and had spent an inordinate amount of time on it. Where others had come up with ten or fifteen, Conner's list was several dozen long. It even impressed the professor.

"What's the matter?" Walker asked, jolting Conner back to the present.

"Nothing. Nothing. If you are ready to apologize, then get yourself over to the coach's office."

Walker was out of the room before the second syllable of Conner's last word. Here Walker had thought that his college career, likely his professional prospects, would be over. Now he had been given a second chance.

Conner smiled.

At the same time, Walker ducked his head back around the door frame. "Thanks," he said, very uncharacteristically.

"Go get 'em," Conner called after Walker.

----- ----- -----

When they got to Carlson Fieldhouse, Conner felt a burst of excitement. He had worried about not being able to return, not to get the rush of the crowd and not to have this source for his mission. Even empty, the place made noise, even in the locker room.

"Ready to play?"

Conner looked up. It was Walker.

"I most certainly am. I'm glad to see you here."

"Me, too. I mean I'm glad to be here."

There was an awkward silence.

"Thanks," Walker said.

"You're more than welcome, my friend," Conner said and stood up.

The two men shook hands warmly.

"You got some points in you?" Conner asked, breaking the slightly uncomfortable moment.

"I do. You got some defense in you?" Walker countered.

For a second, Conner wondered if God had inhabited Walker, then dismissed it.

"I do."

"Then let's do it," Walker concluded as several other players entered the locker room.

Walker, to his credit, simply said to everyone "I'm back, I'm bad and I'm sorry."

The rest of those present either fist shook with him or said something welcoming. Then everyone turned to getting ready for this evening's foe, the team's eleventh conference game.

After the warm-up, the coach had them assemble in the locker room. "Gents, I feel an air of confidence about the rest of the season." He seemed unusually cheerful. "Tonight is the first step back. The Bulldogs have been playing well and a win would be nice. We'll start with Kline, Walker, Forrester, Obumje and Dixon. I plan on substituting a lot."

He looked around. All eyes were on him, even Walker's.

"I won't say that this is a dirty team but I will say that it will be the most physical team you faced since the University of Texas/Mesquite."

Someone called out "That team wasn't physical, coach. They were more like thugs."

"I know. That's behind us. I tell you about their physicality because I don't want anyone losing his cool. If there's an altercation, you let the refs sort it out. If anyone – and I mean anyone – gets in fisticuffs or, if he isn't playing, gets off the bench, there will be repercussions."

He looked around.

"I'm serious about this. Do you all understand?"

"Yes, coach!"

"They're a good team. We're a better team. Do we have a W in us tonight?"

"Yes, coach!"

"Good. Well, don't sit around here. Get out there."

When they got out there, before anything else, Obumjc said "Foul line," and was followed there by everyone on the team, Walker included. A marvelous hush came over the crowd and it sent chills throughout the many who knew what was going on. As much as it could, the crowd silenced, almost as though the public address announcer had asked for a moment of silence. Without being asked, Obumje led the prayer. He thanked the Lord for bringing the team back together again, both in health and in spirit. He ended, much to Conner's surprise, with "Bless us on this mission, one bigger than this or any other game."

When they broke the circle, the crowd gave them an immense cheer. It was as though this was a long-standing tradition. Conner hoped that it was for the right reasons. As they headed back to the bench, Conner trotted over to Obumje, put his arm around him and said "You, my friend, are an astounding influence. Keep it up."

Obumje smiled warmly but said nothing.

----- ----- -----

The game seesawed back and forth throughout the first eleven minutes. Wright kept his starters in for that time. Conway fouled hard but clean. No technical fouls were called. At 26-all, Conner and Shedrick checked in. The roar from the crowd was surprising. It was almost as though this was the last game of the season and the one player who hadn't played all year was getting a chance. The visiting players looked over to see what was going on, then were called back to the huddle by their coach. "Stay focused, men!" he yelled at them.

Before the whistle was blown, Conner said a silent prayer. He wondered if he needed to take a more active role, especially since he would be speaking with boosters. If he was viewed by them as a more important part of this team, they would be more likely to have some flexibility in their positions. At least he hoped so. Yes, he thought, I need to be a more important part of this victory.

The Bulldogs inbounded. As usual, the Eagles' big men knew to limit the visitors to one shot and Shedrick knew to press the shooter, forcing him to the middle. When the shooter stepped around Shedrick's pressing defense, Conner stole the ball and fed his roomie for an easy dunk. This happened two more times before the shooter decided that it was not pure luck. The next time, he thought drawing Conner in would result in an easy pass but Conner picked that one off and fed Shedrick for his eighth straight point, now the difference in the score, 34-26. Needless to say, the crowd was delirious. Although they had scored eight unanswered points, the Eagles had yet to inbound the ball since Conner and Shedrick had checked in.

Shedrick and Conner had developed a recognition handshake for one another following one of these breakaways. It was something that had come naturally, not contrived, as were many others. No chest pounding or other I-am-great histrionics. They even entitled their recognition, calling it 'Glory.'

After a score, Shedrick would trot back on defense and swing by Conner. They would fist touch, point briefly at each other and then point upward, holding that a bit longer. By the fourth time they had done this since checking in, fans were beginning to imitate them.

The visiting coach called time out. Although he didn't have a strategy to combat this defense, he proceeded to yell at his team for being sloppy. Meanwhile, on the Eagles' bench, the coach didn't say anything, a rare instance for that to happen.

Realizing that penetration was not going to work, the shooting guard put up a distant three and made it. Even the crowd was impressed. However, it was not likely that shots like that were going to be very successful. Shedrick apologized to Conner who said "Let him shoot from half court if he wants. He won't make ten percent of those." Shedrick nodded, glad to be supported.

Now the Eagles were up by five. When Conner got the ball, his man pressed him. With no trouble, Conner blew past him and scored an easy layup, then stole the inbound pass and scored again. The lead hopped to nine, 38-29 with five minutes left to play in the half. The crowd loved it.

After another wild shot, this one not finding the net, the Bulldogs went back on defense. When Conner got the ball, his man backed off him a little, giving him room to shoot from the outside. Even

though he was tempted, Conner knew that he was a
lousy shot. Instead, he served a soft lob into
Forrester who had an easy dunk.

Once again, Conner stole the ball and scored on
an uncontested layup. The visitors called another
time out. Coach Wright put Walker and Kline back
in. Forrester, Obumje and Dixon had played the
entire first half but the coach didn't feel the need to
substitute for them. They were fine.

When the Eagles took the court, there wasn't
exactly booing not to see number seven out there,
but there was clearly disappointment. However,
acknowledging that they were up by thirteen with
three minutes to play in the half, it wasn't an active
protest. It was more displeasure in not having the
catalyst in the lineup.

The crowd started a chant. "Seven, seven, seven,"
it sang. Spontaneously, the number was recited in
groups of three. "Seven, seven, seven," then a brief
break, repeated by "Seven, seven, seven," on and on.
Conner sat on the bench and bowed his head,
appreciative of the support but embarrassed by it.
He went to prayer.

When Brantley got the ball back after a Bulldogs
score, Walker hit a three pointer and was fouled in
the act. He made the free throw, thus achieving a
four-point play, one of the rarities in basketball. At
the end of the half, the score was 48-33.

In the locker room, the coach assembled his
squad before they did anything else. "You see what
we can do?" he asked.

The players mostly nodded.

"Do you?" he repeated.

"Yes, coach!" they now exclaimed as one.

"This is a good team but they look like rookies when we play our game. Let's continue. Now get ready." Then he turned and left the meeting room.

The second half began with the same Eagles starting five. Halfway into that period, Brantley had added two to its lead, the score standing at 78-61. At that point, Coach Wright substituted liberally but he kept Conner on the bench. When the crowd saw this, they began their "Seven, seven, seven" refrain.

The coach came over to Conner and leaned down to say something private to him while the fans continued their chant. "I want to give some of the other players a chance," he said.

Conner looked up to judge for himself the sincerity of this statement. He wasn't sure but nodded his agreement. Then, before the coach withdrew, Conner asked "You're still gonna set up appointments with the boosters, right?"

"Absolutely," said the coach. "You earned it," he added.

"Then I have no problem, coach," Conner said.

The visitors made a slight push against the bench players and the game ended 94-81. The players from each team exchanged handshakes and then Obumje led the team to the foul line. Shedrick offered the prayer. None of the visiting players joined.

Richard Means was the first one to grab Conner after this. Although other media wanted his attention, Means got to privately ask Conner what he thought of the fans' support.

"Fantastic," he said. "I am very appreciative of the reception that I have gotten."

"You turned the game around almost singlehandedly," Means noted and waited for some sort of response. Conner neither said nor did anything. "To what do you credit that? How can you make such a difference in such a short period of time?"

"You know that I praise the Lord, Richard, and to him give all the credit. You know my background and you know how true that statement is."

Before Means or any other press representative could ask other questions, Conner said "Thanks" and ran into the locker room. The media turned to those who remained on the court, especially the coach and Walker. That was fine with Conner and fine with the two individuals still remaining for interviews.

----- ----- -----

The next day, Conner knocked on the coach's door.

Coach Wright looked up. "Yes, yes," he said, holding his hands up defensively. Then he searched around his desk and was able to find a slip of paper. "I made an appointment for you to have dinner with the McKenzies tonight. I assume that you are available?"

Conner had a big smile on his face. "I'll take that as a positive," the coach said. He gave Conner the paper. "That's their address. They are expecting you at 6:30."

"Anyone else?" Conner asked.

"Anyone else what?"

"Am I the sole guest or will others be there, as well?"

"Not from the team, if that's what you mean. Other than that, I have no idea."

"And I take it that I should go alone, without a date?"

"Listen, Conner," the coach said, slightly agitated. "You wanted time with the boosters. I got it for you. Now just go there and don't piss them off."

"Got it, coach. Thanks."

----- ----- -----

Conner, Esther and Shedrick met for ice cream. Conner shared both his excitement and nervousness at meeting with these boosters. Both Esther and Shedrick were encouraging. "Don't you always say that God will give you the words when you need them?" Shedrick had challenged.

Hoisted on his own petard, thought Conner. "Yes. Matthew 10:20," he said, smiling. "It's as good as gold. *Don't worry about what to say in your defense because you will be given the right words at the right time. For it won't be you doing the talking — it will be the Spirit of your Father speaking through you.* Thanks for the reminder," Conner added.

They then discussed what he should wear, deciding that a sports jacket without a tie would be appropriate. They ended this conversation with a prayer for success.

Chapter 48

The McKenzie grounds were gorgeous. One drove for about two hundred yards before reaching the actual house. It looked like something in a movie. Conner wondered what living a life like this would feel like.

The door was opened by what appeared to be a butler. He wore a black vest over a white shirt and had on a bowtie. He wore black slacks. "Mr. Ramsey, I believe," he said. "Please come in." Conner entered. "Please follow me." Conner was led into a huge den, for lack of a better descriptor. It was an open area that really didn't have a ceiling. Instead, it was more like an atrium. Its height extended to the roof of the two-story structure. It probably encompassed close to 1,000 square feet by itself, had an enormous fireplace with bookshelves along each wall. There were animal trophies wherever the bookshelves permitted. All throughout, there was Brantley basketball memorabilia – pictures, basketballs, all sorts of things. There were several leather sofas and a myriad of other expensive furniture throughout the room. Conner marveled at the sight of all this, somewhat stupefied by the wealth as well as the devotion to Brantley basketball.

"Good evening, Mr. Ramsey," came a voice from behind him. He turned to see an elderly man making his way across the room. "I am Gordon McKenzie. My wife will be down in a few minutes. I am glad that you could find the time to join us for dinner."

By the time he had completed that opening, he was across the room. The two men shook hands.

"Please," he said, motioning to a seat. Conner did as his host bid. McKenzie sat down across from him. "May I get you something to drink?" Before hearing the answer, he turned in his chair and called out "Martin," in half a demand and half a question. Immediately, the butler appeared. Then McKenzie turned back to Conner for an answer to the question.

"Um, club soda would be delightful. Thank you very much."

"With or without lime, sir?" Martin asked.

"With, please," he responded.

"I'll have the usual," McKenzie instructed.

"Very good, sir."

"He'll be back soon," McKenzie said. He was quiet for just a moment. "Quite a game against the Bulldogs," he began. "You turned a close game into a comfortable victory."

"Thank you, sir," Conner said.

"I didn't realize that you were quite the talent that you are. It's good to have you on this team."

"Thank you, sir."

"If we are to get along, young man, I will have you address me as Gordon. Okay?"

"Yes, sir. Er, I mean, yes, Gordon." Both men smiled. This exchange reminded Conner of when he had first met Coach Wright. I guess that nobody likes to be called sir, he said to himself.

"Speaking of young man, that's not exactly what you are. I mean you are to me but you must come across as a grandpa to your teammates, especially your sidekick, Harris."

Conner smiled.

"They're not put off by it?" he asked.

"Not so far," Conner said. "They cut me some slack."

"When you can do some of the things that you do, it's not a wonder."

"Thank you, sir, er, Gordon."

"Listen, Conner," he began as he sat back in his chair. "I think that we both have objectives in meeting today. I'd like to get to them before my wife comes down. She doesn't like my talking business."

"Fine with me…Gordon."

"I want a winning team. I had toyed with buying a professional franchise but didn't really want to tie up my money without being able to get involved. Aside from minor league basketball and some small market NBA teams, nothing was either available or within my budget."

He took a thoughtful breath, then continued. "Consequently, I looked in my own back yard. Lo and behold, there was my alma mater. Now, obviously, as a supporter, I'm limited by the NCAA in what I can do. I can't pay you or give you things. On the upside, however, I can make life for you a whole lot better after you graduate." He stopped for a moment and looked at Conner as though inspecting his face. "Am I getting through to you, son?"

"Loud and clear, sir." Being called son made it much more logical to employ sir.

"Good. Now, from what I hear, you have an evangelical spirit about you. Is that correct?"

"It is, indeed."

"And what does that mean?"

"Well, sir, Gordon, my priorities differ from many others, at least those on the team. At least I think that they do."

"Keep going," McKenzie requested leaning forward.

Conner also sat forward, trying to mirror McKenzie's posture. This was a wise body language move. Like McKenzie, he took a deep breath, before offering his thoughts. "I believe in God. I believe in the Trinity. I believe that there is a heaven and hell. I believe that God gives us mercy and grace. I also believe that he offers us salvation through him. I want to do what I can to have as many people as possible achieve that salvation." He stopped for a second. "That's pretty much it in a nutshell."

"I see," McKenzie said, holding his lips in a manner that would suggest reflection. "I see," he repeated.

"May I ask you a question, sir?"

"I reckon."

"Do you have a walk with the Lord?"

"I do."

"If I am not being too intrusive, might you share your testimony with me?"

McKenzie looked over at Conner and squinted, perhaps wondering if the question was for real or just playful. He determined pretty easily that it was for real.

"I don't have a special testimony, son, but I do believe in God, I go to church periodically and I always contribute to my church. I think that they call it tithing these days."

Conner smiled. They've been calling it tithing for a few thousand years, he said to himself. "That's superb, sir. Therefore, you can see why it is very important to me."

"I'm not sure that I can, son. Oh, I think that it's important but once you accept Christ, then your eternity is pretty much made, isn't it?"

Here was one of the toughest theological questions of all time and Gordon McKenzie simply wanted a yes or a no. Conner wondered how he could handle this. He thought about a passage he had read just the night before. It was James 2:14-17.

What good is it, my brothers and sisters, if someone claims to have faith but has no deeds? Can such faith save them? Suppose a brother or a sister is without clothes and daily food. If one of you says to them, "Go in peace; keep warm and well fed," but does nothing about their physical needs, what good is it? In the same way, faith by itself, if it is not accompanied by action, is dead.

"Something like that," he responded. "People debate about how much one has to do beyond accepting Christ but you're certainly in the ballpark."

McKenzie sat back with an approving nod, suggesting that he reaffirmed his position such that he would be in heaven.

"Mr. McKenzie…"

"Gordon."

"Gordon, it is clear that you believe that there is a heaven and hell. Correct?"

"I do."

"Excellent. And you believe that the choice is ours as to where we spend our eternal lives. Correct?"

"Heaven or the hot place," he answered with a reflective smile.

"Okay. You want as many people as possible to attain heaven. Correct?"

"Well...not really, son. I want my family, my friends and those people who are good to spend the rest of their time in heaven. As for Hitler, Mussolini, Osama Bin Laden, Jack the Ripper and people like that...no, I don't. They can fry for all I care."

"I appreciate your candor, sir. I really do."

"Do you agree with that?"

"Not exactly. But let's not dwell on what I believe right now. We can come back to it if you wish."

"Okay."

"Let's just take that pool of people whom you love. You want them to get into heaven. Right?"

"I sure do."

"And you would do whatever you could to enable them to do so. Correct?"

"I surely would."

"Mr. McKenzie – Gordon – that's all I am doing. The only difference between you and me is that I have a larger pool of people that I want to make it into heaven. That's all."

McKenzie chewed on that, clearly wrestling with it. Before he could respond, in walked Mrs. McKenzie. Conner stood up immediately. McKenzie struggled a bit to stand up but managed to do so.

"Mr. Ramsey," she said with a delightful though not recognizable American accent. "My husband has been raging about what a gift you are to the university."

"How nice, ma'am," Conner said. "And your husband has been raging how lucky he is to have the gift of you. And now I can see why."

McKenzie beamed like the Cheshire Cat in Alice in Wonderland. Whether real or fake, Conner could see just about every single one of his white, straight teeth.

"How sweet of you to say so," she said. "Have you gentlemen solved the world's problems?"

"We were just getting started, my dear. Another five minutes and we would have finished with world peace." He winked at Conner who smiled back.

"That's lovely, dear," she said. "I will let you resume your work immediately after dinner. Right now, though, please join me."

They made their way into the dining room. Conner was again taken aback thinking that they could fit a couple of dozen people around the table. The place settings were ridiculously situated for a dinner like this. Mrs. McKenzie sat at one end, Mr. McKenzie at another and Conner right in the middle. Even though the house and dining room were remarkably quiet, they actually had to talk a bit louder to hear one another.

Mrs. McKenzie was not a basketball fan. She rather tolerated or even encouraged her husband much like a wife might do for a golf lover. She knew little of the school's history of success, virtually nothing about the horrors of this year and little about Conner's skills. It was likely that Mr. McKenzie had given her last-minute preparation on their visitor. It was probably just as well since this allowed the dinner conversation to be on non-basketball topics.

Eventually, Mrs. McKenzie got around to asking "What are you studying?"

"I am working on a degree in Biblical Studies."

"What degree is that?" she asked.

"It's a master's degree."

"How interesting. I share fellowship with some lady friends of mine. We meet every two weeks. My husband does not necessarily share my passion but we do attend church. What do you plan to do with your degree when you complete it?"

"I'm not exactly sure, Mrs. McKenzie."

"Call me Doris."

"Yes, ma'am…er, Doris. I want to do something in the faith world but I'm not exactly certain what it will be."

"My, my," she said. "Wouldn't it be nice if more people went into the faith world?" she mused.

"It would, indeed," he said.

There was no follow on to this and the three proceeded to enjoy their meal. The butler was serving it and it was clear that a chef was in the kitchen preparing it. Conner had caught a glimpse of the kitchen staff when the butler had come through the door separating the two rooms. There might even have been more than one other person in the kitchen, although Conner wasn't sure. What a life, he thought.

For as fancy a setting, there was not much pretense in table manners. Mrs. McKenzie was much more polished than her husband but she, too, could have benefitted from table etiquette lessons. Mr. McKenzie looked as though he would have been more comfortable on a cattle drive. It was a funny contrast. Conner just kept to himself, answering questions and asking his own without being intrusive.

The meal, itself, was magnificent. They had prosciutto with melon for the first course, salad for the second, roast beef, English peas and Yorkshire pudding for the third, black forest cake for dessert and tea for follow up. This was certainly the most elegant meal that Conner had consumed in a long time, if not ever. He regretted that Esther had not been with him. Maybe in the future. It would have been a fun experience to share, one that would have provided many laughs in its remembrance.

Once the meal was through, Mrs. McKenzie said "I will leave you boys to talk your basketball talk. That's more Gordon's thing. I look forward to seeing you again in the future, Conner. Good luck with your studies."

Conner stood up. "Thank you, Mrs. McKenzie. This has been a wonderful, wonderful evening. I look forward to seeing you again soon, as well."

When she had departed, Mr. McKenzie said "Come on. Let's get back to our little chat. But let's do it in the other room."

They retired to the den and reclaimed their same two seats.

"Now, where were we, son?"

Conner remembered exactly. "We were agreeing that we wanted the same thing to happen, that of people getting to heaven, but that you were a little bit more restrictive in the number of people you thought should get in."

"Yes, yes. Exactly." He nodded his head in agreement. "Yes, that's exactly it. Make heaven available to everyone, except some of those…" His voice tailed off and it was obvious that he didn't want to finish. Then he lightened up, adding "And anyone from the University of Illinois." Both of them laughed at that. It was a good moment that they shared.

After time to savor that, Conner said "Mr. McKenzie, Coach Wright said that some folks did not appreciate my interest in achieving what you and I want to achieve."

It was a brilliant move that he was making in putting the two of them on the same side of the discussion. He continued.

"He suggested that I confirm our common destination because you are, by far, the most influential member of the booster family."

By his body language, Conner could see that his host was not going to deny that recognition but that he was not going to crow about it either. Realizing that Mr. McKenzie had nothing to offer to this conversation at the moment, Conner continued.

"I am not planning to do anything radical. In fact, I have no plans for anything at the moment. My hope this evening was to make certain that I was on the same page as you, to gather your advice as to how to proceed and to see if you had any ideas of how I could invite others to the kingdom of heaven. I believe that you, sir, have a meaningful role to play in God's plan. Your encouragement of me is part of that."

With that, Conner knew it was time to stitch his mouth closed. He did so.

Again, McKenzie pressed his lips together, clearly thinking about the issue and what to say regarding it. Finally, he spoke.

"You are improbable," he began, actually a good description of Conner. How good, he could not have fathomed.

Conner said nothing. He just listened. McKenzie continued.

"But I can see that you are right on target. I like the fact that you have a head on your shoulders and a glorious purpose in mind. I like that we can make a difference to where people spend their eternity."

He stopped again and it was apparent that he was envisioning something. While he did so, Conner thanked God silently and remained quiet. McKenzie gathered his words and continued.

"I don't have anything specific in mind at this moment but I will give it some thought. As you think of things, I want you to share them with me. Perhaps together we can do something special."

Conner wanted to jump up and scream "Yes!" and make a fist pump like a golfer sinking a 70-foot putt on the final hole of a major championship to win by one stroke. However, he knew that he had to play second fiddle to this man of influence.

"I suspect that the best ideas will come out of you, sir, but I will put my gray cells to work on it. I can promise you that."

"Excellent," McKenzie said. "Excellent," he repeated. "If God is listening to us now, I'll bet he is pleased with what we have decided to do."

You don't know the half of it, Conner thought. "Yes, sir. I'll bet that he is, indeed."

McKenzie stood up, again slightly struggling to do so. Conner arose, as well. "I guess that you need your beauty rest," he said. "I do, too."

"This has been a privilege for me, Mr. McKenzie, er, Gordon. A real honor. The thought of working with you on something this important... Well, I couldn't have foreseen having someone this influential as a colleague, if you will allow me to presume."

"Presume away, son. Presume away. Onward Christian soldier and all that."

They smiled at one another. "Now to bed," he said. "And for you, I will look for wonderful successes on the court but also to your ideas off the court. Yes, this is good. Very good."

They shook hands and Conner departed, escorted to the front door by the butler whom his host had somehow summoned without Conner realizing it. Once in the car and on his way, Conner shouted

"Yes!" He felt his face breaking from the size of his smile. "God, you are amazing!" He paused briefly, then yelled "Amazing!"

Chapter 49

Several stories on the basketball team dominated the sports pages in the *Sentinel*. One focused on the team's blanketing defense. Another highlighted Conner's change-the-game influence. A third, less high-profile and considerably shorter, dealt with how faith-based this team had become and how the crowd was responding.

'The respectful silence that comes over this crowd when the team assembles at the foul line is truly something to behold,' it read. 'There is almost a feeling that one is in church instead of in Carlson Fieldhouse. Truly astonishing.'

"Hey, check this out," Shedrick said to Conner in their room. He set the article on top of Conner's books, interrupting his study.

"What?" Conner said, engrossed in his studies and a little annoyed about being interrupted from it.

"Read it. You want to reach others? You're doing it."

With that as a promo, Conner couldn't help but read the article. As he did so, he smiled. When he had finished reading it, he said "That's great. That's really great."

"It is, it is," Shedrick said. "It is, it is," he repeated.

When the two of them got to the gym for practice, Coach Murphy leaned into the locker room and said to Conner "Coach wants to see you."

"Be right there."

Conner finished dressing and hustled to the coach's office.

"Yes, coach?" he said by way of salutation.

"Close the door and sit down, Ramsey," he began.

It wasn't a tone of friendliness but it also wasn't exactly a tone of impending reprimand. Conner did as he was told and waited.

Once seated, the coach said "What the heck went on at the McKenzies?"

"Excuse me, coach?" Conner said, looking for some guidance as to the way that this conversation would be headed.

"You heard me, Ramsey. You deaf and old, too?"

"I thought that it was a wonderful evening, coach. Did something happen that I don't know about?"

"Yes. Old man McKenzie called me and just sang your praises. He said that he was glad to have been reminded that there are more important things than basketball."

Conner was leery. "And that's good or is it bad?" he queried.

"It's good in that he likes you. It better not be bad in that he doesn't contribute the way he always has."

Personally, Conner was elated. However, since the result threatened contributions to the Brantley basketball program, he decided to mute his excitement.

"Thanks, coach. You had me worried there for a minute."

"You should be worried," the coach continued. "Don't you go redirecting basketball money to the holy roller stuff."

Conner stayed silent.

"Do you hear me?"

"I hear you," Conner said, not committing to agreement.

"Now get out of here."

"Coach?"

"What!?!"

"You're still going to set up another appointment for me, aren't you?"

"You're still going to set up another appointment for me, aren't you?" he mimicked, although in much more of a baby voice. "Yes, provided that you wipe the smile off of the Wisconsin/Geneva mascot when we play them."

"I'll try," he said.

"You better do more than try. Now beat it."

Conner laughed good naturedly as he left.

----- ----- -----

Practice went well. The team seemed to gel in a way that had not been the case up to this point in time, certainly not recently. Nobody could identify anything in particular but all of them had the sense of being a family unit. The practice and the meeting afterwards were both productive and enjoyable.

Aside from the one class that they shared, Conner hadn't seen much of Esther. The two had agreed to have dinner after practice. With fond memories of a great pizza, they went back to Bruno's.

"I really like you," she said. It wasn't easy for her to say this first but she wanted to tell him.

"What a coincidence," he said, "because I really like you."

"Tell me more about your visit with the McKenzies." Conner had given her an executive summary of the dinner over the phone that evening. Now, she was excited to hear all about it, to get some play-by-play.

He told her about their pre-dinner conversation. "That's great" she said. Then he told her about the dinner. "Wow. Sounds yummy." And he concluded with the magnificent after-dinner conversion, as he now called it. "That is fantastic," she said. "You are amazing."

It was at this moment that Conner wanted to tell her about God and the genesis of this ministry. However, he held back doing so for two reasons. One, he didn't want to stretch his credibility with her. Two, he still remembered his bleacher conversation in the recreation center with the player who turned out to be God, reminding him not to explain anything about this to anyone.

"The descriptor 'amazing' belongs to God, Esther." For some reason, Conner felt strongly about the use of this word. "I feel his direction and I am going with it. He is the one who is opening the doors. If we can reach a few…"

"You have already reached more than a few," she commented.

"If we can reach a few, we can reach many more. That's our destination."

"You're well on your way," she said. "I just love your passion about this, your humility and your, well, just your goodness. I feel really good about sharing this journey with you."

"And I with you. You're not just a passenger, you know. You're an inspiration, a strategist, a soldier, a recruiter and a dozen other things."

"Yes, sir," she said and saluted, a great big smile shining on her face.

He smiled with her but then got serious. "I hope that it continues this well," he said.

"Why shouldn't it?"

"Oh, I don't know. Injury or something else."

"Hey, listen," she said, taking his hand. "I doubt that anything is going to happen to you or that a huge boulder is going to drop onto the road. But, if it does, God is there. 'If he brought you to it…'"

"…he will bring you through it," Conner finished. "Yeah, you're right, of course. They don't call him 'The Man' for nothing!" With that, he did a rat-a-tat-tat on the table and the joviality of the evening returned.

They enjoyed the evening together before each turned in. Tomorrow was to be a busy day and each had things to prepare, including homework.

"See ya tomorrow."

"God willing."

"God willing. Amen."

----- ----- -----

That weekend was the away portion of the home-and-home competition with Wisconsin/Geneva. Coach Wright never liked losing to them, on the road or at home. He worked the team pretty hard, especially emphasizing handling picks and foul shots. Two days before the game, he softened up. This was uncharacteristic. Typically, he lightened up the day before, not two days before. Everyone noticed but no one said anything.

The bus ride was only about two and a half hours but the coach liked them to arrive the night before. They rolled into the area Friday night before the Saturday afternoon game. Surprisingly, the game was going to be televised on ESPN as part of Dark Horse Week, a promotion that the station emphasized each year. Other games on the docket had similar implications.

"First national telecast," Shedrick said to Conner. "ESPN."

"Yeah. That's cool. Good chance for us to shine."

"If you play well, we'll shine," he said.

"I meant our ministry," Conner corrected.

"Oh, yeah. My bad. What was I thinking?" he said sarcastically, slapping his forehead. "There are millions of people watching basketball and all you can think of is God."

Conner didn't say anything. He just looked at his roomie.

"Okay, okay," Shedrick said, "I lost perspective." This time he really meant it.

"We need to play hard and it will be great if – no, *when* – we win. But let's not forget what's even more important, okay?"

"You got it," Shedrick answered.

Chapter 50

Before the game began, the Eagles went to the foul line for their pre-game prayer. The Wisconsin/Geneva fans, never having seen this before, were doing catcalling and booing, thinking it an affected move by the visitors. Conner ended the prayer with "Let us be models of our faith and models of our basketball skills."

After saying amen, everyone in the huddle felt better and more relaxed.

The Eagles sent their regular starting five to the scorer's table. The Wildcats, wearing their home colors, started a team that not only had a 17-4 overall record but an 11-1 conference record, including the earlier victory over Brantley. They had a certain swagger to themselves, probably well deserved.

As he almost always did, Forrester won the opening tip. Immediately, Kline drilled a three pointer. Wisconsin/Geneva missed one from the corner and Kline drilled another. Six nothing and the game wasn't even a minute old. The fans were dead silent.

After that hot start, though, the Eagles went into the freezer. They couldn't buy a bucket, even missing easy layups. On the opposite end of the spectrum, the Wildcats couldn't miss anything. The volume control for the crowd went from mute to loudest possible. Conner thought the crowd noise at an away game was always louder than what he heard at their home games. He probably felt that way because the roar at a traveling site was always when things didn't go the Eagles' way. And they certainly weren't at the beginning of this game.

Nine minutes into the game, the Wildcats led 30-16 and the crowd was loving every second of it. For many years, Wisconsin/Geneva had been a powerhouse basketball program. After some lean times, they now felt that it was again time to shine. Had they been able to do so, they would gladly have won the game 100-16 without blinking an eye.

Conner and Shedrick checked in for Kline and Walker, the latter two frustrated at having been stymied thus far. To their credit, they encouraged their teammates. Wisconsin/Geneva also made some changes, going to what appeared to be a taller line-up.

The Eagles came out in a man-to-man defensive scheme rather than playing zone. Apparently, though, the Wildcats had studied films of the Conner-Shedrick backcourt. As such, they had a plan for it. The new guards, both considerably taller than the two they had replaced, went underneath, much like where forwards would position themselves. Their forwards now played guards. Doing it this way allowed for two things to happen. One, Conner and Shedrick would not be outside to challenge the ball. Two, in this way, the rebounding edge would go to the taller players, this time not the Eagles.

Two trips down the court resulted in five points for the home team, an uncontested three pointer and a feed underneath to Shedrick's man for an easy layup. On the other end of the court, the Eagles managed to score four points. The scoreboard read 35-20 and the crowd screamed for more. Before Wisconsin/Geneva could inbound again, Brantley called time out.

"Smart plan," Coach Wright said calmly, even smiling. "Not strategic, though. Let's switch to a two-one-two zone. If your men go underneath," Wright said to Shedrick and Conner, "let 'em go. If your men go outside," Wright said to the big men, "let 'em go. If they decide to pack everyone in, then keep them outside the paint and on your back. Harris, you can go inside if they do that because you can jump. Ramsey, you stay outside because you can't jump over a toothpick." Everyone in earshot started laughing. Those who weren't able to hear what the coach said but could see laugher on the players' faces were wondering what a team down fifteen points could find funny. "I want everything stolen and no second chances. Got it?"

"Yes, coach!"

"Good. Stay with the zone for a while, even if they go conventional. Now, let's turn this thing around. Hands in. Eagles on three."

"One, two, Eagles!" they shouted.

"I know what the coach said about your going inside," Conner said to Shedrick. Don't get tangled up in there because it will slow down our fast break. I don't want to take a lot of shots."

"How come?"

"Just because," Conner responded.

"Great answer," Shedrick commented.

The Wildcats' regular guards brought the ball up but handed it off to their forwards at pretty much the outside limit of a makeable three-point shot. The forward who got the ball from the guard did not dribble, thus eliminating Conner's speed. Instead, he held the ball over his head and looked for someone underneath. Conner could not jump high enough to cause a problem. For the moment, he was neutralized. Meanwhile, underneath, the Wildcats were setting elaborate picks. Eventually, one worked and resulted in an easy layup.

Everyone started up court with the Eagles inbounding. Conner called them over, using his ten seconds in the backcourt to share something with them. He had to shout because the crowd was roaring its approval for how the home team was playing. "When they inbound, pick a man to shadow until you get to your position. I am going to force them to pass it to one of the other players. You should have good opportunities to intercept." The other four nodded their understanding.

The Eagles' trip down the floor resulted in Shedrick hitting a three pointer. The Wisconsin/Geneva coach was furious, yelling at his players to cut off the outside shots. Although he was heard, nobody acknowledged his shouting.

Instead of picking up the ball at or after half court, Conner guarded the player inbounding the ball while his teammates shadowed individual players, keeping one eye on the ball. This flustered the inbounder and he forced a pass that could not be handled, it going out of bounds. Shedrick put the ball in play and Conner immediately scored on a layup.

Again, Conner hounded the inbounder while the others played a temporary man-to-man coverage. Forgetting that he needed to keep the ball over his head, he tried to make a bounce pass to his teammate. Conner stole it before it hit the ground. His quicker-than-the-eye-could-see layup made the score 37-27.

For their next effort, the inbounder held the ball over his head. Conner, realizing that he could not do anything under this condition, backed up to the foul line, hoping that his speed would eliminate the short pass. The Wildcats were able to inbound but Conner joined Forrester getting all over the player with the ball, who just happened to be their center. Typically, as it was in this case, being the center meant not having ball handling skills. Between Forrester and Conner, the other player was like a deer caught in headlights. In bringing it back over his head, he lost grip of the ball and threw it into his own bench. It clonked a player sitting there before it rebounded back on court. Eagles ball.

Now the Brantley bench had come alive and could be heard above the ever-quieting local crowd. Shedrick, feeling it, as he said later, dropped in a three to bring the score differential to seven. Again, with Conner backing up to the foul line and double-teaming the player getting the inbounds pass, the

Wildcats were at a loss as to what to do. They turned it over again and Shedrick hit another uncontested three. What had been a fifteen-point lead was cut to four. And virtual silence dominated the arena. The home team called another time out.

"Move the ball," the Wisconsin/Geneva coach yelled at his players. "Don't let Seven get anywhere near it. If he's close to you, lift it over your head and pass it. If he's not, then pass it. Make sure that he is neutralized. And keep guarding them. You're giving them unchallenged threes. Come on. Let's do it!"

At the other bench, there was newfound energy and excitement. What had looked as though it would be a Wildcats blowout now was a nip-and-tuck affair. Artificially, the crowd got back into it when the players walked back on the court, spurred on by the Wildcats mascot. However, it wasn't cheering with confidence. More like hopefulness and 'come on, guys' encouragement.

The urgings from the Wisconsin/Geneva coach seemed to do nothing to stem the tide. By halftime, Brantley was up by two, 42-40, much to the chagrin of the crowd.

The second half was pretty much all a cat-and-mouse game between the coaches. The ten starters were in, and kept it close, the score never favoring one or the other team by more than three points. When Conner and Shedrick checked in, the game became considerably more frantic but pointedly favoring the Eagles. Each time that Brantley went up by double digits, the coach would change backcourts and substitute underneath. When it got within three, he would go with the Ramsey-Harris combination. The final score was 72-64 for Brantley.

This time, when they went to the foul line for their post-game prayer, there was considerably more interest on the part of those fans who had remained in the stands. Some dismissed it as a post-game celebration. Others felt that it was something more special. Either way, it caught more people's attention.

The bus ride home was fun.

Chapter 51

During the week following this victory, it seemed like everyone and his brother wanted to interview Conner. He was as accommodating as he could be but it became overwhelming for him. Finally, he decided to go to the coach and ask for help, perhaps suggesting a moratorium on all but a scheduled few interviews. He also wanted to have another appointment with a booster. The coach hadn't volunteered a second name and time. Conner didn't want to lose valuable momentum.

"Hey, coach, two things for you," he said as he stood by the coach's open door.

"Okay," said the coach, putting down his pen and looking up.

"First, I'm getting swamped with interviews, both scheduled and impromptu. I'd like to have a bit more structure in order to have increased privacy."

"Wasn't publicity what you wanted in the first place? Be careful what you wish for and all that."

"I still want visibility. I just want more structure. It would be like playing three conference games one after the other. Eventually, as much as we might love the game, enough is enough."

This analogy resonated with the coach. "Okay. What do you suggest?"

"Instructions from you limiting interviews to specific times and always in the gym."

"I can probably do that. Let me think on it a little. What was the other thing?"

"Another booster interview," Conner asked, carefully managing his inflection.

"Oh, yeah. That." He sat back in his chair. "You know, Ramsey, I'm not sure that the last one went where we hoped it would go."

"I thought that it was wonderful."

"Not so wonderful for the basketball program."

"Coach..." Conner looked at Coach Wright and it was much like a school teacher would look at a student who was misbehaving.

"Coach nothing. I have a few things on the top of my must-do list. They include being successful on the court, avoiding embarrassment for the university and raising money for the program. We dominate revenue for the institution. If we get put on probation or if we have supporters lessen their contributions, the university is in a world of hurt...and I'm coaching basketball for six-year olds in Nowheresville."

Conner smiled. "And I'm sure that you'd do a mighty fine job at that, too," he quipped.

"Funny to you, smart guy. Not funny to me."

"What are you saying?"

"What I'm saying is…" he hesitated, searching how to phrase what he wanted to communicate. "What I'm saying is that I need to be careful about who you speak with and what you say."

By now, Conner's positive demeanor that he had brought with him into the coach's office was gone. It was replaced with disappointment, concern and a tinge of anger.

"Coach," Conner began, struggling to stay both calm and persuasive. "In the first place, I don't think that the McKenzies will lessen their contributions to the program. Have they said anything to you to that effect?"

"Well, no…but it certainly seems that way."

"If they do, I will speak with them again. As for others, you and I had a deal. Haven't I delivered on my end?"

"Well, yes, but that's just one game."

"And you want me to deliver in other games?"

"Of course I do, Ramsey. But between long-term giving and one season, I'll have to go with the long-term giving. There will be other Klines, Walkers and Ramseys. There always are."

"Fine." Conner turned and left the office, hoping that this action would have more impact than mere words. As he walked toward the exit, he could hear the coach calling after him. He ignored the coach's efforts. As he approached the final door, the coach, somewhat out of breath, caught up with him.

"Ramsey. Confound it! Why do you have to be this obstinate?"

Conner just looked at him.

"Look, I know that we had a deal and I'm a man of my word."

Conner wondered about that but, since he had no proof either way, he dismissed it.

"I'm not saying that you can't speak with another booster. I'm just saying…well, could you wait a couple of weeks?"

"Why? So you can see if we have turned this season around?"

Caught with his hand in the cookie jar, the coach sputtered a bit, much like a car that couldn't get quite enough gasoline. "Well… Um… Look… Okay, you're right. I'm reneging on my promise and that's not right. I'll get you a name."

"When?" asked Conner, not willing to be stalled any further.

"By tonight," the coach answered.

"And not just some yokel, coach. If McKenzie is number one, then I want number two."

Reluctantly, the coach agreed. "By tonight," he said.

----- ----- -----

Conner typically turned off his cell phone when he met with the coach, practiced with the team, played in a game, went into class, studied, spent time with Esther or otherwise wanted to give undivided time to someone or something. When he checked his phone after this meeting, he was not surprised to see that he had several calls. One was from Richard Means at the *Sentinel*. Another was from Esther. A

third was from Pete Carlyle, his friend at the
recreation center.

He called Esther first. "What's up?" he asked as
part of his salutation.

"Hi," she said, more traditionally. "What did the
coach say?"

"He wasn't going to give me another introduction
but I *convinced* him to do otherwise." He accented the
word convinced.

"Did you get him in a headlock?"

"Something like that. At least I was successful. He
promised the name of someone tonight."

"Speaking of tonight, would you like to go see a
movie? They're showing 'Conner Ramsey and His
Christian Ministry.' It's supposed to be a barn
burner, a sure thing for an Oscar."

"And who's playing the leading role? It must be
Tom Cruise, Russell Crowe or Mel Gibson."

"Actually, Pee-wee Herman."

Conner laughed as he remembered the comic
fictional character, the nerd's nerd.

"Thanks a lot, darling."

"And I'd like to be your agent for the next few
movies."

"You got it. You've already proven your worth."

"...or worthlessness, eh?" she offered.

"Actually, I really need to study. But I'd like to do
that with you. Could we have a study date?"

"How romantic," she teased.

"Best I can do."

"You're on." They made arrangements about
when and where to meet.

His next call was to Pete. "Hey, man, Conner here. How are you?"

They chatted for fifteen minutes about life back home, the step up to major college basketball, the fact that members of the Colts, Pete's recreation team, were tracking his successes and a multitude of other one- or two-sentence topics.

"When would it be a good time to come up there?" Pete asked. "A few of us want to see you up close and personal, as the saying goes."

"I guess that the best would be to come watch the conference tournament. It's being played in Chicago this year."

"Really? Where's that again?" he asked sarcastically.

"I'm not sure. Somewhere north of Texas. I'd love to see you."

"Let me check with the guys and see what works for them. We'll get you at least for a dinner, right?"

"Count on it."

"By the way, how's your Jesus Crusade?"

Conner laughed. Nothing easy from his friend. "Slow but steady," he replied. "When you're ready to join the army, you'll be more than welcome."

"Thanks. I'll consider it," he said with absolutely no sincerity. "Don't save me a chair," he added.

They shared a few other memories, some additional kidding and mutual good luck wishes, then hung up.

The third call was to the reporter. "Glad you called, Conner," he said. "Your celebrity status has inspired the editors to ask me about a two-part personal profile. One part would be written, the other would be on our sister station, WELG. It could be dynamite for you."

Conner hesitated, not saying anything in response.

"…and your ministry," Means added quickly.

"Sounds inviting," Conner said "but I'll have to speak with the coach. I think that he's instituting some sort of moratorium on this sort of thing."

"How come?"

"I think that he's concerned about too much publicity detracting from our revitalization. You'll have to ask him."

"I will. Trust me, I will."

----- ----- -----

On the way back to his dorm, Conner was approached by an attractive co-ed, reaching that conclusion because of her looks, her age and the fact that she was carrying textbooks. "Mr. Ramsey," she began cautiously, "I belong to a sorority. It's a Christian-based sorority," she added quickly. "We have weekly meetings that focus on individual topics. In the next two weeks, we plan to discuss role models and, er, um, we were wondering if you would come speak with us."

Conner smiled, clearly flattered with the attention.

"I guess so," he said reluctantly. "It all depends on the timing."

"We could work around your schedule," she said.

"Why don't you give me contact information and I'll call you."

He waited for her to provide him with either a card or that information written on a piece of paper torn out of one of her notebooks. Neither was forthcoming.

"Could I call you?" she asked. "I don't have a cell phone and the sorority can sometimes be really loud. If you just tell me when, I will call you."

Although that sounded a bit odd, Conner figured that it would be okay. He wrote his cell number down on a piece of paper that she provided.

"And what's your name?" he asked.

"Mine? Oh, it's Penny. Penny like the money."

"Nice to meet you, Penny. Do you have a last name?" he asked playfully.

"Of course I do, silly," she said.

He waited. No response.

"Penny?"

"Yes?"

"What's your last name?"

"Oh," she giggled, "it's Diamond. Penny Diamond. That's me."

"Nice to meet you, Penny Diamond."

"Nice to meet you, too. I'll call you soon. Thanks." She waved and exited stage left, so to speak, because she just seemed to slide away more than turn and walk away.

Strange, he said to himself. Attractive but strange.

By the time he had entered the dorm, he had all but forgotten the exchange.

----- ----- -----

Right before practice, Coach Wright handed Conner a piece of paper. On it were the names Chester and Elizabeth Applegate. Their address and phone number were also listed. Circled at the bottom was 'Tonight, 7:00 PM.' Conner wanted to protest the time but did not want to miss the opportunity. He wondered about calling them to see if he could bring along Esther, then thought better of it.

"Thanks, Coach," he said.

He ran outside and called Esther. She wasn't available. He left her a voice message explaining what had come up. "I'd love you to join me but I don't want to upset the applecart." He laughed silently thinking about Applegate and applecart. "I'll call you after the dinner. Thanks for understanding."

Then he hustled into the locker room and dressed for practice.

They tried a number of different things at this practice – a three guard lineup; shuffling Kline, Walker, Shedrick and him into different pairings; a more intricate weave; more pick and rolls; transition offense; and two dissimilar defensive zones. The time flew by. Everyone was surprised when the practice was over.

----- ----- -----

The Applegate mansion did not stand in the shadow of the McKenzie estate. Both were opulent, but in slightly different ways. Driving up to this one, Conner determined that they were more likely to be outdoors types than Gordon and his wife. For one thing, there were several racehorses on the property, although Conner didn't know a thoroughbred from a nag. They just looked young and healthy. For another, of the three cars that were parked in the spacious driveway, two were sporty convertibles, one with the top down. As he got closer, he recognized one as being a Porsche and the other a Ferrari. Must be nice, he thought.

As with the McKenzies, he was greeted by a butler and shown into a large den. Although every bit as large as what he had seen at the first booster's home, this one was more stylishly appointed. There were no trophies and no dramatic references to Brantley basketball. Everything seemed to be tastefully arranged. Instead of one fireplace, this one had two. Just what every house needs, Conner thought to himself. Whatever happened to understatement? he wondered. Don't be covetous, he chastised himself, drawing from the Ten Commandments.

Not long after Conner came into this room, a fiftyish year-old man entered. He had a spry step and was very handsome, but in a natural sort of way. He had a full head of white hair that was neat but not perfectly combed. He wore a "Where's my horse?" t-shirt, blue jeans and loafers without socks. All told, he looked as comfortable as could be. "Chester Applegate," he said before they were close enough to shake hands. "Friends call me Chet. What a pleasure to meet you."

"Conner Ram..." Conner started to say.

"I know. I know. Your reputation precedes you."

"Thank you, sir. And thank you for tonight's invitation. I very much looked forward to meeting you and Mrs. Applegate."

"Yes, yes," he said. "The boss will be down in a few minutes. Meanwhile, how about a refresher?"

He was as charming as could be.

"I'll take water, club soda or tea, please."

"We have all three," he prompted.

"Club soda, please."

"My, my. Quite the athlete, eh?"

"Well, right now, it's time to stay in shape. Go Eagles!" he added, somewhere between serious and funny.

"Go Eagles is right," Chester said. "I played on the team, majored in engineering, graduated in '79, worked for an oil company in Texas, started my own oil company, got lucky and sold it for a nice buck seven years ago. Since then, I've been doing some investing and supporting Brantley basketball. It's been a lucky life. It sure has."

People like that, Conner thought, are usually too modest - truly or falsely modest. He thought of Bill Gates, Steve Jobs, Mark Cuban, Michael Jordan and Wayne Gretzky.

"Reminds me of a Lee Trevino quote," Conner said.

"What's that?" inquired his host.

"The harder I practice, the luckier I get."

"Well, nice of you to say. Some of it, I'm sure, is due to hard work and talent but lots of it is due to pure, unadulterated good luck."

"I can't argue with you, Mr. Applegate. I haven't gotten there. Therefore, everything that I say is purely anecdotal."

Applegate laughed. "Good point. Please make yourself comfortable," he said, pointing to any of the

many seating accommodations that were arranged
throughout the room.

"Thank you." Conner chose something that had
what looked like a firm back. He didn't want to sink
into the chair as he had done at the McKenzie home.

Chet grabbed what looked like a dining room
chair, easily spun it around and sat down. It was
pretty clear that his host was in good shape.

"It looks like you stay fit," Conner noted.

"That's one of the benefits of my lifestyle. I have
a personal trainer out here four days a week. It's one
of my most cherished times. Working out has always
been important to me."

"Me, too," Conner said, "but in somewhat less
luxurious settings."

"A spare bedroom, an old basement, Gold's Gym
or one of these fancy schmancy spas...you can get a
workout if you really want one."

Applegate took on a serious countenance, one
that Conner took to be the preface for being asked
serious questions. Conner didn't know what the
interrogations might be but he told himself to relax
about them. He had prayed before coming into the
house and drew upon that as well.

He was floored by the first question.

"Give me three Biblical excerpts that you cherish,
other than John 3:16," Applegate said.

"Wow," Conner observed. "I love Colossians
3:23..."

"*Work as unto the Lord*," Applegate said. "Also in
Matthew, Ephesians and Philippians."

Conner's eyes widened in amazement.

"Go on," Applegate implored without changing facial expressions.

"Well, I also like Matthew 6:25, the one about…"

"Not worrying," Applegate completed for him. *"Who of you by worrying can add a single hour to his life?"*

This time, Conner was less surprised, although still very impressed.

"And…?" Applegate asked.

"Philippians 4:13."

"Perhaps my most favorite," Applegate said. *"I can do all things through him who gives me strength."*

Conner sat there in amazement. Had the roles been reversed, he could not have done what his host had just done. At least not verbatim.

"That's impressive," Conner said. "Inspiring. I don't know what other words to use but I'm…"

"…surprised," finished Applegate. "Do you know why you're surprised?" he asked.

"Tell me," invited Conner.

"Because in today's world, people are thought of as having one god, be it a deity of a super-celestial nature, money, fame or whatever. And many of today's preachers tell us we must make a choice. And they pick Matthew 8:21 or 1 Timothy 6:10 to talk about this choice."

"I agree."

"You agree with what?"

"That we must make a choice."

"I agree, as well. But, in many cases, we do not have to make a choice. Sometimes, lo and behold, our secular wealth comes as a by-product to our faith. It's not money that is the root of all evil. It's the *love* of money that is the root of all evil. People forget that. Otherwise, we could determine that all rich men were faithless sinners and all poor men were faithful saints."

Conner was nodding his head during this explanation. He loved it. He was shocked to be hearing it as it was the last thing that he expected. Nevertheless, he was thrilled. Wow, he kept commenting to himself.

After a brief interval, Applegate spoke up again. "Coach Wright thinks that I have chosen the path of Brantley basketball worship," he said. "Not true. Much like you might enjoy reading, running, playing solitaire or golfing, I like watching and supporting Eagles basketball. But, and this is what is critical, if you ask me where my heart is, it's in the Lord. I just don't advertise it that much around here."

"The parable of the Pharisee and the tax collector," Conner said, referring to the chest-pounding Jew who paraded his holiness before others in the synagogue versus the lowly tax collector who truly had faith.

"Exactly," confirmed Applegate. "Now, let me be clear about one thing."

Conner gave him undivided attention.

"Although a few other boosters would lean to this side of the scales, there are others — one, in particular — who lean the other way. We definitely do not speak with one voice."

"I see," Conner responded, not knowing what else to say.

In the next moment, Chet stood up. "Let me introduce you to the boss," he said. "Liz, this is Conner Ramsey, the interesting member of the Brantley basketball team."

Conner immediately jumped up and turned to greet Mrs. Applegate. She was absolutely gorgeous, although dressed very modestly. She wore a multicolored, long-sleeve buttoned shirt with the sleeves rolled up, blue jeans and moccasins. Her long hair was pulled back in a ponytail and her smile was magnificent. Together, they may have easily been the Mr. & Mrs. advertisement for a fashion magazine.

"Chet is delighted with your presence on the team," she began. "But I'll tell you something," she said, pretending to whisper as she held her open hand to one side of her mouth, "he likes your walk with the Lord far more than your basketball skills."

Wow, wow, wow, Conner said to himself.

"…and he likes your basketball skills to the roof," she added, just to put things in perspective.

"Thank you, ma'am," he said.

"Liz," she said. "And I'm starved. How about you?"

The dining room in which they ate was one of two that this house provided. It was the size of a typical dining room in a nice house and the three of them sat in arm-touching distance of each other. It was much more comfortable than what he had experienced at the McKenzie home.

Although the meal had several courses and was served by helpers, it was much more relaxed. Following a cup of the most delicious cream of tomato soup, they had grilled salmon ("Hope you like fish"), yams ("Much healthier than simple baked potatoes"), broccoli ("My favorite greens") and buttered carrots ("Not everyone likes these but we certainly do"). Dessert was a tofu pudding that was unusual but undeniably delicious.

"Mrs. Applegate…"

"Liz."

"Liz, this was incredible. Unlike other times enjoying meals like this, I don't feel quite as packed down in the middle as I did then. Thank you very much. I truly appreciate the hospitality, warmth and extraordinary food. This has been such a treat and inspiration for me."

"Conner," Chet said, changing subjects, "you seem to be on an important mission. What can we do to support you?"

Had Conner been asked to say what would have been the least likely offer he would have expected to receive that night, Mr. Applegate's proposal would likely have been it. He was dumbfounded. Both his host and hostess gave him a moment to collect himself. He appreciated that.

"At the expense of being offered one piece of candy and asking for three, I have a few things that your generosity has invited me to suggest. That is, if I'm not being too selfish."

"Ask away. You might hear 'no' but you'll never hear 'yes' unless you ask," Chet said with a smile.

Conner took advantage of this encouragement to ask for three things:

1. Ideas on how to reach the next level of his ministry, explaining it as modestly as possible without divulging anything he promised God not to illuminate;
2. Ways of reaching other influential individuals to make this a movement rather than a one-person initiative; and
3. Ways of soothing the coach's fear that 'converting' boosters to this mission meant losing them as contributors to Brantley basketball.

When he had finished sharing these ideas, Chet said "I'm impressed. Not one thing for you. Not one request for money. Quite different, eh Liz?"

She smiled and nodded her affirmation.

Then, at Chet's invitation, the three of them went into his study. There he opened a well-hidden whiteboard and they developed ideas about how to address those three things. Conner did take time out to call Esther and apologize for the change of plans. She understood and encouraged him to take advantage of this visit with the Applegates.

Chapter 52

The next two weeks moved rapidly but ended on a sour note. Coming into his dorm room, Conner kicked off his loafers as he headed toward his bedroom. He liked to do that. He would slide his foot most of the way out of the loafer, leaving it sort of dangling on his toes. He would flip that one up. It would do a single revolution and land comfortably in his hand. Then he would do the same thing with the other one. Almost at the exact moment when Shedrick heard him and yelled "Don't take off your shoes!" he stepped on a broken piece of glass and gashed the sole of his foot. It required his going to the emergency room and getting eleven stitches, effectively ending his basketball playing for at least a week.

Prior to that accident, Brantley had taken its record to 8-17, 6-9. With Conner out, the team lost three more games. At the end of the regular season, its record stood at 8-20, 6-12. It was unquestionably clear that the only way that the Eagles would get an invitation to the NCAA playoffs would be if they won the conference tournament. The good news was that it appeared Conner would be able to play again pretty much when the conference tournament began. They finished the regular conference season as the seventh seed in the tournament. To win the championship and qualify for the NCAA Tournament, they would have to prevail in four straight games. It was doable, even though it had never been done before. And, of course, there were a lot of good teams in their conference that stood in Brantley's way.

When Coach Wright was asked about the draw, he simply said "It doesn't matter. We can't place second. That means we will have to beat everyone. And, by the way, that's what we plan to do."

His statement was taken by a few as confident, by some as arrogant and by most as idiotic. He was okay with what the writers and others felt. Although nothing was guaranteed, he knew that he had the squad to achieve this lofty goal.

----- ----- -----

By now, the second semester was about halfway through and Conner was starting on his next set of eight-week courses. Conner loved his courses, felt fortunate to get Professor Bags again and appreciated the brain food that went along with everything else he was experiencing. He wanted to maintain the straight-A average he had achieved in the first semester and seemed poised to do so.

----- ----- -----

Esther and he had grown even closer. Their original connection was through school. Like Conner, she had achieved a straight-A average during the previous semester. Once again, they shared a single course. They had spoken about a few things, particularly about taking summer school together and perhaps even hinting about something more permanent between them. Their primary common thread, though, was Conner's mission. And now Esther's, as well. They agreed that nothing was more important than that.

----- ----- -----

Local press coverage was positive, but interest in Brantley basketball on the regional and national scales was pretty minimal. Conner was treated as a rarity, more a matter of human interest than as a bona fide athlete, especially since he did not start for the team. The coach kept him pretty insulated from the media. He didn't want a circus. Coach Wright correctly reasoned that, if everything worked out the way he hoped it would, ample media coverage would find them. If they won the conference tournament, it would make for a good story. Having Ramsey on the team would add to it. Eventually, the press would be all over them…he hoped.

----- ----- -----

Conner periodically attended the fellowship to which Winger had introduced him. He liked it when they discussed theological issues but didn't like it too much when they acted like basketball groupies. He wasn't ever able to schedule time with Penny Diamond's sorority, although she called several times. He promised to do this before the semester was over.

----- ----- -----

As for seeing other boosters, Conner throttled back his requests to meet with them. He didn't tell the coach that he was satisfied with having only met with the McKenzies and the Applegates but he didn't push the coach to set up other meetings. His attention became focused on a project that the Applegates and McKenzies had promised to support, both with contacts as well as financially.

They called it Project 2312, drawing the name from 2 Peter 3:12 *You should look forward to that day and hurry it along – the day when God will set the heavens on fire and the elements will melt away in the flames. But we are looking forward to the new heavens and new earth he has promised, a world where everyone is right with God.*

----- ----- -----

Although Conner's personal prayer life had grown, he missed the in-person sessions with God. He asked for them but did not expect them. He knew that God wanted him to do his utmost on his own. He also knew that God was always with him. As for challenges, his had been few. With more likely to come, he relied on 1 Corinthians 10:13 *But remember that the temptations that come into your life are no different from what others experience. And God is faithful. He will keep the temptation from becoming so strong that you cannot stand up against it. When you are tempted, he will show you a way out so that you will not give in to it.*

----- ----- -----

Finally, he and Penny connected on a date for him to visit the sorority. "Can I bring a friend?" he had asked, hoping that Esther would want to attend.

"Well, actually no," she had said. "We get lots of requests for friends and others. Our facility is very small. In fact, considering the interest your presence is generating, we might even find a better location for it. Anyhow, we made it a rule not to allow outsiders, other than our guest speaker. I hope that you don't mind."

Conner did mind but figured that it wouldn't be worth arguing. He'd only be there for a little while and that would be that. They settled on the Wednesday following the team's first conference playoff game. They would have an early afternoon game and then he would go to the meeting that night. That would allow him to have a late lunch with Esther and still get to sleep at a good time. If they won the first game – when they won it, he said to himself – they would have another afternoon game on Thursday. Everything looked as though it would work out quite satisfactorily.

Chapter 53

Game one of the tournament pitted Brantley against Ohio Western. These were two of the teams that had poor seeds, although Ohio Western held a better conference record and was thus designated as the home team. The only advantage to being the home team was that you got to wear your home whites. Brantley wore its dark blue road uniform.

Conner had been lightly working out, trying to avoid too much stomping action on his right foot. The bleeding would occur if he literally stomped his foot or if he ran and suddenly either stopped sharply or dramatically changed direction. Unfortunately for him at the moment, starting/stopping and zigging/zagging were the moves of which basketball players were made. The problem with doing too much of that was the stress on where the stitches had been. Conner, understanding the importance of the Eagles winning this tournament to qualify for the NCAA tournament – the Big Cheese, as some players liked to call it – was willing to suffer some discomfort in order to help Brantley achieve this victory and the three that he hoped would follow en route to being the conference champion.

Knowing the situation, Coach Wright hoped that he would not have to play Conner that evening, lessening the wear and tear on his difference-maker.

Through the first half of the game, it was pretty much nip-and-tuck. Walker and Kline were hot but so were Ohio Western's two guards. Conner did not play in the half and it ended 52-51 in favor of Ohio Western. At this rate, it would be a shootout. The coach's pep talk wasn't much of anything, other than to play good defense and to eliminate second-chance points.

At the ten-minute mark in the second half, Brantley started to pull away. Not by much, but inch by inch. With five minutes to go, the Eagles had an eight-point lead, the score standing at 82-74. Coach Wright had left Kline and Walker in for most of the game, spelling them infrequently with Shedrick. That was okay except for what the long-term impact might be in this four-games-in-a-row sequence.

With a minute and a half to go and Brantley still up by eight, it became a foul fest. Ohio Western couldn't afford for Brantley to run any additional clock. They would hustle the ball down court, shoot a three and immediately foul whoever had the ball. About half of their threes were good but Brantley's free throw shooting was almost perfect. Ohio Western could only close the gap to six before the game ended.

One down and three to go. Best part was that Conner hadn't played at all in this one.

As with before the game, the Brantley players – all of them – went to the foul line and offered a prayer. The coaches refrained from joining. Nobody from the other team participated.

As the team was walking off the court, Conner heard his name being called. He recognized it and looked around. Sure enough, there was Pete Carlyle, his friend from the recreation league.

"I came all the way from home to watch you grab pine?" he asked.

Conner made a sympathetic face and then explained why.

"Wow. That's bad timing," Pete said. "Will you be able to play tomorrow?"

"Actually, I was able to play today. Had the lead not been maintained in the second half, the coach was going to put me in."

"Oh, Mr. Difference Maker, eh?" Pete chided him.

"It's been working thus far," Conner responded modestly.

"Well, then, I hope that tomorrow's game is close. Can you join us for a bite...as promised?"

Conner looked around to see where the coach was. "Uh oh. I'm not sure if he has plans. Let me find out. If he says it's okay, I'm with you. If not, we'll have to make some other plans. Can you hang here and let me find out?"

"Sure," Pete said. "Bob and Drew are sitting up there." He pointed about forty rows up. Bob and Drew stood up and waved. Conner recognized them and waved back.

"It's cool that you're here," Conner said. "I'll probably play tomorrow. Anyhow, wait here and I'll be back in a jiffy."

Before Pete could razz his friend about 'in a jiffy,' Conner was gone. He didn't return for almost fifteen minutes. When he did, he apologized. "Coach called a short meeting."

"No worries. I kinda figured something like that. I didn't think that he was giving you the game ball for your sterling play today."

Conner smiled. "You're incredibly sweet. Our next game is at 2:00 PM tomorrow. I'll try to do better."

"So…?" Pete asked, accentuating his impatience good naturedly.

"So what?" Conner asked, not understanding.

"Can you join us for something to eat?" Pete said, exaggerating his articulation of the question.

Conner laughed. "Oh, yeah," he said. "I'm sorry. Too many things going on for this little brain. I'd like to bring my roomie and my girlfriend, if that's okay with you."

"Girlfriend?" Pete said. "Already? How do you have time for everything."

"Just gifted, I guess," Conner kidded back.

"Yeah. Sure. How about if we meet at the south entrance of this stadium in, say, twenty minutes?"

"You got a deal," Conner said.

"Girlfriend," Pete said aloud to no one in particular, as he returned to his friends. They were in no rush, now watching two other teams getting ready to tip it off.

As Conner trotted back to the tunnel, he stopped where Esther had been sitting. "That's Pete, the friend who got me on the court in the first place."

"Oh…" she said, immediately understanding the connection from an explanation Conner had provided one evening over pizza.

"How about if you, Shedrick and I join the three of them for a bite?"

Conner could see that she was a little disappointed. However, she shrugged it off quickly and said "Sure."

"You're great," he said as he leaned over and gave her a peck on the cheek.

"You're not too bad yourself," she responded, "…for the fifteenth best player on the team."

"You mean for the worst player on the team."

"Well, you came in first of the worst," she said, holding her thumb and index finger of her right hand to form the letter L across her forehead. This was the teasing look for a Loser.

"Nice," he said.

"You know that I'm kidding."

Other than smiling, he said and did nothing.

"Right?" she asked, just a little bit concerned.

"Of course," he responded. "Hey, I'll be back here with Shedrick in a couple of minutes. Wait for me, will ya?"

"Depends on what offers I get in the meantime," she said, smiling and winking at him.

"You're a piece of work," he said, shaking his head and moving off to the tunnel.

Just a moment later, Esther remembered something she had to tell him. "Conner!" she called. "Conner!" But by then he had turned the corner, was out of earshot and was on his way to the locker room. She told herself to remember to speak with him about it after dinner.

Chapter 54

Dinner was great fun. Esther and Shedrick immediately connected with Pete, Bob and Drew. It was almost as though the six of them had grown up together. Even their individual stories felt familiar to one another. All of the men, in respect for Esther, were selective in what topics they addressed and how they did so.

The three visitors were about to dive into the rolls and appetizers when Conner said "Gentlemen, let's give thanks for this bounty. Esther, would you mind leading us?" Although surprised, Esther was not only delighted to offer a prayer but particularly eloquent in doing so.

"What are you doing with him?" Pete asked Esther after the prayer, his question referring to Conner.

She shrugged her shoulders and delivered her beaming smile. "It's tough," she said. "Very tough. I'm glad that you can appreciate my troubles."

Pete, Bob and Drew ate like there was no tomorrow. They each had ribs, massive side dishes, beer and dessert. Bob, in fact, got a second order of à la carte ribs, something that seemed surprising to Esther. "That's a lot of food," she commented, then chastised herself for saying anything. "I'm sorry," she stumbled along. "That's really none of my business."

The guys burst out laughing at her discomfiture. "No problem," Bob said. I was gonna eat it with or without your approval."

More laughter.

"That's a woman for you," Pete said.

"That's why I love her," Conner chimed in, putting his arm around Esther and giving her a kiss above her ear. She appreciated his care of her.

Shedrick and Conner had chicken, Esther salad. The ballplayers were encouraged to eat well but eat lightly. Esther always seemed to be wise in her eating choices. All three had tea.

After a while, Drew asked "Are we gonna see you tomorrow, Conner? After all, we didn't drive all the way here just to have dinner with you."

"Yes, we did!" Pete said. But, as he said this, he turned to Esther. "And what a delightful experience it has turned out to be."

"I didn't mean that," Drew hollered over the noise.

"I know," mouthed Esther, shooing away his defense.

"We've got a much better team to play tomorrow, now that we're into the main draw," Shedrick said.

"What do you mean?" Pete asked.

"The first round of most tournaments are what the players call either play-ins or mercy kills."

"Come again?"

Shedrick continued. "A play-in is where two mediocre or lousy teams play for the right to get into the main draw. A mercy kill is where the number one seed plays the worst team in the draw."

"Oh, I get it," Pete nodded. "Your first game was the equivalent of a play-in, eh?"

"Roger that," Shedrick confirmed.

"That means you'll play, Conner?" Pete asked.

"If the coach decides."

"You'll play," Shedrick said with certainty.

"I hope so," Conner added.

"To Conner," Pete said raising his beer.

All the others raised their beverages and said "To Conner!"

"Fifty points and fifty steals," Pete added.

"Fifty steals will suffice," Shedrick said. "I'll take the points."

All of them laughed, especially Shedrick and Conner.

Later on, Pete, Bob and Drew went back to the arena to watch other games. That was part of the fun of coming to tournaments like this. You got to see a bunch of games with loser-goes-home implications. For a team like Brantley, losing also meant that your season was over. With their record, Brantley didn't stand a chance of getting a wild card bid into the national post-season tournament.

Since it was still early, Shedrick decided to go back to watch the next game or what was left of it. That would still allow him to turn in early, as well. "Maybe I'll see the one unique flaw in someone we play that will let us win," he said.

"Not necessary," Conner said.

"Huh?"

"We're gonna win the next three by forty or fifty points."

"Oh, yeah, sure, okay. Thanks. Then I'll just walk around looking for pretty ladies."

"I got the last one," Conner said.

"Oh, aren't you sweet?" Esther said.

"Maybe she's got a twin."

"That I don't know about," Esther said.

"Maybe," Shedrick said.

"I guess that it's worth the whirl," Conner said.

The three laughed as Shedrick turned to join the three visitors already headed out of the restaurant.

"That leaves the two of us," he said.

"And so it does," she said. "And so it does. Would you like to go to a movie?"

"Can't. Gotta participate in a sorority fellowship this evening."

"Oh, oh, oh..." Esther said, as though she had just spilled hot coffee on her lap.

"What's the matter?" Conner asked, concerned that she was somehow injured.

"I forgot to tell you."

"What?"

She slowed down, took a breath and said "There's a little bit to the story so bear with me."

"Okay."

"Yesterday, on campus, the reporter from the *Sentinel*..."

"Richard Means," Conner offered.

"Yes. He came up to me looking for two things. One, somehow he knew that we were dating and wanted some background on me. I put him off, setting an appointment next week. I just didn't know if it was in your or our best interest..."

Conner spun Esther's chair around, put his hands on her shoulders and said "You are absolutely the best."

She smiled in appreciation. He leaned over and gave her a kiss which she was happy to return.

Both, a little bit flustered, weren't sure what to do at that point.

She cleared her throat and said "The other thing was that he wanted to get in touch with you, something about your speaking to a sorority. That's what made me think about it just now."

"What did he want? Did he tell you?"

"Yes, well, sort of. He told me to tell you not to do the interview or fellowship or whatever it was."

"Why not?"

"He called them the Devil's Daughters."

"The what?"

"Devil's Daughters. That's all he said."

Conner just stared at her, not knowing what the title meant while understanding that Esther had no additional information.

"I wonder what he meant by that."

"Why don't you call him?" Esther suggested.

"Yeah. Yeah, I'll do that. Let's go outside where we can have a little more peace and quiet."

With the music still blaring from inside the restaurant, they took the revolving door out into the comfortable evening air.

----- ----- -----

"Richard Means," came the phone response.

"Richard, this is Conner Ramsey."

"Hey, Conner, how's it going?"

"Fine, until a few moments ago."

"What happened?" the journalist asked.

"The Devil's Daughters," Conner responded. Esther stood next to Conner and nodded her head, although she could only hear one side of the conversation.

"Oh, yeah, that. I almost forgot about it. I take it that you spoke with Ms. Penny?"

"Actually, no, at least not recently. Esther Conrad said that you had mentioned it to her."

"By the way, she's lovely. Far too good for you," he quipped.

"Yeah, yeah. Everyone tells me that." He rolled his eyes and Esther could imagine what they were talking about.

"Anyhow, you told me that you were going to be participating in a fellowship with a bunch of sorority girls."

"Right."

"And you told me the sorority name."

"Right."

"Well, I've been around Brantley for a lot of years and I've never heard of it."

"The sorority?"

"Correctimundo," Means confirmed. "I decided to look it up, just in case it was a new one on campus since I had last checked."

"And?"

"And there's no such sorority on campus." Silence.

"In fact, there's no such sorority anywhere." More silence.

"After a while, second guessing myself, I figured that maybe I had gotten the sorority name wrong, although I will say that there was no name on campus anywhere near that. Okay, maybe I goofed. I decided to contact Penny Diamond. Guess what?"

"No such person."

"Not exactly."

"What exactly?"

"She works at the Broadway Club."

"What's that?"

"Take my word for it. It's not a 'your kind' of place. You wouldn't want to visit it."

"Why?"

"Oh, for crying out loud, Mr. Squeaky Clean! It's a strip joint. You know? Women take off their clothes and men cheer them on."

"Oh."

More silence, this with Conner trying to process the information and Means rolling his eyes wondering how anyone could be this naïve.

"Why would she want to have fellowship?" Conner asked.

Esther, standing right there but only hearing what Conner was saying couldn't make heads nor tails of what the conversation was about or where it was headed. She had a totally puzzled look on her face.

"Hellooo, Conner," Means said mockingly. "She didn't want to have fellowship in the way you think she wanted to have fellowship."

"What!?!"

The journalist started to laugh. This guy is something, he thought. I wonder if it's a good thing or a bad thing to have people this inexperienced in the world? he pondered. If everyone was like him, the world would be a nicer place. But everyone isn't like him and that makes for problems for the innocent ones. It took Means about two seconds to process his conjecture.

"My guess is that she wasn't interested in you for just you."

"I only met her once!"

"Will you hush up for a second, please?" Means ordered.

"Go on," Conner allowed, now curious to find out what had happened.

"Here's what I think. And I'm guessing that it's pretty close to accurate."

"Wait a minute," interrupted Conner. "How do you know this?"

"How do I know what!!!" Means said. "You won't let me finish a bloody sentence!"

"I'm sorry. Go ahead."

"Thank you," Means said caustically.

For effect, Means let the stillness resonate. Conner got the message and told himself not to say anything until everything was put on the table. He smiled weakly at Esther and held up is index finger to indicate that he would be able to share what was going on in a minute. Turns out that it took more than a minute.

"Okay, to lay this out for you, no pun intended, Penny Diamond is not a person."

"What?"

Means determined not to answer, becoming impatient with Conner's constant interruptions. "Here's the deal, lover boy," he said. "Either you shut up or I hang up. It's your choice."

"I'm sorry," Conner again apologized.

"Are you going to let me tell you what I know?"

"Yes."

"And you're not going to interrupt me?"

"Yes. Er, no."

"Good. Let me start again." Once more he took a breath and then began anew. "Penny Diamond is a stage name. She works at the Broadway Club. For those of you uninitiated, that's a take-off-your-clothes, no-holds-barred strip joint. Usually, they're raided by the vice squad about once a month."

"What does she do there?" Conner asked, voiding his promise to be quiet.

The humor of the question offset Means' frustration with Conner's interruptions. "Well, she's not the company pastor, if that's what you're asking."

"Huh?"

"She's a stripper at a strip club. Got it?"

"Not really, but go ahead."

"It's my guess that she wanted to lure you into a compromising situation and use that to undermine whatever you're doing."

"Why would she do that?"

"Somebody must have put her up to it."

"Why do you say that?"

"Because she uses four-letter words and has a two-digit IQ."

Silence from Conner.

"In other words," Means explained, "she wouldn't have any reason to fellow with you, share a conjugal evening with you or have the brains to set you up for some sort of bribery…since you're dirt poor, overly godish and not married."

'Overly godish' was a weird expression but it made sense to Conner, even if it was intended as a compliment. Actually, he liked being godish and didn't really think anyone could be overly godish. It was like the conversation that he had shared with God about having too much faith. But that was a different topic for a different time.

"Let me see if I understand this," Conner said. "Penny Diamond…"

"Her name is Linda Mason," Means updated.

"Penny Diamond, Linda Mason, or whatever her name is, pretends to want me to attend her sorority fellowship."

"Right."

"But there is no sorority and there never was going to be any fellowship."

"Yup."

"She does this in order to get me to do something that would discredit me."

"And your ministry."

"And my ministry," Conner echoed. "But she doesn't do it for or by herself."

"Oh, she surely did do it for herself. I'm quite certain that she would have gotten a nice piece of change if it had worked out."

"She does it because someone else put her up to it."

"There ya go!" Means said, finally able to bring the explanation to a close.

"Do you know who was behind this?" Conner asked.

"Not yet," Means said. "However this journalist knows a thing or two about getting to the bottom of things. I wasn't always a sports reporter, you know."

"I'm thankful for that," Conner said. "I really can't thank you enough. That would have been disastrous. It could have discredited everything that we've been trying to do."

"Yup," Means said proudly, more pleased with himself than with what catastrophe he had helped avert.

"What now?" Conner asked.

"Well, for one thing, I wouldn't meet Ms. Diamond anytime soon."

"Yeah, okay."

"Meanwhile, I'll rummage around a bit and find out who put her up to this…if I can."

Neither man said anything for a couple of moments. Esther, realizing that something bad had happened, was lightly holding onto Conner's arm, mostly as a show of support. Her restraint at not asking what was going on was quite remarkable.

After some thought, Conner said "Richard."

"Yeah?"

"Thanks. I really appreciate what you did for me. For us. For the ministry. It really means a lot. You showed me something special and I'm very thankful for it."

"Okay. I mean, you're welcome. There's something about you, about what you're doing and about the growing number of people who are buying into it that is, well, intriguing, if not something more."

Conner smiled. "You're welcome aboard," he offered.

"Maybe. We'll see. Meanwhile, I have some work to do."

"Thanks."

"Keep your nose clean, hang onto your girlfriend – she's a good one – and play some basketball."

"Will do."

"Good. See ya."

"See ya."

Conner hung up and just stood there, more in a daze than in a stall to explain what he had just heard. Esther, to her credit, didn't press him. She remained standing there with her supportive hand on his arm and waited. She was allowing him to process the conversation, intuitively understanding that silence showed more support than inquiry or supposition. While doing so, Job and his three friends came to mind. They spoke when they should have been silent, she remembered. She was encouraged by thinking about this.

Finally, he more or less snapped out of it, even shaking his head as though clearing it of cobwebs. "That's unbelievable."

"What is?"

"That student, Penny Diamond, I was going to see tonight for the sorority fellowship."

"Yes?"

"That's not her name, she doesn't belong to a sorority, she isn't a student and she was only looking to get me in trouble. Means doesn't know who put her up to it but he is fully convinced that it wasn't her doing."

Esther smiled. "How did you make it to thirty-four?"

"What do you mean?"

"How did you get this old while being so, so…I don't know, trusting?"

He shrugged.

"Let's let it be. So, now, are you up for the movie I suggested we go see?"

"Which one is that?" he asked.

"I didn't suggest one. Would you like me to make the selection?"

"Yeah. You pick. I seem to have made too many wrong choices lately."

"With me?"

"No, Esther. Not with you. Not with you at all. You're definitely a right choice. You're a right, right, right choice."

"Well thank you, kind sir," she said in her best southern belle accent.

Just then, Conner's phone rang. He looked at the number and recognized it as being the one from Penny. He showed the screen to Esther and said "Penny." Then he hit the ignore button and turned the unit off. "Enough with that," he said.

Esther gave him a thumbs up approval. They shared a smile with one another as they headed off to the car.

Chapter 55

The two Wednesday games were the qualifiers. Brantley and Conway emerged as winners. Today, instead of two games, there would be four. Conway now faced number one seed Iowa Central while Brantley faced number two seed Wisconsin/Geneva. The four-five matchup, Indiana Northern against Kingman, would begin at 11:00 AM. It would be followed by the three-six matchup, Illinois Central against Coleman. Brantley could reasonably expect to take the court at about 5:00.

In the first game, Indiana Northern walloped Kingman with a tenacious defense and superiority under the boards. The final score, 82-66, did not represent the disparity between the two teams. It was a complete thrashing.

In the second game, it took overtime to enable Illinois Central to defeat Coleman by a score of 77-75. As exciting as that entire game was, the last few seconds were heart-pounding. In fact, Coleman had the ball with ten seconds to go. After calling time out, they decided to go for the win. Their guard drove inside and had what appeared to be an easy shot when he passed it to one of the forwards in the corner for an uncontested three pointer. The ball rattled around the rim and then fell out as time expired.

The two games on Wednesday and now the first two games today had all ended with the favored teams winning. Brantley, the seventh seed, was next up against the second-seeded Wisconsin/Geneva Wildcats. The Eagles remembered that Wisconsin had the tallest team, including a seven-foot center and two six-ten forwards. If there was vulnerability at all, it resided with their foul shooting and ball handling. They had one excellent guard who was all conference but then the drop-off was pretty dramatic.

"How's the foot?" Coach Wright asked Conner in the locker room as they were getting ready.

"It feels really good. I was moving around on it without much trouble."

"Well, let's hope that we can get by one more game without you, or at least as little as possible. The more you stay off of it, the better." The coach smiled at Conner, but it was not a comfortable smile. He wished that he had his sixth man in tiptop condition.

"It'll be fine, Coach. You just play me as much as need be. I'm okay."

"We'll see," was all the response Conner was given as the coach moved along to interact with other players on the team.

One of the security officers came into the locker room. "Coach?" he asked, looking around.

"Right here," Coach Wright replied as he came around a row of lockers.

"Ten minutes to warm-up."

"Ten minutes?"

"That's it, Coach. I was in here ten minutes ago and provided a twenty-minute warning."

Coach Wright shook his head, then said "No problem. Thanks."

As the security officer left, the coach yelled out "Ten minutes, everyone."

Various versions of acknowledgement floated back.

"You still doing your prayer thing?" the coach asked Conner.

"Yes, sir."

"Don't forget to include the final score."

Conner laughed. "No, sir. I won't forget it. What margin would you like at the end? That way I can have our prayer request customized in delivery."

"Well, now that you ask, let's make it eleven. I don't want to get too greedy but I don't want to have ulcers in the last quarter."

"Roger that," Conner said as he saluted. "I'll report it upstairs."

"You do that, Ramsey. You do that."

Conner bowed his head for a personal prayer.

----- ----- -----

When it was time to go on the court, the team entered together. They trotted out to their bench pretty much at the same time as the Wildcats. The cheers from the crowd were loud. Since both teams appeared at roughly the same time, it was difficult from the noise to determine which had more fans. However, it was not difficult to make that judgment by looking at the crowd. Three quarters of them wore orange, the Wildcats' primary school colors.

These fans were definitely present to root their second-seeded Wildcats to victory, and they wouldn't mind some revenge for their unexpected loss to Brantley during the season.

A more modest fan base was dressed in dark blue and cheered for the Eagles. In among these fans were Esther, Pete, Bob and Drew. All four now wore Eagles singlet number seven with 'Ramsey' stitched on the back. Had someone guessed without otherwise knowing, they would have surmised them to be family members of the player. In a manner of speaking, they were.

Conner led the team to the foul line. At the same time, in a wonderfully spontaneous display of support, all those in dark blue stood, faced the team at the foul line and remained quiet. Many of them put their hands over their hearts, as though they were about to sing the national anthem or say the pledge of allegiance. Many of them said "Shhh," as though asking for silence in a movie theater. Most of the rest of the crowd responded.

The folks in orange also stood, some not remembering and some not knowing what was taking place but surmising that they had missed a public address announcement. Most of them looked at each other to see if they could determine what was taking place. Not able to gather any relevant information, they followed what everyone else was doing, silently standing. The public address announcer and the organist both remained silent, not knowing if they were to do something. Both figured that, perhaps, they had missed some instructions, as well. Better quiet than sorry, each thought.

The Wildcats bench, not remembering the tournament protocol, stood and faced the same direction as everyone else. By coincidence, the American flag was in a straight line of the Wildcats' bench and the Eagles at the foul line. With the Wildcats facing in that direction, everyone else more or less did the same, too.

In this surprising silence, Connor offered a prayer that could almost be heard by many, although he did not raise his voice. He prayed for safety, enjoyment, healing and glory to God. When he ended with "Amen," many in the crowd echoed it. Then the Eagles returned to their bench and everyone, the Wildcats included, proceeded with what they had been doing. It was almost as though that had been planned by the tournament committee.

When they got back to the bench, the coach, with a smile, asked Conner "Did you ask for the eleven-point winning margin?"

"I did earlier," Conner replied with a wink. "Nothing to worry about."

"Just making certain," the coach said.

The team huddled around the coach. "Defense and boxing out. This is a big team. We need to keep them out of the paint." He looked around. Everyone was focused. "Eagles on three," he said, leading them to their break cheer.

Kline, Walker, Forrester, Dixon and Obumje took the court. The five for the Wildcats, especially their front court, were considerably taller and heavier than those of the Eagles. The men dressed in orange could easily have been linemen for the school's football team. Actually, one of the forwards did play both sports. The ten players shook hands, acknowledged the three refs and took their places on the court.

For the first five minutes, there was a lot of banging taking place underneath. For the most part, the refs let them play. Once or twice, tempers flared and that was when the refs cracked down a bit. When things returned to 'competitive' but not 'personal', the refs lessened their use of whistles. Thanks to Forrester, Dixon and Obumje neutralizing their big men, Kline and Walker were able to outplay the Wildcats' two guards. At that point in time, the Eagles led 15-12.

Instead of making wholesale changes to his lineup, Coach Wright flowed individual players into the game. Shedrick rotated in and out with the starting guards while the three big men caught breathing spells one at a time. The Wildcats had the luxury of having six big men and could thus substitute three at a time. The Wildcats' talented guard, however, had to stay in for the entire game, the coach being fearful that turnovers would escalate if he was on the bench.

The seesaw nature of the game continued through the first half, which ended at 48-46 in favor of Brantley. However, Dixon, Obumje and Walker each had three fouls. Since Wisconsin's bench was deeper at most positions, this favored them for the second half. Conner still had not played in the tournament.

Although he appreciated the coach's careful handling, he was anxious to get into the game and get some playing time. And, of course, he wanted to make a difference. Even beyond that, he felt that his ministry would not get the necessary attention if he were to sit on the bench all the way through.

In the locker room at half-time, the coach expressed some of his anxiety. "This is a one-and-done tournament, gentlemen," he began. "And, for us, it's a one-and-done-for-the-season tournament. We must, and I mean must, get up on them. We cannot leave the game in the hands of a lucky last-minute shot. If their guard had hit that half-court shot at the buzzer, we would be trailing right now. If that happens at the end of the game and he actually hits it, we're toast."

He looked around.

"Anyone wanna be toast?" he asked.

Various negatives were given in response, from clear 'no' answers to pretty much inaudible grunts.

"Anyone wanna be toast?" the coach asked again.

"No, coach!" came the unified response.

"Then let's get out there and do something about it, for crying out loud."

Again he surveyed his team.

"Same starting lineup. Let's do it."

Everyone stood up, knowing where to go and what to do.

Within thirty seconds, both Walker and Obumje had picked up their fourth fouls. Coach Wright debated what to do. He substituted Shedrick for Walker but left in Obumje, with stern instructions.

"No arms. They're calling you for using your arms to keep your man out or get inside of him. You have to use your body. You're faster than that guy. Take advantage of it."

"Yes, coach," came the commitment from Obumje.

The Kline-Harris combination was not a particularly good one. Kline had somewhat limited mobility and Harris was not a shot-maker. Neither were good passers and, aside from Obumje, none of the big men were able to find space against the zone that the Wildcats were now employing. The score went from Eagles up by two to Wildcats up by five with fifteen minutes to play.

"Ramsey!" Coach Wright bellowed.

"Yes, coach?" Conner responded.

"Let's see if your foot has healed," he said, pointing to the scorer's table, silently instructing Conner to check in. "Give Kline a spell."

"You got it, coach," Conner said and stood up to pull off his warm ups. When he arose, nobody in the crowd said or did anything until Pete and his pals started yelling. "Yeah, Seven!" "Seven, seven, seven," they began chanting, unknowingly echoing a chant that had been used earlier in the season for a home game. Many other Eagles' fans took up the cheer and it continued until the refs called time out for the substitution. Conner went in for Kline, each sharing a word of encouragement for the other. Perhaps the most vocal player in support of Conner was Walker, quite a difference from how they had interacted for the first part of the season.

Down by five, fifteen minutes to go and having the ball. "Our turn," Conner said to Shedrick.

"Well, old man," Shedrick responded, "it's about time. I sure hope that you're rested from all that bench time."

Conner looked at his roomie and made an artificial frown. The two smiled at one another. Conner looked for Esther in the crowd and smiled at her. She smiled back. She raised her fist and moved it slightly in encouragement. He winked at her. She winked back.

Wisconsin had its starting lineup on the floor. Shedrick inbounded to Conner who immediately returned the ball. The Wildcats were playing man-to-man and picked up Shedrick just inside half court. He got the ball to Conner. The other guard, not the one who was the ball handler, came up very close to Conner, his hands waving. "Come on, old man," he said.

Conner looked for someone open. Nothing.

"Come on, old man," the guard taunted as he inched even closer.

Appreciating that the ref was counting to five and that he had to do something, Conner went past his defender in a flash, slowed down enough to allow their center to rotate over and dished to a wide-open Forrester. Blam! Forrester jammed it through the hoop with two-handed authority, hanging onto the rim for just a moment or two.

The Wildcats brought the ball up. Shedrick knew to take away his man's outside shot and force this good guard into the middle. With somewhat renewed energy, Forrester and his two compatriots kept themselves between their men and the basket, forbidding them easy access into the paint. The refs watched closely to make certain that there were no serious fouls.

When the guard went to pass to his mate, Conner stepped in, stole the pass and led Shedrick for another two-handed dunk. Conner and Shedrick shared their unique handshake as they both went on defense. Now they were down one with quick momentum. "Seven, seven, seven," shouted Pete, his friends and an increasing number of Eagles fans.

The ball handler brought the Wildcats up court, looking for an opportunity to create an opening. Seeing that Shedrick was playing him to the outside, he attempted to drive toward the middle. As soon as he did this, Shedrick let him go and started racing up court. For those watching the game as a whole, it looked like one player was totally out of whack with the other nine on the court. Even one of the refs had a puzzled look on his face.

However, Shedrick's confidence in doing that was quickly rewarded when Conner took the ball from the dribbler and lobbed a pass down court. Shedrick let it bounce, caught it at the top of its arc and jammed it home, much to the delight of the Eagles crowd and the dismay of the Wildcats coach. He immediately called time out, his team now down one with twelve minutes to go.

"Let's stick with this for a while," Coach Wright said. Then, turning to Conner he asked "How's your foot?"

"So far, so good, especially since I haven't had to run or stop sharply."

The coach nodded.

"Everyone else okay?" he asked. Shedrick, of course, had a wide grin. "Oh, yeah," he said.

"Your points go up astronomically when you partner with Ramsey," the coach noted. "No wonder you look like the cat that ate the mouse."

"Yum," Shedrick responded with a smile.

"Okay, up one. Let's widen it," the coach said in conclusion.

And widen it they did, Coach Wright throwing wrinkles into his lineup periodically. These included a Kline-Ramsey-Harris backcourt with Forrester and Obumje underneath. Although this seemed to invite mismatches below the foul line that favored the bigger team, the fact that the three guards pressed their ball handlers made it difficult to see underneath. Each time that the Wildcats guards tried to penetrate to the basket, Conner seemed to be there with a take away.

Interestingly, however, he didn't steal the ball each time. His logic was to leave the other team with some belief that they could succeed with penetration. Otherwise, they would take that option out of their repertoire and find another approach. Conner tried to make his presence significant but not overwhelming.

With two minutes left, the Eagles led by nine. Although Obumje fouled out shortly thereafter, the Forrester-Dixon combination continued its effective defense underneath. With seven seconds left and the

Eagles up by thirteen, Shedrick was fouled. He sank
the first but missed the second. One of the bench
players from the Wildcats got the rebound, dribbled
twice and launched his first shot of the season from
almost three quarters of the court. It seemed to be in
the air for quite a long time before going through the
basket without touching the rim for an exceedingly
long three-pointer. The end-of-game buzzer went
off as the ball went through the hoop. At first, he
was excited, then realized that it was anticlimactic.

Brantley was now into the semifinals, slated to
face third-seeded Illinois Central. As the players filed
pass one another as is the tradition in college
basketball, all had kind words to exchange. When
Conner got to the young man who had made the
three-pointer, he stopped and said "Great shot. They
should have had you in there earlier."

The young man smiled. "Thanks," he said, clearly
beaming about it. "I'm sure that God took my errant
shot and redirected it."

"Praise God," Conner said.

"Praise God," the young man said, as they shared
a quick hug.

When Conner had gotten through the players line,
he stepped back and looked up to where Pete had
been sitting. The three were still there. He raised his
fist.

"Seven, seven, seven," they started chanting again.

Conner just shook his head, smiled and looked
down. Then he playfully pointed at them.

Next, he looked for Esther. She, too, had not
moved from her seat. He ran up the aisle to where

she was, gave her a peck on the cheek and said "Thanks for your support."

"You're welcome," she said, a bit surprised. "I always support you," she said.

"I know. That's what I mean. I wasn't solely referring to this game. I was saying thanks for your partnership. You're pretty nice," he added impishly.

"Pretty nice?" she said, feigning hurt.

"Yeah. You're pretty and you're nice," he answered.

She smiled as he hustled down the aisle on the way to the locker room. They had selected a place to meet afterwards. They both looked forward to it.

Chapter 56

"Nice game," Coach Wright said. "Ramsey, you and Forrester join me for the post-game interview."

Conner did a double take. During the regular season, there were few times that players accompanied the coach to the interview room. Once in a while, he would allow someone to join if he had played an unusually strong game. Although Conner would have seemed to qualify at least twice, the coach kept him out of the limelight, mostly not to annoy what he thought would be the boosters' attitude. In this quarterfinal game, however, Conner and Forrester had clearly been the difference makers. They deserved the accolades and the press would be demanding their attendance.

"You don't have time to shower," Coach Wright said. Forrester, who had gone with the coach a few times over several seasons, as had Kline and Walker, knew this. However, it was new to Conner. He had already taken off his singlet and shirt when he learned that they needed to be put back on. He did it and hustled after the other two, not certain where the interview room was situated in this arena.

Before dashing out, he called over to Shedrick who was pretty much unclothed himself. "Hey, Shedrick, do me a favor, please?"

Shedrick gave Conner his attention without saying anything.

"Please tell Esther and Pete that I'll be in the interview room."

With an exaggerated sigh and a smile, Shedrick nodded his willingness and started putting his uniform back on. The coach was very particular that players on the team either wore their uniforms fully or didn't wear them at all. In other words, no singlet with blue jeans or shorts with alternate tee shirts. Thus, Shedrick had to put his entire uniform back on and make it game presentable.

When the coach, Forrester and Conner arrived at the interview room, they were asked to wait in the wings while things were prepared. A long table with three individual microphones had been set up. It sat on a stage in front of a sea of folding chairs, each occupied. The front rows were allotted to journalists. There were, however, a few rows available to the public. These were typically taken up by family members of those being interviewed. Esther, Pete, Bob and Drew grabbed four of them before the interview began.

Huge lights poured down on the table. An enormous backdrop eliminated distractions behind. It was light blue with the Plains Conference logo and name alternating throughout in a neat but not busy pattern. In due course, Coach Wright and his two players were instructed to take seats. Name tents had been printed for the press. These also allowed the three interviewees to know where they sat. Coach Wright sat to one side, Forrester in the middle and Conner at the end.

A moderator walked onto the stage. He waited for the audience to quiet. "Ladies and gentlemen, allow me to introduce members of the winning quarterfinals team, the Brantley Eagles. On your left is Coach Jason Wright. Next to him is center Clyde Forrester. And next to him is guard Conner Ramsey."

There was polite applause. He raised his hand, asking for additional quiet in the audience. When he received it, he continued. "Let me read the statistics and then open it up to questions. When you are selected, please wait for the microphone to reach you before beginning. Also, please limit yourself to one *brief* question at a time."

He looked around to make certain everyone had heard. Then he proceeded. "The final score was 94-83, an Eagles victory by eleven points."

Coach Wright looked over at Conner, suddenly realizing that the margin had been as promised! Conner was smiling back at him. Had it not been for that wild three-pointer at the end, the difference would have been fourteen points. Conner thought about what the young man had said about the shot being divinely directed. That player may well have been right about that, he thought to himself.

Then the moderator quickly read off the individual statistics. Kline led all scorers with 32, Harris with 20, Walker with 18 all the way down to Ramsey with five. However, when it came to steals, Conner himself had more than the entire Wildcats team. Once rebounds and foul shooting figures were delivered, the moderator said "We'll have remarks from Coach Wright and then open it up for questions."

All eyes turned to the coach. "Not much to say about today. Wisconsin is a tough team. We played well, especially in the second half. I was surprised to win by eleven." Here he leaned forward slightly and looked again at Conner who returned the look with a smile.

"Kline was hot from the outside. He's got a great eye. Harris and Ramsey work well together. Walker can make his own shot when necessary, although he got in foul trouble right from the start. Forrester and his friends were in among the trees but managed to hold their own. That team is big, isn't it?"

The coach looked for reaction but couldn't see very well into the bright lights. He shaded his eyes, as though he was outside in the sunlight. It didn't really help.

"Nothing much else to say."

The moderator then invited questions, recognizing a reporter in the middle of the room first.

"Waitt from the *Wisconsin Gazette*," he began. "Coach, how was it that this team finished this low in the regular conference season? You certainly don't look like a seventh seed."

"I agree. As you know, we had a bunch of injuries to key players. Kline, Walker and Ramsey went out in one game alone. It was weeks before any of them returned. Then Ramsey cut his foot. We're still monitoring that. We understand the critical nature of this tournament. If we don't win the next two games, we won't be going to the big dance. I'm hoping that we can play well and earn an automatic bid."

"Pilmer from the *Illinois Reporter*," began the second journalist. "Forrester, as the only true giant on the Eagles team, how did it feel playing against five or six others of your size or bigger?"

"I thought that I was in the Redwood Forest, to tell you the truth," he said with a smile. "I'm glad that our guards bottled them up outside. Otherwise, we would have gotten many more fouls and the result may have looked very different."

"Shaffer from Channel 5. Coach, I noticed that you twice shared a smile with Ramsey at the end of the table when the score differential – eleven – was mentioned. What's funny about that?"

Coach Wright smiled. "Well…" Again, he looked over to Conner who looked down, although he was smiling. "As you may know – or if you don't, you should – Conner is our…" Here, he stopped. "What the heck are you, Ramsey?" he queried.

"A guard," Conner responded with a smile. Everyone laughed. Then, because of the silence, Conner continued. "Jesus is my lord and savior. He is my primary driver. In following him, I try to bring others along. Some of my teammates have called it a mission or a ministry. Whatever it is, God deserves the glory."

"What does that have to do with the eleven-point difference at the end of the game?" Shaffer followed up.

Conner answered. "Well, the team likes to pray together. That's what we do before and after the game when we create the circle at the foul line."

Those in the audience were nodding their heads, some making notes, others shooting pictures.

"Before the game, the coach came over to me and asked that I include in my personal prayer the wish for a more comfortable margin of victory. Somehow, we settled on eleven. When that turned out to be the actual score, the coach was playing *Twilight Zone* music in his head, I'm sure."

"But it was just a Hail Mary shot in the last seconds from a bench player that brought it to eleven," Shaffer continued.

"Yes, it was. But what's particularly odd is that he commented about God's influence in directing that shot. You can ask him. Anyhow, coincidence or not, it caught Coach Wright's attention."

"And yours?"

"Not that much."

Chapter 57

"Great job with the interview," Esther said when they were together again.

"Yeah, but super-great job on the floor," Pete added, referring to the game. "You pretty much turned it around."

Bob and Drew also gave him high fives for how he changed the course of the game.

"Thanks," Conner said, knowing that it was much more Esther's compliment that meant something significant to him. However, he did want to appreciate what his three pals were sharing with him.

"What now?" Pete asked.

"Well, we don't have our semifinal game until 5:00 PM tomorrow. How 'bout if we go grab something to eat?"

"Sounds like a winner," Pete said, speaking for his two traveling buddies. They nodded in agreement.

"Maybe I should let the four of you just have a boys' night out?" Esther offered.

"Nooo!" came the chorus of protests.

"In the first place," Conner said, "If forced to make a choice, I'd rather be with you than with them."

He got a humorous thumbs down from Pete and Bob.

"In the second place, we're not doing the boys 'thing' tonight. I'm trying to stick to a resting routine. I won't be out as late as these no goodniks anyhow."

"In the third place," Pete added, "we'd rather be with you, Esther, than with him. In fact, your joining lets us tolerate Reverend Ramsey."

They all laughed as they started walking in search of a place to eat.

----- ----- -----

Richard Means had been a successful journalist because he had an eye for news; he knew how to investigate a story; and he was a skilled writer, one who could provide facts within the framework of an interesting story. With this story of Penny Diamond and what he tentatively entitled 'The Sorority Fellowship Caper,' he recognized that he was onto something worthwhile. It was a combination of sports, human interest and mystery. It also promised to be something longer than a one-article piece.

Right off the bat, he decided to visit the Broadway Club. Perhaps he could get a sit down with Ms. Diamond or even find out who had put her up to this. It might even lead to some law enforcement action. Mostly, though, it would address his insatiable appetite for intrigue, something he did not often encounter on the sports beat.

----- ----- -----

Late the next morning, Coach Wright met with his team to discuss Illinois Central. He didn't feel the need to search out a gym in which they could practice. However, he did want to remind them of a few things. He was particularly critical of foolish fouls.

"If you're picking your man up near half court, don't foul him. If he beats you with a shot from out there, give it to him again. We'll do better than him. If he blows past you, that's why you have teammates. However, from that far away, you shouldn't be pressing him anyhow. Thus, there's no reason for him to blow past you."

As he liked to do, the coach scanned the players. They were all paying attention, although not with captivated interest.

"Am I getting through to you?"

"Yes, coach!" came the military-like response.

"Listen. I know that we're supposed to stay focused on our current game. I want you to do that. However, I also want you to remember that two more wins and we get invited to the Big Dance. That's our immediate prize. We're better than anyone in this league and now we're healthy."

He looked over at Conner.

"Pretty healthy," he corrected. "I want the rest of you to play well enough to keep him on the bench. Okay?"

"Yes, coach!"

"Coach Bromberg will be reviewing a few things with our forwards and centers. Coach Wilcox will be doing the same for our guards. I'll see you back here for the game." He looked over at Conner once more. "Let me talk to you for a minute."

Conner followed the coach to a quiet corner of the hotel lobby. The other two coaches had taken their players elsewhere – Murphy to the pool area and Wilcox to the vacated breakfast nook.

"Listen, Ramsey," Coach Wright began. "I think that we've done well by each other."

"Yes, sir," Conner confirmed, very curious as to where the coach was headed with this one-on-one conversation.

"And I think that you've upheld your end of the bargain."

"Yes, sir," although Conner wasn't quite certain what the coach meant by bargain. Conner assumed that it referred to his making a difference on the court in exchange for introductions to boosters. Rather than seeking to clarify the exchange, he chose to remain silent and attempt to deduce the specific topic from what would follow. Conner's heart rate was clearly elevated in anticipation of what the coach was about to tell or ask him. It was obvious that the coach was pondering whether or not to say the next thing. The longer he waited, the more Conner worried that it was bad news, getting worse by the second. It was difficult for Conner not to ask the coach to get to the point.

"Well, I was approached by the *Chicago Tribune* for an interview with Reverend Ramsey," he half said and half laughed. "Although they are interested in your basketball skills, they are also interested in your mission, ministry or whatever it is that you are calling it now."

Conner raised his eyebrows in somewhat surprise. Bad news? Absolutely not. Good news? Yes. Great news, in fact.

"And you told them that it was okay?" Conner sought to confirm.

"I did," the coach replied, "pending your interest in doing so."

"You dog," Conner said. "You had me worried big time."

"That's what coaches do," came the response.

"Wow! Coach, that's great. Thanks a lot. When will it be?"

"They wanted this afternoon but I didn't want us breaking routine. I told them it could either be tonight after the game or tomorrow morning. They chose tonight. You gonna be okay with that?"

"Okay? Oh, yeah, I'll be okay. Whenever they want works for me. Even halftime tonight."

Coach Wright gave Conner a parent-like look of displeasure. Conner smiled at him.

"Okay, not at halftime." He let a few seconds pass and then added "How about at the beginning of the game since I'll just be riding the pine anyhow?" he asked playfully.

"You'll be riding it longer than that if your head isn't in the game from the get-go," the coach reminded him.

"Is that it, coach?" Conner asked.

"How's your foot?" he inquired, changing subjects.

"I think that it's pretty good. I'll avoid making fancy dunks," he said with a smile.

"Why? Did they lower the basket to six feet?"

"Very funny. Very funny," Conner replied. "I *choose* not to dunk. If I wanted to do so, I'd ask God for some additional skills and be able to dunk with my feet."

"Yeah, right," the coach replied. "Now get out of here."

"Thanks again, coach. That interview means a lot to me."

"I figured. Just make certain that it's a victory interview."

"Yes, sir."

Conner turned to go, then stopped.

"Coach?"

"Yeah?"

"You want to choose a margin of victory?" he asked.

Coach Wright just shook his head as Conner departed. Maybe I should have picked a number, he said to himself. Twenty or thirty would be nice, he decided, then dismissed the thought.

Chapter 58

The game against the Illinois Central Ducks turned out to be easier than expected. It was close through most of the first half. Then, when Kline and Walker started drilling threes, the tide turned in favor of the Eagles. Conner got to play a little but didn't need to do anything spectacular to assist his team. He made a few steals off of dribbles and a few more off of passes but, otherwise, kept a pretty low profile. Brantley won by nine, but the difference felt a lot larger. It would have been larger, in fact, had not the Ducks scored six unanswered points at the end.

Immediately after shaking hands with the other team and going to the foul line for the post-game prayer, Conner was approached by someone with whom he was not familiar. The man was dressed in a tie and sports jacket. He was about fifty-ish years old, wore glasses and had a serious look about him.

"Mr. Ramsey, my name is Tony Weston and I work for the *Chicago Tribune*. Coach Wright…"

"Yes," Conner interrupted. "Coach Wright already told me about the interview. Where would you like to meet?"

"Will you be in the post-game interview today?"

"No, I strongly doubt it. I didn't play enough to even earn an asterisk on the scorecard," Conner said with a brief but genuine laugh.

"I didn't think so," Weston said without particular enjoyment.

Conner wanted to gig him for his lack of humor, then thought better of it.

"There are interview rooms available to the media," he said. "I've reserved one."

"Great. Ya want me to change and meet you or come as I am?"

"I'd prefer right now," the journalist responded.

"Lead away," Conner instructed. Then, noticing Esther standing with Pete and his two buddies, he said to Weston "Wait just a moment." The reporter stopped, understanding the purpose of the interruption.

"Got that interview now," he said to them, having already shared his excitement about it earlier in the day. "I'll call you when I'm done. Okay?"

"Good luck, big boy," she said, squeezing his hand.

"Knock 'em dead," Pete added. The other two simply waved to him.

"Okay, I'm ready," Conner told Weston and off they went to the interview room.

----- ----- -----

In the other semifinal game, the Iowa Central Falcons thrashed Indiana Northern, 106-80. The Falcons were the highest-scoring team in the conference and third in the nation among Division I teams. They averaged 92.2 points per game during the regular season and were averaging 103 in their two games against Conway and Indiana Northern. In this tournament, they had beaten the Conway Bulldogs by thirty points, 100-70. Thus, their average margin of victory was 28.

During the regular season, Iowa Central had beaten Brantley twice, 110-62 in Iowa and 107-76 at home. On the basis of all this, the finals looked like a mismatch in favor of the number one seed over the number seven seed. On top of that, the Eagles were about to play for the fourth consecutive day. In the history of the conference tournament, no team had won with anything worse than a sixth seed.

On the other side of the coin, neither Kline, Walker nor Ramsey had played in the first loss. Kline and Walker had returned for the second loss but were clearly less than game-ready for it. Kline had scored eight points on three-for-eleven shooting. Walker had scored sixteen points on six-for-fourteen shooting. Had not Iowa Central substituted liberally in both games, there is no telling what the margins of victory would have been.

On the gambling circuit, the odds were approaching 7-to-1.

----- ----- -----

Once they sat down in the small interview room, Weston took out his recorder and placed it on the table.

"I presume that you don't have a problem with my recording this?" he asked.

"None whatsoever," Conner responded.

"Excellent," Weston said as he pressed the record button. Then he spoke in the date, place and person being interviewed. He concluded with mentioning his name and newspaper affiliation. Conner looked around the room while he did so. There was nothing interesting about the room. It had four walls with only a clock on one of them, no windows, a four-foot rectangular table and four chairs. It could just as easily have been an interrogation room as an interview room. Perhaps, at times, it was.

"Let me tell you what I know and then we can move forward from there," Weston suggested.

"Fair enough," Conner replied, happy to hear this approach.

Weston then proceeded to lay out a pretty complete biography for Conner, even including a thing or two that Conner had forgotten. He included information on Conner's family, elementary education, middle and high school education, college, work, graduate studies, athletic career and even a little bit about his religious life. It took about five minutes. When he was done, he looked up and asked "Is there anything else that would be helpful?"

"Not that I can think of," Conner responded, "other than that my first dog was named Scamper, my second dog Scooby, my parakeet Tweets and I named all of my aquarium tank fish." He paused, then added "And we had official burials for each fish that died."

While Conner was adding this bit of silliness to his background, Weston was writing down every word. Conner, looking for a smile from the man sitting across the desk from him, determined to cut the humor and stick to the facts. There's no telling how he might interpret something that I intend as a joke, he told himself. Conner sat back in his chair, indicating that he was through with his supplement.

"Excellent," Weston commented without expression. "I have a number of questions written down for you. I will ask them in this order unless something you say has me add a question or change the sequence. Is that okay with you?"

"Just Jim Dandy," Conner replied.

"Excellent," Weston said again.

----- ----- -----

As it turned out, Richard Means was able to meet Penny Diamond, aka Linda Mason, convince her that he worked for a big time newspaper and assure her that he knew plenty of agents who handled budding actresses, especially those who had not yet been discovered but who were what he called "Diamonds in the rough. No pun intended." She had promised to meet him for coffee after her last shift. It turned out to be 2:00 AM but, to Means, was worth the lengthier night.

When she did come into the diner, he invited her to have something to eat. Much to his surprise, she told him that she was starved and ordered steak and eggs. Means hoped that he would get this reimbursed at work, although his boss had been cracking down on expenses lately. He could almost hear his boss now: "So, ya met a stripper at 2:00 in the mornin' and ya want me to pay for your breakfast? Come on, now, Ricky. Whatcha take me for, some sorta moron?" Means smiled to himself. Even if he wouldn't get compensated for the meal, it would be worth it.

Means put enough on the table for Penny to want more information, it in exchange for material that the journalist wanted. Their negotiating continued for over an hour, Means recording the discussion, although he did not do his customary alert to that fact. If necessary, he would voice in an introduction and claim that she had agreed to the recording.

What he found out was illuminating, surprising and disheartening, all rolled into one. The man who had paid Ms. Mason to lure Ramsey into a compromising circumstance was not her handler, nor her employer at the Broadway Club. Instead, it was one of the Brantley boosters, Justin Goudas.

"I don't know why he was mad at this nice man," she had said. "However, he gave me one hundred dollars to set it up and promised me one thousand more if I could do some things in a room that he would have in the hotel. I tried but Mr. Ramsey never showed. I was saddened by that, both for missing the money plus Mr. Ramsey seemed like a really nice man. I wouldn't have minded fooling around with him a little. I sort of felt some energy between us, if ya know what I mean."

Means just rolled his eyes, although he didn't let Linda notice. "I'm sure that you two would have made a wonderful couple," he said.

"Ya think so?" she asked.

He didn't bother answering.

Chapter 59

"The two things that my readers want to know," Weston said, "involve basketball and religion. I want to ask some questions about each and then, perhaps, explore how they overlap."

"Fire away," Conner said.

"Excellent. Tell me why you picked up basketball all of a sudden after a sports lifetime of not really having played it at all."

Conner shared with Weston that it had always been a third or fourth schoolyard sport and that he never had any particular skill at it. Even with his friends, he was never particularly good. Besides, he always preferred baseball and soccer, sports that one played outdoors.

"Well, then, how did basketball jump out of the woodwork for you?"

Conner explained the events of the recreation center pickup game that he had been 'forced' to play with his friend Pete, omitting anything about his interaction with God. "Had Pete not brought me out on the court, I doubt that this talent would have had occasion to blossom."

"And it's just out of left field, through an odd set of circumstances, that you discovered your talents on the basketball court?" he asked with just a tinge of incredulity creeping into his tone.

"I know that it sounds odd but, yes, that's it."

"And from there, you all of a sudden decide to go to graduate school and try out for the basketball team?"

"Yeah, that's pretty much it."

"Don't you think that it's a little improbable for this situation to have occurred?"

"It's not likely, that's for sure."

"You wouldn't say that it's improbable?"

"You're splitting hairs here, Tony. My belief is that I was gifted late in life in order to communicate a message…two messages, actually."

"Like what?"

"Well, for one thing, there's the classic bottom-of-the-ninth scenario and you hit a homer. It's a Kirk Gibson sort of thing."

"Meaning?"

"Everyone wants to do something unlikely, especially if it's in the later stages of a game or later stages of one's life."

Weston offered no comment, although he did quickly envision some winning scenarios that fit his own world.

"Think how many fantasy camps exist around the country for all sports, especially baseball and basketball. You know why? Because people want to relive their glory years or make new memories, maybe even first-time remembrances."

"In other words you see yourself as an inspiration for couch potatoes and over-the-hill types."

"Could be," Conner responded.

"You said that there were two messages. What's the other one?"

"The other one is the more important one…by far." Here Conner stopped and considered how to word what he was about to say. "Tony, I'd like you to listen to the message rather than the words that I use here. If you deliver this only with my sentences, we will both have missed an important opportunity."

Weston looked at Conner without any outward facial expression, although what Conner had said was growing on him. "I'll try," he acknowledged.

"From a secular perspective, I'd like to encourage others, both young and old, to keep their dreams alive as well as to be part of a stay-in-better-shape program."

Weston nodded his understanding of this first message.

Conner continued. "The second message has to do with people finding or renewing their faith."

"That's where people are getting lost," Weston said. "What has basketball got to do with people finding – or renewing – their faith?"

"That's a great question, Tony, and I'm not certain that I can answer it, although I feel it in my heart and soul."

"Give it a try," Weston encouraged.

"When I used to watch college football, I loved watching Tim Tebow, even though I wasn't a Florida Gator fan."

Weston nodded and smiled, thinking the same. "Me, too," he commented.

"Remember how he wore Bible quotes for the blackout under his eyes?"

"Yeah."

"I loved the way that he represented the Lord. In a funny sort of way, I wanted him to succeed. At the same time, I wanted him to continue his Walk. I also wished that I could be in his shoes. Think about it. Wouldn't it be great to evangelize like that?"

Weston daydreamed with Conner. "Yeah," he said abstractedly.

"Well, in many ways, that dream has come true for me, although on a much smaller scale, I guess."

"So far," Weston said. "So far," he repeated, referring to the size of the dream, not that it was coming to an end.

"So far," Conner agreed.

Both men sat quietly for a few moments, each lost in his own thoughts. Weston was the first to return to the moment.

"What do you want your message to be?" he asked.

"Overall, to believe in the Lord, to accept his invitation and to follow his two primary commandments."

"Which are…?"

From this question, Conner understood that Weston was not a strong believer, or at least not a Bible student.

"To love the Lord and to be good to others."

"Yes, that's right," Weston said, seemingly remembering something he had once known but had not been able to call up at that very moment.

"If I can encourage others to see that we are all Davids facing Goliaths, that we are all loved by the Lord and that he wants us to spend eternity with him, then I will have done something significant." Pause. "At least I hope so."

Just then, Weston's cell phone rang. "I'm sorry," he apologized as he reached into his pocket to retrieve it. "Let me just turn the darn thing off."

As he took the phone out, he glanced at the number. "Oh, no," he said. "It's my boss. I really need to take this. Would you excuse me for a second? I'll keep this as short as possible."

"Sure," Conner said as Weston stood up and exited the room.

----- ----- -----

Conner sat there for a few minutes playing the conversation over in his head. He wasn't pleased with how little he had taken advantage of this great opportunity. He vowed to do better when Weston returned.

A moment later, the door opened and a security guard stuck his head in. "Everything okay in here?" he asked.

"Yes, sir," Conner responded, smiling and not thinking much of it.

"Are you sure?" the guard probed.

Odd question, Conner thought. "Yes, I'm sure," he responded, just a smidgen exasperated at the guard's persistence.

"Then what are you complainin' about?" the guard now asked.

Conner scrunched up his face and looked at the guard. "What are you talking about? Complaining about what?"

The guard stepped into the room and the door closed behind him. He walked over and sat at the table in the same seat that had just been occupied by the journalist. This is odd behavior, Conner thought.

"Complaining about not taking advantage of this opportunity."

Conner started to say something and then stopped. He looked at the guard, a man probably in his sixties, although clearly in good health and condition. He had a full head of grey hair but it wasn't particularly neatly kept. He had a two-day growth of beard and, on further inspection, his uniform was poorly cared for.

"Are you...?"

The guard smiled.

Conner smiled. Still, he wasn't sure.

"Is your name Emanuel?" Conner asked carefully.

"Among others," came the response.

"Where have you been lately, on vacation?"

"I have a few other people to tend to, you know," came the soft reply.

"You're something else," Conner said, smiling with real joy in his heart.

"Listen, son, you're the one who's something else. I'm quite proud of you."

"Do you always interact with your designated mission people like this?"

The guard looked at him without responding.

"You know, like the prophets, Moses, David and loads of others since the days of the Bible?"

His visitor laughed, very much reminding Conner of Santa Claus. "Well, truth be told," he began.

Conner shook his head and, with a smile, completed the sentence "…if I tell you, I'll have to kill you."

"Bingo."

"Okay, no more questions from me. It's your nickel, as the expression goes."

"How can I answer a question with a question if you don't ask me a question?"

Conner smiled. This guy, no matter what body he is wearing, is a hoot. "You're a hoot," he decided to say out loud, although he realized that God had probably already read his mind.

"I'll take that as a compliment."

Conner nodded, confirming it was meant as such.

"I really just stopped by to tell you to stay the course. You're doing the right things."

"I appreciate that encouragement, especially since I often wonder if I'm going down the right path. Besides, it feels really slow."

"There is no prescriptive path for this sort of thing. You are going to make right and wrong decisions. Overall, though, you are making many more good ones than bad ones."

"That's good to hear."

"As far as the pace, I don't see how you can do it much faster. This is rather like a seedling needing the time and nourishment to grow into a tree. Aside from yours truly, there's no one who controls time."

"Well," Conner concluded, "if you're okay with the direction and pace, then who am I to question it? I'll continue along the same way."

He paused.

"Unless you have additional instructions, that is."

"Nope. Stay the course and all that. If I need you or want to tell you something, I know where to find you."

"Need me?"

"It's just an expression."

They both smiled.

"On the other hand, if you need me, I'll be floating around."

"Also an expression?"

"Sort of."

Again they both smiled.

"Let me ask you a question," Conner began.

"What?" God interjected, happy to toss in that bit of humor. Conner gave him little more than a polite smile, one that said enough is enough. God made a silly face back at him.

"Should I be addressing theological issues or just sticking to the Great Commission?"

"How do you differentiate between the two?" God asked. "I can't see you doing one without the other?"

"I can," Conner replied. "I can model good basketball skills, have people want to be like me and show how my faith leads my life…"

"Or?"

"I can discuss issues relating to the existence of you, the church, the afterlife or evil."

"Well, you definitely want to do the former. As far as the latter is concerned, provided that you preface your statements with 'this is my belief' – and substantiate it with Bible references where possible – you're as qualified as the next person to share your thoughts."

"Hmmm," said Conner, semi-amazed at this response.

"You know the expression…"

"What?"

"Opinions are like belly buttons…"

"Everyone has one," Conner finished the saying.

"Bingo."

"Well, it's time to go."

They both smiled.

"Drop by anytime you wish," Conner joked.

"Without an invitation?"

Conner thought about that for a second. How interesting, he thought.

Just as the security guard left the room, in walked Weston.

"I'm sorry for the delay," he said. "My boss is an answer-my-call-immediately person. He's got a bit of an I-am-important attitude. I hope that you weren't put off with that."

"No, thank you. I spoke with God while you were gone."

Without batting an eye, Weston said "It's always good to pray."

Conner chose not to correct him. "Did you see the security guard who just left?" he inquired, wondering if God could literally be seen by others.

"The one with gray hair?"

"Yeah."

"Of course. The one who left just before I returned?"

"Yeah."

"I did. Why? Was there a problem?"

"Just curious."

Weston looked at Conner a little more closely, not understanding the reason for that question. He let it ride.

"Now, where were we?" Weston wondered, checking his notes and restarting the recording.

Conner held up his hand. "You asked me about the second message I wanted to share."

"And you said something along the lines of believing in God while being nice to your neighbors. Or something like that," he added.

"More or less," Conner commented.

"Would you like to package it differently?" Weston offered.

"Maybe instead of being 'nice' to one's neighbors, being 'meaningful' to one's neighbors might be more accurate."

"Makes sense," Weston said. He made a note on his writing tablet and then continued. "Let's drill down a bit further. How do you respond to the person who says that you can't prove the existence of God?"

Conner sat back and smiled. Here comes the theology. Okay, give it your best shot, he thought.

"As a general rule, regarding any question involving God or his works, it doesn't make sense to debate or try to force-feed anyone. It just doesn't work that way. Although you may get short-term compliance, like from a child, it won't last. If there is not an opening for him, her or them to consider the merit of what I or other apologists offer, then I will withdraw from the discussion and leave the victory to them. Does that make sense to you?"

"It does. Keep going."

"I don't want to be childish in responding to your question about the existence of God but part of the best answer includes that one cannot prove that he does *not* exist." Here he emphasized the word 'not' in contrast to the question that Weston had asked.

Weston showed his attention without saying anything.

"I once heard someone say that a watch proves the existence of a watchmaker and a universe proves the existence of God. In my opinion, things like fairness, trees, miracles and love cannot be explained otherwise. If someone is stuck on these just being happenstance, like a roomful of monkeys and typewriters eventually resulting in the typing of the Declaration of Independence, then I leave them to their thoughts. To me, it's a bigger leap of faith to believe that than it is to believe in a Supreme Being."

Conner thought for a moment, Weston allowing him to do so.

"Christians talk about coming to know God, to experience him. He is no more a formula than how he constructed us. We are unique and we have free will. Our DNA, even our fingerprints, are one-of-a-kind."

"Okay," Weston said.

"May I ask you a question?" Conner said. This time he emphasized 'you' in order to flip their roles.

"Sure."

"Are you Christian?"

"What? Why do you ask?"

"Because it makes what I say either easier or more difficult, depending on your answer."

"Yes, I am Christian. However, in my writing, I always try to maintain my objectivity."

"Good. That's important."

Weston reassumed the role of the interviewer. "Do you have any Scriptural reference to your explanation relating to the existence of God?"

Without initially understanding how he was able to call it up, Conner said "John 10:30 *I and the Father are one* comes to mind."

"Meaning?"

"Jesus was and is part of the Trinity."

Weston tried to process this, especially thinking about how he would explain it in a newspaper article. "Anything else?" he asked.

Conner chuckled. "Listen, I'm not a Bible scholar. You're lucky that I remember anything. However, John 14:9 *Anyone who has seen me has seen the Father* is a good one, too."

"Yes, it is," the journalist commented. "Indeed, indeed," he added.

Silently, Conner thanked the Lord for the references. Keep it up, Lord, he said silently.

"Oh, gosh!" exclaimed Weston almost standing up as he glanced at his watch. "I didn't realize that so much time had passed. Let me ask you two other questions and then, perhaps, we can schedule a follow on for this interview. Would you be willing to do that?"

"Sure," Conner replied.

----- ----- -----

Esther, Pete, Bob and Drew were able to connect, even with the constant flow of bodies moving in the arena, some exiting, others wanting to observe the many player and coach interviews that had resumed on the court.

"Where to now?" Pete asked.

"Wasn't that wonderful?" she asked, ignoring his cut-to-the-chase question.

"It was," he commented. Bob and Drew had to lean in to hear their conversation, the arena still pretty noisy.

"Outstanding. I wouldn't have missed this for the world," Drew said.

Pete looked at him with a reprimanding glance.

"It's just an expression," Drew explained.

"Conner was great, wasn't he?" asked Bob, although it was more a conclusion than a question.

There was no need to respond to the obvious.

"Where to now?" Pete reiterated.

Esther provided a suggested plan and they were happy to agree with it.

"I'm gonna see about getting another Seven jersey," Bob informed them.

Esther smiled. She was very proud.

"Me, too," Bob said and off he went.

"Just we two," Pete said, not knowing what to suggest. "Should we ditch 'em?" he asked jokingly.

"I don't think so," she said with a smile and a slight tilt of her head.

"Okay, let's go find them. I might even want to get another singlet, too, if any are left."

----- ----- -----

"Christians are being persecuted pretty much all over the world," Weston stated.

"I know. Many religious and political beliefs are experiencing such oppression."

"Let's just stick with Christians for the moment."

Conner nodded and Weston continued.

"What, in your opinion, is the second worst thing happening to Christians?"

"Persecution."

Weston looked at Conner curiously. "Maybe you didn't hear my question," he began.

"Oh, I heard it," Conner replied. "You asked me what was the second worst thing happening to Christians. And I answered it. Persecution."

"You are telling me that there is something worse than persecution?"

"I am. It's materialism."

Weston stared incredulously at Conner but said nothing. Conner continued.

"Individuals who suffer and die for Christianity do so for the Lord. They understand what they are doing. Philippians 1:22 *For to me, to live is Christ and to die is gain.* Others, who worship 'thing' gods, are not even aware that they are selling their souls to the devil.

"I must say, Conner, that you have totally surprised me. I definitely did not expect you to say that. If anything, I would have thought that persecution would be worst and something related to it next-to-worst."

"But what I am saying is true. You can read about places where persecution of Christians is rampant and you will find them praying – for Americans! It seems counterintuitive but it's true. When you think of how short life is, you can see the accuracy of that conclusion."

Weston said nothing, pondering what he had just heard. He nodded his head, although he remained silent. "I'll leave that one for elaboration at a later time. Let's turn to my final question of this session. There's a bumper sticker that I see from time to time. It says the word COEXIST in ways that signify many religions. Each letter is a symbol representing a creed."

"I've seen it," Conner confirmed.

"Coexist is one thing, but I wonder if the underlying message is a bit more forceful than that. Might it be saying that heaven waits for anyone who follows any God-believing conviction? How do you respond to it?"

"Perhaps there should be a question to precede that one. Maybe it is '*Do* you respond to it?' rather than '*How* do you respond to it?'" He emphasized the first word of each question. "Unfortunately, in many instances, silence does not advance the cause. Let me give it a shot."

Weston smiled.

"People who advocate this coexist approach suggest that the journey's end is the same for all religions and that the route taken to it does not make a difference. In today's let's-get-along world, leave everyone to his, her or their traditions."

"And?"

"The problem is that when someone Christian says God, he means something very different from the Hindu view which is very different from the Buddhist view which is very different from the Muslim view. In point of fact, to complicate the matter, there are different beliefs in Hinduism, itself."

He paused and smiled, then explained. "I took Comparative Religions last semester and became somewhat more knowledgeable about other major religions. Hinduism looks to many gods - Brahma, the creator, Vishnu, the preserver and Shiva, the destroyer."

The journalist listened intently.

"Muslims say that there is no God but Allah. Period. There's not much coexistence in that, is there?"

The journalist continued his silence.

"Buddhism is about finding enlightenment. Hinduism is about reaching Nirvana, a word used in Buddhism but meaning something entirely different. But here's what's important." Conner paused, then continued. "In Christianity, instead of the person making the voyage, it is God reaching out to the individual. In John 14:16, Jesus says *I am the way and the truth and the life. No one comes to the Father except through me.* Even Judaism, closely aligned with Christianity, does not believe that Jesus was the Christ. They are still waiting for the *first* coming of the Messiah. That's pretty different right there, wouldn't you say?"

Weston was smiling, although he was writing fast and furiously.

"Coexistence is wonderful. The fact of the matter is that, unfortunately, not all of us will choose the path to salvation."

"You mean eternity."

"No, not really. We will all have an eternity. Christians will be enjoying theirs while others will not. Read Luke 16:20 for the story of the beggar named Lazarus. It's a sobering story. The difference will be the salvation offered by Jesus that each of us can choose to accept or reject. The choice is ours. It is our free will."

After a pause, Weston took a deep breath, exhaled and said "Your theology is even more fascinating than your basketball playing."

"It's not my theology."

"You know what I mean."

"I do know what you mean and I certainly don't want to quibble. However, the reason that I make that comment is because it's not some deep, dark mystery, available only to those with magic keys. The information is plainly available to all as well as open to all, regardless of ethnicity, age, gender, education, income, nationality or anything else."

"Okay."

"Each person explains it a little bit differently and not every person understands all the pieces — actually, nobody does — but the cornerstones are there. I believe God will accept all who build upon those cornerstones."

"Great." Weston looked at his watch by way of apology. "This has been great, Conner. In addition to getting terrific material for a column, this has been personally instructive to me. I look forward to a follow up to this. Can we schedule something now?"

"I don't have my calendar with me. Can you give me your card and I'll call you tomorrow?"

Weston reached into his jacket pocket and produced one. "Call my cell phone," he instructed. "I don't want to miss the call."

"Will do," Conner said.

"I'm really sorry to have to run off. However, I probably have enough to try to digest for one sitting. Thanks again." He reached out and the two men shook hands.

"Thanks to you, Tony. Bless you."

"Thanks," Weston said, a little uncomfortable with Conner's salutation but wishing he had offered it, as well.

Conner went out a minute later, casually looking for the security guard but not finding him.

----- ----- -----

After a light snack with Esther and the boys, Conner turned in for the night. Although he had not exerted much effort in the game, he felt exhausted. Perhaps it was the interview. Perhaps it was anxiety associated with the next day's conference championship. Esther, Pete, Bob and Drew appreciated where he was coming from, and let him go without a fight.

"But tomorrow," Pete said, "you will have no excuse, especially after winning the conference tournament and qualifying for the NCAA Tournament."

"None whatsoever," Conner agreed. "None whatsoever," he repeated.

Chapter 60

The team had a light practice at 10:00, then was told to take it easy for the rest of the day. The championship game would be played that night at 7:30. They needed to plan their day accordingly, coming to the arena at 5:00.

"Listen, guys," the coach said, "these boys think that it's gonna be a walk in the park. After drubbing our backsides twice during the season, they are cocky. But they are forgetting one thing - We've got all our guns back in working order. Payback is gonna be painful."

Following the practice, Conner had a quiet lunch with Shedrick and Esther. Then he and Esther went for a walk, talking about the ministry, the interview the night before, the game, school, their faith and a few other things. Conner really enjoyed walking and talking with Esther. She listened well, asked thoughtful questions and participated. Their conversations were typically well-balanced and touched on subjects important to each and both of them. They loved to hold hands.

"Good luck," she said, when they were ready to part.

"Thanks. I really appreciate your support."

"You deserve it. Not many people in your shoes would be keeping their wits about them. You've got basketball challenges along with ministry challenges."

"I like to look at it the other way around – ministry along with basketball."

"Gotcha," she said. "Whichever way, your plate is pretty full."

"Well, I've got God and you. It couldn't get much better."

"God and you are an unbeatable team. I'm just an extra."

"You're definitely not an extra. That's something that I'd like to talk with you about after the tournament."

"Well, Mr. Ramsey, you certainly have my attention."

"Well, Ms. Conrad, I better have it."

They kissed softly as they headed off in different directions.

----- ----- -----

At 6:30, they were able to take the floor. They did it with their practice jerseys, although everything else they wore was for the game. All the stretching, taping and massaging had been done. They were as ready as they could be.

At 7:15, they came back on the floor after getting final instructions from the coach and changing into their dark blue singlets. Once they threw their towels on the bench, all the players headed over to the foul line. As they were going there, Conner noticed that Gordon McKenzie and Chet Applegate were sitting together in expensive, first-row seats. McKenzie waved and Applegate gave him a thumbs-up. Conner waved back and mouthed a thank you, which only Applegate saw and was able to decipher. Several seats away but also in the front row, sat Justin Goudas, another booster. Conner recognized him from various pictures, although the two had not yet met in person. Goudas was much less conservative than his compatriots, not at all minding having a woman half his age fawning all over him.

After the prayer, they headed back to the bench, a few of the players looked over to the Iowa Central bench. The other team was as loose as could be, oozing confidence, almost showing disregard for their opponent. For some of the younger players on the Brantley team, that was an ominous sign. For the elite members of the team – Forrester, Obumje,

Kline and Walker – that was disrespect, the kind that needed to be forcefully rejected. Walker, in particular, was hot.

"Ooo, I can't wait," he said, almost too hyper for a good start.

"Easy does it, tiger," Obumje advised. "We'll have plenty of opportunity to wipe their smirks all over the floor."

"I'm counting on it."

Those four, with Dixon, hit the floor for the Eagles. The Falcons brought out their starting lineup. They were somewhat bigger than the Eagles but their swagger was particularly noticeable…and irritating to the Eagles fans, as well. Had one not known anything about either team, body language alone would have suggested that any wager should favor the Falcons.

With the preliminaries completed, the game began. Both teams looked to be a little tight. The Eagles went one for their first five shots, it being a Kline three-pointer. The Falcons went two for their first six shots, a three-pointer and a gimme layup. Thereafter, they settled down. Ten minutes into the game, the score was 26-17 in favor of Iowa Central. There was no loss of swagger from the number one seed.

At this rate, Esther thought, the final score would be 104-68, roughly what had been the result of their regular season matchups. However, she knew that Brantley was better than this and also knew that there was plenty of time to right this ship. She gave a silent prayer to put Conner into the game and turn this thing around. "Please," she added aloud.

At the time-out, Coach Wright switched backcourts, inserting Harris and Ramsey. "Let's see if we can't turn this thing around right now," he said, hopeful that it would happen. All five players knew what to do. Shedrick would press the shooter and force him to the middle. Conner would play a little off the other guard, giving himself room to make defensive plays. Forrester, Obumje and Dixon would keep their men out of the paint and eliminate second chances.

Apparently, though, the Falcons had a plan for when this Eagles backcourt entered into the game. In effect, they took Conner out of the game. Whoever he guarded moved to a shooting position away from the ball. Then it became four-on-four with the ball-handling guard looking exclusively to pass into one of its three big men. Try as they might, Forrester, Obumje and Dixon could not handle their picks. Over the next five minutes, even with Conner in the lineup, the Falcons upped their lead, now standing at 39-25.

"Not good," the coach said, as he put in his original backcourt. "Not good at all."

At halftime, the lead was 55-37 and the game looked to most fans as to have already been decided.

In the Eagles locker room, the coach was surprisingly calm. "Looks like we've laid out the red carpet for them," he said. "Since they won the regular season and are the number one seed here, that makes sense. Too bad, though. If we had beaten them, we'd have defeated the first, second and third seeds."

"Hey, coach," Kline said.

"What?"

"You're talking past tense. This thing ain't over."

"Oh? Really? You want to play another half? You don't want to just concede it to them?"

"I don't," Kline said.

"Me neither," Shedrick piped up.

Everyone either said or grumbled their agreement.

"Well, in that case, do you think that we can win?"

"Yes, coach!"

"Do you want to win?"

"Yes, coach!"

"Are you ready to win?"

"Yes, coach!"

"Then let's do it," he said, as he turned and left the room.

Forrester called them together and they put their hands in the center of the circle. "Eagles on three," he said.

Once on the court, Coach Wright told them that they would play a three-guard lineup. "Kline, Walker, Ramsey with Forrester and Obumje underneath. The only way this works is if the two of you are in your man's face. Walker, you take their shooter. Kline, you take the other guard. Forrester and Obumje, I want you at the first position in the paint, where the defensive man stands waiting for the other team to shoot the foul. If they try to lob against Ramsey, you need to swat it away. Are we clear?"

"Yes, coach."

"Great. Then go turn this thing around." He looked at the five, then added "And don't take a long time in doing it. My stomach is already in knots."

They all smiled.

"How's the foot?" the coach asked.

"It'll be fine," Conner replied. "No need to worry."

"I hope not."

The Eagles got the ball to start the second half. As usual, Conner pretty much stayed out of the way. From time to time, he would touch the ball but then return it to Kline or Walker. Kline drilled a three and the half was underway.

When the Falcons brought the ball up, Kline and Walker got in their opponents' underwear. At least that's what it seemed like. The two guards really had no opportunity to shoot and passing was made very difficult. The only thing that they could do was drive. And that was what Coach Wright hoped would happen.

The first two times, Kline's man tried to drive. Once past his defender, the Falcons guard felt confident about going uncontested to the rim. Instead, each time Conner came away with the ball and fired it to a wide-open Kline for two easy layups. The next two times, Walker's opponent tried to take advantage of the overplay. One time he experienced the same fate as his backcourt mate. The other time he launched what looked to be a silly shot from way beyond the three-point line. Forrester corralled the rebound. Now with the ball, the Eagles trailed by nine, 55-46. They had cut the deficit in half, from eighteen to nine. Kline again swished a three-pointer, causing the Falcons coach to call a time-out.

"Nice," was Coach Wright's initial comment. "Think you can shut them out for the entire half?" he asked with a smile.

"Sure, coach," Forrester said. "Want us to go get you a pizza, too?"

The coach made a face and shrugged his shoulders as though he was considering it, then said "After the game. And it'll be on me if this continues."

Meanwhile, at the other end of the court, the Falcons' coach was fuming. Although the Eagles couldn't hear what was being said, they could imagine. His face was red, he was in each of the starting players' faces and one could hear plenty of volume but few distinct words. Periodically, one would drift over. "Candy," "soft," "losers" and then, in what sounded quite odd for the moment "relax." Every player on the Eagles was glad that he was in this rather than the other team's huddle, even though the other one held a six-point lead.

When the other team returned to the floor, they had modified their lineup to include three guards, as well. The likelihood was that they wanted to occupy Conner in guarding someone who might shoot.

Kline, Walker and Conner quickly huddled. "Who's the weakest of those three, when it comes to scoring?" Conner asked. Since the other two had

Tap In   510

played against the Falcons a couple of times, perhaps they remembered.

Kline and Walker stepped back and looked at the three guards. "Twenty-two," they both said at the same time.

"Jinx," Conner said. Kline and Walker looked weirdly at Conner. "Okay, never mind," he said. "I'll take twenty-two. Hey, how about if we pick them up at half court?" he added.

Kline and Walker looked at one another, smiled and then each nodded in agreement. "You got it," Walker said. "You sure that you won't get too tired, old man?" he jabbed.

"I'll give you tired," Conner said. "Bet I outscore you from this point forward."

"Yeah, right," Walker said. "In your dreams."

"Pizza at Bruno's," Conner suggested.

"Start borrowing money, grandpa," Walker fired back with a smile.

Conner smiled. Now they were loose. Conner looked over at the two boosters. They were deep in some discussion, neither looking over. Then he looked for Esther. There she was, sitting pretty as a picture, looking straight down at him with a big smile. She stood up and turned around. Apparently, at halftime, she had donned her number seven Eagles jersey with Conner's name on it. Then she turned back around and blew him a kiss. What a woman, he thought.

Pete, Bob and Drew weren't sitting with Esther. He did a quick scan to find them but just couldn't do so. A moment later, he heard "Seven, seven, seven"

come out toward his left. Although he still couldn't
see them, he had a general sense of where they were.
He waved to the area, hoping that they would
appreciate the individual attention.

Iowa Central inbounded the ball with about
seventeen minutes remaining. Walker stayed on his
man, Kline on his and Conner roughly near his. If
this guy can hit a bunch, then we'll have to make an
adjustment. The likelihood is small, he hoped. They
picked up their men at about the midcourt line.

Once in the front court, the three of them went
into a weave. It resulted in an uncontested dunk and
a huge roar from the Falcons' fans. Walker missed a
two and Iowa Central went back on the attack,
something of the swagger returning. Again, they
went into a weave until they were able to drive to the
outside. This time, Forrester delivered a hard but
clean foul.

Before the shooter went to the line, Conner called
the other four together. "Okay, we can handle this.
We three stay in a zone outside while you two play
man underneath. If one of the guards goes
underneath, Walker you go with him. They'll have to
be very precise if they're gonna mess us up."

Nobody said anything but all of them were in
agreement. The shooter made both shots. The lead
was back up to double digits, 59-49.

Walker penetrated and delivered to Obumje who
slammed home two.

As for defense, the three-zone-plus-two-
underneath took a little while to become natural.
Coach Wright, who hadn't instructed them to defend

in this way, looked on with surprise but did not interrupt. The first time the Eagles tried to defend, the Falcons freed up a guard who took a three-pointer. He missed and Obumje rebounded.

On the other end of the court, Conner penetrated and dished to Forrester who slammed home two. The lead was back down to six.

When Iowa Central came up the next time, Conner stepped in, stole a lazy pass and made a layup. Now the Falcons fans were quiet while the Eagles crowd was erupting.

Iowa Central's next effort at a weave was met with a much more knowledgeable defense by Brantley. Kline and Walker, positioned at the ends of the three-man zone, kept the outside unavailable for the opposing guards. If they were going to drive, it was going to be through the foul line. Again, the Falcons decided to shoot from the outside and the rebound was gathered in by Forrester. He passed to Conner who passed to Kline who touch-passed to a speeding Walker for a windmill jam. Iowa Central called time-out, now leading by just two points.

Once again, the Brantley huddle was loose while the Iowa Central coach was screaming at the top of his lungs. Had organ music and normal crowd noise not been able to drown out most of what he was saying, there would have been a collection of four-letter words for those in the nearby rows to hear. All the while he yelled at his players, the coach kept his hands pinned to his sides. Conner guessed it was a mechanism he used to avoid striking someone. It looked really odd to see someone yelling almost uncontrollably while somewhat standing at attention.

Conner stayed in for the next seven minutes while Shedrick rotated in for Kline and then Walker. Dixon spelled Obumje for a couple of minutes. Forrester remained in the entire time. By then, the score had swung in Brantley's favor, 73-65. Those Eagles fans were having a much more enjoyable time than those who were wearing Falcons colors. Nine minutes and change remained. There was plenty of time for either team to win, even by a large margin.

Connor's foot had been hurting him a bit for the last few minutes. When he sat down during the time out, he unlaced his shoe and took it off. His sock was soaked in blood. When the coach saw that, he sent him off with Coach Murphy and told the team doctor seated a few rows back to go with them. Conner hadn't put his shoe back on and hopped to the locker room assisted by the coach. Many people on that side of the court, especially those seated near the playing level, could see the problem and a buzz began to fill the arena. Eventually, news of what had happened spread throughout, much like the motion wave one sees at many sporting events.

Chapter 61

The doctor took off the bloody sock and examined the sole. "You've torn the place where the stitches were," he reported.

"I figured something like that," Conner said.

"It doesn't look too good," the doctor offered.

Conner wanted to say "Duh" but refrained, instead asking "Can you just close it up temporarily, doc?"

"That's not going to be good for it, your playing on it further," he stated.

"I know, doc. However, this is kind of important and I'm willing to deal with it. We won't have our next game for a couple of weeks. That will give me time to heal."

"Well…"

"Doc, please just do it," Conner requested.

The doctor patched it up and used some gauze to limit the additional damage that would occur from change of direction steps. Conner committed himself to slowing down, knowing that even at that speed he would be faster than his opponents.

Once treated, Conner put on a new pair of socks, got a different pair of his sneakers and stood up. It hurt somewhat but he could tough it out for however many minutes remained in the game. Inside the locker room, the doctor had asked the attendant to turn off the radio. Unlike some, he needed quiet to study the damage and do what he could to make repairs.

By the time Conner was ready to return to the court, he had no idea how much time remained or what the score might be. "Let's go, let's go!" he said as he limped a bit toward the tunnel. Coach Murphy followed. The doctor remained to clean up and repack his medical bag.

When Conner reappeared coming out of the tunnel, a giant roar erupted from the Eagles fans.

Conner looked up at the scoreboard. It was 88-86 in favor of the Eagles. One minute and ten seconds remained. There was a time-out just coming to an end and the Falcons had the ball.

Conner limped to the bench.

"So?" Coach Wright asked, partially concerned for his star player, more concerned for the game's outcome.

"Sew buttons on your underwear," Conner responded.

Coach Wright rolled his eyes. "What am I gonna do with you?" he asked.

"Play me. I can survive for seventy seconds."

"You sure?"

"Do it," Conner instructed.

Coach Wright nodded and sent him in. He checked in at the scorer's table. It would be Kline, Walker, Ramsey, Forrester and Obumje. The crowd was delirious. The Eagles fans were excited to have Conner back while the Falcons fans were exhorting their team to take charge. The tension was enormous, just the way a true sports fan would have liked a championship game to end.

Conner limped out, although he tried to minimize the emphasis. He looked up and saw Esther. She was standing with her arms together, her hands under her chin and a concerned look on her face. He smiled at her and gave her a thumbs-up. All the Eagles fans who saw him do that, interpreted it as being for them and a thunderous bellow resulted. He and she smiled at each other, knowing that this was a moment for them to share. He pointed up. Looking at him, she did, as well. Seeing this, Eagles fans started doing the same thing, some even imitating the handshake that Shedrick and Conner had devised for the court. It was pretty emotional stuff for all involved. When Conner turned to Shedrick and did the actual handshake, another few decibels were added to the volume.

Iowa Central went with the three-guard formation, hoping that Conner would not have as much mobility. They, too, had seen his bloody sock, now observed his limp and correctly surmised that he was less than his best. They incorrectly concluded what went on inside of him.

At half court, the three Brantley guards picked up a man, then stayed in the zone that had worked for them before. Once again, perhaps forgetting Conner's ability, they made an ill-advised pass that he stole and fed Walker for an easy two. Forty-seven seconds and a four-point lead.

Same defensive formation for the Eagles on the Falcons' next possession. Trying to get the ball into their center, Forrester made a wonderful tap of the ball but it was headed out of bounds. Even with Conner's speed on a good foot, he would have been challenged to reach it. Now, with one foot seriously injured, he probably shouldn't have gone after it at all.

But he did.

With two quick steps and a dive, he tapped the ball to Obumje, landing in the first row of spectators. Chairs went spilling and he tumbled to the ground. Obumje immediately called a time out with thirty-five seconds to go. It was their next-to-last last time out.

Conner, sprawled on his back, rocked backwards, his knees coming to his face, and then rocked forwards onto his feet. Feeling a little bit the ham, he responded to the cheers with a wave and a huge smile. The ovations went on for the entire time that it took Obumje and Conner to walk to the bench, escorted by Forrester, Walker and Kline.

"You're a mess," Coach Wright said.

Conner didn't know what he was talking about until the trainer came over and put a wet towel to his eyebrow. When he took it away, it had a decent amount of blood on it, as well. Apparently, when Conner had gone into his acrobatics, he had caught part of his face on a chair and done that damage.

The ref came over and said "Can't play with an active bleed," he said, following the required rules.

"Put something on it," Conner said. The doctor came over and took out some medicine, then applied something else and ended by putting on a strange bandage that pulled at Conner's eyelid, somewhat distorting his sight. He certainly looked like he had gotten the worst of a backyard brawl. Nevertheless, with his adrenaline flowing, he was immune to the facial cut and willing to tolerate the foot discomfort for the remaining game time.

The referee inspected the bandage, noting how it pulled his eyelid.

"Can you see?" he asked, more as a parent than as a ref.

"Well enough," Conner said with a smile.

"Okay. Your funeral," he said, walking to center court. He blew his whistle to have the players return to the floor. When Conner walked out, the same ref came over to examine him once more. "You sure that you're okay?" he asked.

"Couldn't be better," Conner responded.

"You're one tough guy," the ref commented.

Conner said nothing.

Needing ball control, Coach Wright had substituted Shedrick for Obumje. "No threes," he had yelled to them as they started to walk onto the court. Although he had meant for them not to allow threes, he didn't mind them knowing that they weren't supposed to take threes either.

"Who's in?" Kline asked, meaning who would be inbounding for them.

"Shedrick," Conner instructed. "Remember where they're not," he said to Shedrick. His friend nodded. Then, to the others, he said "You three get down court." They looked at Conner like he was nuts but followed his instructions.

Seeing this, Coach Wright started to yell at Forrester, Kline and Walker. He looked over at Conner and was greeted by a bruised but smiling face. He dropped his protest and sat down. Immediately, he hopped back up.

The Falcons played man-to-man defense in order to either steal the ball or create a quick foul. Two of the defenders were down with the three Eagles, one was at midcourt, one was glued to Conner and one was on the inbounder. The ref blew his whistle and Shedrick raised the ball in a baseball motion. The defender at half court immediately retreated to defend his basket while the other two stuck with Shedrick and Conner. The crowd was totally silent.

Then, behind his back, Shedrick threw the ball toward his own foul line. It was totally counterintuitive to what one should have done in this situation. Coach Wright was stunned by this seemingly idiotic move. He was speechless. His mouth was totally open.

Conner ran over and retrieved it. The clock started. Shedrick ran up court, his defender following him. The player guarding Conner came over to foul him. Instead, Conner started dribbling and moving in a way that totally evaded the man guarding him. Falcons fans were screaming for their player to foul Conner but he could not get close. Before ten seconds had elapsed, Conner crossed the half court line, thus avoiding a backcourt violation. The player guarding Shedrick was instructed by their coach. "Foul him! Foul him!" he yelled. "Foul him! Foul him!" he repeated. Precious time ran off the clock.

Then another defender was called upon to join the other two in getting Conner. Just when they had him boxed in, Conner threw a pass to Shedrick who dunked it over his head, what he liked to call his signature move. Fifteen seconds remained and the score was 92-86.

The Falcons coach called his last time out. Conner and his mates walked to the bench. Now he felt the pain on his eyebrow as well as the pain in his foot. He smiled, looked up and pointed to the ceiling. A huge cheer went up from the Eagles crowd and most of them pointed up, as well. Esther started to cry. Even stoic Pete had a tear or two. Bob and Drew were just amazed at the excitement, exceedingly pleased to have experienced this.

The three Eagles guards were now Kline, Walker and Conner. They lined up a few feet into the Falcons' backcourt, forcing the inbounding team to touch the ball immediately, thus starting the clock. Forrester and Shedrick remained underneath their defensive basket just in case Iowa Central decided to throw the ball the length of the court. They did not choose to try the long heave.

Once the ball was inbounded and touched, Conner picked up the dribbler. Not able to dribble around Conner, he passed to his mate and Conner hustled over to guard him, as well. This disconcerted the new ball-carrier and, in trying to get rid of the ball, proceeded to throw it into the stands. Six points and five seconds remained. Shedrick inbounded once more and Conner dribbled out the remaining time without being touched.

The celebration on the court was exciting. In a spontaneous move, Conner was lifted onto his teammates' shoulders, although he was terribly uncomfortable with that decision. After just a few steps, he managed to slide down. Then he told his teammates to line up to shake hands with the Falcons players. Completing that ritual, they returned to their celebration.

Conner held up his hands. Some of the players thought that he was expressing his excitement.

Shedrick, though, knew that he was seeking attention. "Hey!" Shedrick yelled, only getting a reaction from two or three players. "Hey," he repeated. Eventually everyone turned, including the fans who were already on the court. Shedrick pointed to Conner and those immediately around him quieted down.

"Prayer," was all he said. Everyone, players and fans alike, shuffled to the foul line. It had to be a shuffle because of the mass of humanity in that small space. When they got there, many of them said "Shhh!" and the request for silence spread throughout the arena. Although not totally silent, the raucous facility was much more hushed. Many fans, particularly Eagles fans, understood what was happening. A large percentage of those wearing hats took them off. Even Falcons fans showed a similar respect, while trying to exit the arena.

Conner's prayer was short but meaningful. He thanked God for all the blessings that they received, including being able to play in this tournament, much less winning it. He thanked the Lord for their abilities. He asked for prayers over those who most needed it. And he asked for the determination of everyone to help spread the Word. There was a loud "Amen" when he finished.

Straightaway, they returned to the celebration.

By then, Esther had managed to come down to the second row. Conner saw her and started toward her, only to be intercepted by fans, media and his teammates. He kept his eyes on her and saw her shrug, smiling all the while. Then she did the

Shedrick handshake from that distance. He laughed and blew her a kiss. He felt like crying out of happiness.

Before talking with anyone, Conner made a point of giving the endlessly-smiling coach a hug. Then he looked for Gordon McKenzie and Chet Applegate. Their seats were vacant, clearly a wise choice since the human pinball had rolled over where they were sitting. Scanning the lower rows, he saw them heading up one aisle. He ran and caught up with them.

"Thanks for coming," he said.

"You're thanking us?" Chet said. "That was an incredible game. If anyone wonders whether or not we're still Brantley boosters, you be sure to tell them we are."

Conner smiled.

"As for Project 2312," Gordon said, "it's alive and well."

Conner's wide smile got even wider.

"Bless you," he said.

"And bless you," Chet responded on behalf of the two older men.

Chapter 62

The post-game interviews and fanfare lasted for a long time. Somewhere in the hullabaloo, Conner found a semi-quiet place to call Esther on her cell phone. He asked her to find Pete, Bob and Drew, then to have something to eat. He would call them when he got done with this ordeal.

"You need to enjoy it," she said.

"I do. It's just that between my foot, my eyebrow and my girlfriend, I'm feeling needy."

She laughed. "And she needs time with you, as well,"

"Good deal. I'll call you later," he said as a reporter tugged on his shirt.

"Okay," she was able to respond before the call was terminated.

----- ----- -----

Before any of the individual reporters could significantly launch into their one-on-one interviews, Coach Wright and his assistant coaches herded all the players into the locker room. Everyone else was temporarily barred from it. Arena security guards, along with local police, were able to enforce this action.

When the team was assembled, Coach Wright held up his hand. They quieted down.

"Men, I'm so proud of you. We had a few times out there when quitting would have been lots easier than pushing the boulder up the hill. Not one of you quit, neither those on the court, those on the bench nor those who weren't able to suit up."

Applause acknowledged this compliment.

"I also want all of us to thank our wonderful assistant coaches." Here he named off each one, applause recognizing them one at a time.

"A couple of quick things and then we can do what winners do."

Cheering ensued. He held up his hand again.

"I want us to remember that our season is not over. We have won this tournament only to enable us to get into the next one," referring to the NCAA Tournament.

More cheers.

"We need to stick with our practice schedules…and heal our injuries," he said, turning to Conner, bruised and battered.

Cheers and applause.

"For an old guy, you're kinda tough," the coach commented.

Some of the players tossed in their own loving insults to supplement the coach's kidding.

"Many of you will be participating in interviews, both large and small. I want you to remember to be humble, to respect the teams we will be playing…"

Obumje interrupted with "…we will be beating!" A big cheer went up for that, of course.

The coach continued. "…respect the teams we will be playing, remember that you represent Brantley University to its students, its faculty, its staff and all its supporters. Do not embarrass us."

He looked around at everyone to drive home that last point.

"Our job is not done. Aside from representing Brantley University, we now represent the Plains Conference. I'm hoping that at least two other teams get an invitation. Iowa Central certainly will and I'm optimistic that Wisconsin/Geneva will, as well. The better all of us do in the tournament, the better will become the reputation of the Plains Conference. And that will be part of your growing legacy."

"When will we find out our seed, who we play, when we play and where we play?" someone shouted out.

Coach Wright smiled. "Let me start with the first part of your question. We will have a low, low, low seed, I suspect. In case you didn't notice it, we ended our regular season with a record of 8-and-20, 6-and-12 in the conference. In other words, we won barely over 25% of our games. How many teams do you think will be playing in the NCAA Tournament with a losing record, much less with a winning percentage like that?"

The same individual shouted "Yeah, but we ended up 12-and-20," emphasizing the 12. The rest of the team laughed and hooted.

"Oh, excellent," said the coach. "That would lift our winning percentage to somewhere around 35%. Yeah, that's much better," he said sarcastically.

"And not many teams can say that they won their last four games, now can they?" the shouter boldly proclaimed.

"No, they can't." The coach paused, obviously thinking of something. Then he resumed. "If we do this right, what with winning six games in the upcoming tournament, we'll have an 18-and-20 record with a ten-game winning streak. Anyone want to end the year like that?"

There was loads of laughter and side talk resulting from what the coach had just asked.

He repeated his question, this time much more loudly. "Anyone want to end the year like that?"

"Yes, coach!" they responded.

"Good. Me, too."

Cheers.

"Okay, before we go, does anyone have anything that he wants to say? And let's not have everyone talking or we'll be here 'til the cows come home."

"Moo," someone commented.

"You guys are a piece of work," the coach commented with a smile.

Nobody raised his hand. "Reverend Ramsey," the coach said, "you must have something to offer."

Conner stood up.

"Did you win the fight?" someone else shouted out from the back.

Conner smiled. "We did!" he said, raising his hand like a winning prize fighter, much to the delight of the team.

More cheering.

"Let me say just a few things and then conclude with a prayer."

Everyone quieted down. There was something churchlike that now pervaded the air.

"You guys are great. What a privilege to be playing with you."

He looked around, especially offering visual thanks to Shedrick. It was returned with affection.

"Also, you guys have embraced our mission or ministry or whatever it is called in a wonderful, wonderful way. I know that God is pleased with our progress."

He thought about how true that was and wished that he could share his full story with them.

"But we have more to do on the court and much more to do off the court. I hope that we will be successful at both but…" He held up his hand to quell the cheer that was about to begin. They quieted quickly. "…but I more fully hope that we are successful with our mission off the court. In the whole scheme of things, that is far more important. Remember this: Even in our lifetimes, this event will be wonderful but it will just be one of a number of things that will highlight our lives. When you think about eternity, this will be less than one drop in the ocean of time. Let's keep it in perspective and invest our talents wisely."

The room had gotten totally silent. Either the players were reflecting on what Conner was saying or he had put a wet blanket on their celebrating.

"Let's end with a prayer." Conner then delivered a brief prayer, making certain to include Coach Wright and all supporters of the Eagles basketball family. He concluded with "And let's not forget to enjoy today's victory! Amen."

Amid cheers, "Amens" could be heard throughout, several times repeated as a cheer itself.

"Okay, men," the coach said. They quieted down again. "Enjoy, but be smart. Nice going!"

The celebration returned.

Coach Wright tapped Forrester, Walker and Conner, telling them that they would be joining him for the televised post-game interview. Although Conner was not overly thrilled with being selected, he understood the importance of participating.

"I'll be there in a minute," Conner called to
Forrester. The big center gave a slight wave of
recognition with his right hand as he took lumbering
strides toward the interview room. Coach Wright
and Walker were several steps ahead.

Conner went into the restroom. As he entered,
someone was exiting. Conner held the door for him.
Nobody else was in the lavatory. He walked into one
of the stalls and latched the door, then sat down. He
didn't have to go to the bathroom. Instead, he
wanted to collect himself and speak to God. He sat
there in silence for a few seconds.

"Lord," he began, "you are amazing – mysterious
yet direct, serious yet funny, predictable
yet…unpredictable," he concluded, not finding a
better word. Conner smiled, knowing full well that
he was being both heard and listened to. Whether or
not God immediately responded did not change
Conner's message. There was no question that He
was listening.

After another moment's silence, Conner thought
of *Sergeant York*, referring to his all-time favorite
movie. It starred Gary Cooper as the famous World
War I soldier. No matter how many times Conner
watched the movie, he would get teary. It was such a
wonderful blend of action and faith, a brilliant story
of heroism and transformation. Conner liked so
many parts of it but he was most touched each time
when the title character would say things like "The
Lord sure does move in mysterious ways."

"You are amazing," Conner repeated. "What a
journey." He paused. "Thank you, Lord," he said

simply. Then he stood up, unlatched the door, exited the bathroom and headed to the interview. As he did so, he wondered what opportunities and obstacles lay ahead. Many of both, he supposed. Many of both.

----- ----- -----

End of Book

Made in the USA
Monee, IL
06 December 2021

83979668R00308